The
Twisted
Path

Christen Stovall

ISBN: 978-1-7362662-0-5

Contents

Acknowledgements

ACKNOWLEDGMENTS

Rachel Gegen for providing the spine and back cover, as well as refining the front of the book. Alisha Mattingly for editing. Jen Deslaurier for helping me with the final rinse. Crystal Roberts for her love and support. Amanda Little for providing feedback and the lyrics. Last, but definitely not least, my mother for always believing and encouraging me.

CHAPTER 1

Daughter of the Vashirat

Kenna lay in her bed staring up at the filmy canopy that surrounded her. The sun was not yet risen, but she'd been awake for hours. This was the last morning she would wake in this house. It was the last time she would leave her bedroom and join her parents and siblings on the veranda for the morning meal. This would always be her home, and yet, soon it would not.

In a matter of hours Kenna would begin the long trek to the neighboring kingdom of Venallis. She would leave Arthan's golden sea of dunes to marry a man she'd only met once before, and build a life with him in a land of emerald hills and winding streams. Ian was handsome and kind, and Kenna had every faith that he'd make a fine husband. But every beginning marked the end of something else. This one marked the end of Kenna's childhood. Excitement, sadness, and apprehension were warring for dominance inside her, and it made any further sleep impossible.

There would be many adjustments. The governance of her own country was vastly different from the monarchy of Venallis. Arthan was made up of ten clans, known as Vashirats. Each Vashirat had a leader, usually the eldest daughter of the previous leader. The leaders of the Vashirats met twice a year to decide upon matters of state and pass verdicts on crimes too serious to be judged by one person. This method of governing had been in place for over a century, and though there were rivalries between some of the Vashirats, the foundations of Arthan were strong. As the third daughter of the leader of her own Vashirat, the Rihtall, Kenna was well educated in the history and laws of her homeland, but Ian's homeland was run by one, a King who held power over all who lived within its borders. Kenna knew she would have to adjust and adjust quickly.

Bird calls pierced the air outside, drifting through the open bedroom windows. Kenna sat up with a sigh and pushed the netting aside to climb out of bed and greet the morning. She loved the sight of dawn's rays spreading across the sandy peaks that lay beyond the oasis city of Rihta, home of the Rihtall. According to legend, if one looked at the peak of the farthest dune at the moment of the sunrise, they would catch a glimpse of the summer goddess, Shavri, in her palace of light and pearl.

In her eighteen years of life, Kenna had yet to prove the stories true. Not that she often woke early enough to test the theory, or even thought to do it every time she did. But she liked to think there was something of truth to the ancient tales. The world held plenty of magic, both in truth and in spirit.

Kenna possessed a great desire to see as much of the world as she could. It was one of the reasons she'd approached her parents with the idea of a betrothal to a family outside Arthan. There was something exciting in the prospect of striking out from the familiarity of home to build a new life in a far-off land. She looked forward to the chance to immerse herself in the customs and traditions of another culture. The prospect held a promise of adventure and purpose.

Kenna sighed and focused on the present. Now wasn't the time for flights of fancy. Her family's rival Vashirat, the Stratham, was growing bolder with each passing day. Her mother and father needed the military support that an alliance with a noble family of Venallis would bring. High Lord Edan's troops were known for their discipline and prowess on the field of battle.

The High Lord himself was a respected general in his youth, and had fought at King Fergal's side before the throne was established and Fergal was crowned King. By aligning themselves with such a family, the Rihtall would receive a small contingent of men, and their own forces would be trained in the same techniques that had helped unite a kingdom. In exchange, the High Lord's family would gain trade routes through Rihtall territory and access to the nearly unbreakable metal produced therein, not to mention the prestige that came with allying themselves to a family as old and respected as Kenna's.

The door to her bedroom opened and shut. It pulled Kenna's attention from the daydreams of sunrise and returned them to the demands of reality. In the shadows of the room, she could just make out the form of her friend and handmaid, Mairi. The other woman was moving through the room stealthily, obviously unaware that Kenna was already out of bed. Kenna made a small noise to alert Mairi to her wakefulness before stepping away from the window.

"Oh!" Mairi started slightly but then laughed at her own moment of fright. "I suppose I should have guessed that you'd be awake early this morning. I know I could hardly sleep with all the excitement of what today will bring."

"It will be an adventure. But don't you worry you'll miss your family?" Kenna asked. She was thrilled when Mairi agreed to come along and serve as her lady-in-waiting, but she worried that her friend had agreed out of a sense of obligation and would have preferred to remain closer to her family and the comforts of serving in the household of the Rihtall.

Mairi shot her a look of playful reproach. "And leave you to have all the fun? Not likely. How many times must I assure you that I'm happy to come along?"

"Maybe just once or twice more," Kenna replied, anxiously biting her lower lip. "It's not as if we can come for a visit whenever we like. It takes three days to reach the mountains that border Arthan. And the journey over them takes weeks. It could be years before we'll be back here."

"I know that, Kenna. I also know that I won't leave you to face such changes alone. This Ian will have me to answer to if he doesn't make you as happy as his letters promise." Mairi took Kenna by the hand and led her to a chair in front of the vanity. She reached for the brush and ran it through Kenna's dark hair before pulling the long, straight tresses into an intricate netting of jade and pearls.

Kenna blushed a little. Their first and only meeting lasted two weeks, but was enough to solidify Kenna's belief that this was the right course for her. When Ian visited Rihta Kenna's thoughts turned from duty to dreams of a happy future. He was confident, educated, and had a warm and open nature that made it impossible to dislike him. They'd spent hours together, discussing their hopes and dreams as they toured the gardens, enjoying playful archery contests, and taking their first careful steps into a future together. Since his departure, Ian had been quite diligent in his attention to their courtship.

"I have every confidence that Ian will make me happy," Kenna stated, setting aside thoughts of her future husband to turn the conversation back to Mairi. "But I worry you're putting on a brave face for my sake."

"Kenna, in all the years you've known me, have I ever hesitated to speak my mind with you?" Mairi asked. She finished with Kenna's hair and put the brush into a satchel for travel.

Kenna quirked a brow at her. "No, which may prove to be a problem for you in Venallis. The people there are quite careful with their words."

"That is precisely why I should go along," Mairi shot over her shoulder. "Now get dressed so I can pack your nightgown and we can get something to eat before it's time to start our little venture."

Kenna shook her head with a laugh and reached for her traveling clothes. As always, Mairi cut directly to the point. They only had a short time left in the home of their childhood, and there was no point in wasting it with worry.

No, I can save that for the journey there.

Though the hour was still early when Kenna and Mairi stepped into the screened pavilion where her family took their informal meals, Kenna's parents and siblings, along with her two elder sisters' husbands, were already seated around the table. The youngest of her siblings squirmed impatiently. They were not accustomed to having to wait to break their fast, and didn't hide their relief at seeing the person of honor arrive at the table.

Kenna's mother smiled approvingly when Kenna walked through the door. Lady Isla was a presence in any room, even when that room was populated by her husband and children. As the head of the Rihtall Vashirat, her mother was the person to whom all their kin and tenants looked for guidance and protection. She was a tall, willowy figure with striking golden-brown eyes and raven hair that fell below her hips when it was unbound. Kenna, like most in the Vashirat, admired and respected her mother and found her to be an intimidating example to equal.

Her father, Consort Veruth, was the only person Kenna knew who did not display reservation around his wife. He was an equally impressive figure. Tall and handsome, with broad shoulders and dark hair that was peppered with gray at the temples. He was a skilled and respected diplomat in Arthan. The two were well-suited to one another. Their own marriage had been arranged, but their hearts were turned to it long before the vows were exchanged.

"Mother, Father," Kenna said as she dipped in a low curtsy. "I trust I did not keep you waiting for long."

"Ages, actually," her brother Jaik answered, jumping in before either of their parents could respond. "As twins, one would think you'd share my impeccable sense of time. But alas, you do not. I hope your new husband does not mind tardiness."

Their mother looked at him with a single brow raised. That was all Lady Isla needed to do to command silence. She turned back to Kenna. "You did not. I gathered your siblings early so that all would be present when you arrived."

"Thank you, all of you," Kenna replied. She smiled around the table at her three sisters and three brothers. Her twin pulled the chair beside his out for her. Kenna accepted it, heart clenching with sadness. *After this morning that seat will be empty.*

Jaik was her counterpart in so many ways. As twins they'd always been together. They shared in each other's hurts and triumphs. Leaving him behind would be one of the hardest things she did.

It's inevitable, of course. One day he'll marry as well, and both of us will have our own families to look after. She took a deep and shuddering breath. That fact didn't lessen the pain of their impending separation.

"I've had the kitchens prepare your favorite breakfast," her father said as he took his seat. He fixed his large, deep brown eyes on Kenna. "I've also had them write down instructions for the cooks in your new home so that you may share these dishes with your husband's family."

"I've heard the people of Venallis do not season their foods at all, that they consider it too indulgent," her sister Sazia commented as her plate was placed before her. "I've also heard that they rarely express affection, and that they're only allowed to wear certain colors or they risk punishment from the King."

"That's an exaggeration," Kenna corrected her. Sazia was the second eldest. She'd never been interested in places beyond the borders of Arthan and didn't make any effort to understand Kenna's fascination with the wonders of the outside world. Their relationship had never been a close one.

Kenna scooped up a spoonful of sweet boiled grain and dried fruit as she began to elaborate on the customs of the people she would soon call her own. "They are more reserved than we are, but they season their food, and they do express affection with one another. You'll have to come visit me sometime and see for yourself, Sazia. You might enjoy it."

"I'm quite content within the confines of Arthan," Sazia sipped from her goblet. "And besides, I'm too busy running my own household to make such a long journey."

"Oh, Sazi, do stop putting on such airs," Jaik said, rolling his eyes. "You're just jealous because Kenna will be a far prettier bride than you were, and that you didn't get nearly as many wedding gifts when you married."

"I married the man I love. That is gift enough," Sazia replied. The pinched set of her lips confirmed that Jaik hit closer to the mark than she liked. "A happy marriage requires more than beauty. Beauty fades with the passage of time."

"I think you are quite dazzling, my darling. I treasure you above any worldly gifts." Nattan, her husband, lifted Sazia's hand to his lips and smiled at her. "Besides, I believe it was access to my family's mines that played a key point in negotiating some of the details of the betrothal." Nattan winced, and turned quickly to Kenna to apologize. "I did not mean to imply that you have no value beyond that."

"Thank you, Nattan, I know," Kenna replied gently. Her brother-in-law was endearingly awkward, and utterly besotted with Sazia. She smiled at him. "And I appreciate the part you played in all of this."

"Please send Ian my love," Iyari, Kenna's eldest sister, tactfully cut in before Sazia could make further comment. "And tell him that my daughter adores the doe that he carved for her. She keeps it on the table at her bedside and speaks of him daily. I think if you were not to marry Ian, Lali would put in a bid for his hand herself. The fact that he is over twenty years her senior seems not to matter in her mind."

"I'll let him know he made a favorable impression," Kenna laughed. "We'll have to see if we can come visit for her next birthday so Lali can spend more time with her Uncle Ian."

"I hope you will come visit as often as you can," her mother stated. "Your father and I will do the same. Although there will be no need for visits at all if we never finish our meal." She smiled at her family. "Not that I am in too great a hurry to see my children spread across the sands."

Kenna took another bite, blinking back tears as she did. She would miss seeing these faces each morning. The laughter that they shared, even the petty squabbles that happened from time to time, were all precious elements to Kenna's life. Now that the hour of her departure was near at hand, she wasn't sure how she would get through the days without their familiar presence.

The rest of the meal was kept on a carefully jovial tone. Kenna's final farewells were exchanged in the burgeoning gardens that set the entrance to the domed palace of Vashirat Rihtall ablaze with color. Kenna squeezed each of her beloved siblings in turn, weeping openly when she picked up her littlest sister. Veda was just three years old. Kenna had doted on her since the day of her birth. Knowing that Veda wouldn't remember much of their time together was heartbreaking.

"Promise me you'll be a good girl," Kenna kissed Veda's chubby little cheek, tears running down her own cheeks. "I will come back to see you as soon as I'm able, dear one."

Veda nodded and wrapped her arms around Kenna. She was too young to understand what was happening, but she reacted to Kenna's weeping with confused concern. For that, Kenna was sorry, but she couldn't maintain her composure enough to hide her sadness.

After a long hug, she released the toddler and turned to her twin. Jaik's eyes and nose were red, but he offered her a smile before he pulled her into a tight embrace. Kenna clung to him, wishing he was coming with her, but his place was here. She was marrying into the Venallian nobility to strengthen her Vashirat's position against the Stratham Vashirat. Jaik was one of the best warriors in the Rihtall army. If their enemy chose to attack while Lady Isla and her husband were away, Jaik's skill would be needed.

"I've waited so long to see far off places, but now that the hour is come, I wish I could put it off a little longer," Kenna cried on his shoulder, clinging to him.

"If he doesn't treat you with the love and respect you deserve..." Jaik whispered, his voice choked up at the end.

"He will, Jaik. You met Ian. You know he's a good man," Kenna reassured him.

"Still," Jaik persisted, pulling away from her. "You have but say the word, and I will come for you straight away."

Kenna nodded and sniffled. "I know you will, Jaik. You had better come for visits regardless."

"Sand drakes could not keep me away, dearest sister," he promised.

Kenna pulled him back to her and hugged him even tighter than before. *It's time to leave, and now I can't think of anything I want more than to turn back time and be a little girl playing hide and seek in the water gardens with all of them.*

"Daughter," her father called from the carriage. "It is time. We have a long way to go before we can safely set up camp."

Kenna released her twin brother slowly and turned to join her parents. She looked down at the carriage step and took a deep breath before she climbed into the vessel that would transport her to Venallis.

Determined as she was, Kenna still had to fight to keep the tears at bay when their traveling party started to move. She stuck her head out the window and waved back at her brothers and sisters for as long as she could see them. When the gates that surrounded her home closed behind her, Kenna settled into her seat and looked to the road ahead.

* * *

The journey from Rihta and through mountains dividing Arthan and Venallis took over a month to complete. They moved at a steady but careful pace through rocky cliffs and ravines that created the natural barrier between the drastically different realms, stopping frequently to give the horses and the drivers a break from the harrowing trek. Nights were spent with wheels locked in place, and wagons pressed against the umber cliff faces.

Kenna and Mairi passed much of the time in the mountains clinging tightly to one another's hands and avoiding the temptation to look out the windows as the group crept along the narrow roads. It was terrifying to see nothing but steep rock walls on one side of the carriage and a dizzying drop on the other. They tried to distract each other by recounting ancient legends of magic, the stories of how the desert of Arthan came to be so different from the lands around they neighbored.

The first indication that they were nearing their destination was when the red and orange peaks shifted to grey stone, with veins of deep purple running through it. The trees grew thick and green, with pointed tops and feathery branches. Gradually, the road began to slope downward, and grassy expanses, dotted with pink and yellow wildflowers spread out from the bottom of the mountain range. Venallis seemed to be welcoming them with all the banners of spring on display.

They drove on for several hours after leaving the mountain range behind. In the evening they set up a little city of plum and sage-green tents in the midst of a blossoming meadow. The last portion of their journey would be completed the following day and in the company of their hosts. According to Venallian custom, a member of Ian's family would meet them to escort Kenna the rest of the way to Britwylde, the estate of the High Lord. In Ian's last letter, he'd spoken of a younger brother, Niall. It was Niall who would lead her the final leg of the journey. Kenna went to sleep that night with a heart full of hope, even though her stomach twisted with anxiety.

The next day was as lovely and temperate as any that could be asked for. A warm breeze drifted through the painted canvas of Kenna's tent, sending the silk curtains and table coverings fluttering. Venallis was not as arid as Arthan, and even their warm weather felt chilled to Kenna. She preferred warmth over cold. It was another thing she would miss in her new life. Yet, her family needed this alliance with High Lord Edan's, and marriage was the safest way to ensure their interests remained aligned.

Kenna shivered slightly; whether from the cooler air or nervousness she could not say for certain. Up until now, she'd been able to focus on the good of the family and the prospect of spreading her wings. But as she awaited the arrival of her future brother-in-law her enthusiasm was losing ground to apprehension.

I wish Ian was the one coming to greet me. He'd explained that sending an official representative was to show honor to the union, but Kenna thought it seemed an odd and rather cold custom compared to those of her homeland. She took a deep breath and tried to steady her nerves. *This is the first of many changes, but I am ready, and I do not face it alone. Ian will help me navigate the differences.*

Just thinking of her intended made Kenna smile. Though this marriage was made for reasons outside the realm of romance, affection for Ian came easily. Few people of their standing married for love, and while Kenna wouldn't say she was in love with the man, she did care for him. With time, the friendly bond they shared could easily turn to something deeper. She dearly hoped that would be the case for them.

Another breeze drifted across the grassy plains. This one carried with it the sound of hoofbeats on earthen paths and jingling bridles. Kenna drew another deep breath. She smoothed her skirts and nervously twisted a lock of hair between her fingertips. The moment had arrived, and she would face it with all the courage and dignity she could muster. Years of study and training had prepared her to handle these sorts of situations. Yet it was not the hours spent poring over books that she took solace in now. It was the courage and confidence her family's love had instilled in her that strengthened her resolve. She was doing this for them, and that was reason enough to embrace whatever the future held.

Once she was satisfied with her appearance, Kenna rose and waited for Mairi to announce the new arrivals. She didn't have to wait long. Mere seconds later, her friend stepped into the tent and hurried over to Kenna.

"The High Lord's son has arrived, my lady." She dipped into a perfectly refined curtsy before dropping all formal pretense and flashing Kenna one of her bright and infectious grins. "It seems both his sons are easy on the eye. Though this Niall is not as tall as your Ian, he has the same noble countenance. I've never seen such golden curls. I wonder if they're common here in Venallis."

"Mairi, this is meant to be a formal meeting. You should focus on our purpose." Despite her words, Kenna couldn't help but chuckle at Mairi's bubbly mood. She crossed to the entrance of the tent and peeked out of the flaps. Ian's brother was not as tall or muscularly built, but the younger son of High Lord Edan was inarguably attractive. Even from here she could see that he had a quietness to him that was intriguing. The glossy golden hair atop his head was perfectly groomed, falling just below his ears, wavy with gentle curls at the tips. A small part of Kenna wondered if it might be as soft as it looked.

She glanced over her shoulder at her friend. "But those curls do glisten quite spectacularly, don't they? As far as I know, he's not entangled with anyone romantically. Perhaps you'll make an equally memorable impression on him."

Mairi huffed a disbelieving laugh. "As if anyone would notice me when you're around. My family hardly holds the appeal yours does. Besides, I'm sure there are plenty of eligible bachelors for me to pick from. There's no reason I should settle on the first one I set my eyes on."

Kenna laughed again, though her nerves were once more breaking against the dam of her composure. Through the narrow opening between the panels of deep plum fabric, she could see her mother and father greeting the newcomers. It took a minute or two to complete the formal pleasantries and then they turned to make their way toward the tent.

Kenna jerked her hand from the canvas and retreated to the center of the room. The last thing this meeting needed was for her escort to stumble over her on their first encounter. She ran her palms down her skirts again in an effort to clear them of the sweaty sheen that was beginning to form.

Sensitive to Kenna's moods, Mairi wrapped a reassuring arm around her shoulders. She gave Kenna a gentle squeeze before ensuring everything was in order. "All will be well. You have only to get through this meeting and then we can finally settle into our new home." The words were uttered quietly but rang loudly with friendship and honesty.

Kenna straightened her shoulders and lifted her chin. *I am the daughter of one of the oldest and wealthiest families in Arthan. I'm educated, strong, and determined. This is the course I've chosen, and I will see it through with the courage and devotion that my parents have always demonstrated and instilled in me.*

With a sudden swish, the curtains opened, and Kenna's mother swept into the room with so much command and poise that she seemed to fill the space.

"Master Niall, I present my daughter and your future sister, Kenna of Vashirat Rihtall."

"Master Niall," Kenna curtsied and then stood tall to meet the eyes of the man who came to accompany her to Britwylde castle. She was immediately struck by the vivid, periwinkle of his irises, a color rare among her own people. "Thank you for your escort. I look forward to seeing my new home and becoming a part of your esteemed family."

Niall looked taken aback for an instant before he inclined his head. He said nothing at first, then shook his head minutely, and stepped forward to take her hand and place a brief kiss on the back of her fingers as he offered a more polished bow. "Well met, Lady Kenna. I—My brother is equally eager. To meet you that is, or rather see you again." His cheeks took on a distinctly crimson tint. "We should depart as soon as you're ready. It is not uncommon for the weather to turn rainy this time of year."

"We can leave as soon as your horses are refreshed," Kenna replied. She studied Niall closely. There was something about him that struck her as closed off, distant. The contrast to his brother could not have been more stark. Ian was a confident man, quick to smile, with an open and relaxed demeanor.

"Then we can depart straight away. The manor is not far." He nodded politely to Kenna and then bowed to her mother before turning on his heel and exiting the tent.

Kenna's shoulders relaxed. She exhaled slowly. The first, and hopefully most awkward, part of this day was over. Ian would no doubt be waiting at the gate for her, and having him at her side when she was presented to the household would take some of the pressure off of the momentous occasion.

"He's an odd one," Kenna's mother commented once the sound of Niall's boots grew distant. "I suppose each family has their black sheep, though. At any rate, he seems anxious to be off."

Mairi draped Kenna's cloak across her shoulders, and without further conversation they stepped out of the tent. The horses were already saddled and waiting. In truth, they'd been ready for hours. Kenna and her family were eager to settle into their quarters at the estate and be done with the business of travel for a time. Everyone was ready for a hot bath and a night in a real bed.

As soon as Kenna, her family, and their personal attendants were atop their horses, the party took off down the road that twisted through the Venallis' countryside. The rest of the company remained behind to strike the camp. They would see that everything was stored up properly and follow along after.

For a time Kenna rode at her parents' side. She was content to enjoy their company and the splendor of

Venallis' lush, blossoming scenery. Movement was far easier than waiting. Patience was not a virtue Kenna possessed in abundance when she was sure of her course and had decided to take action. This morning of waiting was a trial for her and provided for too much time to overthink the days ahead.

Her future brother-in-law rode a few paces behind the guards at the head of their procession. Niall sat straight-backed and rigid in the saddle. He never turned to admire the streams and meadows, or looked over his shoulder at those who followed. It struck Kenna that even though he was surrounded by people, Niall was a creature set apart from the world around him. She'd never seen anyone so alone.

That simply will not do. This man is to be my brother. Kenna hoped they could be as close as she was with her siblings by birth. She tapped her horse's flank with the heels of her boots. Trotting past her parents, Kenna maneuvered the animal alongside Niall's and held the pace there.

Niall's blue eyes shifted to her. He swallowed, looking as uncomfortable as he had upon their first meeting. "Is there anything you require?"

Kenna tilted her head to the side and offered him what she hoped was a charming smile. "Nothing at all. I thought we might use the ride to your home—or rather, our home—to get to know one another a little better."

"It's not a long ride," Niall replied quickly. He winced slightly, then glanced at her. He looked away just as quickly. "Or—uh—very well then. What would you like to discuss?"

"Perhaps you could tell me a bit about yourself?" Kenna hadn't expected him to respond this way, and now felt as though she were intruding on his solitude, but the conversation was started and ending it now would be even more awkward. "Your brother enjoys falconry. It's something he and I have in common. Do you enjoy the sport as well?"

Niall took another deep breath and shifted in his saddle. "I—no. I'm afraid I've never been as keen on the activity as Ian. I'm not partial to hunting in general."

"Oh." Kenna bit her lower lip and tried to think of another question.

He seemed to take her reaction as disapproval. "I do accompany Ian on hunts from time to time. I simply prefer more academic pursuits. Reading and the like."

Kenna seized on what she hoped would be an interest they could share. "You enjoy reading, that's lovely! My father has an extensive library. I've spent many a happy hour there, lost in poetic volumes. I brought some of my favorites with me. I'd be happy to let you borrow them if you like."

Niall looked supremely uncomfortable. He remained silent for some time before making any effort to speak. It seemed to Kenna that some sort of conflict warred within his mind. She was near to turning her horse around and leaving Niall to his loneliness when he finally spoke again.

"We're nearly there now. If you look just beyond those trees, you can see the east tower." Niall indicated a pointed roof in the distance, upon which fluttered a sapphire blue flag. He glanced at her, and for the first time Kenna thought she detected something other than discomfort. It was a smile, with one corner of his mouth twitching up slightly. "Our library is housed there. We have a small collection of poetry, though most of the books in the library contain the history of Venallis and the campaign to unify the clans."

Kenna saw the olive branch for what it was. "I will be certain to visit the library as soon as I'm able, for the poetry, and to learn more about my new homeland.

Perhaps that is something upon which we might build a friendship."

The glimmer of a smile faded from Niall's face. He offered her a polite nod but said nothing. Kenna stifled a sigh. Whatever his reasons, Niall was obviously hesitant to move past anything but the formalities. *I wonder if Sazia was correct about the lack of affectionate demonstrations? If so, Ian didn't seem concerned with clinging to such formality. Maybe our betrothal eliminates any need for such rigid distance in public.*

"There, the castle gates are open. I believe that my brother already rides out to meet us," Niall spoke suddenly, drawing Kenna from her thoughts.

All of Kenna's concerns for her relationship with Niall faded from her mind, as did her earlier nerves. Riding toward them, on a great grey steed, was the man to whom she would soon swear her future. Ian was as impressive and noble a man as she remembered. Even from a distance and atop a horse, one could see how tall and muscular he was. His light chestnut hair shined in the bright morning sun, straight and thick. The wild locks fluttered in the wind as he raced toward her. It only added to the air of eagerness that he exuded. Amid the swirling changes of her life, Ian felt like a grounding point.

Forgetting any concerns for the eyes of those nearby, Kenna nudged her horse to a trot. As the distance that lay between the two of them shrunk, she could see a wide, joyful grin spread across Ian's attractive features. It was infectious, and her own lips curled in a returning smile.

"Kenna!" Ian exclaimed. He slowed his horse and dismounted before the beast came to a complete stop. In a flash he was at her stirrup and offering her a hand down. "Seeing you here is like seeing the sunrise for the first time." His grey eyes were twinkling with delight and obvious adoration.

Kenna allowed him to lift her out of the saddle and blushed despite her determination to be an image of poise and dignity. She couldn't help it. After the awkward attempts at conversation with Niall, this greeting was so warm and affectionate that it made her stomach flutter. Ian didn't act like a man marrying a woman for any kind of strategy, but rather, a man who was embracing his sweetheart after an overlong separation.

"Niall!" Ian released Kenna's waist and greeted his brother. "What do you think of your future sister, my soon-to-be wife?"

"She is as lovely and as gracious as you've been relentlessly claiming, brother," Niall answered solemnly. He smiled in earnest then. "But I did not expect to meet you outside the gates. Surely mother and father wished you to remain with them, as tradition dictates."

"They did suggest I was being impulsive," Ian gave a slight, nervous laugh. It reminded Kenna of how one of her younger siblings would react when caught sneaking sweets meant for a party. "But I simply could not wait. Especially since they insisted on observing tradition and sent you to meet Kenna and her parents."

"I'm flattered you were so eager to see me again, and in truth, I'm happy to see you as well," Kenna straightened her riding clothes. "But perhaps we should continue on to the castle. I don't want my future family to think they've made a mistake or that we're entering into this recklessly."

"You're right, of course," Ian looked at Kenna with utter admiration, then beamed proudly at his brother. "Did I not tell you? She is as clever and sensible as she is beautiful."

"Yes, Ian, and thank the gods, for you have too little sense," Niall replied, but beneath the cool response, there was genuine affection in his voice. "One of you needs to observe the niceties of tradition."

Kenna felt her cheeks grow hot. She was delighted by Ian's enthusiastic greeting but overwhelmed as well. This was more than she'd expected, even if such devotion was to be hoped for. She placed a gloved hand on Ian's shoulder as her parents approached. "I think your brother offers sound advice. I'm sure the evening's festivities will provide us with ample time to reacquaint ourselves. Besides, we have our entire lives together. I think formalities can be observed for these few beginning moments."

Ian gave her another smile, lifted her fingers to his lips and kissed them gently. "As you wish, my darling." He slipped his hands around her waist and lifted her back into the saddle as if she weighed nothing at all.

Kenna watched him exchange a quick look with his brother, who simply shook his head and turned away as an amused grin spread across his face. The bond of brotherhood the two of them so obviously shared softened the otherwise serious young Niall. Ian returned to his own horse, and side-by-side with the man who would be her husband, Kenna rode through the gates of the High Lord Edan's estate.

The courtyard was festooned with banners and garlands of wildflowers, but the atmosphere among those waiting to greet her was austere and formal. Kenna studied her new home with a careful eye. Though the décor of her greeting was festive, the attitude of the High Lord and High Lady was what set the tone. There could be no forgetting that this marriage was a business matter, and not a romantic affair of the heart. Even if her intended was all smiles and joy.

Kenna sat confidently in her saddle, with her chin held high. She schooled her expression to one of practiced politeness and prepared herself for the formal introduction to the household. Now was the time for custom and tradition. She pulled her horse to a stop and waited for Ian and Niall to address their parents.

The High Lord Edan and his wife, High Lady Carene, stood at the head of a small crowd of people. At a glance it was obvious that Ian favored his father. The High Lord was an older, bearded, and more somber version of his first son. The younger of their children bore a stronger resemblance to the High Lady, with the same pale hair and blue eyes.

Without turning to look behind her, Kenna could sense her parents' arrival. Her mother's hand on her wrist a moment later confirmed their presence. Kenna placed her own hand over her mother's, glancing to the side. "All is well. I'm ready for this."

"Of that I have no doubt, my fierce little hawk. But you are still my daughter, and I will ever worry for you," her mother replied under her breath. She pulled her hand away and dismounted. Though they were in Venallis, their own customs dictated that Lady Isla should speak for their family. "High Lord Edan, High Lady Carene, we come with joy in our hearts, and hope for the union that will be forged between our two families."

The High Lord stepped forward and greeted Kenna's mother with all the honor due her station. "Good Lady Isla, we are as hopeful regarding this union as you. Even now a banquet is being prepared for the evening, to honor the arrival of you and your family. This day is a welcome one indeed."

"A hearty meal and time with friends are always welcome after a long journey." Lady Isla smiled regally.

It was an expression that Kenna knew well. This smile was that of the head of their family, a woman set to the business of the Vashirat. "But there will be plenty of time for celebrations. I believe there are still a few small matters of business we must complete before our children, and our families, are joined."

Kenna's stomach twisted uncomfortably, a ridiculous response to her mother's practical and necessary concern for the technical aspects of this union. She knew it was proper for business to be attended, but when Ian met her outside the gates, Kenna almost allowed herself to forget that there was more at stake than her happiness.

"It is easy to see why you're so respected among the other leaders of your homeland," High Lady Carene said as she moved closer to her husband's side. "Thank you for being so sensible. My husband and I were hoping to speak with you and your daughter about the details as soon as you were settled in."

"Father, mother," Ian stepped forward. He cast an apologetic look in Kenna's direction. "Surely such things can wait until tomorrow. Should we not see that Lady Kenna and our other guests have had a night's rest before we bombard them with the tedium of business?"

Kenna's mother smiled at her future son. "You forget that I was the one to speak of business first. I appreciate your concern for our comfort, but I will sleep better knowing all is settled."

"My mother is correct," Kenna added when it looked like Ian might press the matter. "The sooner we see to the final details of our betrothal, the more quickly we'll be able to begin the festivities."

Ian studied her face, then nodded slowly. "It's hardly romantic, but I suppose you're right." He helped her dismount again and offered her his arm. "Very well, then: would you at least allow me the honor of escorting you inside first?"

"I will," she answered, happily slipping her hand into the crook of Ian's elbow. One of the things Kenna most enjoyed about her intended was how genuine and informal he was. All the nobles Kenna knew were well-practiced in hiding their true emotions and motivations. His openness was refreshing—endearing even—and filled her with anticipation for the future they would build together.

* * *

A short time later, Kenna was alone with Mairi in the room she would inhabit until her wedding night. Most of her belongings were taken to the chambers that she would share with Ian after they were wed. For now, she would be housed in one of the finest guest rooms in the estate, with only the items she required between now and the wedding day.

With the official greetings over, Kenna was feeling the effects of so many days on the road. She lazily flopped back onto the bed, closed her eyes, and allowed her thoughts to drift to Ian. Seeing him again pleased her more than expected.

"Kenna? Did you hear me?" Mairi asked. She was standing nearby with a gown draped over each arm.

"Forgive me, I wasn't paying attention," Kenna admitted with an apologetic smile. "I think the cream and gold dress would be suitable for the evening. It's neither my family's colors nor Ian's."

Mairi set the other dress aside and moved to help Kenna change. "I suspect you could arrive in rags, with brambles in your hair and mud on your face, and Ian would say you were the loveliest woman in attendance. The man is clearly smitten. As I think, are you."

"I doubt that," Kenna laughed. "And shouldn't an engaged couple be fond of one another?".

"He is far more than 'fond' of you," Mairi replied without missing a beat. She grinned at Kenna impishly. "Tell me, is the view from that pedestal he has you on as dizzying as the mountain pass?"

"Tease all you like. Your day will come, and when it does, I shall be sure to give you just as much grief." Kenna pulled off her riding gloves and playfully chucked them in Mairi's direction. She could almost imagine they were in Rihta, chatting away in her bedroom. In time, she knew Britwylde would grow as comfortable and familiar.

They continued to banter playfully as Kenna stripped out of her riding habit and washed. Nearly an hour later she was dressed, and Mairi was fussing over the placement of a jeweled hairpin, when there was a knock at the door. Mairi settled for an expedient pin position, then hurried to meet the visitor while Kenna fretted over her gown.

At the threshold, she could hear a low male voice greeting her maid. "Apologies, but I was hoping to speak with your mistress before our families met to discuss final terms and we're swept up in the night's festivities."

Kenna's cheeks grew warm and a soft smile graced her lips. Propriety suggested that Ian should not be paying her private rooms a visit, but his presence was a welcome one. Kenna crossed to the door to greet her intended.

"My Lord, should we not wait until we meet with our parents?" Kenna asked.

Ian's eyes lit when they settled on her. "We should, yes, but I wanted a chance to speak with you without being concerned for the business end of things. Have I acted out of turn?"

"No, I don't mind, though it could raise a few brows if you're seen here." Kenna cast a conspiratorial glance at Mairi. "But I'm glad you came."

"Well, then," Ian replied with another one of his impossibly charming smiles. "Would you be willing to raise those brows with a stroll through the gardens? Your lady's maid could come with us. I would not impugn your honor by asking you to join me alone."

It was a silly, impulsive thing to do. Kenna knew she should decline his offer. Yet, there was something about this man that made her feel free. She liked him, and she found that she wanted to fly in the face of proper courtly protocols when he was around. The idea of walking through the gardens with Ian, not as any part of a negotiation, but simply as two people, was an enticing one.

"I will, thank you," she finally answered.

"Thank you," Ian replied. He offered her a slight bow, then stepped aside to allow her to pass. "I wanted to share some time with you, without the pressures of everyone's expectations hanging over us and examining our every interaction."

Kenna laughed, allowing him to lead her down the hall. "They wish for us to be happy in this arrangement. I don't know your parents well, but if they're anything like mine, they would sacrifice the material gains if they thought a marriage between the two of us would be unhappy."

Ian nodded thoughtfully and continued to move without further comment. They strolled through the castle until they came to a small and unobtrusive door that opened out to a quaint, well-tended garden. Mairi discreetly settled on a bench as Ian and Kenna continued to walk the perimeter. The area was not large, and she would be able to see them even from across the colorful flowerbeds and herb planters.

"You said that your parents would not agree to our marrying if they thought such a union would make you unhappy," Ian finally broke his silence. "Is that true?"

"Of course. My parents understand the needs of our people, but they love me and would not allow my happiness to be the price," Kenna explained. She didn't look up at Ian, but heard a long, slow sigh that sounded relieved. Suddenly, and despite his displays of joy, she worried that she'd misjudged his earlier greeting. *Perhaps, he was only putting on a performance and sees a way to free himself of our betrothal now.*

"Then... you do want this?" Ian asked quietly. He brought them to a stop, searching her face. "You wish to marry me?"

"Well, yes. The entire thing was my idea. Then I met you and..." Kenna slid her fingers from his elbow to take his hand in both of hers. "When I met you, you were so kind, so thoughtful. Being here with you again has only strengthened my resolve. I want this, I want you, Ian. I look forward to our life together."

A slow, radiant smile spread from ear to ear across Ian's handsome face. His stormy eyes glistened, making the contrast with his chestnut hair even more striking. "Bless you Kenna, for you have certainly blessed me!"

"Then you want this as well?" Kenna asked breathlessly. Her heart was beating wildly in her chest, her knees a little wobbly.

"I do. I didn't think I would when my father first spoke of an arranged marriage. But from the moment of our first meeting I knew the gods had drawn me to you."

Kenna squeezed Ian's fingers. Something deep inside told her that his words were more than sweet nothings. She could feel the gravity of them, this moment had a sense of fate to it.

"Would you think me too forward if I kissed you?" Ian asked sweetly, almost shyly.

"Not in the slightest. In fact, I would likely kiss you back," Kenna replied. She set aside all her years of careful instruction and allowed herself the simple luxury of being a young woman with the man she would soon marry.

Ian's arms wrapped around her waist. He moved slowly to close the distance between them. Then he lowered his head and gently pressed his lips to Kenna's. The kiss was soft, sweet, and over quickly, yet the warmth of it tingled on Kenna's lips, and replaced the tension she'd been feeling with a sort of longing that made the wedding day feel impossibly far away.

Chapter 2

Son of Britwylde

Freed of his charge, Niall spent little time in the courtyard with the others. He hurried inside his family home and to his bedroom. His mind was trapped in a whirlwind of thought. The upcoming festivities were for his brother and not something he resented. Niall loved and admired Ian, just as everyone else did. His brother was an easy man to respect. All of his life, Niall watched favor fall upon Ian, and he'd never envied it, never wished for that which was given to his brother. *Not until the moment I saw her.*

Niall stopped himself from traveling too far down that line of thought. Any form of pointless longing had to be stomped out of existence before it could take root. Niall would not allow anything to come between Ian and himself. *No, Ian will inherit the family's lands and run them with the same skill that our father does. I will return to my place at court and continue to serve at the King's side. That is the path I've been set on, and that is the one I will walk. Anything else is a fanciful dream that I will not indulge.*

Niall tossed his riding cape and gloves onto the bed and reached for the pile of scrolls he brought from Rosehaven. There were stacks of ledgers to be balanced, reports to be read and sorted according to their level of urgency. He was entrusted with organizing the business of the realm, and being ready to provide King Fergal with whatever information he might need. Busying himself with the details of his work always helped to instill a sense of balance for Niall. At the moment his mind was spinning itself into knots around the woman his brother was about to wed. He inhaled slowly, then exhaled with equal care as his eyes ran over the lines scribbled on the parchment.

Concerns for the business of court brought their own set of anxieties. King Fergal's health was declining, and he had no heir to follow in his steps. The court was in a virtual frenzy of rumors as to who would sit upon the throne next, most of which Niall ignored. If the King had decided on an heir to the throne, he hadn't shared that information with anyone but his closest advisors. Niall was the King's own godson, but that didn't mean he was privy to the sensitive information of the succession. Thinking of a world without King Fergal was difficult. He admired and cared for the King like a second father. *In some ways I feel more at ease with the King than I do with my father.*

Niall was a favorite among the young people at court, at least when it came to the King's opinion. The fact that his father was one of King Fergal's two most trusted friends had presented Niall with opportunities not available to most. His place was secure as long as the King lived, and he continued to perform his duties with diligence and loyalty. He hoped to forge a future of his own making, one in which he could see the world he'd spent so many hours imagining during his childhood frailties. In that way, Niall had far more freedom than Ian, and he valued the ability to have some control in his destiny.

Eventually, the details of holdings, town coffers, and percentages due turned Niall's mind from the health of the King, the events of the afternoon, and the conflict of emotions that stormed inside him. He hardly noticed the passage of time and didn't realize the sun had gone down until the lighting was too poor for him to continue reading without the aid of a candle.

Niall looked out the window and cursed under his breath. Dinner would already be over with, and the family, along with their visitors, would be gathering in the great hall for dancing and storytelling. He would have been missed by now. Of that there could be no doubt; nor could there be doubt that his father would be displeased by the absence. There would be more than the usual level of tension between them. Apologies would be expected and were due. His actions could easily be construed as disapproval. Niall didn't feel ready for his brother to marry, for his family to change, but he did not disapprove of something that brought Ian such obvious bliss.

He pushed aside his work and hurried to the looking glass to make sure he didn't have ink smeared on his face. *Clean, thank the gods.* He reached for one of his finer tunics and pulled it on quickly. His stomach was growling, but there was no time to stop by the kitchen for something to eat. He'd have to hurry to the hall and hope that some kind of food was still being passed around for the guests to nibble on. *If not, I'm sure I can convince Brona to take pity on me and bring a plate after.*

Niall dashed through the family quarters, pounding down the hallways of the castle until he drew closer to the banquet hall. He slowed his pace and casually straightened his tunic as he rounded a corner. Working with the King, he'd long ago learned how to move with haste and cover any evidence that he might have been running down the hallways like a street urchin. Outside of an emergency, such behavior from a member of the King's household would have been frowned on to the extreme. It was all part of the facade of the court, an illusion meant to demonstrate certainty and control to the people of Venallis. The reality was a nest of vipers, all vying for the upper hand.

Sounds of laughter and music drifted from the room ahead. The doors were flung wide, as was the custom in their household during celebratory feasts. This was to symbolize that the joy of the occasion was meant for all, from the highest noble to the lowest peasant. It was a practice held at court as well. Whatever food was left uneaten would later be distributed among the common folk, so that they might also take part in the bounty and fortune of the evening. Tonight's gala would be but a sample of what the wedding feast would offer.

The great feasting hall of Britwylde castle was festively adorned. Bouquets of pink and yellow wildflowers overflowed from ornately sculpted vases. The tables were cleared of dishes and pushed against the walls to make room for dancing. The colors of both families were proudly displayed. Banners of blue, pale gold, purple and green were draped from one side of the room to the other. Numerous candelabras filled the space with flickering firelight.

Just as Niall had expected, his father spotted his entrance immediately. *No doubt he's been watching the doors for me.* Even across the multitude of dancing couples and merrymaking, he could see the High Lord's disapproval.

Niall grimaced and quickly snatched a goblet of wine from a servant passing by. He would need to do something to squash any rumors his late arrival might give fuel to. Gossip was a pestilence among the nobility, many of whom were present to celebrate Ian's marriage. Their family was one of the highest-ranking in Venallis, and his father was one of only two men who bore the rank of High Lord. The rank was second only to the King's.

Fixing a well-practiced smile on his face, Niall raised his cup and loudly cleared his throat. "Honored guests, might I beg your indulgence in interrupting your conversations and draw your attention to a toast. Allow me, kind family and friends, to salute my brother, Lord Ian, and his bride, the Lady Kenna."

The buzz of conversation died down slowly as one pair of eyes after another, turned toward Niall. His stomach twisted beneath the polished veneer learned at court. He didn't enjoy being the center of attention, but had learned how to hold it nonetheless. "Family, friends, guests from afar. It warms my heart to see so many here to celebrate an occasion that brings great happiness to my brother and the rest of our family, which will soon include the members of Vashirat Rihtall. Though King Fergal himself could not be in attendance, he has sent gifts of silk and wine to celebrate this union. I ask you all now to raise your glasses with me, and His Majesty from a distance, to offer hope and love to the happy couple. May their lives be long and filled with joy. May tonight be but a glimpse of the prosperity the future holds for them."

A chorus of well-wishes and words of approval erupted for an instant, followed by a brief silence as everyone sipped from their cups. A few people greeted Niall and complimented his toast, but most went back to the conversations and activities they were engaged in before he interrupted. Niall caught his father's eye again and was granted an approving dip of the head, though one eyebrow was raised. This was High Lord Edan's way of saying the mistake had been remedied but should not be repeated. Niall would have to mind his time with better care for the remainder of this visit.

"Well done indeed, little brother," Ian remarked, emerging from the crowd. He was beaming with his future bride at his side. "Though it would have gone well with dinner. Where were you? You arrived so late last night and then vanished as soon as you returned today. It's almost as though you were in Rosehaven still."

Niall winced. "I am sorry. I was distracted by work brought from the palace and I lost all sense of time. I promise it was not an intentional slight, nor an indication that I feel anything but joy for your upcoming nuptials." That last part had slipped from his lips unintentionally, and he hoped it would not garner attention that could lead to further questioning.

"Of course, it wasn't, Niall." Ian slapped his shoulder affectionately. "You've been at court far too long. I don't read treachery and double meaning in every word and action. You're my baby brother, and beyond that, my most trusted friend."

The tension in Niall's shoulders eased. He lifted his cup to his lips, casting a glance at the woman who was to be his sister. Kenna studied him closely with those dark, intense eyes of hers, the gold flecks in the irises made more vibrant by the colors of the gown she wore. If she didn't share Ian's opinion, she said nothing to indicate it. Niall pulled the goblet from his lips and put aside his habit of watching everyone for signs of intrigue.

"Thank you again for your kind greeting at the borders," Kenna said graciously. Her voice and expression were as warm as a summer's afternoon. "Your brother tells me you don't visit the family estate as often as he'd like. I hope that will not be the case in the future."

"It was my duty to escort you to our home, and one I did willingly for my brother," Niall replied carefully. "Ian wrote of his great admiration for you. I would do much for his happiness. But sadly, my time is governed by the needs of the King. I rarely have leave to be away from court."

The sparkle in Kenna's eyes dimmed slightly at his response. Guilt flooded Niall's conscience. His words had been intended as a compliment, but one that kept his own emotions at a distance. She'd obviously detected that distance and misread it as dislike.

"How long did King Fergal give you leave from your duties this time?" Ian asked, seemingly oblivious to the exchange. Niall knew his brother was more perceptive than most gave him credit for. The question was a deliberate distraction from the growing tension.

"A few weeks. Long enough to attend your wedding, and to remain for the celebrations to follow," Niall said. "He might have granted a longer stay if things were not as they... It's a busy time at court, and the King depends on the assistance I provide him." Niall curbed his tongue. The King's weakened state was not widely known, and there were some things that required discretion in public, even when speaking to Ian.

"Then promise one thing, Niall," Ian said sternly. "You can consider your compliance a wedding gift."

Niall drew a deep breath and shifted uneasily. "And what is that?"

"Try to remember that you are here for happy reasons and leave your work behind," Ian's tone was serious, but his eyes twinkled merrily. "The night is a pleasant one, all our family and friends are gathered, and in less than a week I shall be wed to the most gracious, intelligent, and beautiful woman ever born." At this, he fixed Kenna with a look of utter adoration, eliciting a soft blush across her dusky cheeks.

Niall suddenly felt like the awkward and sickly boy he had once been. At court he could conduct himself with as polished and cool a demeanor as any of the nobles surrounding the King. Here in his home, he struggled to retain that sense of confidence. He was once again, the youngest son. The child who had been forced to spend so many hours in bed, recovering from one illness after another. "Of course, Ian. I'm thrilled to be here to share in your joy. Kenna, you are... I'm very happy for you, of course."

Kenna was the one to come to his rescue, speaking up sweetly as Niall verbally stumbled. "Your brother is far too generous in his compliments to me, but I do hope that we'll find time to get to know one another better while you're here. Ian is equally generous in his praise of you."

"I very much doubt that," Niall replied quickly. He could feel his own cheeks growing hot and knew he was the one blushing now. She was as enchanting as Ian had described, and it made something inside Niall ache for a life that was not his to claim. "I'm monopolizing your time. I should let you see to your other guests. Excuse me."

He bolted before either of them could say another word. Niall managed to melt into the crowd quickly and did not look back. Kenna was kind, well-spoken, obviously intelligent, and beautiful. She was also completely out of reach for anyone but Ian. Niall fervently hoped that this match continued to bring his brother joy.

The wedding will take place soon, and then I can return to the life I'm building for myself. The goings-

on here at home will return to normal, and I'll forget all about the way her eyes lit up when she spoke of poetry, or the generosity of her smile. I have little interest in marriage at this point. It serves no purpose for me to be miserable over Ian's.

The evening festivities went on well into the night. This wedding was a symbol of the stability Venallis now enjoyed. The peace had been hard-won in the King's youth, with Niall's father and the other High Lord, Dempsey, at his side. The combining of such a highly ranked house in Arthan to that of a noble family in Venallis served to emphasize that victory to the wider world.

The delegation from Arthan, with their raven hair and golden-tanned skin, stood out among the fairer population of Venallis. They carried themselves with a sense of pride and distinction. Their customs differed from the rigid codes of conduct in Venallis, but not so much that the different peoples weren't able to find common ground. The joy felt by Ian appeared to be shared by everyone assembled, and the warm glow of hearth and home permeated the bustling room.

I wonder if Kenna is as happy with the pairing as my brother? Niall pondered idly as he watched the two of them dance. He hoped she was, for both their sakes.

"We missed you at dinner, Niall," his father commented, coming to stand at Niall's side. "It's not a wonder to me that Fergal holds you in such high esteem for your diligence. He writes of you often."

"The King appreciates my efforts, but I'm sure he doesn't value me any more than the countless others that work toward the well-being of the realm," Niall answered. He knew it wasn't true, King Fergal made no secret of his fondness for Niall. In the absence of children of his own, King Fergal had often shown favor to both of High Lord Edan's sons. The fact that Niall received more attention than Ian was undoubtedly due to proximity and nothing more.

"You aren't at court now, son. You do not have to be so humble, nor close yourself off to your family." His father frowned, studying Niall. "Perhaps I allowed you to go to court too soon. You were young to enter into the service of the King. I shall write to His Majesty and ask that he grant you more time to remain with us. It will do you good to be with the family. It will give you the opportunity to know Kenna better."

"I don't regret my time at court, father," Niall answered sharply. He felt a growing sense of irritation. "I'm building a life for myself there. I love you all, of course, but I have the freedom to seek my own path in Rosehaven. This will always be home; however my duty lies elsewhere now."

"You are there because I saw fit to send you there. You still serve our family, whether here or at the side of the King. Don't mistake distance from this place with freedom from it." His father's expression was stormy. It was one that Niall knew well, having seen it many times during his childhood.

More than one person glanced furtively in their direction, their thoughts casually concealed behind a goblet or handkerchief. Niall felt the blush that colored his face grow darker. There was but one option, and it was to play the role that fate had put in place for him. "I do not forget, father. I assure you. I only meant to demonstrate that I know my place. The family holdings go to my brother. My contribution to our family is in carrying favor with the King."

His father's shoulders slumped. "Niall, that was not my meaning." He moved to stand in front of Niall, cupping his face in his palms. "You are my son. I worry for you, especially so far from home and surrounded by so much ambition. It's all too easy for a person to lose themselves in the midst of that."

Niall swallowed his frustration and the instinct to argue as he considered his father's words. He nodded obediently. To dispute the matter further would risk his father petitioning the King to release him from his duties at court altogether. His objections could wait for another time. This was Ian's night. Discord would only sully what should be a perfect evening.

His father patted Niall's cheek and released him. He summoned one of the servants to refill their cups. This was often how disagreements between the two of them played out. Niall's mother insisted that it was because they were cut from the same cloth. Niall, himself, thought it more indicative of their differences. Regardless, the argument was over for now, and any further discussion would surely happen behind closed doors before his return to Rosehaven.

Resigned to this, Niall made a point to remain at the party until all but a few of the guests retired. Those remaining were too muddled by wine to take note of the comings and goings of their fellow guests. The castle hallways were practically deserted as Niall made his way back to his rooms. In the quiet and peace of the night, he was able to think with clarity. As eager as he was to return to his duties, there was still something to be cherished and enjoyed in the simplicity of his childhood home.

His gut twisted with guilt at his own performance throughout the day. *I've not appreciated being back here. I'm pouting like a petulant child and wasting time that I could be spending with the ones I love.*

Soon Ian would be married, and their childhood would truly be at an end. The bond they shared would have to take a back seat to the one Ian would form with his wife. He would be starting down a path that would leave Niall behind. It felt as though the world was about to change forever, and he simply wasn't ready for it.

Niall cursed himself. *Why must I cling to melancholy and dread when others see only joy and the promise of the future?*

Footsteps echoed off the stone walls, pulling Niall from his brooding. Even in the dim candlelight, he recognized his brother's silhouette. Ian was rounding the corner that led to the finer guest chambers. No doubt he'd escorted Kenna to her rooms and bid her goodnight after leaving the party. Now was as good a time as any for Niall to put a better foot forward.

"Ian!" Niall hailed his brother urgently. "I'm happy to have caught you. Though I think it might be best I not offer comment on how near to your intended's bedchamber you are at such a late hour."

Ian's face turned an amusing shade of red at that remark. "Nothing inappropriate happened. We were only discussing the wedding, and we were chaperoned the entire time."

"Ah, of course you were, brother," Niall teased. Before Niall left for court, he'd helped his brother out of more than one visiting lady's chamber. Not that Ian was a notorious lothario. He was the heir to a sizeable estate and likeable. He had no shortage of admirers. Even so, he would never allow things to go too far or to tarnish the young lady's honor. "I know you care for Kenna, and at any rate, you'll be wed soon. Who would know if the two of you grew too impatient to wait for things to be made official?"

His brother scoffed indignantly. "Even were she to agree to such a thing, I would not risk sullying her reputation with rash behavior. Niall, what I feel for Kenna is more than some infatuation that can be satisfied with a quick tryst in the night. I love her. Deeply."

"Then this isn't just to appease father or carry out your duty to our family?" Niall asked, realizing as he did that a part of him hadn't believed his brother's smiles to be completely genuine.

"I never expected to feel this intensely, not when father broached the topic. I agreed to meet her out of a sense of obligation." Here Ian paused, and another, softer smile touched his lips. "But I agreed to marry her after spending a matter of hours in her company. Even then, I knew I loved her and would for as long as I drew breath."

Niall looked down in shame. "I'm sorry. I've returned home and done a terrible job of supporting you in all of this. I suppose it wasn't real to me before I was back inside these walls. I see now that this marriage, arranged or not, is what you want."

"You should spend some time with Kenna. I know that once you understand her better, you'll see why I love her so," Ian ruffled Niall's hair. "Besides, I know you. One of these days you'll meet some nobleman's daughter and be completely enthralled. You'll pine and swoon, and spend hours writing poems of her perfections. You'll make an even bigger ass of yourself than I've been doing."

"That is ridiculous," Niall declared, pushing his brother's hand away and putting on a production of smoothing his hair back down. Satisfied that his dignity was restored, he tried to stare Ian down with the same disapproving glare their old tutor used to turn on them when they were being unruly, but he couldn't maintain the performance for long. Niall laughed. "Come on, you ass. I've brought a bottle of wine back from the palace. Let's break the seal and toast to your bride. We should thank the gods that any woman has the forbearance to marry you."

They started down the hall toward Niall's bedroom, but Ian stopped them before they reached the family quarters. "Wait! I've a better idea!"

"Better than a bottle of the King's finest vintage?" Niall asked incredulously.

"What is wine without a platter of meats and cheeses to go with it?" Ian answered, doing a reasonable impression of their father's steward. "I happen to know there's a fine assortment of both in the larder."

"For your wedding!" Niall proclaimed, as if his brother didn't know what the extra stores were for. "If we're caught pillaging the larder, we'll—"

"We'll what? Get our ears boxed by Brona?" Ian laughed. He grabbed Niall by the arm and began tugging him toward the kitchen. "We're grown men. I'm about to be married, and you're working for the King."

"That will not matter to Brona. Not when she has a household full of guests to feed," Niall argued, he tried in vain to break free of his brother's vice-like grip. Brona was the head of the kitchens, a kind and doting woman, but protective of her domain, and strict. It made no difference to her that they were the grown sons of the High Lord of the estate. If they were caught meddling with her kitchen there would be dire consequences, and their father would do nothing to shield them from Brona's ire. It was a lesson learned repeatedly during their childhood. "Nor will father be pleased by such foolishness. I've already fallen on his bad side once today. I don't need to add to the pyre."

Ian only laughed and continued to drag Niall through the castle, despite his protests. It was just as it had been when they were children. Ian led the way, and Niall followed, no matter what the sport may be. Even when Niall was too frail to go out and play with the other children, Ian always found a way to include him in adventures. Sometimes he'd load Niall into a cart from the stables, piled with blankets and furs. Then off they'd go, with Ian pulling the cart and Niall laughing from his perch.

Now Niall was healthy and could move without the aid of a cart, but it was still Ian who led the way. He suddenly realized that no matter how their lives might change, this would always be the case. Ian would be there to drag him out of his doldrums and Niall would embrace the fun. Of course, they would each come to have other obligations, but there would always be a close bond that Niall could rely on.

Working in tandem, Ian and Niall were able to pilfer a small feast of cheese, sausages, and even a few of the sweetcakes prepared for tomorrow's dinner. They hurried back to Niall's room with their prizes arranged on a plate, stealthily hidden beneath a cloak. Most of the estate was in bed, but a few servants walked the halls as they finished the last of their work for the night. Ian and Niall would nod at them pleasantly, hoping that a round of cheese wouldn't drop from their stash and roll across the floor. No one would have reported back to Brona if they had been caught, but there was a level of fun in pretending their activities came with true risk.

Once they were safely behind closed doors, they settled in chairs beside the fire with their stolen banquet. Niall listened patiently as Ian told him of his courtship with Kenna and the wonders he saw during his visit in Arthan. He spoke of their father's plans for the estate and all that Ian hoped to accomplish when his own time to run things came about. When he finished, he turned the conversation to Niall's hopes for the future.

"So, what is life like at the King's side?" Ian popped another chunk of cheese in his mouth and leaned back in his chair. "You've come back twice as serious as you were during your last visit."

Niall took a long drink before answering. "It's complicated. Here people are honest about their intentions. We speak plainly with one another. At court everything is a game, and everything has more than one meaning. Everyone at court seem to have their own twist on the rules."

"That sounds terrible. I remember there being plenty of greed and peacocking, but you make it seem full of treachery."

"Things have changed since your last visit," Niall answered frankly. "I shouldn't speak of this, but King Fergal is not well."

"Yes, father received word of his illness, but surely his doctors have the situation in hand," Ian replied. "And if not the doctors, then he has access to the magical healing of the Soulbound."

Niall caught his brother's eyes. The King was weaker than most were aware. The only reason Niall knew the depth of the monarch's illness was because the King often needed an arm to lean on when he walked. As King Fergal's godson, few questioned Niall's presence at the monarch's side.

"Is it truly that bad?" Ian asked. His jovial demeanor suddenly turned solemn, revealing the true depth of the man.

"There is no proof of it, but some suspect that poison is involved." Niall admitted slowly.

"And not even magical intervention helps?" Ian considered the information with a frown on his face. When Niall remained silent, Ian drew a deep breath. "Have you considered that being at the side of a dying King isn't the safest place for you?"

"He needs me. Would you have me abandon our King, one of our father's greatest friends, when he needs someone he can trust at his side?" Niall placed his goblet on the small table between them and moved to the window, staring out into the darkness. "I love and serve our family, but I can't stay here and pretend the world outside doesn't exist. What happens in Rosehaven will have repercussions for all of us. This estate is your future, your life. My place is out in the wider world."

Ian put aside his own cup and moved to still Niall's pacing. "I would never suggest you abandon your duty to the King." He waited until Niall looked at him before he continued. "But no matter how old you get, or where life may take either one of us, you will always be my little brother. Niall, I want you to find the joy that I have. Ambitious people will not hesitate to strike when they see weakness, and a dying King could be perceived by many as a weak King. If someone were to act against him, the people closest to King Fergal will surely be at risk as well."

"King Fergal may be ill, but there is still fight in him. He could recover. Only a handful of people know how sick he is, or that poison is suspected." Niall wasn't sure if he was trying to convince his brother or himself. "The King would never have let me leave if he thought the danger too great."

"You are as stubborn as a mule, you know that? Even when you were shaking with fever and coughing so violently that you couldn't breathe, you'd always insist all was well," Ian grumbled.

"I'm still here, aren't I?" Niall said doggedly. He hated feeling like people were hovering over him. He'd fought that most of his childhood, and even though he'd been of sound body for many years, his family still fretted and worried. "I'm not that sick little boy anymore. Besides, the King has assured me that he's made provisions for my continued well-being after he passes."

Ian sighed heavily. Niall could tell that he'd won the argument for now. His brother had never been good at concealing his thoughts, and the set of his jaw spoke volumes: he couldn't deny Niall the bounty a King's favor could provide, nor could he match it.

"Shouldn't you be worrying about your wedding night, rather than your little brother?" Niall asked, making his tone light and jovial. It would be best to steer the conversation toward simpler topics.

"You have a terrible habit of worrying about everyone else when you should be taking care of yourself," Ian was quick to reply, but the returning twinkle in his eyes indicated that Ian was willing to go along with the change. "As to my wedding night, I feel nothing but happiness and anticipation."

"No need to conceal your trepidation with me," Niall teased. He turned round and plopped back in his seat, casually refilling his goblet. "Perfectly natural for a man to be nervous about his upcoming nuptials and trying to hide it behind concern for mundane business."

"I have nothing to worry about. Kenna is far greater than any woman who would ever look in your direction," Ian shot back.

"She is stunning, but I do question the sanity of any woman willing to marry you."

Ian plucked a piece of cheese from the tray on the table and tossed it at Niall. "Someone sounds jealous." his expression turned thoughtful. "Why don't you like Kenna?"

"I don't dislike Kenna," Niall answered quickly. Too quickly perhaps. "I don't know her. She seems perfectly lovely."

Ian shot him a look. "I know you, Niall. That is exactly the sort of thing you'd say about someone you have no interest in allowing into your life."

Niall frowned, carefully sorting through his thoughts to choose his next words. "She will be your wife. I will love her as a sister. I just doubt we have much in common."

Ian made a sound of disgust. "Stop playing court, Niall! At least give her a chance. I think you'd see that the two of you have quite a lot in common actually." He rose from his chair and stormed through the room for a few minutes, making Niall wish he'd answered differently. Ian stilled and stared moodily into the fire, then looked up as though he'd been struck by brilliance. "Join us tomorrow! We're going for a picnic and perhaps a bit of hunting after. Kenna is quite skilled with the bow."

"Tomorrow? A hunt?" Niall looked at Ian dubiously. "Ian, you know I'm not much for hunting. I'm wretched with a bow." He frantically grasped for any excuse that would spare him the agony of tromping through the woods, only to humiliate himself with one shot. "She'd likely back out of the entire marriage if she saw me shoot."

"Oh yes, because our future happiness depends on your ability to fire a decent shot," Ian snorted.

"Please, don't ask this of me," Niall pleaded. "Anything but that. Please, Ian, Humiliate me another way, if you must. It's bad enough I can't get out of the stag hunt for the wedding feast."

"No, no," Ian downed the rest of his wine and fixed a triumphant grin on Niall. "Every other moment between now and the wedding is filled with official business. It's a picnic and hunt, or nothing until the next time the court can spare you. I'm making this my official wedding request from you."

Niall groaned and spent a few miserable minutes trying to figure a way out of it. He came up empty-handed. "Oh, fine, then. But I swear to the gods, I will not have a single ounce of pity for you if one of my arrows lands firmly in your hind end."

Ian merely laughed. "Unlikely, considering how clumsily you handle a bow." He ruffled Niall's hair and moved to the door. "Sleep well, Niall; you'll want to be well-rested for our outing." There was still a triumphant grin on his face when the door closed behind him.

Niall finished the last of his own wine, tossed the remaining crumbs from their midnight meal in the fire, and changed into his nightshirt. Tomorrow was sure to end with sore muscles and ample humiliation. At least tonight could offer some respite.

He snuggled into his bed and listened to the familiar sounds of the estate. In the quiet darkness and solitude, Niall had time to reflect on his day. Inevitably, regret followed reflection. There was a tension in the air that spoke of more than the chaos of all the visitors and wedding plans. The world was charged with the nervous energy of impending change. It felt like the wind before a storm, dark clouds on the horizon, moving rapidly across the fields. Rather than embrace his family at such a time, Niall had been distancing himself from them.

He rolled over and pulled the blankets closer. He needed to set aside the cares of the realm for this visit and allow himself time to relax. Tomorrow, hunt or no hunt, he would do his best to ensure everything went well for Ian. His brother deserved nothing less than that.

Niall forced his muscles to relax. The sensation had become foreign to him, but it was a welcome relief. He closed his eyes and rolled onto his side. The warmth of the wine in his veins and exhaustion caused by weeks of relentless stress blotted out any remaining anxiety. Sleep claimed his mind within minutes, giving way to desires Niall refused to allow purchase in his waking thoughts.

CHAPTER 3

Picnics and Portents

Kenna laughed with abandon, spurring her horse past Ian's as they raced across the verdant countryside. The morning had been filled with the business of greeting more guests and finalizing plans for the wedding ceremony, but the remainder of the day was theirs to enjoy as they pleased. Ian had arranged for a picnic and afternoon of hunting in the woods near the family estate. His brother and Mairi were along to serve as chaperones for what Kenna hoped would be the first of many happy days to come. It was the first time in all the formality of political courtship that Kenna and Ian were able to enjoy an activity for the sake of pleasure alone.

Though Kenna loved Arthan and appreciated its beauty, she found the lush, green fields, and dense woods of Venallis enchanting in a different way. Venallis had a quiet wildness to it. The country felt alive with forces that could not be seen by mortal eyes. *It's not a wonder they say that the door to the faerie court is hidden somewhere within its borders,* Kenna thought.

Once, when she was a child, a band of traveling entertainers made the long trek over the mountains from Venallis to her family's home. She'd listened with rapt attention as they told tales of the spellbinding places they'd traveled. Even so, their plays and songs had not prepared Kenna for the untamed beauty of her current surroundings.

Away from the expectations and business of the occasion, the tension that hung over every conversation evaporated in the sunlight. Even Niall seemed more at ease than he had been the day before. He remained quiet and reserved, but he smiled on occasion and was less awkward in his responses. Mairi seemed to take this as an encouraging sign, and prattled on at his side several paces behind Kenna and Ian. From some of the looks Niall shot in Ian's direction earlier, she guessed he was only politely listening to her friend's monologue.

The woods were within sight. Kenna tapped her horse's flanks with her heels to urge the beast to greater speed. By the terms of Kenna's challenge with Ian, whoever reached the trees first would be declared winner. The loser would have to attend the winner's every whim for the remainder of the day. It was silly, really: Ian had demonstrated a dogged determination to see to any desire Kenna might give voice to from the moment of her arrival, and according to Ian, for the rest of their lives.

With the trees only a few paces away, Kenna leaned over her saddle and gave the horse a final nudge. It jumped forward and closed the remaining distance with a defiant snort. Kenna laughed again and eased the animal to a slower pace. She turned back to beam triumphantly at the others. "I believe the race is mine, my lord."

"And one I'm happy to concede to you," Ian replied with equal delight. "Though you hardly needed to win the race to claim my service. I am yours, now and after we wed."

"And yet, win I did," Kenna replied playfully. She turned from Ian and dismounted, pretending to survey the bright green wood before her. Ian had a way of making her forget responsibility. She liked it—it was so different from anything she'd experienced before. Her entire life had been made of expectations. Ian seemed to want nothing more than to shower her with utter love and devotion. The man was all warmth and sunlight, and he created a kind of charmed bubble for himself and those around him.

Ian hopped out of the saddle with a chuckle. He took their horses to a nearby tree and hitched their reins to one of the branches. Kenna noticed him stare pointedly at his brother when Niall and Mairi caught up. The younger brother drew a deep breath and climbed down from his own mount. He looked like a man burdened with an unwanted task.

Kenna's mood soured slightly. *I wish Ian wouldn't push Niall to engage with me. He clearly has no interest in doing so.*

Ian had assured her that Niall's distance was not personal, that he was simply reserved with people until he knew them better. It was difficult, but Kenna was willing to trust Ian's instincts with his brother. If it was time that Niall needed, trying to force a friendship would only make things awkward and spoil the afternoon.

"How are you enjoying our afternoon out?" Mairi asked. She hooked her arm through Kenna's, all bright smiles and eagerness.

"Well enough. As are you, it seems." Kenna replied. She raised an eyebrow, trying to put her frustrations aside and enjoy the day. When Niall walked by to speak to his brother, her smiled dimmed.

"What's the matter?" Mairi asked under her breath. She pulled Kenna a slight distance from the brothers. "Are you having second thoughts? You know if you voice them your parents will understand."

Kenna glanced back at Ian. He was busy chatting with his brother as he pulled bundles of food from their saddlebag. She shook her head and forced her expression to relax. "No, Ian is everything I could have hoped for, and he's made our arrival a merry one. I already care a great deal for him. We'll be happy together."

Mairi's eyes narrowed slightly, darting between Kenna and Ian, then settling on Niall. "Is it his family?"

"I'm sure I'm reading too much into things," Kenna said, trying to convince herself as much as Mairi. "I just get the sense Niall is disinterested in forming any kind of bond with me."

"He is rather quiet, but I'm sure that has nothing to do with you. Besides, Niall lives at court. You won't see much of him," Mairi pointed out.

"I suppose you're right. I don't even know why it bothers me so much." Kenna sighed. She was used to a household full of siblings. They laughed and shared stories and treasured their time together. But as she thought about it, Kenna realized a desire for a familial bond wasn't the reason Niall's distance bothered her. She felt compelled to make a connection with him, to know who he was. He intrigued her for reasons she couldn't put a name to.

"I'm sure it's just nerves, Kenna," Mairi whispered reassuringly. She wrapped her arm around Kenna's shoulder and gave her a gentle, one-armed hug before steering her back toward their companions.

Ian had a large bundle in his left hand but held his right arm out for Kenna. She tucked her hand into the crook of his elbow and allowed him to lead her down the shaded path through the trees. Here and there beams of radiant sunlight managed to pierce the leafy canopy overhead. It dappled the violet-blanketed forest floor with light and made the color of the blossoms even more striking. Gossamer spiderwebs stretched from tree to tree, sparkling with faerie dust. Normally, any sign of arachnids would have sent chills down Kenna's spine, but here the webs shimmered like strings of dazzling gemstones. It was easy to imagine they were precious garlands set in place by the spirits of nature themselves, rather than the work of spiders at all.

"Keep an eye out for faerie rings. They say if you wander into one of their circles, they'll pull you into their world between realms and keep you there for a hundred years," Ian said, his tone casual and relaxed despite the warning. He smiled at Kenna. "Don't worry, as long as we stay on the path there's little danger of faerie mischief."

"Back home we're more concerned with being snared in the dreamworld of the djinns," Kenna replied. "I think I would prefer the mischief of the faeries to the nightmares of the djinns."

"I once read a story about a man who captured a djinn with an enchanted net," Niall piped in. His voice held more interest than Kenna had ever noted before.

She looked over her shoulder, happy to have caught his attention for more than just a polite response. "Yes, my father told me a similar tale. Though in his version it was a rope made of seaweed."

To her surprise, Niall offered her an unguarded smile. "I often wonder if such tales could be true." He looked thoughtful for a moment. "It seems a bit silly that something as simple as a net or a rope could entrap a being that exists in the realm of dreams."

"Though if the tools were magical themselves it would level the field," Kenna replied. She released Ian's arm and slowed her pace so that Niall and Mairi could catch up and they could converse more easily.

"Still, it seems strange, don't you think?" Niall asked. He glanced furtively into the shadows of the forest. Occasionally, the sunlight caught his hair and caused it to flash like polished gold.

"'Tis strange indeed, but so often the most complex problems have simple solutions," she replied quickly. It was something one of her tutors often said, and she'd found it true on more occasions than expected.

Niall's eyes met hers, and for the length of a breath the guarded barrier was gone. Then he blinked and quickly turned away again. "And sometimes complications are best left to resolve themselves."

Just like that, the momentary connection was lost. Kenna sighed. She sensed a depth and intelligence in Niall that fascinated her. She suspected that they had more in common than one might think, and longed to be able to engage him beyond a superficial level. *It's a pity he holds the world at arm's length. But I have a life to build with Ian and that is where my focus must remain.* Even as she told herself this, Kenna knew she would continue to try to forge a bond with Niall, for the sake of peace in the household if nothing else.

Ian cleared his throat and shifted the bundle in his hands. He looked mildly annoyed but then quickly turned to gaze down the path. His expression brightened. "The river is just ahead. You can hear it now. I thought we could have our picnic on the banks."

"And a hunt after that?" Kenna asked. She was eager to see what sport her new home offered.

"If we're not too full after our meal. I think Brona may have sent us with half the pantry," Ian answered, he hefted the load of food to emphasize the weight of its contents.

"If we can't manage a hunt today, we can simply wait for the hunt tomorrow," Niall added, not concealing the hope in his voice. "It's customary for the groom to fell a stag before the nuptials, to demonstrate his commitment to provide for his betrothed and for the lands he will one day preside over. On a more practical level, it helps to feed the tide of guests."

"I had hoped to postpone the hunt for a day to allow your family another night of rest, but father insisted," Ian explained apologetically. Leaning closer to Kenna, he whispered, "Just as well, I suspect Niall would have tried to get out of going if he had more time to come up with a valid escape from the activity."

Kenna looked at Niall curiously. "So, you dislike hunting stag as much as you dislike falconry?"

"I prefer indoor pursuits," Niall replied quietly. He looked miserable at the prospect of it. "Archery is the popular method of hunting here, and I've never been skilled with a bow. The moment I let loose with a shot everyone will wish I'd stayed home."

"Perhaps Kenna could help you improve," Mairi piped in cheerily. "She's an excellent archer."

Kenna shot her friend an annoyed look. Niall barely seemed willing to carry on a conversation with her. The last thing she wanted to do was force lessons on an unwilling pupil.

Niall looked utterly panicked. "Oh, I don't—there's hardly time for—"

Ian started laughing and tried to cover it with a cough. "I'm afraid it would take more than an afternoon to help Niall, no matter how skilled the teacher might be. His aim is excellent; the problem lies with his ability to handle the bow itself."

"I'm sure he isn't that bad. Some people simply do not have an interest in archery," Kenna said. She didn't want to further strain the tension that Niall displayed around her. She pulled Ian forward, focusing on the river ahead of them. "The day is beautiful. I suggest we forget archery and simply enjoy our meal. If the food packed for us is even half as tasty as the dinner your dear Brona prepared last night, I expect we'll all be too stuffed to move, let alone hunt. I assure you, Master Niall, I won't force the issue."

"Thank you, my lady." Niall's relief was evident to Kenna even without looking at his face. The tone of his voice made it so obvious that one might have thought he'd just escaped a grisly execution.

The matter was dropped without further discussion after that. They spread a blanket on a patch of dry grassy ground next to the river and turned their attention to the delights of their picnic. The kitchen had been generous in its efforts, supplying meat pies of quail and berries, and a round of rich, creamy cheese. For dessert they were given cakes drizzled with a sweet honey glaze that complimented the elderberry mead Niall brought from Rosehaven, a gift he'd received from the King on his last birthday. It was a perfect moment of contentment, one in which Kenna was happy to indulge.

The gentle breeze that wafted through the trees carried the scents of honeysuckle and lavender. Birds sang merrily with the accompaniment of the rushing water. The conversation turned to details and plans for the wedding, which included elements from both cultures. The ceremony would take place outdoors to honor Kenna's traditions, and would include a formal handfasting to honor Ian's. Thankfully, the two cultures didn't differ greatly on the words of the vows to be made.

They were still picking at the last crumbs of their lunch and filling their goblets with the final drops of wine when the shadows around them began to twist and darken unnaturally. The air, which until then had been warm and pleasant, took on a strange chill that settled deep in the bones. Kenna shivered, reaching for her cloak as the gusts rustled through the trees.

An odd splashing sound drifted across the river, standing out above the typical rush of the current. Ian pulled Kenna further from the river and reached for his bow. He caught Niall's eye, and both jumped to their feet, the younger pulling a knife from his boot as he rose. The sense of peace and cheer that Kenna experienced moments before was replaced by a sickening dread that made her regret eating such a large lunch. She silently cursed her decision to leave her bow and quiver with the horses.

"Do you see anything?" Ian asked his brother in hushed tones. He had the stance of a trained warrior, alert and ready to jump to action if an attack should come.

Niall shook his head, drawing closer to the riverbank. Another sound joined the distant splashing: a soft keening cry. The weeping grew louder as the wind whipped their hair and garments. The sound wasn't quite human but so close to it that it made the discordance even more disturbing. It was clearly audible over the rushing water, and the leaves that were being brutally ripped from their branches by the violent gales. Kenna felt the urge to cover her ears, but somehow sensed this sound could not be blocked out so easily.

"What is that?" Mairi asked. She'd scooted closer to Kenna and clutched her hand tightly. Kenna squeezed her fingers, hoping that lending comfort to her friend would strengthen her own courage

Ian remained near them, but Niall continued to approach the river's edge. He didn't look back, nor offer explanation, just stared at the distant shore, narrowing his eyes as if he were trying to focus on something. Kenna followed his gaze and then violently pushed herself backward, gasping in shock and disgust. To her abject horror she realized what was holding Niall in such thrall.

On the opposite shore was a horrifying specter. A woman in a tattered, black gown knelt at the water's edge. Every second that Kenna stared at the disturbing being revealed a new and terrible detail. The woman's face was a mask of horror. Her skin was grey and gaunt, stretched and broken over a skeletal head with empty, black pits where eyes should have been. She plunged what looked like bloody rags into the water, as though trying to remove the stains. When the garment did not come clean her moans intensified, lamenting her failure.

The sound grew louder and took on a frenzied tenor. A voice reverberated through the cries, adding a haunting song to the eerie wails. Though the creature's lips did not open and close, it was obvious that the song emanated from her. It was not the ghostly combination of sound that froze Kenna's blood, but the words that filled the air.

"Hands will join in fasting. One death will herald more. Harken ye my words, for sorrow stands at your door." The woman's empty-pit eyes seemed to fix on Kenna and bore into her.

Ian snatched an arrow from his quiver and pointed his weapon at the distant specter. The arrow sailed across the water and passed through the woman's torso without effect, as if she were nothing more than thin air. Niall tensed and shifted suddenly. His face was white, and the expression it bore was one of unmistakable fear. He raised his arm and threw the dagger in his hand with such force that it sailed across the entire breadth of the river without wobbling or wavering.

The woman stared at the weapon as it approached then vanished seconds before the blade sliced through the empty space she'd occupied a second earlier. With her disappearance, the howling of the wind died down, but the warning it brought continued to echo in the air.

"Wh—what was that?" Mairi asked. Her voice was a terrified, shaking whisper.

"A banshee," Ian answered gravely. He lowered his bow and began to gather the supplies of their picnic. "We should go." Ian looked at his brother, who continued to stare across the river, posture rigid. "Niall, we need to get Kenna and Mairi back to the castle quickly."

Niall jumped and turned around slowly, as if he'd forgotten their presence entirely. His face remained ashen and his eyes looked haunted. "I heard the banshee's song, Ian."

"We all did. That's how it works. Those who see its face hear its voice," Ian took a step toward his brother. He held his hand out to the younger man, as if Niall was a frightened animal. "Let's go home. There's nothing to be gained from staying here. Come Niall, take my hand."

Niall looked back over the water. "I shouldn't leave my dagger, it was a gift from our parents. Will you come with me, Ian?" Ian nodded and the two of them moved a few feet up river to a place where there were rocks laid out closely enough to cross.

Kenna took a deep breath and focused on Mairi, who continued to cling to her hand with cold, trembling fingers. When Mairi stopped shaking, Kenna was able to focus her attention on the task of cleaning up the remains of their meal. By the time Ian and Niall returned everything was stowed away and they were able to leave.

The ride back to the house was a somber and quiet affair. Their earlier cheer was replaced by solitary contemplation. Where the countryside was beautiful and wild before, it now felt like eyes followed their progress all the way back to Britwylde castle. Kenna wanted to ask Ian more about what happened, but she feared speaking of the encounter would somehow invite the banshee's return. Further discussion could wait until they were safely within the confines of the family home.

Unfortunately, peace and quiet was not to be. The courtyard was bustling with activity when they rode through the gates. A number of new guests had arrived during their outing, and were issuing instructions to their servants, or chatting with one another as their belongings were unloaded. As the bride and groom, Kenna and Ian could not pass through the throng without being noticed.

Many of the newcomers were nobles from court who recognized Ian's younger brother immediately. They greeted Niall with waves and smiles that looked like perfectly painted masks. Ian and Niall exchanged an anxious glance. Whatever message passed between the brothers was a mystery to Kenna. Thought the encounter undoubtedly weighed heavily on their minds, Ian's and Niall's faces betrayed no signs of distress. Niall immediately moved ahead to intercept his fellow members of court, distracting them as Ian helped Kenna out of the saddle.

"Do not speak of what happened at the river. Such omens are easily misinterpreted, and it could cause panic among our guests. It would be best to discuss what happened, later, when it can be done in private," Ian whispered in her ear. He looked back at his brother. "Niall's far better at dealing with those prancing peacocks than I am."

It was apparent to Kenna that Ian was not as comfortable in the company of the nobles from court as he was with his family and other members of the Britwylde household. Niall, on the other hand, navigated the interactions with surprising ease. Kenna had seen her mother and father conceal their own emotions in a similar way. It was a strange contrast between the brothers. It was even stranger when Kenna considered how uncomfortable Niall was whenever he spoke to her.

"I take it we won't be spending much time visiting your brother at the palace," Kenna whispered back, all too willing to avoid thoughts of the banshee for now. Perhaps with some time and distance she would be able to think about the encounter without feeling the dread its presence evoked.

The muscles in Ian's jaw tightened. He eyed the men and women his brother was speaking to with barely concealed contempt. "I wish he would spend less time at the palace. I believe Niall's presence there has had a negative impact on him. He smiles less, and grows increasingly distant and guarded. He's more like them every time he comes home."

"I understand your concern, Ian, but surely it's wise to have your family represented at court," Kenna pointed out, careful to keep her voice pitched for Ian's ears alone. It was no secret that King Fergal lacked an heir. His death could bring a great deal of uncertainty and confusion. "The King won't live forever. Perhaps

Niall sees an opportunity to keep a set of eyes and ears where important decisions are made."

"That's exactly the sort of thing Niall says whenever I voice my concerns," Ian grumbled, but seemed relaxed slightly.

"And he's right." Kenna laid a hand on Ian's shoulder. "We should be thankful to have a connection at court to defend Britwylde's interests when needed."

Ian nodded and said no more of it. Niall was approaching with another young man at his side. He was tall, with light brown hair, that contrasted attractively with a pair of stunning green eyes. Yet it was the mischievous quirk to his mouth that drew attention. His every movement radiated a kind of casual confidence that seemed to put the people around him at ease. From the smile that spread across Ian's face Kenna sensed a kinship that ran deeper than that shared with the other nobles present. Both Ian and Niall were obviously at ease with him.

Kenna's shoulders relaxed. She concentrated on the warmth and brightness of the sunshine, and the people surrounding her. Turning her attention to the ordinary made it easier to set aside her fear and concentrate on duty. This was the beginning of her role as the future lady of this region, and how she conducted herself during these early moments could set the tone for years to come. She'd spent much of her life being educated in the fine dance of politics. Now it was time to put that knowledge to use. Judging from Ian's reaction to the presence of the courtiers, it was likely going to fall to her to navigate the ever-changing moods of those in power.

"So, this is the lady of the hour." The newcomer spoke to her before Ian or Niall had offered introductions. There was a flash of a brilliant smile, then a flourish and playful bow before Kenna.

"My lady, this is Lord Cathal, son of the High Lord Dempsey," Ian put a hand on his friend's shoulder as he rose.

"It's a pleasure to meet you, Lord Cathal," Kenna replied, returning Lord Cathal's smile with one of her own. She liked him already, and it was clear that his presence delighted Ian. His friendly reception and easy-going nature created a feeling of belonging. Kenna hoped he would be a regular fixture in their lives.

"I assure you, my lady, the pleasure is undeniably mine."

"Cathal spent half of his summers here. He's practically family," Niall supplied the details of their association.

"You're late, you cad! I expected you with Niall." Ian pulled him into a hug, clapping his back.

Lord Cathal laughed, returning the embrace. "My father had important business for me. You know how relentless he can be if he thinks his desires are justified. There's nothing else in the world that would have delayed me. I assure you."

"Does that business have anything to do with the rumors that have been flying around court, concerning a possible engagement of your own?" Niall asked.

"You should know better than to take note of such nonsense," Cathal scoffed. "No, it was nothing as interesting as that. Just his usual blather about how I must take my future more seriously among other tedious topics. I escaped as soon as I could, and I'm told I've arrived before the stag hunt!"

Behind them, Mairi whimpered slightly. Kenna turned to her friend and felt a wave of guilt. They'd moved past their own fear and left Mairi alone in the shadows. If anyone were to look at the poor girl, they'd surely see that all was not well. Her cheeks lacked color and her eyes were red, filled with tears that had yet to fall.

"Excuse me, good sir. I'm afraid my poor maid suffered a fall from her horse during our ride," Kenna curtsied to Lord Cathal, hoping that her own cheeks weren't losing their color. Seeing Mairi's distress brought the echo of the banshee's song to the forefront of Kenna's mind. "I must attend to her health. I do look forward to seeing you at the hunt."

"My dear, sweet lady," Cathal turned his attention to Mairi. He approached her horse and looked up with genuine concern. "I'm terribly sorry to hear that a creature as lovely as yourself had to endure such a terrible ordeal. May I help you from your saddle?"

Mairi looked from Kenna to the young nobleman, and a blush replaced the ashen pallor of her cheeks. "Of—of course, my Lord. That would be most kind of you." Her voice still shook, but Kenna could see that Cathal's kindness was helping her recover from her frightened stupor.

He looked at her with an expression of gentle reassurance and held his arms up. Mairi leaned down so that he could wrap his hands around her waist. He lowered her to the ground with tender care, then held her for a moment when she wobbled on her feet. Mairi offered him a strained smile, tucking a loose lock of dark, wavy hair behind her ear.

"There you are, my lady," Cathal said finally. He guided her toward Kenna. "I pray that a little rest will be all that's needed to have you right as rain again."

Kenna took hold of Mairi's hand. "I'll see her to her room and get her settled in bed."

"Thank you, Lord Cathal," Mairi said as Kenna led her away. "That was most gallant."

Lord Cathal inclined his head with a hand over his heart. "It's the least I can do for a lady of such sweetness. What sort of man would I be if I left you to collapse on the cobblestones?"

Kenna stopped at Ian's side as they passed him. He bowed to her, before leaning in to place a chaste kiss on Kenna's cheek. His lips remained close to her ear for a few seconds. "Speak to our cook. Brona keeps a store of medicinal teas. She'll be able to provide something to soothe Mairi's nerves."

"I'll see you at the dinner table, my darling." Kenna was overcome with a wave of affection for him. She turned her face toward Ian's and pressed a kiss to his cheek in return. It was the first time she'd used such an endearment, and the effect was brilliant.

Any remaining tension from their harrowing experience evaporated. The expression on Ian's face was like watching the first rays of the sun touch the amber dunes of Arthan. "I shall count the minutes."

Another whimper from Mairi pulled Kenna away from the tender exchange and the warmth that was blossoming between Ian and herself. She wrapped an arm around Mairi's shoulders and ushered her across the courtyard and through the doors of the castle. Some acknowledged their passing, but no one slowed them with anything more than brief greetings. Away from Cathal's flirtations, Mairi paled again. The lack of color in her cheeks and her shaking hands were evidence enough that haste was required and conversation would have to wait.

Once they were in the privacy of Mairi's bedroom, Kenna helped her out of her boots and riding clothes before tucking her into bed. Per Ian's suggestion, she sought a remedy from Brona, and was quickly supplied with a steaming kettle of lavender tea. Brona brought the brew herself and was as warm and soothing as the beverage. She looked at Mairi with unveiled concern, clucking quieting and muttering about the lack of color in "the poor dear's face."

Kenna assured her that the tea was all that they required, and released Brona to her regular duties. With so many people packing into the place, the kitchens needed its supervisor's attention far more than Mairi and Kenna did. When they were alone again, Kenna settled next to Mairi's bedside and took her friend's hand in her own. "All will be well. Ian tells me that such omens do not always mean what they seem."

"That horrible thing at the river spoke of death, Kenna," Mairi replied. She looked at Kenna with wide, terror-filled eyes. "'Halls of blood.' That's what it said. The halls would turn scarlet with blood."

Kenna frowned. That wasn't what she'd heard, it wasn't even close. "You must have misheard it, Mairi. The song mentioned my handfasting and that one death would be followed by others. That could mean anything, and who's to say that any of this will happen soon or at all?"

"I heard nothing about a handfasting, Kenna," Mairi shook her head adamantly. "It sang of blood and betrayal." Mairi began to cry. "I think it was warning me of my own death."

"No, shhh," Kenna wrapped her arms around her friend. "Try to rest for now, dear one. I know it's difficult to feel safe right now, but you need to allow yourself time to recover. It will be easier to make sense of things once you've rested." Kenna reached for the cup of tea on the bedside table and held it to Mairi's lips. She wished there was more to be offered, well aware that her reassurances were hollow. She had no way of knowing what lay ahead. Yet the urge to comfort Mairi remained; doing so helped to ease her own fears.

"Now drink this down. We're safe here and all will be well."

Mairi offered no further dispute. She drained the contents of the cup and then laid her head back on the pillow. She sniffled a few more times, but the ingredients of Brona's tea were effective, and after a short wait, Mairi drifted into a peaceful slumber.

Kenna would have joined her friend in an afternoon's nap, but she knew she'd only toss and turn and drive herself mad reliving the encounter. The words of the banshee continued to unnerve her, no matter how much she wanted to trust her intended's assurances that the incident could be misinterpreted. The whole thing made her feel helpless, dragged toward a fate she could not avoid.

Kenna attempted to stave off the feelings of impending doom with mundane activities. She washed her face and tidied her hair, trying to make the day feel normal again. Yet the evidence of the fright remained stark in the lack of color in her cheeks and the haunted shadows that lurked in her eyes. Applying a bit of rouge to her cheeks helped, but it wouldn't be convincing to anyone who knew her well. To anyone else, she would blame her strained appearance on weariness and wedding jitters. Certain that she'd done as much as she could, Kenna checked on Mairi a final time and then slipped out of the room, quietly closing the door behind her.

Ian met Kenna in the hallway. He gathered her into his arms and held her tightly for a few minutes before speaking. Kenna snuggled into the warm safety of his embrace and allowed the circle of his arms to build a barrier against the fright of the encounter at the river. With Mairi asleep, she wasn't sure what to do now that her time was her own. She didn't feel up to mingling among strangers, but didn't want to go back to her own room where she would have nothing to do but sit and ponder what happened. Spending time with Ian seemed like an excellent option.

"Are you all right?" Ian asked, finally releasing her to search her face.

"I can't stop hearing that horrible creature's song," Kenna admitted. "Now that Mairi is tucked away in her bed resting, I was hoping we could spend some time together. I don't want to be alone with nothing to do to but fret over it."

"I wish I could stay with you. I need to meet with my father to discuss some of the details of the coming days and tell him what happened. But I can come back to you as soon as I'm finished," Ian stroked the side of her face. "Unless you'd rather rest before dinner."

"I understand, but no, I don't think I'll be able to rest for a good long while," Kenna replied, stifling her disappointment. They'd had so little time alone together. "I just wish there was something I could do to distract myself. If I were back in Arthan I could think of a dozen options, but this place is still so new to me."

Ian thought for a moment then looked around the halls. "Come with me. I think I might have a solution for you."

Kenna followed as he led her through the residential wing to a plain door at the end of a long hall. They stepped through it and climbed up a spiraling staircase to a second door. Ian glanced at her and smiled before he opened it to reveal a large room lined with shelves that were filled with leatherbound books and rolled-up pieces of parchment. He pulled her into the room and moved to the side to offer her an unobstructed view.

"I recall your fondness for reading. My lady, I present the library of Britwylde." He gestured grandly. "These are mostly records and historical accounts, but there's a hidden room that I think will provide the sanctuary you seek."

"Ian, this is wonderful! I don't mind reading Venallian history. You don't need to risk running late to your father just to see me settled," Kenna was already moving further into the library, eyes scanning every corner of the space before her.

He took her hand and gently ushered her deeper into the chamber, then through another after that. "Trust me, you'll like this."

He guided Kenna to a third door on the far wall of the second room. It opened into a small, tidy space that held an air of peace, and the magic that a person's interest and care could give to such tucked-away corners. Ian was correct, she did like it.

The single window that took up much of the back wall was made of many tiny panes of stained-glass. The magnificent image it held was a majestic griffon standing on a cliff and gazing out over a valley. There were two wooden bookshelves, roughly waist-high on either side of the room, with little figures carefully arranged on the tops. In the center of the room was a small desk with a comfortable, cushioned chair behind it. A map was spread out across the desk with several odd little dots marking its surface.

"This is where the books of poetry and legend reside," Ian waved for her to enter. "Make yourself comfortable and I'll come back for you as soon as I finish with my father."

"Thank you," Kenna replied, absently. She was too fascinated by the humble wonders of the room to offer anything else. Behind her, she heard Ian chuckle before he stepped outside and closed the door.

Kenna wasted no time in examining and selecting one of the books on the shelves, and decided on a small collection of faerie legends. Book in hand, she pulled the chair closer to the window and settled in for the adventure such an object could offer.

The pages of the book were lovely, filled with beautifully detailed illustrations, and carefully chronicled tales and songs about the faerie realms. Some of the pages contained little notes in the margins, thoughts, questions, and observations written in a different hand. These were as interesting and thought-provoking as the stories themselves. In no time at all, Kenna was utterly engrossed in what she was reading. The ghastly image of the banshee was replaced with thoughts of speckled faerie wings, and magical, glittering landscapes. Portents of death and destruction were erased by elegant verses of light and laughter.

CHAPTER 4

A Crown of Bones

Niall mentally clung to the composure that the protocol of greeting guests provided. Even so, it took all of the discipline he possessed to keep his knees from shaking, and his hands were like ice. The pretense that all was well granted a slight sense of control, but it was a fragile illusion. Simple things caused the image of the specter to flash through Niall's mind; a high-pitched peal of laughter, the sloshing of a horse drinking from the nearby water trough were easily twisted into the ominous song of the death harbinger.

The banshee had looked directly into Niall's eyes and it seemed to drain him of anything but dread. The encounter provoked a disquieting sense that unexpected change was on the horizon. The banshee's song continued to play relentlessly in Niall's ears. Conversations helped to dull the sound of it, but the words could not be drowned out and eventually they overwhelmed his tenuous hold on the present.

"Beware the poison drip as Fate tightens her grip. A twisted path is near, stained by the blood of a life you hold dear."

Niall jumped slightly, realizing he'd lost control of his thoughts and was doing little to conceal it. The courtyard felt like it was closing in on him. Cathal and Ian were no longer with him, but he was not alone. Someone was asking him a question and he hadn't the slightest idea what it was. Niall swallowed, forcing the world back into focus and concentrated on the person at his side.

"Forgive me, Sir Liam," Niall interrupted his elder quite improperly. He needed to find a place of quiet where he could mull over what happened. "I just remembered that I was supposed to meet with my father when we returned from our outing. I'm afraid I must go." He stepped away from the man without waiting for a reply.

More people tried to pull him into conversations as he pushed through the crowd, but Niall only muttered distracted excuses and bolted for the door. As soon as he was inside his family's home, Niall dispensed with propriety and ran for the residential wing. Most of their guests were outside enjoying the warm spring afternoon, but those that remained indoors cast curious glances in his direction.

The door to his room was within sight when Niall almost ran his mother over. He skidded to a stop and stared at her, panting. Normally running through the halls when they had a household full of company would have earned him a stern reprimand, but he was too unsettled to care. Niall didn't say a word, he couldn't seem to form an explanation. His mother's eyes clouded with concern and she opened her arms to him. Niall fell into the safety of that embrace just as he had when he was a little boy.

"Come, we'll talk in my chambers," his mother stated succinctly. Lady Carene was an astute woman even with strangers; with her children, she was practically a soothsayer. Where Niall's father was disciplined and reserved in his affection, his mother was as warm and gentle as a summer's day.

She ushered Niall out of the hallway and into her chambers with the smooth and reassuring confidence that Niall had relied on through the worst of his childhood maladies. Her chambers were richly and elegantly decorated in shades of pale blue and grey, and filled with all that she treasured. Portraits of her parents, husband, and children hung on the wall opposite the door in polished wooden frames. The chairs were cushioned with goose-feather pillows of the finest brocade available. A harp stood by the window, polished and waiting to be played. The space always provided a peaceful sanctuary for the family during times of uncertainty.

"Now tell me what troubles you, dearest. I can see that it's more than the disagreement with your father last night. What has happened?" His mother situated them both onto a bench beside the fire and stroked Niall's hair away from his face.

"We encountered something in the woods," Niall began slowly. Now that he was away from the noise and bustling of so many people, he could feel some semblance of composure returning, but speaking of the banshee was difficult. "I fear for the changes that are coming."

"Change can often be difficult and frightening," she said and folded her arms around Niall. "Much is changing for our family now. You and your brother have reached an age of transition. Your brother will be a husband soon and a father after that. You're at the side of the king and on the verge of great things. Such times can bring difficult adjustments."

"It's more than that, mother," Niall replied. He pulled away from her and stared into the flames. "I've heard portents of loss, and omens of death on the wind. I saw—heard a banshee's cry."

His mother's grip on his shoulders tightened. She was silent, and when Niall looked at her face he could see shadows in her eyes. The revelation had shaken her, unraveling the calm he'd been reaching toward. Yet, when she finally spoke her voice was strong and steady. "What did you hear, my darling?"

"The banshee sang of poison. And of fate's grip," Niall shuddered. He was certain the unearthly tones of that song would plague his dreams for the rest of his life; however long that may be. "It said there was a path stained with blood." He wrapped his arms around his mother and began to shake. "I feel as though death is preparing to strike, and I can't do anything to stop it."

"No," his mother said firmly. Niall got the impression her response was not as much to him, as it was a single word to defy the banshee's predictions. She held him tightly, smoothing his hair and rocking back and forth just as she had done when he was small enough to curl up on her lap. "Hear me now, Niall, and let my words replace those of the banshee. Death will come to us all one day, but I will stand in the path of fate itself to keep you from harm. You and your brother are my greatest hopes realized. A banshee's song is nothing in the face of a mother's love."

Niall shook his head. "But how can we fight a death that is already foretold?"

"You said the banshee sang of poison," she cupped his face and met his eyes. "We will have every dish and goblet tested by more than one taster. Nothing will pass the lips of those in this house unless we can be assured that it is pure."

Niall nodded silently, despite his mother's reassurances, he couldn't help but feel like he was being stalked by powers far beyond his control. It wasn't only the banshee's words that filled him with fear of what lay ahead. Nothing was simple anymore; every turn held an air of irrevocable resolution.

Niall's mother pulled him close again. "You have always carried the weight of every care on your shoulders, Niall. Allow me to carry this burden for you. Your father and I will do all in our power to ensure the safety of this family."

"Yes, mother," Niall nodded hesitantly. "I'll try to put it from my mind."

"Do the best you can to enjoy the celebrations that lay ahead. It know it is difficult, but you must set aside your concern and live in the moment," she said, smoothing Niall's hair. "We cannot allow fear to blind us to the good that surrounds us. Your brother's wedding is a joyful occasion and should be met as such."

"I suppose you're right. Even tomorrow's hunt will be better than sitting in my room and seeing death in the shadows," Niall conceded. He took a deep breath and offered his mother a weak smile. "Thank you, mother. I admit to missing your counsel and comfort when I'm at court."

"I will be sure to visit you more frequently in that case," she smiled warmly. "I give you leave to spend the remainder of the day resting. You've been busy with one task or another since your return, rest would do you good."

"Father will not be pleased if I miss dinner two nights in a row," Niall replied with a sigh.

"He won't object when he's learned what happened this afternoon." His mother stood up and offered him her hand. "Now, go seek some peace for yourself. We'll speak more after the wedding, when we can do so with greater leisure." She assured him that she would speak with his father right away, and hugged Niall a final time before they both left her room.

Niall returned to his room to change out of his riding clothes and wash up. He was still shaken, but could rest in the knowledge that his parents would take every measure to ensure the safety of their family. To know that he was free from the duty of playing host was a tremendous relief. He would have been able to put on a mask and perform his duties, but the dismay of the encounter would have remained with him for the rest of the day and night. Now he could allow himself time to process everything alone. Even so, he remained in the solitude of his bedroom until the racket in the courtyard settled down and the halls quieted.

Once Niall was certain he'd be able to navigate the corridors without interruption, he stealthily stepped out of his room and made his way to the library. Even after living away from Britwylde for five years, there was a familiar sense of contentment as he climbed the spiral stairs that led to the family's collection of books. This magical place filled with the maps, painted images, sketches, and the written word had been his own private escape as a child. When Niall was too ill to go to the library, Ian would bring books and maps to his bedside. The pages contained within those volumes presented a doorway to the wider world that his weakened state held out of reach.

The library smelled of old parchment and the slightest hint of leather. The light that shone from the windows glimmered with dust motes. As a child, Niall believed it was evidence of the magic held within the pages of books. When Niall was ten his father had the small side room set up as a place of comfort. The space was limited, but Niall loved it all the same. Most of the books of poetry and folklore within the family collection were in this haven, as well as a map that King Fergal sent to Niall on his eleventh birthday. As a small and sickly boy, this room held a form of magic and offered a measure of freedom that illness denied him.

There was not a soul to be seen in the two larger rooms, and in this remote corner of the castle none of the noise from the main wing could be heard. The tension in Niall's shoulders eased and he let out a contented sigh as he pulled open the door to his private reading room. He stopped short the moment he stepped into the room. The chair was pulled from its usual place at the desk and arranged by the window. Kenna sat on the cushioned seat with her legs tucked up underneath her and an open book in her lap.

"My lady!" Niall said, surprised by her unexpected presence. "I'm—I didn't realize anyone was in here. Forgive me for interrupting you." He turned to leave, panicked by the idea of being alone with her in a place held so intimately in his heart.

Kenna looked up with equal surprise. "No, not at all. Ian brought me here before he went to meet with your father. My maid is still resting and I didn't feel ready to face the crowds just yet."

"I should leave you to your peace then," Niall took a step backward. She looked radiant with the light shining from the multi-colored window behind her.

"No, no! There's no need for that. I can find somewhere else to read. It's your home, after all." She said, then closed her book and started to rise.

Niall stopped backing away and took a tentative step forward. "It's as much your home as it is mine now. More so, in some ways. I am rarely here. My life is in Rosehaven now. This is home, but not home all at once."

"Is it not strange how it can be both?" Kenna asked, smiling at him. She moved away from the chair to return the book she to its place on one of the shelves. "I had the same sense as I departed my family's home to come here."

"Strange indeed. As if you're getting a glimpse of what the world will be like when your time in it is done," Niall replied. He forgot his nerves and stepped into the room, drawn closer by the conversation. "Life goes on here without me present. It changes in so many ways but holds the memories of that time all the same."

"A wise man once visited my mother's court and he supposed that all experiences create a sort magical imprint on the places we inhabit," Kenna said thoughtfully, studying Niall's face. After a moment, she blushed and looked down at the desk, examining the map spread out across the top. She leaned closer to it and pointed at one of the black ink blots. "What are these little marks all over the place?"

"Oh, I put those there," Niall admitted. He moved to stand beside her. "I was unwell as a child. Weak lungs, according to the physicians. I spent hours reading about far off lands. These blots marked the places I hoped to visit one day. It helped pass the time and make the world feel less out of reach, I suppose."

Kenna straightened and met his eyes. "And have you visited any of them?"

"No," Niall answered breathlessly. Kenna's thoughtfulness and curiosity were enchanting. No one in his family had ever paid much attention to his little efforts to experience the world from his sick bed, but she seemed to notice everything, to think about it and want to know more. He looked down at her and smiled slightly. "I mean, yes, a few. The City of the Blessed for one, and I once traveled to Wiettan with the king. But our time there was short and we did not go much past the border. What I saw of it was beautiful though."

"Is it true that the lilacs there bloom all year round?" Kenna asked.

"Well, as I said, I was only there for a short time, but my mother's family hails from Wiettan. She has assured me that they do bloom in both the spring sun and the winter snow." The air around them felt warmer, thinner. Niall could happily spend the rest of the day in this room with her. But such thoughts could not be permitted; not in the slightest measure. Niall cleared his throat and moved around the desk to put space between them. He covered by pointing to the section of the map that showed Arthan. "I've heard your own country never sees the chill of winter. Is that true?"

"Yes, though we do get more rain during what constitutes our winter, and it is cooler than other times of the year," Kenna explained. She looked up at him, dark brown, golden-flecked eyes wide and sparkling with an intelligence that was spellbinding. "Have you ever been to Arthan?"

"I haven't, but after meeting you I have no doubt that it must be extraordinary," Niall replied, accidentally giving voice to his thought before he realized the words had even sprung from his lips.

Kenna's eyes locked with his, and the smile on her lips faded. They held each other's gaze for several seconds until the silence grew too weighted. Niall blinked and took a breath. He turned away from the desk quickly and began tidying some of the trinkets arranged on the shelf closest to him.

"That is to say, you speak of it with such, uh—" Niall searched his mind for anything to distract from the intimacy of his previous statement. "You speak of it with such affection. It paints a vivid picture for the listener." He winced a little, knowing his response was less than convincing. They'd barely spoken since her arrival and none of their conversations had been about her homeland until now.

"That's very kind of you," Kenna replied gently. "Your brother has assured me we'll return there often. You'll have to try to join us for one of those visits, if your work with the king allows."

Niall let out the breath he was holding and turned back to Kenna. She seemed as composed as ever, and if she thought his comment inappropriate there was nothing in her demeanor to indicate offense. "We shall see. But I have disturbed you long enough. I should be going."

"I enjoyed speaking with you, Niall," she inclined her head slightly. "We'll have to do so again after the wedding."

"Of course," Niall replied quickly, offering her another, less familiar smile and hurried from the room. He left the library entirely but didn't return to his bedchamber. Suddenly, the idea of being alone was one that invited more thoughts than he cared to indulge. Despite having an excuse to take dinner in private, Niall decided to join the masses at the supper table. The company and the reminder of this visit's purpose was of greater value to his state of mind.

The dining hall was packed to the four corners, and the volume of so many voices was deafening. Niall found a seat next to Cathal and spent the rest of the evening and night toasting to Ian's good fortune, and avoiding any thoughts of banshees or quiet conversations in libraries. When he finally returned to his room, Niall flung himself into his bed—still clothed, and tired enough that sleep came effortlessly.

In the morning, preparation for the day's hunt and his duties as a member of the hosting family kept Niall too busy to worry about anything beyond whatever task he found to lay his hands to. There were so many extra horses in the stables that the grooms were running themselves ragged trying to keep up with the added work. Niall spent most of the morning helping them feed and water the animals, checking the tack, and coordinating where all of the extra livery could be stored until it was needed. It was organized chaos, but it made the hours pass by quickly.

When everything was finally put in order, it was time for Niall to prepare for the hunt. He rushed through cleaning himself up, splashing water on his face and running a comb through his wild hair, picking out the hay from the stables. Then he quickly changed into his riding tunic and made his way down the stairs. Dislike of hunting warred with Niall's desire to please his brother. He left his room and dragged his feet all the way to the main entry.

To his surprise, there were few people assembled in the foyer, though Ian was waiting for him at the doors. His brother looked more pensive than Niall had seen in years. The expression on his face caused Niall's resolve to falter slightly. Ian was a rock and had seemed less disturbed by yesterday's encounter with the banshee than the rest of them. To see him visibly unsettled now made all of Niall's anxiety return.

"Perhaps you should remain here," Ian spoke in low, quiet tones when Niall drew near.

"Why the sudden change? You've made it explicitly clear that you wished me to be present for the hunt," Niall answered. It suddenly occurred to him that Ian's hesitance might not have to do with the banshee. *What if Kenna told him of our encounter in the library?* Niall's stomach knotted. He grabbed his brother's shoulder and guided them to a quiet, secluded corner. "What is this about?"

Ian frowned. His jaw tightened and his face turned pink. It looked like he was fighting back tears. "It was selfish of me to ask you to come. You hate the sport, and you'll be miserable the whole time."

"Try again, Ian," Niall pushed. This was not like his brother; Ian was never afraid to speak his mind. "You don't have to protect me."

"But I do," Ian's answer was full of conviction. "If anything happened to you, I'd never forgive myself. We encountered a banshee, Niall. What if something happens today? If you were to die because I asked you to come along... I won't risk that."

"What did you hear the banshee sing?" Niall asked slowly.

"*A wife for one, a crown of bones for the brother. The die is cast, one will cause the other,*" Ian spoke hesitantly, as if pulling the words from his memory was painful. "Hunting stag can be dangerous. I don't want you put in harm's way."

The words sent a chill down Niall's spine, but seeing his older brother so fearful moved him to courage. "That could mean any manner of thing. 'A crown of bones' could refer to my position with the king," he pointed out, then paused, frowning. What was meant to comfort Ian rang with a heavy note of truth. King Fergal's health continued to decline. Niall cast a quick look around the foyer and leaned closer to his brother. "I heard a warning of poison. Considering the king's condition and the suspicions of those who tend his health, I think it likely that the words we heard refer to that. It pains me to say it, but maybe the banshee was trying to warn us that the king will succumb soon."

"I hadn't considered that," Ian replied. He looked thoughtful for a few seconds. "Still, I think you should stay behind. What if you're wrong?"

"And if I am to die, how do you know my staying isn't what would lead to my death?" Niall gave his brother's arm a squeeze. "The Soulbound have the gift of foresight and warn against falling into this trap of second-guessing every step. Is that how you wish to live your life? Will you forsake the woman you love because marrying her may or may not spell my doom? We will drive ourselves mad if we fret over every choice we make." He shook his head. "I won't allow it. If death and danger await us, I would rather stand at your side when I face it."

The shadows in Ian's eyes deepened, and at first it looked like he would continue to argue the point. Then, he drew a deep breath and released a heavy sigh. "Very well, I can see you've decided on your course. I know better than to try to dissuade you once you've set your mind to something."

"I'm as stubborn as my older brother," Niall answered teasingly, hoping that it would lighten Ian's mood. He gave his brother a look of mock suspicion. "Or perhaps this is just a trick to get me to join the hunt willingly."

That got a laugh from Ian. "I've been caught! And I thought I was being so clever." His smile faded quickly. "Just promise me you'll be careful out there, Niall. I need you. You're not just my brother. You're my closest friend."

"I will be, I promise," Niall vowed solemnly.

"But we should discuss this further when we return, and with father present," Ian insisted. "If you're correct and the prediction was about the king, he should be made aware of that."

A horn blast rang out from the courtyard, echoing through the stone halls of the castle. Niall stepped away from the shadowed corner. "Come, we need to make sure your wedding is celebrated with a proper feast."

The brothers walked out of their home side by side. Where the castle entry had been empty and quiet, the courtyard boasted a small crowd. Those who would be joining on the hunt cried out when Ian was in sight. Niall discreetly stepped away as Kenna approached to take her place at Ian's side. This was their day and he would not stand in the way of what should—and if he had anything to do with it, would—be a happy time for Ian. Banshees and the like could be cast into the netherworld and sing their songs of despair and devastation to the dead.

The general atmosphere of celebration and the way the sunlight bathed the countryside in warm, radiant rays helped to put the conversation with Ian from Niall's mind. To his surprise, he was even beginning to enjoy himself. There were many along for the ride who had little interest in hunting but wished to be a part of things regardless. Niall was able to find a place for himself among their numbers. He chatted with friends from court as Kenna and Ian rode along at the head of the party. Ian seemed content to keep Niall away from those actively engaging in the sport, and Niall was not going to object to being spared the humiliation of demonstrating his lack of skill with a bow.

With a little distance from the troubles that plagued his mind, Niall found that his smile was no longer part of a performance. It felt more like a merry parade through the beloved lands of his youth than an ordinary hunt.

Even so, as they rode past the place where they'd entered the woods yesterday Niall's mind turned back to the encounter. The conversations around him faded to the background, overwhelmed by the sound of his own thoughts. The more Niall considered it, the more convinced he became that the banshee was foretelling King Fergal's death. It made sense when he compared the songs he and his brother heard. The idea of the king's death was a daunting one. Without an heir, the event could easily be the beginning of brutal bloodshed across the country.

It would be the end of a peace that Niall had known his entire life. King Fergal had been on the throne nearly three years before Ian was born, and seven by the time Niall came around. The world they'd grown up in was free of the violence and discord that marred Venallis before Fergal's accession. Now that he worked in the king's service, he was aware of how delicate the country's peace actually was.

Beyond the politics of it all, Niall's heart clenched at the idea. King Fergal was someone Niall looked up to, the kind of man he aspired to be. Fergal was a fair and considerate man. He listened to those around him, but trusted in his own thoughts and intuition as well. Niall would lay down his life if it would preserve the king's.

"And so, you see, Master Niall," Sir Liam's voice broke through Niall's contemplation. "It's out of love for my daughter, and the great respect I hold for you and your family, that I find myself compelled to bring the matter to you."

"Of course, I understand entirely," Niall replied. He didn't, in fact, as he'd been too distracted to truly listen to a word the man was saying.

"Marvelous! My sweet Lisbeth will be delighted, as am I." Sir Liam gave Niall an oddly affectionate clap on the shoulder. "I wanted to speak with you before I broached the topic of an engagement with your father. I'd not put my daughter up for marriage to a man unless I knew the lad would look upon her kindly."

"Marriage?" Niall asked, realization dawning slowly. "You wish to speak with my father to arrange a union between Lisbeth and myself?"

"Well, if you're amenable to it, I can see no reason to delay the conversation. The two of you seem to enjoy one another's company at court." Sir Liam chuckled indulgently, obviously misunderstanding Niall's reaction.

Niall gaped, mentally scrambling to recall the details of what the other man had been laying out to him while he was preoccupied by speculation. "Uh, yes, well Lisbeth is a lovely young lady, and I do hold her in great esteem, but—"

"Then as long as your father agrees, the matter is settled in my mind!" He beamed at Niall. "Truth be told, Lisbeth has spoken of little else since the two of you danced at the winter's ball."

"Perhaps we're moving with a bit too much haste," Niall squeaked. Lisbeth was a pleasant enough person, and they had danced at the ball, but Niall hadn't realized her affections ran so deep as to desire marriage. In fact, he didn't know she bore him any feelings at all. Prior to their dance, she'd barely said two words to him. They never shared much beyond the usual court pleasantries. He'd certainly never thought of her as a prospective wife.

"Don't worry, my boy! I know your father is busy with the business of your brother's nuptials, but we'll need to begin negotiations as soon as we can," Sir Liam countered. There was a glint to his eyes that spoke more of ambition than romance.

"Yes, but it would be improper of me to distract from Ian's wedding," Niall grasped desperately. "Such conversations should wait, lest my brother feel that I'm trying to take from his day."

The other man frowned, but Niall could tell that his logic had hit its mark. "Well, if you insist, but I do think I should approach your father as soon as it would be considered proper."

A cloud drifted across the sun, casting a long shadow over the hunting party. The sudden dimming reminded Niall of the arrival of the banshee. It was only a cloud and not the result of a supernatural being, but paired with the sudden prospect of another wedding it was enough to cause Niall's fears to return. The banshee spoke of a wedding, and he'd assumed that wedding was Ian's. Yet, here he was, being presented with the possibility of a marriage of his own.

He craned his neck, searching for Ian in the crowd ahead with a growing sense of foreboding. "Where is my brother?" Niall asked urgently. The blood in his veins was turning to ice. "Ian!"

Sir Liam looked around the group, obviously bemused by the sudden alarm in Niall's demeanor. "I don't know. The last I saw of him he was riding near the head of the party with Lady Kenna and High Lord Dempsey's son."

Niall offered no explanation, he spurred his horse's sides and charged through the party of oblivious lords and ladies. He didn't have time to be bothered with the niceties of polite conversation. The banshee's song was screaming in his ears again, though the creature was nowhere to be seen. It was more than a remembered fear, though. The hairs on the back of his neck were standing on end. His instincts were on high alert and his intuition warned that something was not right.

"Kenna!" Niall called out her name as soon as he caught a glimpse of her dark hair blowing in the wind. She was sitting atop her horse, conversing with Mairi, and Lisbeth, of all people. The latter grinned brilliantly at Niall's approach, but the greeting was meaningless: Ian was nowhere in sight. "Where's my brother?"

"Cathal's squire spotted the stag going into the trees. Ian and Cathal gave chase," Kenna's expression clouded. "What's wrong? Should I have gone with him? I was under the impression that Ian must make the kill, and Lisbeth and I were having such a lovely conversation I decided to remain behind."

"Cathal was with him? You're certain?" Niall couldn't keep the panic from tinging his voice.

"He was a little behind Ian, but yes," she replied. "The squire, I'm afraid I don't remember his name, was well ahead of them both. Ian didn't want to lose the beast and rode after it without sounding the alarm."

Niall took a deep breath of relief. "But he wasn't alone?"

Kenna had just started to shake her head when a cry rang out from the trees. The blood drained from Niall's face. He knew the sound of his brother's pain, and this was not the sound of a minor injury.

"No, please—no!" Niall took off at a full gallop. He was vaguely aware of the presence of another rider behind him, but cared only for reaching his brother. He'd never ridden so hard in his life, and yet the horse couldn't move fast enough to satisfy Niall's fear.

The trees loomed up and he plunged into their shadows without a care for whether there was a path to follow or not. He paid no attention to the branches that raked his face and tore at his clothes as the animal carrying him barreled ahead. There was only one thing that mattered, and a few scratches paled in comparison.

"Help!" Cathal's panicked calls broke through the cycle of the banshee cries and the sound of Ian's pain echoing in Niall's ears. "Bring help! Quickly!"

Niall's horse exploded through a thick curtain of branches into a nightmarish scene. Cathal's squire was standing near a slight hedge of bushes. His face was pale, and his clothes were torn and spattered with blood. Niall's stomach lurched as he scanned the rest of the clearing. Ian was gasping on the ground a few feet away from the squire. His head was resting on Cathal's lap. The front of his tunic was soaked in blood, and more flowed from ghastly wounds covering his torso, pooling on the ground beneath him. A wounded stag kicked and convulsed nearby. The creature's movement was desperate and sickening. Its antlers were drenched with Ian's blood, and each time it jerked its head, scarlet droplets spattered the surrounding area.

"I told him to wait," Cathal sobbed. He was rocking back and forth as he cradled his wounded friend. Tears were streaming down his cheeks. "Why didn't he wait for me?"

Niall jumped off his horse and stumbled forward in a desperate rush to reach his brother. As he drew closer, he could see that Ian was still breathing. His chest moved up and down in ragged, shallow shudders. Each one came with a horrible throaty whistling sound. Niall practically shoved Cathal away when he approached. He knelt at Ian's side, gently sliding an arm under his shoulders to support him.

"Ni—Niall?" Ian opened his eyes that were clouded with pain and fear.

"Don't speak, save your strength." Niall answered gently. "We'll get the healers and you'll be fine." Tears gathered in the corners of his eyes and spilled down his cheeks. "You're going to be fine. You are—you have to be."

Ian lifted a hand, reaching weakly for Niall's. "It was—in the bushes," He started shaking. "Niall... be careful."

"I'm here, Ian. I'm here. The stag can't hurt anyone else," Niall took his brother's crimson-coated hand. There was so much blood; too much. But Ian couldn't die, he was the strong one. He was getting married soon, it wasn't supposed to be like this. "Stay with me, Ian. You have to stay with me."

"I tried..." Ian looked up at him. His deathly-grey lips were moving, but only a trickle of blood escaped. The hand that gripped Niall's went slack. Ian drew another shaky breath and the rest of his body relaxed.

Niall could do nothing but watch as Ian let out a final sigh and the light in his eyes faded. Niall started shaking his head. The screams and cries of the banshee vanished from his memory, replaced by a strange, dampening silence. "No, no, no, no, no. Ian, no, you can't go!"

A mournful cry broke through the shock that was clouding Niall's mind. Kenna rushed toward them, reaching out for Ian, weeping as she did. Niall numbly released his brother's hand. It slipped to the ground lifeless and limp. He stared at the sight of Kenna clinging to and sobbing over Ian's body. Her pain shook a part of Niall back to life. He gently lowered his brother to the ground and reached for Kenna as others joined them.

"He's gone," Niall whispered softly, pulling her to his chest. She turned her face toward him and sobbed against the front of his tunic.

Niall stared over at the dying deer. Cathal seemed to have managed to get himself under some semblance of control. He pulled a knife from his belt and slid the blade across the stag's throat. The beast twitched for a few seconds more, then went still. Niall could do nothing but hold Kenna and watch the surreal scene unfold before him. His eyes came to rest on the antlers atop its head. "A crown of bones," he mumbled through numb lips.

He wasn't sure how long he sat there with Kenna while the news of the tragedy spread through their group. Sir Liam dismounted quickly and began issuing orders to see to Ian's body. Cathal and some of the other men kept the rest of the hunting party away as a litter was fashioned for Ian and attached to his horse's saddle.

At some point Kenna's sobs subsided, but she still clung to Niall, and he felt no compulsion to release her. Holding the woman his brother had loved so dearly kept a part of Ian alive and whole in Niall's mind. They clung tightly to one another as Ian was placed on the litter and his face covered with his cloak.

"Niall, we're ready to return to the estate," Sir Liam was crouching beside him. "It's time to take your brother home." His voice broke a little at the end.

"Our parents," Niall choked, he felt his throat closing. Someone would have to tell their parents what happened. Father had decided to stay home, he'd wanted to go over instructions for the soldiers who would he traveling to Arthan with Kenna's family. Mother was busy running a household full of guests and preparing for the wedding. Neither of them knew that their efforts were now for naught.

"I can send one of the other men ahead to tell them, if that's what you'd prefer," the older man offered gently. "It is not a burden you must bear."

Niall took a deep shuddering breath. "No. I'll tell them. It will be better coming from me."

"Let me be at your side," Kenna spoke up. She pulled away from Niall. Her face was red and swollen from weeping, but she retained an aura of quiet grace and dignity. "Ian wouldn't want you to have to do that alone."

"Thank you," Niall managed with a slight nod. He closed his eyes and swallowed back the anguish that poured from his heart. He knew the second they left this clearing there would be no denying this new and terrible reality; Ian was gone.

Niall pushed himself off the ground and forced stiff, cold limbs to take one step and then another. He ushered Kenna away from the terrible scene and to Mairi's waiting arms. Once Kenna was cared for, he returned to the clearing and took the reins of Ian's horse from Cathal. The beast obediently followed with its mournful burden dragging silently behind. Niall climbed into his own saddle and gripped the reins tightly.

"What do you want us to do with the stag?" Sir Liam asked.

Niall looked over his shoulder at the bloody carcass. "Burn it. There'll be no wedding feast." He nudged his horse's sides and solemnly retraced his path back to the edge of the woods. The sun was just beginning to set as he emerged from the trees, the sky blazing red and purple on the horizon. Its beauty was an odd contrast to the horror of the afternoon. Niall bowed his head and wept silently as he turned toward home.

Chapter 5

Uncertainty

The sound of Lady Carene's grief was something Kenna would never be able to erase from her mind. It would haunt her as surely as the banshee's song did. Kenna stood at Niall's side, both still wearing clothes stained with Ian's blood. The room was littered with flower garlands that had been meant to adorn the wedding canopy; now they would grace a coffin. Kenna's dreams for a happy future had turned into a tragic nightmare.

"He didn't suffer." Niall's words were a lie. Kenna had witnessed Ian's final moments. She'd seen the devastating damage done to his body: his death was painful, and it had not been instant. She watched Niall as he spoke, seeing how he swayed slightly. The strain of this conversation on him was obvious, and completely understandable. Kenna gripped his hand, and to her surprise felt his fingers curl around hers and cling to them tightly.

Kenna's own grief was lurking just below the surface of her composure, creating an illusion of control in the midst of chaos. Life had been bright and full of anticipation this morning; she and Ian had discussed the wedding and their hopes for the future over breakfast. The idea that he could be gone so suddenly was beyond comprehension. In the span of a few minutes, the future she'd prepared herself for, the life she wanted, had vanished like smoke in the wind. She felt almost numb with the shock of it all, but could sense that the pain of this loss was waiting in the shadows. It stalked her and would surely overwhelm her the second she was alone.

Niall's parents pulled him into a tight embrace, but he didn't release Kenna's hand, nor did she pull it from him. His grip was strong and safe. Kenna was struck by how grounding that contact was. She felt like a tiny bird blown off course mid-flight, and Niall's hand was her tether. A servant had been sent to fetch her parents, but for now, she feared what would happen when that tether snapped.

Kenna stood as a silent observer as the family poured out their sorrow in the comfort of each other's arms. She wasn't sure what to do with herself. If she were Ian's wife, she would have been a member of their family and welcome in the tearful embrace. She had no place among them without Ian—and yet Niall continued to grip her hand.

It was several minutes before the family released one another. Kenna tentatively approached Ian's parents. *I should say something, but what words could possibly convey any meaning at a time like this?*

She tried nonetheless. "I would have cherished Ian, and will cherish every moment that I was granted with him, brief though our time was."

"As he cherished you," Lady Carene responded in a broken and strained voice. Even marred by pain, her tone held consolation. Yet her response was heartbreaking, and more than Kenna could bear. In what had to be her gravest hour, Ian's mother was offering comfort. Lady Carene's face crumpled and a fresh batch of tears streamed down her cheeks. "He had such hopes for your life together."

Kenna started to weep and she couldn't stop herself. Once the first tear slipped past her lashes the torrent was unleashed. Her legs refused to hold her upright for another second. She sank onto a nearby settee, pulling her hand from Niall's in the process. *Ian and his family deserve better than this.* The horrible injustice of it was too much to bear.

Lady Carene stepped away from her husband and son. She sat beside Kenna and wrapped her arms around her. Her hold was so tight that it ached, but the physical sensation was soothing. It helped ease some of the pain pouring from Kenna's heart. A part of her felt terrible for taking comfort from a woman who was surely in greater pain than herself, but she was helpless to refuse it.

They wept in each other's arms for what seemed like hours, though only minutes passed before Kenna's parents were shown into the room. Her mother offered words of sympathy and consolation to the High Lord and High Lady, composed yet genuine. Her father scooped Kenna up in his arms as if she were still a little girl. He carried her from the room and back to their own quarters. All the while, the sound of Ian's mother's tears echoed off the stone walls and tiled floors. Kenna pushed her fingers into ears in a vain attempt to muffle the sound. She would have closed her eyes as well, but knew that if she did, she would see Ian's final seconds of life play out again. She wanted to go home, to hide from this terrible tragedy.

Not a soul stood in their way. Her mother opened the door and stepped back for her father to carry Kenna inside. Once there, he sat on the bed and continued to hold her as the sobs shook her body. They were not Lady Isla and Consort Veruth right now, but parents comforting a devastated daughter. Kenna welcomed their attention. There would be need for strength in the days to come but right now she needed a safe place to fall apart.

The household was quiet and contemplative that evening. Both families took to the privacy of their own quarters. Though the castle was full of guests, no one questioned the absence of their hosts or that of Kenna's family. Eventually Lady Isla and Consort Veruth were forced to leave Kenna and address the entourage from Arthan. Mairi was summoned from her room to care for her, and remained staunchly at her side. If she still feared the banshee, she had the sense not to say so to her mistress.

Hours passed before Kenna mustered the wherewithal to go to her own room and address her physical needs. She changed out of her riding habit and climbed into the warm bath that Mairi drew for her. The water could soothe sore muscles, but it did nothing for the ache that spread through her chest. The tears began again once she was in the warm embrace of the water. These were not the loud sobs that wracked her body earlier; they were quiet and steady, and hurt so much more. The tears eventually slowed and then stopped, but Kenna remained in the tub long after the warmth of the water cooled. She quietly sat there staring at the wedding gown that she'd so carefully hung on a rack in the corner.

The dress was beautiful. It had a long full skirt of the palest pink silk, with airy, flowing sleeves that draped from the shoulders, and a neckline embroidered with birds and flowers. Kenna had chosen each detail with painstaking attention. It was everything she'd dreamed of as a child. Now the dress was a painful reminder that those dreams had turned to ash. She loved it, and she hated it.

It took time for Mairi to coax Kenna out of the bath. She fussed over her, as if any of those little attentions could change the terrible reality of the day. Once she was dressed, Kenna's parents returned with trays of food. The four of them clustered around one of the small tables in the chamber, picking unenthusiastically at their meal. Part of Kenna wished everyone would simply go away and leave her to her misery.

"Under the circumstances, we'll be remaining longer than we planned," Kenna's mother announced as a servant came in to remove the dinner trays. "It's proper that we attend the funeral, and I've offered to remain and help see to the management of the guests while the family mourns. A mother should not have to worry about a house full of people when faced with burying a child."

"That's very kind of you, mother," Kenna answered quietly. She was exhausted; mentally, physically, and emotionally. "Do you know when the funeral will take place?"

Kenna's father reached over to take her hand. "Three days hence. Lord Ian's family wished to lay him to rest as soon as could be arranged. You must stay for the burial, but if you wish to return to Arthan after, I don't believe anyone would feel it was inappropriate. I can take you back while your mother remains."

"No, I'll stay. It's the least I can do to honor Ian." Kenna turned to stare out the window. The night sky was clear and glittering with countless stars. It was exactly the sort of night that poets wrote of in sonnets of love. "He was going to bring me flowers for my hair for our wedding's eve feast tomorrow." Kenna bowed her head, eyes stinging with a fresh batch of tears.

Her parents exchanged mournful glances before her mother spoke. "You should go to your rest early, darling. There's much to fill the coming days, and grieving adds a terrible burden to any activity."

Even as fatigued as she felt, Kenna doubted she would be able to sleep tonight. There were too many nightmares waiting to claim her peace the moment she closed her eyes. She did want solitude though, and it would be easier to convince her parents and Mairi to leave her on her own if they thought she was going to go to bed.

"You're right, of course," Kenna nodded. She wished them all a good night, then pushed away from the table and climbed into her bed.

"Would you like us to stay with you?" her mother asked.

"No, I'd rather be alone for now," Kenna answered the question without looking at her mother. She turned on her side with her back to her loved ones. Tears were brimming in her eyes, but Kenna managed to hold them back until she heard the door close and knew she was finally alone. She cried until sleep overwhelmed sadness and granted the peace of a dreamless slumber.

The day after the accident was one of surreal disbelief for Kenna. Ian's body was cleaned and laid out for the formal viewing and vigil. In death, he looked peaceful. The horrendous wounds that claimed his life were concealed under his finest set of clothes. They were the very clothes he would have worn on his wedding day. Though she was not his wife, Kenna stood with Ian's parents at the viewing, quietly listening to the formal condolences offered by the guests. Honoring the family's traditions gave a sense of comfort to Kenna. It could not bring Ian back, but she cared for him, and for those he held dear. She took Lady Carene's hand when the older woman's face paled and her eyes grew distant with grief, hoping that the gesture would offer some small measure of peace.

Time felt like it could stretch out and shrink at will. Periods of activity rushed by in a blur of unfamiliar faces and quietly offered words of condolence. Yet when Kenna would return to her rooms, or sit with Ian's family in their quarters, the minutes would creep by. The hours spent with the family were often silent, but occasionally there were stories of Ian's youth that would lead to a moment of fond, but subdued laughter. It lightened the mood briefly until the family faded back into a sad stupor.

To her surprise and relief, Niall seemed to linger near her. He said little but was always within sight, with a watchful eye in her direction. His reasons were a mystery to Kenna. She couldn't puzzle out whether he hoped to offer comfort or derive it for himself. In the end, she decided that it didn't matter what the intent. His presence was calming and brought her peace either way. If he felt driven to be near her, Kenna wouldn't push him away with requests for an explanation. She didn't know Niall well, but from conversations with Ian she knew the brothers were close, and that was reason enough for her.

The next day was even more difficult to face. Kenna woke before the sun was up and could not find sleep again. This would have been her wedding day, and now she had no idea how those hours would be filled. This day should have been a time of joining, a wedding and feasts to celebrate the beginning of a new life. Now it was shadowed by the permanent parting of death. The hours passed slowly, and by the time Kenna finally crawled back into bed she felt as though she'd lived an entire week in the span of a single day.

Kenna was still in a state of shock when the morning of the funeral dawned. *I do not know how to face this day,* she thought as she sat up in bed and looked out the window at the overcast world beyond the glass. Even nature seemed to be laden with despair over this loss. Kenna closed her eyes and wished that Jaik was there. He would have found a way to lighten the burdens of her heart. If he could not do that, he would have done what he could to carry them for her.

She sighed and forced herself to climb out of bed. The funeral would happen, whether she wished to face it or not. There was no point in delaying things, but she took her time getting dressed for the funeral anyway. Once she stepped out of her room she would be faced with a deeper sense of reality. But she wasn't ready; yet despite her hesitance, the hours passed at a steady, relentless pace.

"It's nearly time," Mairi said. She was holding a veil of deep, stony-grey fabric, attached to an oval hairpin of silver and onyx. "I'm told this grey is the color of mourning in Venallis."

Kenna took a deep breath as she mustered the energy for a response. She couldn't put the moment off any longer, and the veil Mairi held out to her felt like a physical representation of the devastation that hung over Britwylde. "I was supposed to wear a bride's veil, not a mourner's veil. It is fitting that it matches the gloom of the storm clouds outside."

"I wish we had heeded the warnings of the banshee. We never should have gone on that hunt after hearing such predictions," Mairi stated sadly.

"The banshee's words were hardly straightforward, yet I cannot help but think..." Kenna stopped herself, shaking her head as if the action could dislodge her regret. "We could not have known when death would strike. Is there a point to survival if one avoids living to achieve it?" Kenna took the veil from her friend and placed it on her head. "Ian said the words of a banshee can be easily misinterpreted. We might have spent years closing ourselves behind stone walls and jumping at every shadow." She sighed. "If I cannot share my life with Ian, I will honor his memory by showing courage through this."

Mairi drew closer to better arrange the veil atop Kenna's raven tresses. "All the same, you're my dearest friend, and I feel that I should have done more to spare you this pain."

"Please don't linger on it. There is so much I wish I could change, so many choices—so many places where I think I might have taken a different step and Ian would still be here." Kenna pulled Mairi's hand away. "I can't bear that right now. I need to focus on getting through this day. It's the only way I can see to move forward."

Mairi nodded and pulled Kenna into a warm hug. Kenna closed her eyes and tried to imagine they were back at home and this was a day like any other. It worked for a moment, but the illusion was shattered by the arrival of her parents. She pulled away from her friend, knowing that she could no longer avoid stepping into the harsh reality of the world outside. It was time for Kenna to do her duty and pay final respects to the man who should have shared her future.

Kenna had always possessed a strong sense of responsibility, and it was that dedication to duty that got her through the funeral honors. There were customs to be observed, and so many people there to observe them. She was able to drape herself in the cloak of proper etiquette and obligation. It was a numbing, and oddly soothing, barrier as she moved among the people gathered in the great hall for the funeral procession.

Mournful pipes pierced the air when all was ready. Ian's body was lifted up in its wooden casket and made slow, steady progress through the house. At the insistence of Ian's family, Kenna walked at the head of the procession with them as his body was carried outside. Though not his wife, they assured her that this was what Ian would have wanted. Together, they solemnly trudged to the family's burial grounds.

Kenna walked with her shoulders straight and her head demurely bowed. Her face was safely obscured behind the foggy fabric of her veil. It covered the tracks of tears and offered a delicate buffer from the rest of the world. Beside her, Ian's brother had no such mask. Niall's eyes were red-rimmed but dry. Though no tears fell, the pain he felt was there for all to see. It stirred a deep desire within Kenna to offer him reassurance and provide protection against the cruelties of this loss.

"You're not alone in this," Kenna whispered beneath the haunting lilt of the pipes. She knew that Ian would have been the first to comfort Niall were he here. Though their time together had been brief, Kenna had quickly learned that Ian always sought to spread happiness and contentment to those he loved most.

Niall's eyes remained fixed on the cart that carried his brother's coffin. He swallowed and blinked several times, but said nothing. Kenna could feel her composure cracking in the face of it. Even now, Niall couldn't remove himself from that rigid reservation he usually displayed when she was around. A fresh batch of tears sprang to her eyes.

"Neither are you." Niall's response was so quiet that Kenna wasn't sure he'd actually spoken.

She'd all but decided Niall hadn't said anything when she felt his hand slip into hers. The contact was gentle and genuine, and it brought clarity to his presence the in the days leading to the funeral. He'd been watching over her, quietly providing the protection Ian would have if fate hadn't been so cruel.

Kenna squeezed his hand tightly, sensing a strength in that grip that she'd not expected from Ian's reserved and distant brother. It created a new sadness that mingled with her grief for Ian. There could have been a deep and true friendship between the two of them in time. Now, Niall would be forced to step into his brother's place, and she would return home, unmarried and uncertain of her future.

Venallian tradition dictated that the family remained until the burial was complete. In this way they could bid their loved one a final farewell and accompany him on his first steps into the afterlife. As the final shovelfuls of earth were placed over Ian's grave, clouds thickened and grew even darker overhead. They blotted out what little sunlight had managed to slip through and gleam over the funeral. It gave Kenna the feeling that she was being buried along with Ian.

By the time they returned to the castle, the first drops of rain were beginning to splatter down on the gravel path underfoot. The peaty smell of moist earth filled the air. It was a pleasant smell, fresh and full of the promise of spring. If the day's events weren't so mournful, the scent would have delighted Kenna.

There was no gathering after they returned to the castle. Most of the guests went to their own rooms to navigate the currents of their grief in private. In Kenna's homeland, there would have been a feast to honor the departed: a chance for those who knew the person to share their memories of the one who passed on and to celebrate their years of life. In all honesty, she was thankful that there were no such practices here. The thought of remaining in the public eye was too much after the prolonged process of watching Ian's body laid to rest.

Kenna was about to return to her room to recover when her father pulled her aside. He wrapped an arm around her shoulders and kissed her temple before speaking. "I know you're fatigued, but the High Lord has asked us to join him in his study."

"To what end?" Kenna asked, voice wobbling a little. She hoped she didn't sound as petulant as she felt.

"There are things that bear considering while there are still representatives for the noble families present," the Lord Consort replied slowly, the shift to business in his voice immediately alerted Kenna to the gravity of the request. She could tell from the slight creases on her father's forehead that there was something troubling him.

"What it is, father?" Kenna put aside any thoughts of escaping to the sanctity of her own company.

He looked pointedly to the few people lingering in the hall. "It would be better to discuss the matter in the privacy of High Lord Edan's study. Your mother is already there."

That made Kenna's blood run cold. Her mother was the head of their family, and therefore obligated to attend to business even before the needs of her own children. There was often a difficult balance between being a mother and being Lady Isla of the Rihtall Vashirat. If she was choosing business over a mother's instinct at a time like this, it didn't bode well.

"Then we should join her right away. Whatever is happening, I would rather face it immediately." Kenna gave a quick nod, as much to convince herself as her father.

Her apprehension intensified when they entered the High Lord's study and found that the High Lady and Niall were waiting there as well. High Lord Edan was seated behind a desk of polished mahogany. His appearance was haggard, the weight of his loss written heavily on his face. His wife was seated next to their son on a bench near the fireplace. She held Niall's hand in her lap and stared at the floor with haunted eyes. Niall was the only one that looked up when Kenna and her father entered. From Niall's manner and the concerned look in his eyes, Kenna guessed that he knew as little about this meeting as she did.

Lady Isla was the first to speak. She moved from her own seat to pull Kenna further into the room. "Come here, my sweet. I regret that we must burden you further, but there is a matter to be put before you and the High Lord's son."

"I'm sorry that any of us must bear this burden," Kenna replied honestly. The tension in the room was palpable. "What is happening?"

"Let me answer that, though it pains me more than I can put to words to discuss such things on a day like this," High Lord Edan spoke up. His demeanor was similar to her mother's, sadness hampered by the necessities of business. "Unfortunately, we do not have the luxury of waiting."

Kenna exhaled and slowly sank into a nearby chair. Intuition warned that whatever was about to come wasn't going to be pleasant. Her parents took up positions on either side of her seat. Another knot twisted in Kenna's gut; they were surrounding her protectively.

"I hardly know how to begin. With Ian's passing..." his words choked off. The High Lord cleared his throat and blinked back the tears that glistened in the corners of his eyes. "Despite the pain we all feel now, the reasons for our alliance remain. In light of Ian's accident, Niall is now heir to the estate, and will assume all the duties that come with that."

"Do we really have to discuss this now?" Niall asked. Kenna could see the tension in his shoulders, and the hurt on his face was there for anyone with eyes to observe.

"I'm sorry, son. This is difficult for all of us, but there are issues we must address while there is time to do so," his father answered. "Under the circumstances, I believe the betrothal should remain, with Niall stepping into his brother's stead."

There was a silent and heavy pause after this statement. Kenna's mouth dropped open. It had never occurred to her that the wedding might continue without Ian.

"What?" Niall rose, yanking his hand from his mother's. "How can you even suggest such a thing? Ian is barely in the ground, and you want me to marry the woman he loved?!"

Kenna sat in stunned silence, watching as High Lady Carene reached to comfort her son. No meaningful response came to Kenna's mind, and Niall was giving enough response for the both of them. He was pacing the room in agitation, shaking off his mother's hands when she tried to still him.

"I can't just replace Ian," Niall said in a voice that almost sounded like a sob. He looked so conflicted that if it were possible, Kenna thought he might have split himself in two and run from the room to escape the conversation.

"No one expects you to, darling," his mother replied, finally coaxing him to stop moving. "But your father is right. Both of our families need this alliance to hold."

"Kenna, what do you think of this?" Lady Isla asked. She knelt and looked Kenna in the eyes. "I've spoken to the High Lord and High Lady in great detail. While we want the marriage to move forward, we won't force either of you into an unhappy union."

Kenna stared at her mother as she tried to untangle her thoughts. A betrothal with High Lord Edan's family had been her idea, and at the time she'd only been thinking of the political benefits it would bring, but what had started as a political arrangement turned into something more when she met Ian. He'd gone from being just an idea to a very real person with an open and honest heart that he offered to Kenna freely. He'd loved her with such unwavering devotion, and that had slipped past Kenna's thoughts of duty. She'd wanted to marry him, not just to help her family, but because she could envision a happy future as his wife.

It was jarring to consider the practical elements again; yet the needs of her Vashirat remained. Without the strength of this alliance, or worse, if the Stratham should forge one of their own, it would only be a matter of time before they moved against Kenna's family.

"Kenna?" Her father looked at her questioningly. The role of Lord Consort was set aside entirely and replaced by a father's love and devotion for his daughter. It broke Kenna's heart and strengthened her resolve. Even with all of the feelings she'd come to harbor for Ian, the need to keep her family safe was the driving motivation behind it all and even in her grief she could not set that aside.

There was only one answer to give. "I am willing to honor the arrangement. I'll marry Niall if he agrees to uphold the betrothal as well."

Niall's jaw dropped. He stared at her, brows furrowing together in disbelief. "This can't be happening. How can I be the only one to have a problem with this?"

"No one thinks it is a perfect solution, Niall," High Lord Edan replied. "But now that you are my heir, you must learn to put aside your feelings and consider the greater need."

"Ian loved Kenna! It wasn't a matter of duty for him. I need—I can't be here. Excuse me." He pulled away from his mother when she reached for him again, charging out of the room without another word.

High Lady's Carene's eyes filled with tears. She clapped her hand over her mouth, stifling cries that made her shoulder shake. She turned to her husband. "We should have given him more time before asking this of him."

"There isn't time. King Fergal's condition grows worse by the day. Niall will need the stability and protection this alliance offers," the High Lord replied tiredly. "He doesn't understand what's at stake."

"Then perhaps you should help him understand," she shot back firmly. Her voice held a note of ferocity in it that could have rivaled any mother bear's. She closed her eyes and took a quick breath, then opened them again. "I'll speak with him, but the two of you must find a way to understand and relate to one another. You both need the other, now more than ever."

The High Lord rubbed his temples. "Explanations and understanding will come in time. Until then he must trust in my experience and adjust to his new position."

"He is barely twenty and reeling from the loss of a brother he adored, as well as the future he sought for himself," Lady Carene answered quickly. She started for the door.

"Wait," Kenna spoke up, wishing to help smooth the jagged edges of pain that surrounded her. "Perhaps I should speak to him. We barely know each other. It's not fair to ask him to make this decision when we've only shared a few words."

Lady Carene studied Kenna for a few seconds before she nodded. "Very well. Just... be patient with him. His world has been turned upside down and he's lost the person he relied on most for balance."

"I will," Kenna replied softly. She rose from her chair, forcing shaking legs to hold her upright. "Do you know where I might find him?"

High Lord Edan supplied the answer. "I believe you will find him in Ian's room, he's been spending much of his time there," His voice was calmer now, though weary. "I would look there first."

In a moment of clarity, Kenna realized that the High Lord paid far more attention to his younger son than that son realized. The pain the man was feeling was not just the loss of a child, but the helplessness of seeing the suffering of his second son as well. She bowed her head respectfully. "I know this is difficult for all of us, allow me to carry this much for you. I will speak with Niall. If he still refuses the marriage, let it be on my head and no one else's."

Niall's mother took Kenna's hand and led her to the door. "I see why my Ian loved you so desperately. You have a strong heart. Show Niall that and I think he will find it easier to contemplate the possibility of a future with you."

Kenna nodded and stepped out of the High Lord's study. She'd never been to Ian's room and had to be directed there by one of the servants. The brief walk helped her wrap her mind around the proposal before her, but it didn't prepare her for the conversation she was about to have.

She stood outside the door, trying not to think of how this was the room Ian grew up in, or that their own children might have slept here one day. That path had ended, and as difficult as it might be, she had to consider a different future. Hoping the right words would come to her, Kenna raised a hand and delicately knocked on the door.

At first there was no reply, and she wondered if the High Lord had been wrong in guessing Niall's location. She was about to turn away when she heard the sound of footsteps approach the threshold. There was a pause and then the door opened to reveal a tear-stained Niall. He frowned slightly when he saw her, but it was an expression of surprise rather than displeasure.

Kenna cleared her throat and tried to find a good way to begin the conversation. "I apologize for disturbing you. I thought we might talk about what's happened. It's been a strenuous day and that was a shocking conversation."

Niall inhaled sharply, but he stepped aside to allow her entrance. "I assumed my mother would be the one to track me down."

"She was going to. I offered to speak to you instead," Kenna admitted. She still felt shaky, but she had to believe that the small instances of connection she shared with Niall over the past few days would allow for an honest dialogue between the two of them.

"To convince me to go through with the engagement, you mean," Niall said quietly as he closed the door behind them. He didn't sound angry, just weary and sad.

"No, to talk to you," Kenna insisted. She looked around the room and had to fight to hold back tears of her own. Everything in Ian's room spoke of a man who had been full of life and optimism. There was a collection of hand-carved wooden animals on a shelf near the door, with a small knife lying next to a half-formed fawn. A lute was propped up in one of the corners. Ian had never told Kenna he played. She took a deep, steadying breath. "I want to understand you better, regardless of whether or not we marry."

"Ian loved you," Niall said. He looked thoughtful, and Kenna got the impression he was trying to sort through some sort of personal dilemma.

"He loved you too," Kenna gently replied. "Which is why I'm willing to consider a union between the two of us. Though you are his brother, I believe the respect he bore you was deserved."

"And what if I refuse to agree to it?" Niall asked.

"Then you refuse, and I go home to Arthan," Kenna answered simply. "I won't force a man to marry me against his will. I've no desire to stay where I am not wanted."

"You are not unwanted, Kenna," he answered quickly.

"A poor choice of words, perhaps," Kenna replied. "But as I also said, I will not try to convince you. I only want to speak with you, to understand you better, and to help you understand me."

Niall considered this for a moment then turned from Kenna and walked toward the bed. He sat down on the edge of the mattress, his wrists on his thighs, hands hanging slack between his knees. *He looks so utterly lost and alone.* If she'd known him better, Kenna would have moved to his side to offer comfort. But she didn't know how her attempts at comfort would be received, and she remained rooted to the floor, waiting for him to speak.

"I feel like I'm being asked to replace my brother." Niall didn't look up when he spoke. "It's like I'm stealing his life, and no one cares that it doesn't belong to me. They just keep taking what was meant for him and pushing it into my hands."

Now Kenna did cross to him. She hesitated at the bedside for an instant before sitting. "But you aren't stealing anything from Ian. He was taken from all of us, Niall. He loved your family. I know he will rest easier in the afterlife knowing that you're here to watch over what he left behind, whether or not that includes me. He would want to know the people he treasured were well cared for."

"And is this what you want?" Niall asked, finally looking at her. "To be passed from one brother to the next, like some sort of heirloom?"

"No, none of this is what I wanted. There was an entire life I envisioned with Ian. I didn't want that life to end before it had a chance to begin." Kenna reached over and tentatively touched Niall's hand. "But life rarely allows us everything we desire. I also understand that people like you and me have other concerns that go beyond what we want for ourselves. There's also what our families need and what our positions demand. I need my family to be safe and my family needs this alliance to help with that safety. We are the children of noble houses. Our families must also consider the good of the people who rely on us for protection. It is the price to be paid for the privilege we enjoy."

Niall looked away from her again, but she could see his jaw tightening and his face turning red. She could tell that he was working to keep a hold on his composure. He shook his head and turned back to her slowly. "Ian spoke of another Vashirat in Arthan, the Stratham. Why do they hate your family as they do?"

"The feud started generations before my birth. Some say it was a dispute over lands, others that it was over love. The truth is that it revolves around a struggle for power and the dominance that power brings. Land, marriages—all of those have contributed to the rift between the Rihtall and Stratham," Kenna sighed. There were many legends surrounding the vicious enmity, but none in Kenna's mind justified all the blood spilled and lives ruined. "My Vashirat has always been one with a greater focus on the arts and pursuits of the mind. Our armies have not fared well in the last clashes with the Stratham. They grow bolder each day that passes and push against our borders daily. Something has changed for them. Something must change for the Rihtall as well if they wish to prevail."

"And my father's men are renowned for their skill, both in combat and strategy," Niall said quietly.

Kenna nodded. "And though Venallis is still young, it's growing in power and in influence in the world around it. Just being aligned with one of its noble houses would give the Stratham pause."

Niall frowned at the floor. "Ian was the man you needed. I'm no warrior. I can handle a sword and I'm fair at tossing knives, but I'm a scholar, Kenna. I fear my family's influence as a backing force will dwindle once my father passes the estate to me."

"Earlier today I told you that you weren't alone, I meant what I said, Niall. I'm here for you if you'll let me be. As a friend, or as your wife." Kenna wouldn't have told him any of this if he hadn't asked. It felt like adding more weight to shoulders that were already buckling under tremendous pressure. He shook his head, obviously conflicted. Kenna gave his hand a gentle squeeze. "There is strength in knowledge and in friendship as well."

"May I ask you something else?" Niall met her eyes. "And please understand that my question isn't one of judgement, nor will I judge you for your answer—whatever it may be."

"You may," Kenna replied, wondering what was behind those pain-filled cerulean eyes.

"Did you truly love Ian?"

Kenna's lips parted to answer, but she paused. *I cared for Ian and was eager to marry him. But did I truly love him?* It would be easy to offer Niall a quick yes, and let it be done, but something in his voice told her that what he needed was honesty, not simplicity.

"Never mind, it doesn't matter now." He looked back at the floor. Kenna could sense that he was closing himself off to her again.

"No," she replied truthfully, sad and ashamed though the answer made her. "I cared deeply for him, and in time I believe love would have followed. I wish I could give you a different answer, but you asked if I loved him already, and the truth is that I was not in love with your brother when he died."

Niall took a deep, shaky breath and closed his eyes as her words made their impact. He said nothing in response.

Kenna stood up then and walked to the door. Admitting the truth about her feelings for Ian was painful. It felt like a terrible betrayal, though she had never done anything to dishonor Ian's feelings for her. She glanced around the room and felt her heart break at the sight of his belongings. They were silent monuments to a life cut short. She couldn't bear to be in there a minute longer. The final reserves of strength for this day were used up and she had nothing else to offer. She left Niall to his grief and ran to her room.

Once inside, Kenna bolted the door behind her and slid to the floor, weeping with her back pressed to the door. She stayed there for nearly an hour, until the stone beneath her grew too uncomfortable to remain.

Still sniffling, she pulled herself together and moved to the mirror to examine herself. The day had been a long and difficult one and the evidence was written harshly on the face reflected back at her. The time required to complete the burial, combined with the conversations that followed between her family and Niall's took up most of the day. It was something of a relief to see that the sun was already setting.

After taking a few minutes to wash her face, Kenna sent for Mairi to help her out of her funeral gown. Her friend was there in a flash, obviously waiting for the moment she was needed. She helped Kenna into a nightgown and robe, then settled Kenna in a chair and began braiding her hair.

Kenna's stomach growled loudly as the braid was finished and tied off with a ribbon. She'd missed both lunch and dinner entirely, and though the idea of food held little appeal, her stomach would not settle.

"I can go to the kitchens and have a tray prepared for you," Mairi offered sweetly. "I'm sure no one would be put out by the request."

"Thank you, Mairi. I'll sleep better if I don't have to contend with the grumblings of an empty stomach." Kenna managed a weak smile. Mairi's thoughtfulness helped to slide some of her world back into place. "Could you see if Brona would bring me some of that tea she prepared for you? I'm still feeling quite shaken, and I worry I'll have trouble sleeping without it."

"Of course," Mairi replied. She gave Kenna a little hug before hurrying out of the room.

Mairi was only gone for a few minutes when there was a knock at the door. Kenna sighed and secured the sash of her dressing robe before turning to see who was waiting outside. It was most likely her mother, coming to check on her before retiring for the night.

However, when Kenna turned the latch and opened the door it was not the familiar and comforting form of her mother waiting in the hall.

"Oh dear, were you in bed?" Niall asked, cheeks blazing a vivid shade of pink. "I'm sorry if I disturbed you. It's early still, but I should have considered the events of the day before I called on you."

"No, no, I wasn't in bed. I missed dinner and was waiting for my lady to fetch me something from the kitchens," Kenna answered quickly. After their earlier discussion Kenna was surprised that he would want anything else to do with her.

"May I come in?" Niall asked haltingly. He held a book in his hands, clutching it as though it were a precious gem.

"Oh—of course. I'm sorry," Kenna stammered, and opened the door to allow him entrance. Though they'd been alone in Ian's room, it felt awkward to be alone with Niall now. Even so, Mairi was sure to return soon, and there wasn't anyone in the halls to spread gossip about his unannounced visit. "Is there anything I can do for you?"

Niall stepped inside, looking around the room before speaking. "No. Thank you though."

Kenna closed the door and turned to stare at her visitor. She smiled at him nervously as the awkward silence drew out between them.

"I—I owe you an apology for how I behaved when my father suggested that we... I was taken aback by the idea," he finally explained.

"It was something of a shock for me as well," Kenna admitted. "Nothing about the last few days has been what I expected. There have been many adjustments, and none of them have been easy."

Niall gave a mirthless chuckle. "That's quite the understatement. Still, I don't want you to think that my reaction has anything to do with my opinion of you."

"Thank you, Niall. I appreciate that. I'll admit that it did give me pause," Kenna told him frankly. Silence fell between them again. He was obviously nervous. Kenna gestured to the book he carried. "What's that?"

Niall started, and looked down as if he'd forgotten the book entirely. "It's a gift. For you, actually."

"Truly? That's very kind of you, but you didn't have to bring a peace offering. Your apology is enough," Kenna replied. She twisted the hem of her sleeve and smiled uncomfortably.

"It's not a peace offering. I had intended to give it to you as a wedding gift," Niall explained, holding it out to her. "You mentioned that you enjoyed poetry. The poetry in the library is limited, and I brought this with me from the palace. I thought you might enjoy the collection it holds."

Kenna took the book from him and began leafing through the pages. It was an exquisitely bound volume, with poems scrawled out in graceful calligraphy and filigreed patterns along the top and bottom of each page. "It's beautiful, Niall, but I can't accept it now. It was meant to be a wedding gift and there'll be no wedding."

"That's why I'm here, actually. I thought it might... serve as... a betrothal gift," Niall replied. His voice sounded both hesitant and hopeful.

Kenna looked up sharply. "A betrothal gift?"

Niall blushed intensely for the second time. "Yes. That is, if you're still willing to have me—marry me, I mean."

"Are you certain?" Kenna asked. He'd seemed so adamantly against the very idea of it. "What's changed your mind?"

"You did," he paused and frowned thoughtfully. "When I asked you if you loved my brother, you didn't give me the answer you thought I wanted to hear, or the one you thought would make me agree to the marriage. You told me the truth."

Kenna looked down at the book in her hands. She didn't know how to respond to this. She certainly hadn't expected her answer to convince Niall to accept the idea of a marriage between the two of them.

"I respect you, Kenna. I respect how much you care about your family. That's something you and my brother had in common, and he considered you part of our family." Niall took a deep breath. "He'd want you and your Vashirat to be safe and cared for. If our marrying can help that happen, then I want to honor the agreement made and his word to you."

"You don't have to," Kenna replied quietly. She didn't want to trap him in a life that he hadn't asked for. Yet the memories of their conversation in the library, and of his arms around her when they found Ian, were firmly lodged in her mind. There was more to this man than the closed-off person she'd seen in most of their interactions.

"I know, but I want to. I know you don't love me, and I don't love you. But maybe if we can start from a place of honesty and respect, the love will follow," Niall reasoned.

"What if love doesn't blossom?" Kenna placed the book on the bedside table.

Niall considered that for a moment. "Then you will still be married to a man who will stand at your side no matter what fate brings. You will have whatever protection I can offer, and you'll have my friendship and respect."

"Now it is you who offers the honest answer," Kenna said, considering him thoughtfully.

"The honest answer and a genuine proposal. Though, I suppose I should do it properly," Niall replied. He took a breath as if steeling his nerves, then got down on one knee before her. "Kenna, would you do me the honor of accepting my hand in marriage?"

It wasn't a romantic proposal of poetry or longing, but there was a sort of sweet vulnerability to it. Kenna held her hand out to him as she made up her mind. "Honesty and mutual respect seem like a very good way to start a marriage. Yes, Niall, I will marry you."

CHAPTER 6

The Wedding

The reality shift in Niall's world was drastic and dizzying. Two short weeks ago he'd ridden out of Rosehaven to attend his brother's wedding; but instead of a wedding there had been a funeral. His return to Rosehaven was greatly delayed and utterly in question now, and he found himself at the center of a frenzied storm of activity. He was the heir to his father's estate and to his brother's marriage. It was difficult to catch his balance, to even catch his breath.

The betrothal was publicly announced at the evening meal the next day. Niall and Kenna rose from their seats in the dining hall and stood together before the head table. High Lord Edan and Lady Isla made the proclamation jointly to demonstrate the resolve of both families and the dedication to their alliance. Niall and Kenna joined hands as those present offered a spattering of confused cheers and applause. The circumstances of this new engagement were painful and awkward, and it was obvious the guests were unsure how they should respond. In fairness, so was Niall.

"We still walk in the shadow of pain," Lady Isla's voice lifted above the muted congratulations. "But let the joining of our families herald a future of hope, and be a reminder that the dawn will always come."

Niall tucked Kenna's hand into the crook of his elbow to escort her to a seat on his right. There would be no going back now that their engagement was formally announced. It was real and in a week's time he would be a married man. His stomach twisted tightly with guilt. Ian was laid to rest yesterday and the world was already moving forward without him. Niall hated that he had to step into his brother's place. He'd always known it was a possibility, but knowing something was a possibility and actually experiencing it were two drastically different things.

"I know this is difficult for you, Niall," Kenna whispered once he was settled in his chair beside her. "These are strained circumstances, to say the least."

Too tense to form words, Niall merely turned to her and nodded. He tried to smile, but failed miserably.

Kenna blinked several times, cheeks turning pink and eyes glistening slightly. She quickly reached for her goblet and took a sip. It was obvious to Niall that she was hiding behind the metal rim of her cup.

Fresh guilt surged through him. *She's being so kind, trying to make the best of this terrible, upside-down situation and I'm acting like the very idea makes me feel ill. This will never do: I have to get myself under control before I say or do something that causes her more pain. At court I'm perfectly able to conceal my thoughts and feelings behind the mask of gentility. Why is it so much harder here?*

He looked at his future wife thoughtfully. The last thing Niall wanted to do was hurt her. She'd been through so much as it was. *Kenna will be my wife soon. We promised honesty and respect last night. I cannot wear a mask with her and still hold true to my word.*

"Forgive me," Niall murmured in her ear. "I'm afraid my nerves are getting the best of me just now. I'll try to do better at settling them."

"It's all right, I understand," Kenna replied. Niall could still see the hurt on her face though. "It's a complicated situation."

The urge to soothe her hurts away moved Niall to action. He took her hand in both of his and held it securely. Since Ian's death, Niall had needed to be near her, to see that she was taken care of. It's what his brother would have done. "But we can rely on one another to get through it." He kissed the backs of her fingers. It was a clear demonstration of affection, performed where all could see.

She turned to him and opened her mouth to speak, but before she could say a word, another voice rose above the rest.

"High Lord Edan, I must protest." Sir Liam was standing in the center of the room, face was almost purple with displeasure. "Young Niall has already agreed to marry my daughter, Lisbeth. The matter was settled during the hun…" His words trailed off and his anger looked slightly deflated. "The matter was settled a few days ago."

Niall felt every eye in the room turn to him. Kenna pulled her hand away slowly. The air seemed to grow heavy with tension. He hadn't truly agreed to the match with Lisbeth, and never imagined Sir Liam would bring it up again, not after what happened. Until now, Niall had all but forgotten about the discussion.

High Lord Edan stood up with slow, deliberate purpose. Even gripped by the loss of a child, Niall's father managed to convey a sense of control and authority. Growing up as the son of the High Lord, Niall knew the expression on his father's face well. Sir Liam was treading on dangerous ground.

"And yet, the matter was not brought to me," the High Lord spoke deliberately "There was no request for my blessing, nor even my permission. And if I had given it earlier, Niall's position has now changed. He will be the next High Lord of these lands. As such, his marriage is for me to determine, and I have done so."

"I—Of course, High Lord," Sir Liam sputtered. His mouth kept opening and closing like a gasping trout after being pulled from the water. If he'd hoped to gain the backing of the other nobles by bringing the matter up in public, the stunned and charged silence that filled the room was evidence of his grave miscalculation. "I did not intend—"

"I am well aware of what you intended, *Sir* Liam," the High Lord emphasized the difference in their stations. "I suggest you return to your seat and finish your meal."

Niall caught his father's eye and paled. High Lord Edan's expression was thunderous. The nervousness and disquiet he felt before seemed calm and peaceful compared to the anxiety that was knotting through him now. Nothing about this engagement felt right. If he could have left without making matters worse, Niall would have run from the hall and not given it a backward glance.

"And so begins our very truncated courtship," Kenna muttered as she reached for her wine and took a long drink. Niall exhaled slowly and sank lower in his seat, wishing he could disappear entirely.

The conversations in the room were slow to start up again. Thankfully, the remainder of the meal passed without further incident. When talk did resume, everyone seemed at pains to put forth an air of celebration, while also trying to respect the tragic death of the High Lord's eldest son. It was an uncomfortable mixture of toasts to Ian's memory and wishes of good fortune to the "happy couple."

When the evening finally came to a close, Niall escorted Kenna back to her chambers just as a dutiful future husband should. It was yet another stone in the façade of normalcy that was being built up around the situation. The walk through the castle was quiet. It wasn't until they were well away from the dining hall that either of them spoke.

"I didn't realize there was someone who already held your affections," Kenna said.

"There isn't," Niall replied quickly. It bothered him that the encounter had given her that impression. "In truth, I hadn't been listening to Sir Liam when he brought the suggestion to me. I also never actually agreed to marry Lisbeth. I absently said something about understanding his point, and then he all but set the wedding date."

"And you didn't think to correct him?" Kenna asked.

Niall shook his head. The pain of losing Ian was still so raw, and the conversation with Sir Liam had happened mere minutes before the accident. "There wasn't time before... and then there was so much going on. I hadn't given it a second thought until he spoke up this evening."

"Well, he certainly has a way with timing," Kenna remarked. "He could have at least offered a toast before trying to cancel our wedding."

Niall snorted, caught off guard by Kenna's dry remark. He started laughing out loud, seizing on the moment of levity amidst all the pain and grief. "Ah yes, the old toast and contest. What engagement would be complete without it?"

"So, you do have a sense of humor," Kenna gave his arm a little nudge. "Ian claimed as much, but I must confess, I didn't believe him."

"He always did see the best in people," Niall sobered a bit, but retained a small smile. "And he laughed easily."

"Then I can safely assume there are no other ladies waiting to claim my future husband?" Kenna asked lightly.

"None that come to mind, but I will be sure to inform you forthwith if I suddenly recall one," Niall answered as they came to a stop outside her room. An uneasy silence fell between them. Niall wasn't sure what the proper parting was under the circumstances, and she seemed as lost as he was. It felt like there should be more than a quickly muttered parting, but they were still so new to one another. "Well," Niall started. "I suppose I'll see you in the morning. Wedding plans and all that."

"Yes, of course. Until then, I hope you have a pleasant night." Kenna stood at the threshold, looking anywhere but at Niall.

"Right. Well... sweet dreams." Niall released her hand and smiled. Then, without giving it too much consideration, he leaned in and kissed her cheek. The contact was fleeting and completely chaste. But Niall couldn't help but note the warmth and softness of her skin. Or how her hair bore the scent of jasmine and something else he couldn't put a name to. It sent a fresh wave of guilt through his heart. He stepped back quickly, hoping that he didn't look as exposed as he felt.

Kenna stared up at him with her dark eyes wide. Her surprise was obvious, but there was something else in her expression that Niall couldn't place. She said nothing, and her silence made Niall's impulse to run irresistible. He muttered a second, quick goodnight before turning and walking from her door with as much haste as he could manage without breaking into an all-out run. A few seconds after he turned the corner, he heard her door open and close.

Much to Niall's surprise and relief, his father did not summon him to his study for an explanation concerning Sir Liam's display at dinner. Whether he believed the engagement truly of Niall's doing or not, he seemed to consider the matter settled. *Apparently, the world still holds a few small mercies for me.*

With the betrothal now public knowledge, preparations for a wedding were hurriedly put back in place. The change of groom required many of the plans to be altered slightly. Most of the usual celebrations that would precede a marriage ceremony were deemed inappropriate in a time of mourning. The stag hunt in particular was a custom no one objected to foregoing this time. There was no announcement concerning the matter. A pig was quietly slaughtered for the wedding banquet. No one raised a brow at this, and no one complained over the lack of fresh venison. Such a meal would have been too grave a reminder so close to Ian's accident.

It took a week to make all the necessary changes. A new tunic had to be hastily sewn for Niall. Arthan's custom required certain patterns be embroidered on the groom's clothing for the ceremony. Ian's had been finished long ago and now served as his burial shroud. Niall felt an odd sense of relief, knowing that Ian's tunic could not simply be altered. He already felt like everything that should be Ian's was being adjusted to fit him.

The wedding day arrived with astonishing speed. Niall sat in his room, dressed in his new clothes, keenly aware of each minute that passed. To say that he was nervous about the impending nuptials was an understatement. In less than an hour he and Kenna would be joined as husband and wife. If he hadn't been present for all of the preparations, Niall would have thought the turn of events was some sort of cruel and ridiculous prank. He was still adjusting to his new role as heir to the estate, and now he would have a wife to care for as well.

"You're really going to go through with this, aren't you?" Cathal asked. Under different circumstances Ian would have been the one to help him prepare.

"The wedding is in less than an hour." Niall replied quietly. He turned to Cathal. "It's too late to back out of it now. Besides, I couldn't do that to Kenna. She's already lost one groom; I will not add the humiliation of abandoning her at the altar."

"In that case," Cathal sighed heavily, uncorked a bottle of wine and filled a goblet, holding it out to Niall. "Let us share a drink and toast to your insanity."

Niall accepted the cup but stopped before he touched it to his lips. He wanted to down it in one long swig, but the household was on high guard and the wine had not been tasted. It was a pity, Cathal often had some of the finest vintages on hand, and a strong drink would be a welcome boost to his faltering courage. He'd come close to backing out so many times in the last few days. It was only his growing respect for Kenna that stopped him from speaking up. *No, now that I'm on this path there's no turning back.*

"I can't. It hasn't been tasted. I told you what the banshee sang to me. After what happened to Ian, I won't risk it," Niall replied, wishing it could be different. Cathal was a trusted friend but there could be no exception to the new rules of the house.

"It's from my private stores, Niall. Are you suggesting I would offer you a poisoned cup?" Cathal was filling a goblet for himself, but stopped and shook his head. He stood with his back to Niall, shoulders hunched. "I suppose Ian's death impacts each of us differently."

"I know you didn't poison it, but my mother has lost one son already. If extra precaution helps her to navigate this terrible thing, I won't treat that lightly." Niall explained. "And what if someone managed to tamper with it without your knowing? Or perhaps the cup itself has been meddled with."

"You're right, of course. But you should apply that same caution to your future. You shouldn't rush into a decision that will affect that rest of your life just because it's what your family asks of you or what you think Ian would have wanted." Cathal took Niall's wine carefully poured both cups back into the bottle and replaced the cork. He approached Niall to straighten the collar on his burgundy tunic. "Your brother would be more concerned with your happiness than whether or not you fulfilled some sense of duty to his memory."

A defiant spark caught in Niall's heart. "I'm not marrying Kenna for Ian. I'm marrying her because it's the right thing to do, that is all there is to it. Whether I do it for duty or... It's not up to you, or Ian for that matter."

"I see," Cathal replied. He pulled his hands away from Niall's collar. "Then I've done all I can to save you from your fate."

Niall squared his shoulders. He knew Cathal was trying to help, but it struck an unexpected nerve. He gave Kenna his word and that meant something. She meant something to him, though he wasn't sure what, exactly. He simply knew that he could not let her down. "She needs me, Cathal."

"And what do you need?" his friend asked succinctly.

"The impossible. I need for Ian to be alive and for the world to be returned to what it should have been," Niall answered honestly.

Cathal looked down at his boots. His eyes turned red and haunted, a muscle in his jaw twitched, as if it were all he could do to keep the pain over Ian's passing under control. It seemed that Ian's ghost loomed over all in the castle, casting its shadow over their hearts and minds.

Niall was about to apologize and offer comfort to his friend but a knock at the door broke the grief-laden silence. "Yes? Come in."

The door opened before Niall's invitation was complete. Lord Edan stepped inside, dressed in his finest attire. He looked aged by years rather than the week and a half that had passed since Ian's death. When he saw Niall, he blinked back tears and attempted a small smile. "It's nearly time, son. I thought I would escort you to the pavilion."

"I'll meet you down there," Cathal said to Niall before turning to offer the High Lord a quick, respectful bow. "High Lord Edan, may this day bring many happy tidings."

Cathal hurried out and closed the door, leaving Niall and his father standing in an awkward silence. A wedding was supposed to be a happy occasion, but there was so much pain and loss woven through every detail. It was uncomfortable, and like the strange tension that sometimes filled the air before a storm, there was no way to alleviate it.

"I know this isn't what you expected when you came home," his father said, finally speaking. He reached up to cup Niall's cheek. It was an uncharacteristically affectionate display. "Things have never been easy between the two of us. What you're doing today is a very selfless act, Niall. I want you to know that I am immeasurably proud of the man you've grown into. I respect you deeply. I admit that I am not always good at showing that."

Niall had to struggle to keep his emotions in check. "Thank you, Father. I want to do what I can to make all of this easier for everyone."

"I know you do," his father replied. He gave Niall's cheek a gentle pat and then genuinely smiled. "Now, your bride awaits. Best not to start a marriage by being late, hm?"

An apprehensive groan escaped Niall's lips. The resolve he displayed for Cathal was beginning to crumble in the wake of his father's heartfelt words. He felt his knees shaking and worried that he might trip if he took a step forward.

"Take heart; you don't go to pledge your life to an ogre," his father chuckled gently. "Kenna has a kind heart. I truly believe the two of you will find happiness if you give one another a chance."

"She's been a comfort through all of this," Niall agreed. In fact, it was Kenna's patience that had kept the entire betrothal from falling apart on more than one occasion. If she could manage that, then there was hope that all would work out for the best. "I can see why Ian held her in such high esteem."

The High Lord placed a hand on Niall's shoulder and escorted him out of the room. They said nothing more as they walked through the halls of the family home. A slight and pleasant breeze that wafted through the open windows of the castle. There were concerns that the ceremony would have to be performed in the banquet hall, but favor, it seemed, had turned a kind eye on the affair. After days of rain and gloom the sun was shining down on the estate.

Once outside, Niall's father led him to a wondrously adorned canopy, populated by representatives from most of the noble families in Venallis. His mother was waiting at the end of an aisle lined with garlands of flowers and ribbon. Though the family was still officially in mourning, exceptions were being made for this day. The drab grey of their grief was replaced by garments of color in celebration of the wedding. Yet, the beautiful lace and silk could do nothing to conceal the marks of the sadness they all felt.

Niall's eyes locked with his mother's. She blinked back tears as a sad, gentle smile curved her lips. He wrapped his arms around her and held her tightly for a moment. The embrace she returned was as comforting as those she'd offered when he was a little boy afraid of imagined terrors in the shadows. Niall hoped he was giving as much comfort as he received.

The sound of pipes and a lute filled the air, signaling the bride's approach. The hour was here at last. Cathal already waited at the wooden altar. *Ian ought to be there,* Niall's mind supplied treacherously; suppressing the thought, Niall released his mother and took his place at the altar. His palms were damp with sweat and his heart was racing. Niall suddenly found it difficult to take slow, steady breaths. He kept his eyes firmly locked on the embroidered ribbon that would be used in the handfasting. It was a delicate silver satin, with deep blue and gold patterns woven through the entire length. This was not the one planned for Ian's wedding. That had been painstakingly embroidered by Niall's mother, and would never be used. This ribbon was something new. Even in her grief, Lady Carene had taken the time to craft it. It was not as ornate as the one made for Ian, but held meaning, nonetheless.

The music drew closer as the bridal procession approached. Niall continued to focus on the tiny details of the handfasting sash. He wasn't ready to look up and fully embrace the gravity of this change. Then a collective gasp escaped the guests. The sound broke Niall from his anxious avoidance. He turned slowly and looked up at the woman who was walking down the aisle to meet him. The breath caught in Niall's throat. He blinked a few times, captivated by the vision of beauty and wonder that drew ever closer to him. Kenna's father and her mother followed closely behind her, but Niall scarcely took note of their presence.

Kenna looked like a creature from the realm of magic. She was dazzling in a gown of cream and pale pink silk. A delicate ivory veil, twinkling with strands of silver and gold, was draped over her head and face. It ran the length of her gown and flared out behind her. The glittering lace atop her shining ebony hair reminded Niall of the sky on a clear summer night. She appeared so composed, so sure of her choices, and that calm seemed to stretch and encompass Niall.

As she crossed the last distance between them, Niall had the oddest sense that time around her had frozen, and her passage down the aisle was the only movement allowed to progress forward. He exhaled suddenly, unaware that he'd even been holding his breath. Then she was standing at his side, and time resumed its normal passage.

The cleric smiled at Niall and Kenna before uttering words of welcome to those sitting in witness. He didn't speak of loss or the unexpected changes that this wedding was forced to undergo. Instead, he raised his voice and declaimed words of hope, of duty, of honor, and yes, even of love.

Lady Isla placed her daughter's hand in Niall's. "On this day one part of life ends so that the next may begin. Your pasts have been in the charge of your parents. Your futures belong to one another."

She reached up to lift the veil from her daughter's face before kissing Kenna's cheek, then Niall's. Her portion of the ceremony performed, Lady Isla stepped back to join her husband in the seats reserved for them. When everyone was settled, the cleric offered another round of blessings, then draped the handfasting cord over Niall and Kenna's wrists.

They each took up one of the ends with their free hands as the cleric spoke. "Let this ribbon represent the bond you have agreed to enter into. As you wrap this cord around your wrists, let it be the physical embodiment of the vows you make to one another this day."

"I, Niall, son of High Lord Edan and High Lady Carene, swear to honor you, Kenna, daughter of Lady Isla of Vashirat Rihtall, above all others," Niall lifted his end of the cord and wrapped it once around their joined hands.

Kenna looked up at him as she lifted her end to do the same. "I, Kenna, daughter of Lady Isla of Vashirat Rihtall and Lord Veruth, swear to return that honor to you, Niall, in as much as is given." She wound another loop around their hands.

"To give safe harbor in all storms," Niall whispered, wrapping the ribbon again.

"To be your warmth when the world grows cold," Kenna returned and placed her portion of ribbon over his.

They swore their lives to one another in the light and the dark, in days of health and hours of illness, and to face any challenges at the other's side. With each vow they wrapped another layer of ribbon around their hands until all the wedding oaths were made. Niall and Kenna stood before their families and tied their futures together. When the words were complete, their right hands were locked together by satin and promises.

"May the Gods bless the union of Niall and Kenna, and may this day be the first of many together." The final words of the ceremony came quicker than Niall expected. The cleric raised a chalice to each of their lips in turn and when they'd both sipped from it, he spoke loud enough to carry the proclamation to every corner of the courtyard. "And now may your union be sealed with the meeting of lips."

Niall glanced anxiously at his parents. The closest he and Kenna had come to this level of physical affection was the brief kiss he'd placed on her cheek the night their betrothal was announced. He swallowed hard and looked back at Kenna. She was watching him, her own expression as unsure as his. Knowing she shared his anxiety helped to ease Niall's discomfort a little.

He leaned in slowly, giving her time to meet him in the middle or to back away if she wished. Kenna's fingers pressed against his under the layers of ribbon around their hands. Niall's eyes slid shut as the final space between them disappeared. Their lips met tentatively at first, but then the strangeness eased away, and warmth spread through Niall. He deepened the kiss slightly as his nerves were replaced by the new sensation. Kenna made a small noise in her throat. The sound was a bit surprised but not fearful or displeased. Then her lips were pressing back against his, soft and enticing.

The contact didn't last more than a few seconds before they pulled apart, but it lingered between them as they turned to face the people watching. A cheer rose up, accompanied by applause. Then Niall and Kenna began walking down the aisle, leaving the lives they'd known before behind them forever. They continued to the house and passed through the doors as husband and wife.

Once they were inside there was a brief lull in activity for Niall and Kenna. Niall led his new wife down one of the side corridors, giving them privacy on their way to the banquet hall. It provided them with a few quiet minutes to catch their breath and adjust to the new reality of their relationship.

"You look beautiful," Niall said to her. She did, and it felt best to begin this arrangement with words of kindness.

"Thank you, Niall. I had the dress altered so that it would be something new. The cream overlay and sleeves were Mairi's idea," she replied. She reached for the handfasting ribbon and began carefully unwinding it. "You look very handsome as well. Your tunic goes nicely with my gown. Did you do that intentionally?"

"My mother selected the fabric and trim. I would assume she intended for our wedding garments to complement each other." Niall pulled his hand from Kenna's as she removed the final loop that bound them together. He offered her his elbow and she accepted it. "She has an eye for details and goes to great length to see that everything is as it should be."

"I shall have quite the challenge matching her care and skill when I'm lady of the house," Kenna replied.

"We both will, but at least we'll have each other to help navigate through it," Niall answered. The wedding was done, but they were still practically strangers, and tasked with building a life together. "My parents are both in good health; hopefully such concerns are far from coming to pass."

They made slow progress through the less traveled hallways of the house. The sound of music and voices drifted down the corridors as they drew nearer to the wedding feast. Once they entered the room, they would be expected to formally greet all of their guests and continue the performance of happy couple. These precious moments of privacy would have to come to an end soon.

But the feast was one of the traditions that could not be avoided. Toasts would be made, and dances would be shared. One of the dances was of particular significance in Kenna's culture. It was an intricate series of movements that represented the melding of two lives and the trust between spouses. Niall had spent several hours practicing it for the last three days. Kenna observed the lessons, but it was considered bad luck for the bride and groom to perform the dance together until after vows were exchanged. Ian had struggled to memorize the intricate steps, but Niall saw the poetry in them, and mastered the dance quickly. It was one of the few things that fell into place with ease for Niall amidst the hubbub of wedding preparations.

"I don't know if I'm ready to face everyone yet," Kenna whispered when they stopped outside the doors. "It may sound a little silly, but going in there makes all of this feel so much more real."

"Not at all. I completely understand your hesitation," Niall let out a small nervous laugh. "We could tarry a bit longer if you like. I'm sure our tardiness would be forgiven. After all, it is our wedding day."

Kenna stared at the doors contemplatively. Then she shook her head. "No, better to just step inside and have done with it. I won't start this life by cowering."

Niall nodded, feeling his own courage return with Kenna's determination to move forward boldly. Besides, there wasn't much point to putting it off. If they took too long someone would come looking for them. He squared his shoulders and knocked to signal their presence. The doors swung open to a shower of flower petals. The musicians began playing, and the people inside greeted the newlyweds with a round of clapping and cheers. It was all perfectly orchestrated and outwardly everything a wedding feast should be.

Yet, the echo of funeral dirges seemed to harmonize under the cheerful fanfare. Despite all the efforts to make this day one of celebration, no one present could deny the shadows that lingered in the room. No one put the sadness to words. It was in the tired set of High Lord Edan's shoulders, and the haunted shadows in High Lady Carene's eyes. It was in the way Kenna's parents watched her carefully, and in how the newlyweds interacted with sensitive caution around one another.

But as the afternoon waned to evening and more bottles of wine were opened, the stiffness in the room eased and the mood turned jovial. Laughter mingled with music. People indulged in the many delicacies brought forth. Were anyone to look in from the outside, it would have seemed like any other wedding banquet, at least where the guests were concerned.

It was not as easy for Niall and Kenna to relax and forget the strange circumstances that brought them to this point. They sat in places of honor at the head table. They smiled and accepted the gifts brought to them. That was the hardest part for Niall. So many of the gifts had obviously been intended for Ian. Not that any of them were labelled as such, but the details of color and style were often catered to his brother's tastes. It was a long parade of reminders that his brother and best friend was gone.

It was a welcome relief when the final gift was presented and the dancing began. Familiar dances from court were intermixed with the choreography that was popular in Arthan. It was an interesting and lively blend of the two cultures.

More candles were lit as the evening shadows deepened to night. The tempo of the music changed. The melody was soft, slow, and sweet, brought to life by a quartet of stringed instruments. The musicians of Kenna's homeland had a way of coaxing sounds from their instruments that left the listeners enthralled. And then it was time for the final dance.

Niall joined hands with Kenna and escorted to the center of the room. They circled one another, turning away, then coming back together again. The moves grew more intimate. Palms gently rested on cheeks as each section of the choreography brought them physically closer to one another.

Throughout the dance their eyes remained locked. It was easy for Niall to let the rest of the people in the room fade from his mind. He focused on Kenna, remembering their quiet conversation in the library, and allowing this dance to be more than performing his duty. He put alliances and politics aside, Kenna was the person he was sharing this experience with. This was the start of their journey. That perspective gave him focus and even a little hope, and helped him to connect with his new wife as they moved through the dance.

A final turn together, and then Niall placed his hands on his wife's waist. He lifted her in the air, and spun them slowly around before setting her back down. The final notes of the song came to an end, and he bowed to Kenna as she curtsied. The dance was done, the customs of both families were appeased. There was only one thing left to complete their union, and it would not be accomplished in a hall full of watchful eyes.

Niall and Kenna were escorted from the banquet hall by their families. They were each led to their individual rooms to change out of their wedding clothes and into sleepwear and dressing robes. There had been some discussion of witnesses to this final step, but both Niall and Kenna firmly protested the idea. Under the strained circumstances it didn't take a tremendous amount of resistance to be spared a public consummation. Their parents agreed that an escort to the bridal bed would suffice, and the matter was settled.

Niall had felt his brother's presence all day, and as he stripped off his tunic, that presence changed to a full-scale haunting. It was only his imagination, but Niall felt like Ian was right there, staring at him with accusation in his eyes. During the wedding feast and dance they were surrounded by people, and though husband and wife, that had created a buffer to the intimacy of their new marital status. Soon that buffer would be gone.

Niall could hear shuffling outside his door. Those waiting to take him to the bridal suite were growing impatient. He pulled a nightshirt over his head and reached for his robe. It was time, whether he was ready or not. The nerves that threatened to overwhelm him before the wedding came rushing back in full force. He hesitated at the door to compose his features, not wanting to look like a scared child when he went to meet his wife for the night. After a few minutes, he had to resign himself to his nerves and move forward regardless. Niall opened the door and walked down the hall with his parents, and representatives of visiting noble families.

Other guests and members of the household, as well as Kenna's family, were standing outside the bridal suite when Niall arrived, indicating that the bride was already inside. There were no words exchanged, just an acknowledgement of his arrival. Had this been the wedding that was planned the procession would have been one of joy, with bells and laughter, and not a solemn and uneasy gathering. Niall took a deep breath and opened the door and stepped inside to greet his new wife.

The door clicked shut behind him and the sound of footsteps and the sound of the footsteps outside grew distant. Niall stood with his back pressed to the door. The room was bathed in warm light from the flickering of dozens of candles scattered throughout the chamber. The enormous four-poster bed was draped in swaths of creamy chiffon and garlands of white flowers. Kenna stood near the bed in her nightdress, and a robe of pale blue satin and lace, her loose hair hung down to her waist. She looked beautiful, and every bit as nervous as Niall was. They stared at one another with only the sound of the crackling fire filling the empty space between them.

"It's been an eventful day," Niall commented. The silence was growing uncomfortable. He took a few steps further into the room. If they were to accomplish anything, he couldn't remain rooted to the floor at the threshold.

Kenna laughed nervously. "Yes, and tiring. Many firsts today."

"Indeed," Niall's voice squeaked a bit. He winced and cleared his throat as he tried to force himself to relax. One of them needed to be calm if they were to move past these first awkward moments. "The dinner was very good. I enjoyed those little spiced cakes. Are they a tradition at weddings in Arthan?"

"I'm so pleased you liked them. They're not a wedding dessert specifically, but they are one of my favorites," Kenna replied. The rigid set of her shoulders eased visibly. She shivered a little. Niall wasn't sure if she was cold or her trembling was the result of fear.

"In that case, I'll see to it that Brona gets the recipe before your family leaves." Niall approached her and reached out to rub the sides of her arms in an attempt to warm or comfort her. "I want you to be content—uh, happy here. I know it's difficult to leave one's home."

"Thank you," Kenna whispered. She looked up at Niall, searching his face. They fell back into silence.

Niall's eyes met hers. The little distance that remained between them felt charged. His heart was pounding. "Are you sure you want to do this?"

There was a pause before Kenna responded, and when she did it was not with words. She reached up to stroke the side of Niall's face. Her hands slid down to his shoulders, and she stood on tiptoe to press her lips to his. This kiss differed from their first, and public embrace. There was no one watching them, no need to put on a performance. Niall felt the heat blooming between them. Kenna pulled away for a second, then leaned in and kissed him again, more confidently than before.

Niall inhaled sharply. She smelled sweet, and her lips were soft and warm against his. The anxious knots in his stomach turned to something else. His hands moved from Kenna's arms to wrap around her waist and gently pull her closer. The yearning he'd been careful to avoid up to this point took over Niall's thoughts. He returned the embrace, allowing those feelings to guide his actions.

Kenna's fingers twisted into the collar of Niall's nightshirt. She tugged gently, pulling them back toward the bed, breaking the kiss when they reached their destination. They pulled away from one another, slightly breathless. Niall watched as Kenna lifted trembling fingers to untie the sash that held his robe closed.

He stilled her hands and moved to join her on the bed. He started kissing her again, gently easing her back, ardor growing with every touch. The need to feel something other than pain and confusion took hold, and Niall surrendered to it. Kenna's kisses were inviting, and her presence was like a balm to his battered spirit; he could love her if he let himself.

"I love her, Niall. When you meet her, you'll see how she so easily claimed my heart." Ian's voice broke through the haze in Niall's mind. The memory of his brother's joy came crashing down on him like a raging tidal wave. The image of Ian laying bloody and dying in the forest clearing destroyed any sense of romance or desire.

Niall tensed and broke away from Kenna. "I can't do this." He moved to the edge of the bed; hands clenched together to keep them from shaking as he tried to catch his breath. Kenna sat up slowly. She straightened her clothes and smoothed her hands over her hair. They sat in silence, neither making eye contact with the other.

"I'm sorry, Kenna," Niall finally managed. He felt like his windpipe was being crushed by the weight of his guilt. The sense that his brother was looming in the shadows returned. "Ian was in love with you. I feel like I'm betraying him. It's like he's here in the room with us. I—I can't."

"I understand. I feel it too, Niall," Kenna replied softly.

"I know you're my wife now, but I still think of you as the woman my brother was to marry," Niall confessed. He didn't know how to move past it, but he would have to. They were married and he was the sole heir to the estate, the continuation of his family line rested on their physical joining. "I know children will be expected, but I can't tonight. It feels too soon, and the loss is still too fresh."

Kenna placed a hand on his shoulder. "You don't have to explain. We don't have to do anything tonight; it can wait until we're ready."

Niall stood up and walked away from the bed. He needed physical distance to regain a sense of composure. "You are as kind and understanding as any man could hope for in a wife. I feel like I'm letting everyone down."

"You're not. Niall, there's no reason to rush this. We have the rest of our lives together. It's barely been a week since your brother died." Kenna pulled her legs up and tucked them under herself. She offered Niall a little smile. "Why don't we give ourselves some time to get to know one another, to come to terms with the situation we find ourselves in?"

Niall relaxed slightly. "You'd be all right with that, with waiting until things feel more natural?"

"Of course. You're my husband now," she said gently. "As far as I'm concerned, what we do tonight is no one's business but our own. I say we celebrate our wedding night in whatever way we choose."

"And what would you suggest we do?" Niall asked.

"Well, we could start by pouring ourselves some wine. I don't know about you, but I could certainly use a drink," Kenna laughed a little. She seemed as relieved as Niall felt.

Niall smiled and reached for the pitcher of wine that had been left in the room. He used the time it took to fill their goblets to banish the memories of blood and sadness that plagued his mind. When he finished, he turned and offered one of the cups to Kenna. "To my wife. A woman of astounding grace and understanding."

Kenna accepted the refreshments and took a long drink. She lowered her goblet to look at Niall. She patted the space beside her with a gentle and encouraging smile. "Come sit with me. I'd like to know more about my new husband. Maybe even come to be friends with him."

Niall took another drink and then returned to her side. The wine, paired with her understanding, was already helping Niall relax. "Where would you like me to begin?"

She thought about it for a moment before responding. "Tell me about your childhood and we can continue from there."

After a second of thought, Niall nodded, trying to come up with an interesting story from his youth. "I had something of a dull childhood. As I have said before, I was frequently unwell."

"You seem to be in good health now," Kenna observed, giving him a quick look.

"As to that, it was nearly dying that brought me to the image of health and vigor you see before you," he commented dryly.

Kenna furrowed her brow in confusion. "I'm afraid I don't follow your meaning."

"Then it would seem that we've found a good place for our conversation to begin," Niall smiled at her. He took a breath and thought back. "I was twelve and suffering from the wasting sickness."

"The wasting sickness?"

"Yes, a malady of the lungs. I'd always been prone to coughing fits, but in my twelfth winter my cough was relentless, and paired with a fever," Niall explained. "I grew pale and lost a great deal of weight. They call it the wasting sickness because the sufferers waste away slowly."

"Oh yes, we have that in Arthan as well, but we call it the consuming illness," Kenna said. She contemplated his words quietly. "But, is that not usually fatal?"

"It is," Niall answered. "And it nearly was for me as well. I don't remember much from the worst of it, but my mother tells me that the physicians had given up any hope for recovery."

"Yet, you seem to have recovered all the same," Kenna pointed out. She sipped at her wine and waited for him to continue.

Niall nodded and took a drink from his own goblet. "Through the good graces and kindness of King Fergal. He learned of my condition and sent the Soulbound from court all the way to Britwylde. Lady Aliace was nearly too late, but with the magic she possesses she was able to pull me back from the brink."

"And you have been well ever since?"

"Aside from the occasional chill, and mild maladies anyone suffers throughout life, yes," Niall replied. "I can still remember what it was like when the magic purged me of the illness."

"We have Soulbound in Arthan as well," Kenna seemed to think for a moment. "I've never been healed by one of the Soulbound, but I have seen them perform a healing once. What was it like for you?"

"It was unlike anything I've ever experienced before or since. Perhaps it was because I was so close to death, but I swear I saw her Soulmate. I was lost in darkness and then Lady Aliace was there, soothing the fever away and calling me back to the world of the living." Niall had to concentrate to remember all of the details. The world had become so hazy and dark by then. "There was the form of a man made of light behind her. I could feel both of them with me, holding onto me. I don't know how else to describe, but the words do not truly convey what the experience was like."

"I can't imagine what that existence must be like for them," Kenna mused when Niall grew quiet. "To see and hear the one you love above all others, and yet to be divided by the veil of death, never to touch or be touched; together, but not."

Niall left her side to refill his cup. "Would you care for more?" Kenna held her empty goblet out for him and he obliged her. "It seems like life is full of trade-offs of that sort. The Soulbound must suffer terrible tragedy to unlock their magic, and yet that same magic can prevent others from suffering a similar fate. Were it not for Lady Aliace's magic I would not be here now, drinking wine with my wife."

"Then I'm glad she was there to help," Kenna replied with a sweet smile.

"And now I have told you something about my past. It seems only fair that you should do the same," said Niall as he settled back at her side.

Kenna sighed thoughtfully and scooted backward to lean against the headboard. "Well, let me think. I did not have any near-death experiences. I did meet a lamia once. He was a fierce creature to behold, but he made the finest sitars in all of Arthan. My father bought one of his instruments for me a few years ago, as a gift."

"I didn't know you were musically talented. Ian never mentioned it," Niall situated himself more comfortably on the bed, bringing his legs up to cross them. They could have been the oldest and dearest of friends to anyone looking from the outside. He laughed a little. "Quite surprising, as he could speak of little else beyond your many charms."

"He never asked, and I never had the chance to play for him," Kenna blushed. "I have played the sitar since I was a small girl."

"Would you play for me?" Niall asked, genuinely interested in the prospect.

"When my sitar is unpacked, yes. I could learn your favorite song or play you one of mine," Kenna smiled broadly. "Do you play any instruments?"

"No. It seems you surpass me in that skill, as well as archery."

Kenna put her drink down on the bedside cabinet and fixed a puzzled look on Niall. "Are you truly that terrible with a bow?"

"Are you truly that good?" Niall countered playfully, laughing a little.

"I assure you, husband, I am," Kenna lifted her chin proudly. "I've won contests back home. Several, as a point of fact."

Niall raised his glass to her. "Then I shall leave that in your capable hands, wife. I doubt even a master could help me with the sport."

"Challenge accepted," Kenna raised a brow at him. "Even if it takes the entirety of our lives together."

Ordinarily the prospect of going anywhere near a bow would have made Niall break out in a cold sweat, but Kenna's confidence in her abilities and her ongoing patience made the idea less daunting. He smiled warmly at her, neither accepting nor refusing what was an obvious offer to help him improve.

They continued to talk well into the night, finishing off the bottle as the candles burned down to stubs. The castle grew quiet as Niall listened to the stories of Kenna's youth in avid fascination. She had a way of describing places and people that made him feel as if he'd been right there with her. Though this may not be a traditional wedding night, Niall thought it a good one all the same.

After hours of friendly conversation, the wine and activity of their day caught up with both of them, and they could no longer deny the need for sleep. Niall took a pillow and one of the blankets from the bed and arranged them on the chaise along the wall. They'd taken their first steps to building an understanding between each other, but it was still too new and delicate to be tested. Even without expressing it out loud, they both knew that the following days and weeks would require caution as they attempted to forge a path forward.

CHAPTER 7

The Honeymoon

Married life was not what Kenna was expecting when she left her family home. In the month since their wedding, a genuine friendship was forming between Kenna and Niall. As husband and wife there was no longer a need for a chaperone, and they found themselves with plenty of idle hours in which to become acquainted. In the evenings they often took long walks together on a path behind the house that ran along the river. They could easily slip out of the kitchen door and make their way to the water's edge without much notice or fuss. These walks were peaceful outings that Kenna found herself anticipating with pleasure.

Sometimes one would do most of the talking while the other listened and asked questions. Kenna would sing her favorite songs, including some bawdy tunes she'd learned from the guards back home. If her mother heard her singing such songs, she would have frowned for days. Niall simply laughed and even shared a few of the improper ballads he'd learned at court. When the weather didn't permit such ventures, they would take a bottle of wine up to the library and while away a few hours in the comfortable company of books. It was a courtship as any other, save that they were already wed.

Despite their growing closeness, the topic of consummation had not been broached again in the weeks since their wedding night. Niall and Kenna continued to share sleeping quarters to avoid gossip, but he did not share her bed. Kenna was content to wait until he was ready: until they were both ready. There had been so much change in so short a time, and it was a relief to be granted this peaceful adjustment period without feeling any kind of pressure to move at a faster pace.

With the official time of mourning for Ian coming to an end, Kenna's parents would be leaving soon. She wished they could stay longer, but she knew that her sister and her husband had already been running the family's holding for far longer than they'd expected to. It was only a matter of time before the leaders of the Rihtall Vashirat would announce their return home.

Even understanding that, the day came sooner than Kenna was prepared for. She was sitting in the sewing room with Mairi and Lady Carene when a servant entered and delivered a message that Lady Isla wished to speak with her daughter. Kenna's eyes locked with Mairi's. There was little doubt as to why she was being summoned. Her heart clenched. *It's too soon. I'm not ready to see them leave. Once they're gone this is really and truly my life.*

"Tell my mother I'll be along shortly," Kenna said, setting aside her embroidery calmly; inside it felt like a part of her was breaking. Once her parents were gone, Mairi would be the only person from home remaining in Venallis. "High Lady Carene, if you'll excuse me, I shouldn't keep them waiting." *Calm, composure; that will see me through this.*

Niall's mother reached out to clasp Kenna's hand. "Of course, dear. Thank you for spending your morning with me. All will be well. You are loved here."

Kenna curtsied to her mother-in-law, grateful for her open love and kindness. The High Lady had been an unexpected boon in the midst of so much difficulty. Were it not for her ever-reassuring presence, Kenna would have been at a loss as to how to move forward with Niall. It was heartbreaking to see how the older woman suffered in her grief. Kenna hoped that the time they spent together provided as much comfort for High Lady Carene as it had given her.

Though she knew she ought to move with haste, Kenna dragged her feet through the halls. Taking her time wouldn't change the reason for this meeting, but it allowed her to cling to the hope that her parents were not about to announce their departure. Yet, even at a slow pace she eventually approached their door. The moment she'd been dreading had come.

As Kenna entered, she was immediately confronted with evidence of her parents' plans. Servants were bustling around the area, packing away clothing and other belongings that wouldn't be needed before their departure. The reality of this parting painfully burrowed into Kenna's heart. This was it; they were truly going home, and she was being left behind. This would be her home, and Niall, her closest family.

"Daughter, come to me." Her mother held her arms out, apparently reading the expression on Kenna's face.

Kenna walked into the room unquestioningly and allowed her mother to wrap her arms around her. Suddenly, she felt like a little girl playing house, rather than a grown woman with a husband and a life of her own to build. It had nothing to do with who she married, and everything with the difficulty of saying goodbye. She hiccupped and closed her eyes against the tears that were welling up. A mother's embrace was like no other, and soon this would be something she rarely experienced.

"There, there. No tears, Kenna," she soothed. "We would not leave if we had any concerns for your well-being. You are strong, and this parting will not be the last we see of one another, my brave little hawk."

"I know," Kenna replied, but knowing something in one's head, and knowing it in their heart were two very different prospects, and right now it was Kenna's heart that needed reassurance. "I don't want to say goodbye at all."

Kenna's father set the tunics he was sorting aside and drew near enough to stroke her hair. "Nor do we. Even if you were married to a man in Arthan we would be letting you go to a new home. This is the way of life. Children grow and leave their families to build homes of their own."

Kenna sniffled and released her mother to cling to her father. Still weeping, she nestled her head on his chest and let the tears flow freely. Everything was so different from the expectations she'd held when they left Arthan. Though she'd tried to prepare herself for this day, the idea of losing his safe and familiar presence was almost unbearable.

"You won't be alone. I believe that Niall will do what he must to be a good husband to you." Her father kissed the top of Kenna's head. "He assured us of as much when we spoke to him this morning."

"You spoke to Niall?" Kenna asked, pulling away. "Before you sent for me?"

"We wanted to know him better before we left you here," Lady Isla replied. "After speaking with him we feel that he will do his duty and try to make you happy within his ability to do so."

"He gave me his word no harm will come to you. As serious as that young man is, I believe him," her father added.

Kenna laid her head back on her father's chest. She inhaled deeply, savoring the comforting scents of sandalwood and tobacco that so often soothed away her childhood fears. She had no doubt Niall meant what he said to them, but he was still a new fixture in her life, and there was so much she didn't know about him.

Kenna's mother spoke, but it was the Lady of Vashirat Rihtall that was addressing Kenna and no longer the reassuring parent. "Kenna, before we go, I must ask if you think you could be with child yet?"

"It's only been a month, mother." Kenna released her father and took a step away from her parents. Anger and frustration began creeping in to overpower the sadness of their departure. The fact that she could say with absolute certainty that she was not carrying a child made the question even more aggravating. She was not about to admit to her Vashirat leader that her marriage remained chaste. They were preparing to leave her in a new home, with a husband who was adjusting to a marriage he never expected to be a part of, and unless something drastically changed overnight, a child was a long way off.

"Even so, with the death of his oldest son, the High Lord's line must be carried on through your husband. All eyes will be fixed on you. If a child does not come quickly your husband may be forced to seek an heir elsewhere, regardless of his promises to cherish you," Lady Isla lectured. "Until a child is produced the Stratham Vashirat will view this alliance as an insecure one."

"I am more than—" Kenna bit back a scathing remark. In Arthan a woman's value was not based on her ability to bear children. To have her mother reduce her to that now was shocking. It felt like a betrayal; one that cut deeply.

"Kenna? Is there any sign you may be pregnant?" her mother pushed for an answer.

"No," Kenna replied tersely. She clamped her mouth shut, too angry to trust the words that would pass her lips if she continued.

"Are you certain? Perhaps it's too early to tell," Lady Isla continued to press.

Kenna inhaled deeply and then exhaled with slow purpose, using the action and the seconds it provided to focus past her hurt and respond to her Vashirat leader dutifully. Yet, try as she might, Kenna couldn't completely hide the anger and hurt in her voice when she finally managed a response. "Yes, it is early, but I'm positive that I'm not with child."

Lady Isla's shoulders slumped slightly, adding to Kenna's aggravation. Her mother reached for Kenna and pulled her close. "I'm sorry I must be so blunt. So much has gone so off course with this betrothal. We are at a delicate stage. I do not wish to distress you, but an heir must be produced if we are to be certain this alliance will hold."

"I understand the urgency. This entire betrothal was my idea. You make things more difficult than they already are by making me feel like a failure for something utterly beyond my control," Kenna stated brusquely. She pulled away again and raised her chin, silently daring her mother to push the conversation. "Furthermore, your implication that Niall would be convinced to cast me aside so easily does him a great disservice. He is my husband now, and I will not have his honor questioned. Not even by the Lady of my Vashirat."

"Kenna," her father scolded. "You are still a member of Vashirat Rihtall. Remember to whom you speak."

"How am I to forget? You will be leaving tomorrow, and rather than being my mother and father, you remind me of duty and reduce me to nothing more than a vessel for childbearing," Kenna glared at them both. What she wanted—what she needed—was to be reassured by loving parents. "I have uprooted my entire life in service of our Vashirat. Can you not, even now, just be my parents?"

Kenna's mother reached for her again. The mask of Vashirat leader melted from her face, and was replaced by tenderness. "I am your mother, now and always, little hawk. It is why I worry for you and ask these difficult questions."

Though she was still angry, this response left Kenna somewhat deflated. Her mother governed her emotions with an iron will, and was not often the nurturing figure that High Lady Carene presented. Kenna allowed her mother to pull her close again, but the contact did little to soothe her frayed nerves.

"Farewells are difficult. We're all feeling the weight of this one." Her father's tone was gentle and patient. Where Lady Isla was a force of nature, Lord Consort Veruth was the calm after the sandstorm. "Let us speak no further of expectations. We leave tomorrow after the morning meal. Today should be a day of peace between us."

Kenna nodded against her mother's shoulder. She was still furious, but didn't want to spend her last hours with her parents arguing. Her mother continued to hold her, stroking her hair and kissing her temple. Even with this tender demonstration, Kenna's anger was slow to settle, and her spirit felt battered from all that she'd endured since arriving at Britwylde.

"There now," her mother finally released her. "We must finish with the business of departure. It would please us both if you and Niall would share the evening meal here in private tonight. I've spoken to their cook about preparing a special banquet using the recipes and ingredients we brought from Arthan. Will you speak to Niall?"

"Of course, I'm sure he'll be happy to oblige. He did express a fondness for the spiced cakes at the wedding," Kenna replied in a carefully level tone. She needed time to let her temper cool, and the only way it would be granted was by allowing her parents to think the disagreement had passed. "I'll find Niall and arrange it straight away."

Extending their invitation to Niall was an easy out, and Kenna latched onto it quickly. She left the room with her head held high as if nothing in the world was wrong. On the inside, she felt completely rattled by the troublesome exchange.

True to her word, Kenna went in search of her husband. Of all the people at the estate, he was the only one who knew and understood the pressure they were both under. It was a point they'd been able to bond over.

She found Niall in a stall at the far end of the stables. His tunic was hanging on a peg outside the door. He was quietly brushing down Ian's horse, stroking the animal's neck with one hand as he slid the brush over its flank with the other. He looked peaceful, relaxed in his shirt and breeches. Kenna almost turned away to leave him to his thoughts, but he looked up at the sound of her approach.

"Hello, Kenna," he said. His tone was comfortable and familiar. It was a far cry from the tension that he'd displayed when she first arrived.

Kenna returned his greeting sullenly as she lifted the latch to the stall door and stepped inside. She leaned against the wall, and wrapped her arms around herself. The invitation from her parents needed to be extended, but she wanted to allow the peace of the stables to soothe her rumpled spirits.

Niall studied her for a moment, narrowing his eyes slightly. "What's the matter?"

"My parents are leaving tomorrow," she explained. "They voiced concerns along with their announcement."

"Concerns?" Niall asked. He stepped away from the horse and placed the brush in a burlap bag hanging in the corner. "Have I done something to make them question your well-being here?"

Kenna shook her head. "I'd say it's more a matter of what hasn't been done."

"Ah, then they know we haven't..." Niall let his words drift off, but he gestured vaguely between the two of them.

"No, I didn't tell them that, but my mother voiced hope that I would have fallen pregnant before they left," Kenna blushed as she spoke.

Niall let out a long sigh and gave Kenna a look that suggested she might not have been the only one to receive this sort of pressure from a parent. "Sometimes it feels as though the moment we married we ceased to be their children and became conduits for the future generation."

"Well, it wouldn't be wholly inaccurate," Kenna pointed out. "Children are to be hoped for one day."

"Yes, and I'm sure we will have them someday," Niall replied. "But it's only been a month. Even if we were... working toward that goal now, it's unlikely you'd be with child already. Even less likely that there would be signs of it if you were."

Kenna pushed off the wall and walked over to the big grey-dappled stallion that was casually munching grain from a trough. She envied the beast, so oblivious to the pressures that were placed on her. She reached up to stroke the horse's silky neck, thinking of Ian and wondering if this conversation would have taken place if he were alive.

Silence settled between them. Kenna could hear Niall pacing behind her. After a few seconds he approached her, and a gentle hand came to rest on her shoulder. "Kenna, do you want to... proceed further than we have?"

"No. Or yes—I don't know," she turned to face him. "Things seem to be going well between us as they are. Maybe we should consider it at least."

Niall was quiet, biting his lower lip and frowning, he looked conflicted and anxious.

"Unless you disagree," Kenna added quickly.

"No, I agree that things are going well between us. Better than I would have thought when we agreed to this. To be honest, I'm not sure how I could get through losing Ian without you here," Niall admitted quietly. He was the one that turned away now, gathering the rest of the grooming supplies and heading for the door. He held it open for Kenna and followed closely behind her.

"I'm sorry, Niall. I don't mean to pressure you. It's just difficult to feel like so many are putting their hope on this—on us."

"Don't be, Kenna. I'm sorry that your patience and understanding with me has resulted in difficulty for you." He laid the grooming bag aside and sat on a nearby bench. "Things are going well, but what's between us still feels very new. I worry that having a child now would put pressure on something that's still fragile."

"It's different for you, Niall," Kenna sat down beside him. "I feel like everyone is watching my waist for any sign of swelling."

"I understand why my father's anxious for an heir to continue the family line, but why are your parents so impatient to see it happen?" Niall asked.

Kenna's mind flashed back to her mother's suggestion that Niall would set her aside. "They're concerned that your family will seek to annul our alliance if it seems that I can't..."

"They think I'll blame you and seek a different marriage?" Niall shook his head in obvious frustration.

"My mother suggested as much." Kenna replied. She was still angered by the encounter, even more so now that she could see the impact it had on Niall. "I'm afraid I might have lost my temper at the suggestion."

To her surprise, Niall wrapped an arm around her and pulled her close to his side. "I would imagine so. I didn't think such emphasis was put on a woman's childbearing status in Arthan."

"It's not," Kenna said through gritted teeth. "Her assumption is entirely based on what she thinks your expectations are. I told her she did you a great disservice by even suggesting it."

"Well, I'm glad to know you think more highly of me than that, and that you were so quick to defend me," said Niall with a kind and appreciative smile. He gave her a gentle squeeze. "Try to put it from your mind. This marriage might have come about to satisfy practical concerns and strategy, but it's our marriage. We get to decide how and when to proceed with children, or any other matter. The rest of the world can go hang."

"I'm glad you think so," Kenna answered him, laying her head on his shoulder. "I hope you feel as bold this evening. My mother has requested that we join them for a private meal. You'll likely be subjected to a similar conversation."

Niall laughed. "I'll consider myself warned."

Kenna smiled. She'd come to genuinely enjoy Niall's company, and though she was not in love with him, she felt a growing connection. The progress they'd made in the past weeks was encouraging. Being able to carry on an open conversation made her parents' departure that much less daunting. In fact, she was starting to feel relief at the prospect of continuing to forge ahead in her life with Niall, without the pressure of their expectations shadowing her every move.

"I haven't any pressing business today," Niall stated a little hesitantly. "If you like... we could avoid the pressures of our parents together."

"I can think of nothing I would enjoy more." Kenna lifted her head and looked at him with delight. She nudged his shoulder playfully. "You know, you can be quite charming when it suits you."

"I don't know about that, but I will defer to your good judgement," Niall blushed brilliantly. He stood up and offered her his hand. "Shall we?"

Kenna took her husband's hand and set aside her cares. Having grown up at Britwylde, Niall knew all the secret and hidden places of the property. After stopping in the kitchen for a basket of food, they rode out into the countryside and spent the afternoon in the empty gamekeeper's cottage a few miles away from the main estate. It was a pleasant way to pass the time, and would likely convince their parents that they sought solitude to set about the production of an heir.

Having enjoyed their escape, the dinner they shared with Kenna's parents was not as tense as Kenna feared it would be. Her mother seemed content to put aside her position as leader of Vashirat Rihtall and merely be a loving parent. Niall was not as at ease with her parents as he'd come to be with her, but he managed well enough. Kenna wished they could see more of the man she was coming to know; hopefully, they would with time. By the end of the meal, she had all but put their earlier encounter behind her. It was well past sunset when they finally stood to leave for their own room.

"I think it's best we all seek rest now," Kenna's mother announced when the last of the wine was drained. "Morning will come earlier than any of us wish."

Niall rose from his seat and offered his arm to Kenna. "Shall we retire for the evening?"

"If not now, I fear you'll have to carry me to bed," Kenna answered. She stifled a yawn behind her hand, then turned to her parents to kiss each of their cheeks in turn. "Goodnight mother, father."

Niall shook her father's hand, then leaned in to offer her mother a kiss on the cheek, as was proper. He reached for the door but turned as if he'd forgotten something. "Before we go, I'm afraid there's one last thing I must address."

"Yes, Niall?" Lady Isla smiled at her son-in-law. "What troubles you?"

"It's more a matter of what troubles Kenna," Niall's tone was mild but held a note of steel. "I'm told you have concerns over the stability of our marriage. That you've suggested her value to me is no greater than that of a brood mare."

Kenna's jaw nearly dropped. She looked from her parents to her husband. Niall's expression remained relatively pleasant as he met her mother's eyes, but there was iron in the set of his shoulders. This was not the same quiet, reserved man she'd married a month ago. He was confidently holding his ground, chin tilted in a subtle display of defiance.

"I think you misunderstand our intentions," Kenna's father replied calmly. "We simply have concerns for our daughter's happiness."

"And I have concerns for my *wife's* happiness," he emphasized the word 'wife'. "I will not have anyone dictate her worth to me or to her. As far as children go, that is a matter between a wife and her husband, and I'll thank you to leave it to us to address in our own way and time."

"Is that so?" Lady Isla was studying Niall closely. Kenna could practically see her mother's thoughts turning in her head, and there was a slight quirk to the corner of her mouth. She was impressed, perhaps even a little amused. "And can you promise your father will see it the same way?"

"My father has as much authority in the matter as you do. Which is to say, none at all," Niall smiled at them both, placed his hand over Kenna's, and opened the door. "And as long as we're all clear on that, I leave you both to your rest. Goodnight."

Without another word, he ushered Kenna into the hall, leaving her parents to their final night at Britwylde. It took Kenna several steps before she could overcome her own surprise at the interaction.

"Niall, what on earth possessed you to do that?" she asked, still processing the incident.

"You were upset by what they said earlier. I don't want you to suffer for the kindness and understanding you've shown me," Niall replied. They continued on for a short distance. "I can be bold when the occasion calls for it, I simply choose my battles, and this was one worth choosing. We're in this together, no matter what.

I will always defend you, regardless of who causes you distress."

"Well, if you can stare down the Lady of Vashirat Rihtall, I've faith we'll be able to handle whatever might come our way," Kenna remarked with playful astonishment. She sobered as they reached the door to their room. "Thank you, Niall. Whatever else we are to one another, you're a true friend."

That got a smile from him. Niall opened the door and stood back so she could enter first. Kenna felt something delicate and warm flicker to life inside her as she moved past him. It was an ember that if properly nurtured could grow to a flame. That night she slept more soundly than she had since her arrival in Venallis. Though not in the bed beside her, Niall's presence made their room feel safe and comfortable. For the first time, Britwylde felt like a true home.

It was late in the morning when Kenna and her parents gathered in the courtyard to say goodbye. The castle felt lonelier now that they were leaving her in the protection of a new family. Niall's presence at her side was the only thing that soothed the ache in Kenna's heart, especially after his bold defense at dinner. As much as she appreciated his actions the night before, she was concerned that her parents might have taken offense at Niall's statements, but as it turned out, her fears were unfounded.

"I was worried your young man wouldn't take the bait, but I believe Niall may secretly be as fierce as you. I have every confidence in the world that he'll make you happy, my little hawk," Lady Isla whispered in Kenna's ear at their final embrace. She pulled away and reached for Niall's hands. "As long as you continue to defend my daughter as you did last night, I know all will be well. I expect the two of you to visit as soon as you're able. We will all miss you both terribly in the meantime."

"We will," Kenna replied, untangling the emotions that were twisting through her. Kenna wasn't even sure how to respond to it. There was no time to process what had happened. They were leaving, and it would be months, perhaps even years, before they stood face to face again. So, she did as she was expected, falling back on the dutiful and calm response. "Tell everyone that I love them and that I'm happy. I don't want any of them to worry."

"Of course," her father said. He wrapped his strong, warm arms around Kenna and held her close. She nestled into the embrace, closing her eyes and resting her head on her father's shoulder. When the hug finally ended, he cupped her cheek with tears in his eyes. He looked at Niall. "Take care of her; she is precious to me."

Niall nodded solemnly. "You have my word. I swear she will have anything in my power to give her."

"We'll take care of each other," Kenna assured her father.

They embraced again and tarried for a few more minutes as the last of the trunks were secured. Mairi joined them and wished the Lady and Lord Consort of Vashirat Rihtall farewell, begging them to send her love to her family. With a third and final round of hugs and wishes for a safe journey, Kenna's parents loaded into their carriage and began the long trek back to Arthan.

Kenna remained outside and watched her parents' procession until she could no longer see the dust kicked up by the horses. Niall stayed with her as long as he was able before his father summoned him to the business of the estate. Kenna slipped her arm around Mairi's waist and they went back into the house together to finish the last of their unpacking. There could be no further denial, Britwylde and Venallis were now her home.

"We're going to have to do something about these tapestries, Kenna," Mairi commented as she bustled around the room, fully engaged in the process of making the space suited to Kenna's tastes. Mairi was studying a particularly drab woven depiction of a battle. "Why would this even be in a bedchamber, especially one meant for newlyweds?"

Kenna laughed. "Thank the gods you're here, Mairi. What would I do without you to see to such details? But I agree, it's an odd choice to promote romance."

"I know your mother sent along some silk drapery. It's green with gold embellishments. This room needs some color." She wasn't even looking at Kenna or the tapestry during this declaration, but making her way to one of the chests. "When you're the lady of this house, you'll be able to add as much color as an Arthan flower faire."

"I'm sure we'll be able to find a nice compromise between what's fashionable in Arthan, and the popular style in Venallis." Kenna shook her head with another laugh. "I want to make sure Niall is as represented as I am. Though, I'm sure he'd happily leave all the decorative decisions to me."

"He is rather agreeable when it comes to you," Mairi commented.

Kenna stopped what she was doing and looked at her friend with concern. "Does it bother you that he and I married? I know you were interested in him when we first arrived."

"Oh that!" Mairi blushed, and focused on the task at hand. It was plain that she was avoiding Kenna's eyes. "No, I forgot that quite some time ago. There's someone else who holds my affections."

"Oh?" Kenna asked, curiosity piqued. "Who might that be? A certain green-eyed, flirtatious gentleman, perhaps?"

"Cathal makes me smile," Mairi admitted, finally looking at Kenna. "He's fun to be around."

"And does he enjoy your company as much as you do his?"

An utterly smitten smile spread across Mairi's face. "I've been given reason to believe that he does, though we've made no formal declarations of intent."

"When did this happen? I hadn't noticed the two of you spending any special time with one another," Kenna sat down on the edge of the bed closest to her friend.

"At your wedding banquet actually," Mairi answered, her blush going a shade deeper, her eyes taking on a wistful sparkle. "He asked me for a dance and then spent much of the evening speaking with me."

Kenna felt a prickling of guilt. She hadn't spent much time with Mairi since the wedding. In the past she would have known all about the budding romance between her friend and Cathal. *I'll need to make a better effort to balance my time now that it's just the two of us here.*

"I think it might be the reason he hasn't left Britwylde yet," Mairi continued. She looked truly happy.

"I'm delighted for you, Mairi. I'm sorry it took me this long to realize there was something special going on," Kenna replied. She was pleased, but there was also a note of jealousy. *I wish things were as simple with Niall and me.*

"How are things between you and Niall?" Mairi asked, echoing Kenna's thoughts with unnerving precision. She was looking at Kenna with concern, obviously sensing her disquiet.

Kenna smiled reassuringly. "Things are going well. We're both trying to understand one another and navigate married life. But Niall is kind, and we're finding ways to connect."

She couldn't bring herself to tell Mairi that she was a wife in name only. There were some things that felt too private to be shared, even with those she trusted most. It was difficult and unsettling to feel as though they were locked in a state of limbo. They were more than friends by merit of their marital status, but there was still so much caution surrounding both their hearts.

* * *

The days that followed the departure weren't nearly as difficult as Kenna thought they would be. Sadness still hung over the household, but that was to be expected. Whether the official time of mourning was over or not, the loss of Ian would never be completely healed. With most of the wedding guests gone the household slowly began to find a new sense of normal.

Nearly a week had passed since the party from Arthan had departed. The days were usually busy until the evening meal, where the family gathered to share time together before retiring. Cathal usually joined them, his presence helping to lift the somber mood of the house. The jokes and stories he shared could liven any event. Kenna watched him with a close eye, pleased at how his efforts were focused on Mairi more than anyone else in the room. He was a pleasant man, a bit rambunctious for Kenna's tastes, but he seemed to make Mairi happy and that was all that mattered.

Kenna sat next to Niall, laughing at Cathal's retelling of an incident at court that had resulted in Niall having to distract half the privy council while Cathal was forced to sneak out of a window and through the garden wearing nothing but a strategically placed handkerchief. He spun the tale with enough color and gusto to match that of any of the storyweavers in Arthan. It made the room feel brighter, and the echoes of loss a little quieter.

"And that is why I never drink without hiding an extra pair of trousers in the room." Cathal finished, lifting a glass to his lips.

"It's also why I will no longer allow you to drag me to a game of cards when there is drinking involved," Niall added. He pushed away his plate and laced his fingers through Kenna's.

Kenna glanced over at him, surprised by the public gesture of affection. The contact was as natural and familiar as if they'd been together for years rather than a single month. It made Kenna's heart swell with hope. *This feels good, like happiness.*

"And this when Niall was no more than fifteen?" High Lord Edan asked. He looked less than pleased by the antics recounted. Yet, when he looked at Niall, Kenna thought she detected the slightest hint of a smile curving his lips. In the past weeks Kenna had come to recognize that though the High Lord was not obvious in his attentions, he held a tremendous amount of respect for his youngest son and loved him dearly.

Cathal shrugged and looked away. "Ian made me promise to look after his little brother. I could not let him down."

"As I recall, I spent far more time looking after you than you did me," Niall protested.

"Yes, well—" Cathal began to argue but his words were brought to an abrupt stop when the doors to the dining hall opened to admit an anxious servant, followed closely by a travel-worn messenger in garb bearing the sigil of the King.

Niall's fingers tightened around Kenna's. The mood of the evening was instantly dampened by a growing sense of tension. Lady Carene watched the messenger closely. Her eyes darted from one face to the next. There was something more going on here than Kenna could puzzle out.

The messenger bent to the High Lord's ear, but whatever he said was uttered so quietly that only the intended recipient could have understood it. He passed a parcel to High Lord Edan who signaled to one of the nearby servants. "See that our new guest is given something to eat and a warm place to sleep for the night. In the meantime, as lovely as the meal has been, I think we should all return to our chambers for the night to prepare for tomorrow's work."

Kenna glanced to Niall, who bore an expression of thoughtful speculation. Whatever he suspected, he did not press for an explanation. Instead, he rose from his seat and helped Kenna from her chair. They wished his parents a goodnight and left the room. The frown on his face and troubled shadows in his eyes filled Kenna with concern.

"What news do you think the messenger delivered?" Kenna asked after passing through several halls in silence.

"I'm not certain, but I know the man's face. He's one of the King's most trusted messengers. Whatever the missive held, it was from the King himself," Niall paused, and his frown deepened. He glanced around them and when he saw that the hall was empty, he leaned closer to Kenna and pitched his voice low. "Or those acting according to his express, and potentially, final orders."

"According to his final orders..." Kenna repeated, letting the words sink in. Niall had expressed concerns for King Fergal's health over the course of their conversations. It was something she knew troubled him greatly. "Do you think that was word of his passing?"

"No, my father would have said so outright, but I worry that His Majesty may be close to death. If he is, my father and I will likely be expected to make haste to Rosehaven."

Kenna considered this carefully. If the King died without an heir, it could plunge her new home into chaos. Even if an heir were selected by the King himself, there would almost certainly be those who contested it.

Niall seemed to read Kenna's expression. "It could be something else entirely. At any rate, Rosehaven is over a week's ride from here. Whatever it is, there'll be time to prepare ourselves."

"And here I thought we might have a little peace," Kenna sighed. She started walking again. "Well, no matter what the news is, it's for your father to decide how to proceed."

Niall nodded thoughtfully. Whatever was on his mind, he didn't give voice to it then; but Kenna could have ventured a guess as to what was troubling him. If all had gone as planned, Niall would have returned to the King's side by now. He'd know what was going on, and be in a better position to act in the best interests of his family.

The quiet mood continued even after they were alone in their chambers. Niall pulled off his tunic and settled in a chair by the fire with a book while Kenna stepped behind the dressing screen to change into her nightgown and robe. Despite everything, peace settled over their little corner of the estate.

She didn't push her husband for further discussion. Niall often mulled things over in his own head before he spoke of them to anyone. At first, Kenna worried that it was resistance to their marriage. Now that she knew him better, she understood that it was his way of ensuring that he didn't react rashly or jump to unfounded conclusions. It was one of the things she'd come to respect about him. Her patience and consideration had been rewarded with rapidly growing trust. During their daily walks Niall often expressed the thoughts and ideas he'd had throughout the day. It was actually rather endearing, and it went far in making Kenna feel at ease with him.

"I'm sure all will be well," Kenna reassured him. stepping out from behind the screen as she tied her dressing gown sash. She wished she could offer Niall more than empty words. Especially considering how close he was to the ailing King.

Niall closed his book and smiled up at her. "You're probably right." He grew quiet and contemplative for a moment. "Besides, my place is here now. King Fergal managed most of his reign without me at his side. I suppose he is more than capable of doing so again."

"There are worse places to be," Kenna replied. She met Niall's gaze and her stomach flipped a little. The room seemed warmer than it did mere seconds before. She felt flushed and moved to open the window. The breeze that filtered in carried the scent of fresh grass, and the sound of crickets.

"And I couldn't ask for better company," Niall's response was slow and quiet. He rose from his seat and joined Kenna at the window. "Kenna?"

"Yes, Niall?" Kenna's voice was more breathless than she'd intended. Niall was close, and the air seemed to hold a sense of anticipation. She turned around slowly and looked up at her husband.

"Are you happy?" He was studying her face closely. "With me, I mean."

Kenna nodded, unable to make her lips form words. They were preoccupied with the idea of a different purpose entirely. Without thinking, she placed her hand on Niall's chest. His heartbeat thrummed through the fabric of his shirt; like hers, it was racing.

Niall looked down at her and lifted his hand to gently stroke her cheek. He moved in tentatively. Kenna had every opportunity to pull back, but she held his eyes steadily. As Niall had said before, whatever it was they shared was new and fragile, but there was a pull between them. It wasn't love, not yet, but it was more than friendship. Kenna's eyes began to slide shut and she leaned closer.

An alarmed bark from the courtyard shattered the quiet of the night and the spell that was cast in the inviting glow of their bedchamber. Niall jumped slightly. Kenna opened her eyes and found him staring out the window with a furrowed brow. She turned around and tried to follow the direction of his gaze. "What is it?"

"The beacon on the west wall is lit," Niall responded slowly. He moved away from her and leaned out the window. "Why would my father order that beacon lit? We haven't used it in years. The staircase leading to it has fallen into disrepair."

"Do you think it has something to do with the messenger?" Kenna ran a hand over her hair. The sudden change in mood left her feeling off-balance and dissatisfied.

"Possibly, but I don't know why he'd use the old beacon rather than the newer one." Niall stepped away from the window. He shot Kenna a quick and soothing smile. "I should go see what's happening. Stay here. I'll be back shortly."

Kenna nodded again, and watched her husband leave. She wrapped her arms around herself and looked back out the window. Another dog began barking, then let loose with an oddly gurgled yelp. Silence settled over the estate again. Kenna closed the window and arranged herself comfortably in Niall's chair by the fire. She picked up the book he'd been reading and thumbed through it idly.

A sudden crash echoed down the hallways, followed by shouting. Kenna jumped up, dropping the book on the floor. She thrust her feet into a pair of shoes by the fire. The commotion outside her room continued, growing louder and more frantic. The door burst open. Kenna whirled around, expecting to see Niall, but found Mairi running across the room with wide, terrified eyes.

"There are armed men in the great hall!" She was clutching a dagger, though her hands were shaking so violently that Kenna feared she would drop it. "Gods, Kenna, they were wearing Stratham colors."

"What?" Kenna's chest tightened. She could feel the blood draining from her face. "No, that can't be. They wouldn't dare cross the border into Venallis."

"I saw them. I was—I was with Cathal. They cut down the guards." Mairi began crying. "The poor men barely had time to draw their weapons. There was so much blood."

The crashing grew louder and was punctuated by screams. Men were calling for weapons and the sound of running footsteps echoed down the corridors. Kenna grabbed hold of Mairi's arms and looked her in the eye. "Did you see Niall? Was he in the banquet hall when they breached the doors?"

"Halls of blood," Mairi sobbed. "The banshee said there would be halls of blood. Ian is dead and now we'll be killed too."

"Mairi, we are not going to die. I need you to focus please. Take a deep breath and listen to me," Kenna looked her friend in the eye. "Was Niall in the room?"

Mairi seemed to calm a little. She shook her head. "No, he wasn't there. Cathal and I were, we were. . ." She began crying again. "He told me to run, and I left him behind."

"Hear me, Mairi. We're going to protect ourselves until Niall returns, then we'll all get through this together." She took hold of Mairi's hand, tightening her friend's fingers around the hilt of her dagger. "We are daughters of the Rihtall Vashirat. We are fierce and our hearts hold courage. We will not give into our fears."

Mairi took several breaths and seemed to get herself under control. "Oh Kenna, what have we brought down on these people?"

Kenna's jaw tightened. There would be time for remorse later. She released her friend and moved to pull one of Niall's daggers from a satchel he kept near the chaise he slept on. "We need to be prepared to defend ourselves. Niall will come back for us, I'm sure of that. I won't put him at greater risk by leaving this room and forcing him to search for us."

"Should we bar the door?" Mairi asked. She was still obviously frightened but seemed to have rallied herself for what was coming.

"No, when Niall gets back, we may need to leave quickly. We'll lock it for now and put out the lights. If the Stratham think this room is empty, they may pass it by without incident," Kenna answered, hoping that Niall would return quickly and safely. If he didn't, she wasn't sure what they would do, but she would not die without a fight. "My bow is in my trunk. Go fetch it and I'll lock the door."

Having a task visibly helped pull Mairi from the brink. Kenna hurried to bolt the door. As she drew near the oak barrier the sounds of violence grew louder. A chill ran down Kenna's spine as she fumbled with the lock. Even without witnessing the bloodshed, she could tell that the household was caught utterly off guard and the consequences were dire. There was a tremendous amount of noise, but little of it was the sound of swords clashing. This wasn't a fight: it was a massacre.

The stomping of heavy booted feet was drawing terrifyingly close. Kenna's own hands were starting to shake now, making it difficult to hold the knife and manipulate the lock. She took a deep breath to still her fears and force her fingers to obey. The lock finally slid into place seconds before a shadow showed through the crack at the bottom of the door. The handle lifted, but the lock held. There was a pause, then the door shuddered against a full body impact.

Kenna backed away quickly, grabbing her bow from Mairi. She placed her own dagger on the bed and nocked an arrow to the bowstring. Mairi whimpered slightly as another impact shook the door. Kenna pushed her friend behind her. She would stand and defend them until there was no more fight left in her, even if she had to do it on her own.

The assault continued, wood began to creak and splinter. The next seconds passed in a strange kind of distention of time. Kenna pulled the bowstring back. She focused on her breathing and the way the wood of her bow strained against the palm of her hand. The door burst open. A shadowy figure appeared in the open doorway, obscured by the darkness in the room and the lights in the hall.

Kenna loosed her shot, barely registering where she hit her target, only focusing on the next shape that appeared after her first fell. She fired again, and another body crumpled to the floor. Kenna let a third arrow fly but the next man to enter wasn't caught by surprise. He dodged to the left and charged forward as Kenna reached for another arrow.

"That's enough of that!" her assailant growled. He was enormous, his face hidden by a helmet bearing the crimson covering of the Stratham. Kenna tried to jam the arrow into his eyes, but he grabbed her wrist and twisted it away with such force that pain radiated all the way to her shoulder. Kenna dropped the arrow, but refused to cry out. She cast her bow aside and reached for the dagger on the bed.

Her attacker was frighteningly fast and skilled. He had hold of her wrist before her fingers could curl around the hilt and the dagger clattered to the floor. Kenna threw her weight backward, trying to free herself.

"Get your hands off her, you Stratham brute!" Mairi twisted to the left and moved behind the Stratham soldier. With a quick jump, she was on his back, wrapping her arms around his neck. The impact of her efforts was immediate. He gasped and his grip on Kenna's wrists eased enough for her to pull away.

No longer struggling to hold Kenna the Stratham soldier turned his full attention to Mairi. He clawed at her tiny arms as she choked him. Mairi only squeezed tighter. What they could see of the man's face was shifting from red to purple, but he continued to put up a fight.

Kenna was about to duck down to find the dagger she'd dropped when another soldier charged into the room. He kicked the dagger away from her hand and sneered down at Kenna. His entrance must have distracted Mairi, for her hold loosened slightly. The man she was choking drew a breath, then backed up and slammed her into the wall with astonishing force. Mairi's arms went slack and she dropped to the floor winded.

"No!" Kenna jumped to her feet and tried to run to her friend's side but was stopped by a vice-like arm around her waist.

"Rihtall trash!" The second soldier hissed in a thick Arthan accent. He lifted Kenna off the ground and threw her several feet as though she weighed nothing. Kenna slammed into one of the chairs and skidded across the floor, stunned by the force of the impact. He was on her again before she could gather herself to attempt fight or flight. Fingers curled into Kenna's hair and hauled her back to her feet.

"Your Vashirat believes they're so much better than the rest of us," the Stratham spat as he dragged her across the room. "Did you really think your little Venallian lordling could protect you? Or was it that no Arthan man would have you?"

A cold dread seized Kenna. Niall would have come for her by now... unless he couldn't. Mairi said he wasn't in the great hall—perhaps the Stratham had encountered him before entering. "What have you done to my husband?"

"Taught him the price of meddling in Arthan affairs," her captor hissed. "You should thank me for ridding you of that weakling. His own wife has put up more of a fight than he did."

Kenna's heart clenched with pain. She felt tears welling up in her eyes, but she wasn't going to give this monster the satisfaction of seeing her weep. Instead, she twisted around to meet his eyes, despite the pain it caused. "My Vashirat will dance on your bones." She spat in his face defiantly.

He cursed and slammed her against the wall before pressing a blade to her throat. "Maybe, but you won't be dancing with them."

Kenna tried to push the cold iron from her skin, but the more she struggled the harder he pressed. She could feel the warm wetness of her own blood beginning to trickle down her neck. Mairi was holding her hands out in surrender and pleading for their lives.

"Hurry up and slit her throat, Ghalen," the other man grumbled. "We don't have time for you to put on a show."

The angle of the knife changed slightly. Ghalen leaned in and pulled her head back further. Kenna met his eyes boldly. If this was to be her final moment, she would face it with the courage her mother had instilled in her. She would not shrink from these men like a scared child.

A hand clamped down on her attacker's shoulder. He whirled around suddenly. Niall growled and shoved a sword deep into Ghalen's gut. He pulled the blade free and the man sank to the ground in a quickly growing pool of blood. Behind him, Cathal charged at the soldier holding Mairi.

"Are you all right?" Niall asked, cupping Kenna's face. His eyes settled on the place where Ghalen's blade was pressed to her skin. "I'm sorry. I came as soon as I could, but we had to fight our way through the halls."

"You're alive!" Kenna exclaimed. She threw her arms around Niall, overwhelmed by the surge of relief that seeing him brought. "They said they'd killed you." She released him and straightened her robe.

"No, not yet at any rate. But there are too many for us to fend off." Niall shook his head, leaning in to look more closely at her wounds. He tore a strip of fabric from the hem of his shirt and tenderly applied it to the cut. "My parents are in my father's chambers. There's a hidden passage that leads to the kitchens. From there we can get to the docks and escape on the river."

"Are you saying the castle is lost?" Kenna asked.

"I don't know how they managed it," Niall's clothes were stained with blood, his face pale. "They overwhelmed our guards in minutes. There wasn't even time to sound an alarm."

"Niall, we need to get moving," Cathal interrupted. He was holding a blanket around Mairi's shoulders. "The path to your father's chambers won't be clear for long."

Niall glanced over his shoulder, but turned back to Kenna. "Are you hurt badly? Can you make a run for it?"

"Not badly, battered and shaken, mostly. I'll be fine until we can get somewhere safer than this," Kenna assured him. She hurried to gather her bow and quiver, then nocked another arrow and turned back to Niall. "Lead the way. Anyone who wishes to clash swords will have to face my aim first."

The hint of a smile turned the corners of Niall's mouth. He offered Kenna his hand and led them to the open door. They stepped out into the halls that continued to echo with fighting. One of the serving boys was laid out awkwardly against the wall. His eyes were open wide but unseeing. The horror of the poor child's final moments was written in the frozen expression on his face. Blood covered the floor around him.

Mairi gasped and buried her head against Cathal's shoulder. Kenna gripped her bow with one hand and clung tightly to Niall with the other. She knew once they were away from the carnage the tears of mourning would come. Until then, she would store up her anger and use it to fuel their escape.

High Lord Edan's rooms were near the staircase leading to the library, on the opposite end of the residential wing. It held the promise of a quick exit to the kitchens, but getting there would present a challenge. They managed to navigate a few hallways without a fight, occasionally ducking into empty rooms to avoid detection, but as they drew closer to their destination the sounds of conflict intensified. Niall and Cathal lifted their swords as they inched forward to glance around the corner.

Kenna stepped back to wrap her arms around Mairi. Her friend's face was as pale as Kenna had ever seen it. Framed in dark curls, her skin looked nearly white. She was cold to the touch and her eyes were glassy. Kenna rubbed her arms and tucked the blanket more securely around her shoulders. Mairi needed water and calm. She'd received several brutal blows before Niall and Cathal came to their aid, and she seemed to be in a daze. Kenna worried she'd suffered some unseen and deadly injury.

"Hold tight, Mairi. We're almost there, and then you can rest for a little while," Kenna spoke soothingly. "We'll be safe before the sun rises."

The timing of their attackers felt like a mockery of Kenna's reassurances. Mairi turned to reply, but it was a scream, and not words, that answered Kenna's empty promises. Six men stepped out of one of the nearby bedrooms. Their weapons were drawn and dripping with blood. One hefted a crossbow and pointed it in their direction. There was the slightest movement, a click and whirring sound.

Kenna heard the bolt's impact before her eyes could register what happened. It was a sickening wet thump that curdled her stomach. Mairi's head jerked oddly. Her scream turned to a horrible, strangled gasp that was cut off by the bolt that protruded from her chest.

"Mairi!" Kenna cried in shock. Her friend went slack in her arms. The weight of Mairi's limp body pulled Kenna down to the floor as well.

"No!" Cathal screamed. He barreled down the passage and bowled into the archer before he could finish reloading. Cathal had the man by the shirt front and was slamming his head against the stone tiles with vicious force. He was like a man possessed, screaming and beating the bowman. "Not her! Not her!"

Kenna cradled Mairi, rocking her back and forth, as if the motion could have any effect. Mairi didn't move. The only sound was the cracking of her killer's head on the cold stone floor. The front of her gown was turning the same bloody crimson of the Stratham's face coverings. Kenna couldn't let go, but some part of her mind knew she would have to.

I can't leave her alone and afraid. I can't let her go. Mairi had been so afraid, so shaken.

"Kenna, look at me," Niall was at her side now. He reached for Mairi, gently pulling her away from Kenna.

"No, she needs me," Kenna snapped. She pulled Mairi back to her chest. Down the hall, Cathal was being jerked off of his victim by two Stratham soldiers. He swung at them blindly, kicking and struggling as he continued to scream out his rage and pain.

"There's nothing more you can do for her now," Niall's voice was steady and gentle, but urgent.

Cathal screamed as he was overwhelmed. "Get your hands off of me, killers, savages!"

Kenna's grip on her friend tightened, but reality was starting to press its way past the trauma. Niall reached for Mairi again, and this time Kenna allowed him to pull her away. "I'm sorry, Mairi. I'm so sorry."

Niall settled Mairi's lifeless body on the floor and grabbed Kenna's hand. He pulled her to her feet and around the corner. There was no more time to say farewell to the best friend Kenna had ever known. She had to leave Mairi behind or join her in death. Kenna gripped Niall's hand and followed him through the blood-soaked halls of his home.

No soldiers stood between them and their destination for that last short run. From the increased sound of combat, it seemed to Kenna that the household had rallied somewhat, but with little hope of victory. At the very least, the attention of their attackers was focused elsewhere when Niall and Kenna finally approached the High Lord's rooms. Niall skidded to a halt and tapped out a careful rhythm on the door. There was a pause, that to Kenna seemed nearly endless, but couldn't have been more than a few seconds. The door cracked open wide enough for a single eye to peer out and identify Niall.

"It's your son," a voice from the other side called.

"For the sake of the gods, let him in!" Niall's father's command followed. His voice was strained, the sound of a man in pain.

The door swung wide and Kenna and Niall were pulled in quickly. High Lady Carene was upon them before the door was fully closed or locked. She clung to Niall and Kenna with fierce desperation. Kenna melted into the motherly embrace and returned it with equal intensity. They were far from safe, but her mother-in-law's arms felt like a sanctuary; solid, warm, and reassuring.

"Cathal sacrificed himself so we could make it here," Niall informed his parents. He pulled away from his mother and joined his father at the desk. "You're injured. You should be sitting."

"There's no time for that, Niall," the High Lord answered abruptly. He was leaning heavily against the table. His tunic was torn, and the entire right side was stained scarlet.

Kenna released Niall's mother and looked down at her own nightdress, horrified to see that the front was equally covered in gore. She shuddered and her throat grew uncomfortably tight against the sobs that were fighting their way from her heart.

"Niall, you and Kenna must get away from here," High Lord Edan declared through clenched teeth. He reached into his tunic and pulled out a cloth bag as bloody as the pocket it had come from. "Take your wife and mother to Kenna's family. You'll be safe with them until..." He moaned and his knees buckled.

Niall caught him before he collapsed. "I'm not leaving you behind. We go together."

"I won't make it out of this room, Niall. I'll only slow you," his father replied. The High Lord looked at his son with a sad mixture of regret and pride. "What happens to me now doesn't matter. I should have disobeyed the King and told you—" The thundering sound of boots grew louder. He pressed the bag into Niall's hand. "Go, now. The future of the kingdom depends on your safety."

High Lady Carene went to her husband's side. She stroked his face lovingly. "I will remain with you, my love."

A fist slammed on the door. "Your guards are dead, High Lord. Surrender now and we'll make your deaths quick."

Niall's mother stroked her son's face. "Everything you need is in that bag. You and Kenna should go now."

Kenna reached for her mother-in-law. "We stand a better chance of survival if we stay together. We only have to get to the river. There's no need for anyone to stay behind."

"What happens to the two of us doesn't matter. It is you and Niall who must escape this night. Take care of my son," the High Lady replied. She looked at Kenna and Niall with an expression of heartbreaking love.

"No! I said I won't leave you and I meant it. I've already lost my brother. I will not lose the two of you as well," Niall argued. He crossed his arms. "We all go, or we all stay."

"I agree with Niall," Kenna added. She would not allow the two of them to sacrifice themselves; too many had died already.

High Lord Edan looked at his wife for a moment, then he pushed himself upright. He clung tightly to High Lady Carene's arm, but slowly moved to the far wall and twisted one of the sconces. The nearest panel creaked and opened into a dark passage. "Then we should be on the move."

Niall's shoulders relaxed visibly. He took Kenna's hand and led her to the hidden door. Kenna let out a sigh of relief. The nightmare would be over soon, though morning would dawn with enough pain and terror to keep the memory vivid for years to come. Niall pulled one of the candles from the wall and stepped into the dark, cobweb-filled hall.

"I'm sorry Niall," his father said suddenly. "But the King has made his choice." He slammed the door behind Kenna, and she heard something lock into place. When he spoke again his words were dampened by the thick wood that separated them "Guards, open the doors. If they wish to take my home from me, they will not do it without a fight!"

"Father, don't!" Niall flung himself against the panel. He pushed and kicked at it, but it didn't budge. "No, please don't do this!"

Kenna heard the door to High Lord Edan's chambers burst open, followed by the unmistakable metallic zing of weapons clashing. There was nothing they could do. The door to the hidden passage was barred from the other side. She tugged on Niall's arm. The High Lord and Lady had made their choice, and she would honor it.

"Niall, we have to go," she whispered. "They're giving us the time we need to escape. Staying here now will do nothing but make their deaths meaningless."

Niall's face crumpled. His hands balled into fists on the door and he hung his head. The sound of fighting exploded on the other side of the wooden barrier. There was a thud against the wall, and the sickening sound of someone sliding to the floor.

Kenna gently tightened the grip on Niall's arm. "They wouldn't want you to hear this. Honor their sacrifice tonight. Live and seek justice tomorrow."

Niall nodded. He closed his eyes for a second, then slowly stepped away from the door. In the dim light from their single candle, Kenna could see the stark lines of strain on his face. They said nothing more and moved with as much speed as stealth allowed. The sound of fighting echoed after them, magnified by the empty space they traversed. Kenna held Niall's hand with such intensity that her fingers ached. It was the only comfort they could offer one another.

The tunnel opened into the kitchen just as Niall said it would. The room was in absolute disarray. Food stores were strewn across the floor. Broken eggs and cream were swirled with blood. The bodies of servants were scattered around the room, some so terribly battered that they couldn't be recognized. Poor, nurturing Brona was splayed out on one of the tables, with torn and bloody clothes. The marks of her final, brutal moments were laid bare for all to see. There was nothing of dignity or life remaining.

Kenna watched the impact of every blood-spattered body play out on Niall's face. His entire life was ripped to pieces and broken on the floors of his home. It revealed a night without mercy or remorse. Moonlight shone on the river through the open door, an oddly serene contrast to the horror that surrounded them.

Afraid the candle would alert someone to their escape, Kenna took the little light from Niall and blew it out. The night sky was clear, and the moon full enough for them to make their way to one of the boats tied to the dock without stumbling in the dark. They climbed into the nearest vessel and pushed away from the shore. Niall took hold of the oars and paddled until they were caught up by the current. The screams had all but died down as they drifted away from the estate.

CHAPTER 8

The Next Step

Niall was numb. His thoughts were sluggish on the surface, but down deep they were racing, and there was a strange sort of buzzing in his ears. Sometimes the buzzing would twist itself into screams and the sound of metal clashing against metal. When the clamor threatened to overwhelm him, his hands would shake so violently that he feared he might drop the oars. The horror of the evening didn't feel real. At the same time, it was all too real and unbearable to contemplate.

The smell of smoke filled the air and an orange glow flickered from the direction of Niall's once-beautiful and happy home. They were still close enough to the castle that he could see flames flickering behind the stained-glass window of his childhood sanctuary. Anything that wasn't stone was ablaze. The sight was at strange odds with the sound of the gurgling river and the splash of the oars whenever Niall dipped them into the water.

"Niall? Can you hear me?"

Kenna was speaking. That realization forced the world back into focus. She was here, here with him. Kenna was all that remained of his life, his family. She was crying and holding herself as if to stave off the chill of the night. "Niall, please say something."

"I—I hear you," Niall managed to mumble through sensationless lips. His own voice sounded distant, like it came from someone else entirely. The buzzing turned to sounds of terror again. Niall took a shuddering breath. He needed to focus, for Kenna. His world might be crashing down around him, but his wife needed him to get them to safety "We'll go a little further down river an—and then make for the bank. We can tie off on a tree, or a... a..." He could feel himself beginning to unravel again.

"Do you want me to take the oars for a little while?" Kenna asked.

Niall shook his head quickly. He needed the task to keep himself from falling apart completely. "No, I'll keep going. We'll be far enough away soon."

Kenna pulled her knees in close and wrapped her arms around them then buried her face in the folds of her nightdress. Niall could hear muffled sobs but he couldn't bring himself to offer any hollow comfort. He was too lost for anything like that. All he could do was focus on getting away. He dug the oars in deep and clenched his teeth as he pulled. Rowing and breathing would keep him stable enough to get them to safety. When that was done, he would let himself feel the impact of what happened.

After two hours Niall's arms were burning. The castle had faded from view except for a slight, distant glow in the night sky. They were deep in the midst of the woods with trees thickly lining the shores on either side of the river. Niall lowered the oars again and nearly dropped one of them when he tried to pull it through the water. He was exhausted and nearing the limits of his strength. Niall pulled the paddles out of the river and let the current push them along for a few minutes.

"I think... we can... head to shore," he panted, wobbling a little in his seat. Now that he'd stopped rowing, Niall wasn't sure he could start up again.

Kenna was still clutching her knees, but she was no longer weeping. The tracks of her tears reflected silver in the moonlight, etching the sorrow on her cheeks. Niall rallied what little strength remained in his weary muscles and turned the vessel toward the bank. There were plenty of low-hanging branches they could tie the boat to for the remainder of the night—however long that might be. Even with the moon overhead, it was difficult to guess the hour.

The final push to the riverbank was all Niall had left in him. The second the boat scraped the rocky bottom, his arms and back gave out. He slumped over the oars and sat motionless except for the uncontrollable shaking that seized him. The little wooden vessel began to twist sideways and drift back out into the current. Kenna sprung to action before they lost too much ground. She took the oars from Niall and guided the boat back toward dry land. When they hit the shallows, she jumped out with the rope in hand and waded to the pebble-strewn bank.

Niall managed to pull some last remnants of power from his body. He clumsily climbed over the side and stumbled out of the water to help Kenna loop the rope around a tree branch and secure the wooden craft. Then he leaned against the trunk of the tree and slid to the ground. His arms hung limply at his sides, hands stinging and blistered. He watched as Kenna rifled through the few items that were on the boat. She came back with an armful of rough, lumpy fabric.

"There's a stack of empty grain sacks in the boat, but that's it," she explained, kneeling next to Niall. "Do you think we can light a fire?"

"I don't know," Niall mumbled. "If anyone saw us leave, they might be watching the river for signs of our location."

"I don't think they did, but I'd rather not find out by waking with a sword in my face," Kenna replied. She shook out the sacks in her arms then draped one of them over Niall. "I think these should help against the chill on the wind."

"The wind feels good," Niall answered honestly. He was sweating from his efforts, and the breeze that rustled through the trees was a cooling balm.

"You should drink some water," Kenna studied him for a moment before she turned and started back toward the river.

"No! Don't go!" Panic jolted through Niall. Even though the river was a few feet away it felt like Kenna was too far. He was too worn out to go to her if something happened and the idea of being alone was terrifying. Niall tried to push himself up. "Please, I'm fine. I just need to rest. We both do. Just come back and sit with me for a little while."

Kenna looked down and closed her eyes for a few seconds before returning. She sat on the ground at his side, then nestled against Niall, arranging the grain sacks over her chest and legs with a shiver. "I'm sorry, Niall. I'm so sorry for everything that's happened."

"It's not your fault," Niall replied drowsily. He rested his cheek on the top of her head and closed his eyes.

"It is, though. They were soldiers from the Stratham Vashirat. Your family..." Kenna started crying again.

"Gods, Niall, your family! They're dead because you married me."

"Please don't, Kenna." Niall whispered roughly. His fingers clenched. He couldn't face this. *Not now, not yet.* The tears were so close, but if he let even one escape he wouldn't be able to hold back the tide; it would annihilate him. It was too much to feel right now, and he wasn't strong enough to even contemplate it.

Kenna stiffened against him and started to pull away. The absence of her warmth turned Niall's blood cold. His eyes jolted open and he threw his arms around her to pull her close again. "Stay, please. I don't blame you. I just—it's too much right now. I can't."

Kenna slowly relaxed back into his embrace. She twisted her fingers into his shirt and her tears intensified, mingling with the sweat that already dampened the fabric. Niall held her but had little else to give. He couldn't even find the energy or courage to think beyond the present. He sat and stared up at the heavens as his wife mourned for them both. In time, exhaustion won out and sleep numbed the anguish.

* * *

It was nearing midmorning before Niall opened his eyes again. He was no longer leaning against the tree, but was slumped over on the ground, one arm draped across Kenna's waist, the other serving as a pillow for her head. Niall shifted, instantly regretting the action. His muscles were stiff to the point of resisting any exertion, and they angrily protested the previous night's abuse.

The horrific details of the attack came flooding back to Niall's mind in a tidal wave of loss. The sound of birds and the rushing river turned to sounds of fear and death in his mind. He clenched his jaw tightly to bite back the scream of rage and grief that threatened to burst from his lungs. His entire body tensed, sending ripples of pain through his limbs. The physical soreness was almost a relief. That was something tangible that would ease in a day or two. He didn't know how he could ever escape the agony that gripped his heart.

Kenna's breathing changed abruptly. She lifted her head and looked around. The expression on her face was haunted. "I know it's foolish, but I hoped I would wake up and find that it was all a nightmare."

"It is a nightmare," Niall replied quietly. He didn't voice the idea that he'd rather hoped he wouldn't wake up at all. He slowly pushed himself into a sitting position, wincing with each movement.

"You should have let me do some of the rowing last night," Kenna admonished gently. She sat up and studied her bloodstained nightgown and dressing robe. Her nose went red and her eyes glistened with tears. "We should try to clean ourselves up a bit."

Niall looked down at his own clothes, surprised by the amount of dried blood spattered across the once pristine fabric. A wave of nausea rolled over him. Soreness aside, he jumped to his feet and stumbled a few steps before he bent over and started heaving up what little there was in his stomach. Blood didn't make him queasy, but this wasn't just blood, this was all that remained of his home and family. Tears refused to fall, but he couldn't stop this reaction.

"Don't fight it, Niall. It's all right, let it out." Kenna was at his side in an instant. She put a small, warm hand on his back and rubbed gentle circles while Niall's stomach wracked an already punished body.

It took a few minutes, but eventually Niall's stomach ceased its convulsions and he was able to sit back and catch his breath. He stared at the river, shaking as he tried to find the will to carry on. And still he could not cry. He knew he should—that he needed to—that he would eventually. It just couldn't happen until they were safe. It was something that loomed before him like a waiting predator. The loss would catch up with him, and when it did Niall feared his grief would utterly devour him.

"Give me your shirt." Kenna interrupted his thoughts, holding a hand out. "We can't travel looking like this. We're safe enough here, for now. I think we should stay for the day and rest while we figure out the best course of action. We won't make it far in our current state."

"We'll have to backtrack," Niall said. He pulled his shirt over his head, careful to avoid studying it too closely, lest he become ill again. "The river flows away from Arthan."

"Niall, we can't make it all the way to my family's holdings on the river. We haven't any food, nor vessels for carrying water. Even if we made it through the mountains, we would perish in the dunes that surround my home," Kenna replied as she slung his shirt over her arm and headed for the river.

Niall jumped to his feet and followed her, heedless of his body's protests. He needed to stay close to her. "There's a trading post on the river. We can't be far from it: perhaps a day's journey downstream. We could sell the boat once we're there. It's a good sturdy craft, should fetch enough to buy a horse, maybe even a few supplies. If we need more, I can sell my sword. I doubt they see many of its quality there."

Kenna placed his shirt on the side of the boat and began untying her dressing robe. Niall could see her fingers shaking as they fumbled with the gore-encrusted silk. She pulled the sash open and froze at the large brownish-red stain on her nightgown beneath.

"I'm sorry we couldn't save Mairi," Niall offered mildly. He'd promised Kenna's parents protection and had failed so miserably.

"Could you go into the trees, or further along the bank? I need to clean this, and want to wash myself." Kenna didn't look at him when she spoke.

"No, I'm not leaving you alone," Niall replied quickly... too quickly. His heart was racing and he heard a strange, disembodied roaring in his ears.

"Niall, we're alone here. No one knows where we are. I'll be safe for a few minutes," Kenna insisted.

Niall shook his head vehemently. He could not bear the idea of being away from her company. "No, we stay together. Besides, I'm your husband. There's nothing improper about it."

"A husband who doesn't share my bed and has never seen me unclothed. I'm not comfortable undressing in front of you," her voice was tinged with frustration. "I have my bow. I can protect myself if it comes to that."

"We stay together," Niall persisted. He reached into the boat and pulled out two of the remaining grain sacks. Using the dagger he tucked into his belt the night before, he cut a hole in the bottom of one of them, then another hole on each side. He ripped open the bottom of the second bag and handed them both to Kenna. "Here, you can wear these while you clean your clothes. I'll turn around while you change."

Kenna looked at the improvised garments skeptically. "I want to bathe as well."

"I—I don't want to be alone," Niall finally admitted. He swallowed and held the grain sacks out to her again. "I've lost everyone I hold dear," he took a calming breath. "Everyone except you. I swear I will not look while you clean yourself. Please, don't ask me to wander on my own."

After a moment of consideration, "I understand," Kenna said, taking the rough shirt and skirt from him. "Sit on the other side of the boat while I bathe. Then we can wash our clothes together and see if there's anything nearby that we can eat."

"Thank you, Kenna," Niall sighed with relief. He obediently moved to the other side of the boat and situated himself with his back to the river. It was silly to think she would never leave his sight; they'd each need privacy at some point. For now, though, the memories of last night's attack were still too fresh and raw to allow for solitude.

After a few minutes, the sound of splashing water abated. Niall nearly turned to reassure himself that Kenna was still there, but he'd given his word he wouldn't look, and he was not going to allow fear to cause him to break another promise to his wife. After everything they'd been through, it was the least he could give her.

"You can turn around now," Kenna finally said, to Niall's unparalleled relief.

He stood up slowly and turned to her. Kenna was standing in the crudely constructed and shapeless garments he'd provided. Her raven hair was wet and dripping down her back, her arms and legs below the knees were exposed and glittering with droplets of water.

"I look like a madwoman," she commented, examining herself. "But this will serve until my clothes are clean and dry."

"The fault is with the tailor, I assure you." Niall managed half a smile. "At least I know I can rule that out as a future career." The conversation almost felt normal. Almost. There was no way to banish the shadow that hung over them. It filled the air with looming terror and danger.

"We should see to our clothes," Kenna replied, looking away from Niall as she gathered up the discarded clothing. The moment of semi-normalcy was over.

The chilly river water was not as effective in cleaning their clothes as either of them would have liked. It removed the worst of the gore, but the garments remained stained even after several minutes of intense scrubbing. When it was obvious the clothes were not going to get any cleaner, they gave up and draped them over nearby branches to dry in the breeze that filtered through the trees. There was little else to be done until they could acquire unsullied replacements.

It was harder to cope with their situation when there wasn't a task to keep them busy. The idle hours passed in near silence. Niall was forced to contemplate their situation in more depth than he wished to. His family was gone, his home was destroyed and almost certainly stripped of anything of value. Technically, he was the High Lord now. *But High Lord of what? Ruin and devastation?*

Niall glanced at Kenna. She'd only married him as a means of securing an alliance that would strengthen her family against its enemies. Not that it had done any good in the end. Those enemies had simply turned their ire on his family and eliminated any benefit their marriage could have provided to the Rihtall Vashirat. *It isn't Kenna's fault, nor her parents'. No one could have imagined that the Stratham Vashirat would turn such vicious hatred on my family.*

"I think our clothes are dry enough to wear," Kenna stated, pulling Niall from his contemplation. She tossed his shirt to him and reached for her nightdress and robe. "Turn around, please."

Niall obeyed without question and busied himself with pulling his own shirt over his head. He hated putting it back on. His skin crawled at the pale brown splotches that were splattered across the fabric.

"I think we should find something to eat," Kenna called over to him. When Niall turned, he found her bending over the side of the boat. "I have my bow, thank the gods. I should be able to get a rabbit. A squirrel if nothing else. Do you know what vegetation is safe to eat around here?"

"Some. It's a bit early for berries, but there will be herbs and possibly some mushrooms growing nearby. We might find some watercress along the river's edge," Niall answered thoughtfully. He didn't feel hungry, but it was well into the afternoon and they hadn't had anything to eat since dinner the night before. *Hungry or not, I need to keep my strength up if I'm to take Kenna safely back to her family.*

Kenna leaned further into the boat, her torso disappearing behind the wood of the hull as she reached for something in the bottom. When she stood back up she was holding the pouch from Niall's father. As she shook it, Niall heard the jingle of coins. Kenna approached Niall and silently placed the purse in his hands.

Niall held it for a few seconds before summoning the courage to pull the top open and look inside. There wasn't much there. Enough coin for them to secure passage on a caravan, a small portrait of the family that his father had always kept secreted on his person, and a folded square of fabric that was stained with his father's blood.

Niall reached inside to grab the portrait, but when his fingers brushed the cloth square beside it, he felt a

lump encased in the stiffened folds. He pinched one of
the corners between his fingers and shook, not wanting
to touch the fabric any more than he had to. A single,
round, gold and sapphire object fell on top of the coins
with a slight tinkle. It was his father's signet ring: the
ring of the High Lord of Britwylde estate.

He wrapped his fingers around the band that was so
intricately woven into Niall's perception of his father,
and carefully drew it out of the pouch. It should have
gone to Ian upon their father's death. It shouldn't be
going to anyone yet. His father should be wearing it,
alive and well. Now it belonged to Niall and he couldn't
bring himself to put it on.

"He was a good man. I wish I'd had more time to
know him," Kenna murmured. "I wish..."

"As do I," Niall managed. His eyes were burning
with the tears he held locked inside. He started to shove
the ring back into the pouch but stopped himself.
Though he wasn't ready to wear it, he wanted it closer
than loosely packed in a bag of coins. Niall pulled the
bloody fabric from the bag and carefully slipped the
ring back inside its folds. He tucked the little parcel in
a hidden pocket that was sewn into the underside of his
shirt. Someday he might put it on, but until then he
would keep it close.

Once Niall had his father's ring safely tucked away,
he was able to frame his mind more clearly around the
practicalities of survival. With the coins his parents had
provided they had enough to travel safely beyond the
borders of Venallis. It was a relief to Niall to know that
he wouldn't be forced to sell his sword to scrape
together enough money to make the trip to Arthan. He
didn't want to be on the road unarmed.

But before they could book passage, they needed to
attend the needs of their bodies. Though young and
healthy, they would weaken quickly without food. To

that end, he followed Kenna into the woods and foraged for mushrooms and herbs while she managed to bag a fat rabbit for them.

They spent the remainder of their day at the river's edge, resting and gaining strength for the journey to come. Tomorrow they would take the boat and make their way downriver to trade for the means to make the trek to Arthan. Niall didn't have a definitive course after that, but he would not ask Kenna to remain chained to a man who had nothing to offer her.

They did what they could to make their little camp as comfortable as possible with so little to work with. The sky grew cloudy in the evening. With few other options for shelter, they dragged the boat further onto the bank and turned it upside down. It wasn't much, but it kept them from getting completely drenched when the rain began.

Sadness was never far though, and no amount of physical comfort could take away the atrocities they'd fled from. For the second time in their marriage, they slept in one another's arms as the rain pattered down on their makeshift shelter. It was still early enough in the spring that the nights were cool, especially in the soggy weather. But it wasn't the chill that compelled them to cling to one another: both felt the need for closeness. Once again, Kenna wept until sleep overtook her, but Niall remained dry-eyed.

They woke early the next day. broke camp at dawn, and were well away from the woodland sanctuary by midmorning. This time Niall and Kenna took turns rowing and allowing the current to propel them forward, only using the oars to guide the vessel away from rocks, or waterlogged branches. At first Niall was sure of their course. They drifted down the river and all seemed well, but as the day wore on and the sun began to drift back toward the horizon, concern clouded his mind.

He frowned and twisted in his seat. "We should have seen some signs of civilization by now. I thought we were only a few hours from the trading post."

"Could we have passed it our first night out?" Kenna asked.

"I don't think so... But it's been years since I was there. I might be misremembering. I suppose it could have closed down or moved." Niall put the oars into the water and started to direct them toward shore. "I haven't lived on my family's lands for five years. I'm afraid I didn't stay informed on the details of the holding."

Kenna bit her lower lip thoughtfully. It bothered Niall to see her troubled, especially when it was his fault. Their present situation was the result of the lack of interest he'd shown in his family lands. He'd been foolish to become so wrapped up in his place at court.

"I think we should go ashore," he told her. "We've already traveled several miles away from the Arthan border. If the outpost was closed, we don't want to add any more time to our journey." He continued to row away from the center of the river.

"We'll need to look into something for dinner, in that case," Kenna pointed out. She reached for her bow and laid it across her knees.

Niall hopped into the water as soon as the bottom of the boat scraped against the riverbed. He dragged the vessel further in by hand and tied it to a branch that hung out over the river, then went back to help Kenna out and carry her to the shore. He was already half-soaked, there was no reason she should suffer through wet clothes a second night.

"I'm sorry. I thought this was our best option," he apologized, feeling that he'd failed her as a husband.

"You don't need to put this on yourself, Niall. We'll find something for dinner and reassess the situation in the morning." Kenna flung her quiver over her shoulder and looked at him solemnly. "You didn't expect to inherit these lands. There was no reason for you to assume something would happen to your brother. You were building a life for yourself in Rosehaven. You gave it up to honor an agreement you had no part in arranging."

"You gave up your life too, and you've suffered for it," Niall replied quietly. "We haven't consummated our union. I won't hold it against you if you choose to return to that life once we reach Arthan."

Kenna looked off into the underbrush. She was quiet for some time before responding. "There's not much point in discussing that right now. We're far from my family. If we don't feed ourselves, we'll never make it to them at all."

Niall nodded and felt another part of himself beginning to break. "Please, don't misunderstand. I'm not trying to push you away. I just don't want you to feel obligated to remain bound to me when I can't uphold my end of the alliance."

"No, I understand, and my parents will likely push for an annulment. But we really ought to focus on the immediate necessities," Kenna answered, still obviously avoiding eye contact. She turned from him and started into the trees.

"Of course," Niall said through a throat that felt like it was clenching closed. He followed in her tracks, eyeing the ground for nuts or mushrooms, and trying to convince himself that the silence that lingered between them was only to avoid scaring away potential quarry.

It took more than an hour before Kenna was able to find any game, and even then, it was only a squirrel.

Niall gathered a spattering of wild sage and chives, as well as another batch of mushrooms. The meal would have been scoffed at in Rosehaven, but it would ease the pangs of hunger. They'd survive another day at least.

By the time they were nearing the place where they had tied off the boat, the tension from their earlier conversation had eased and they were discussing the best way to prepare squirrel. However, before they could make good on any of their limited cooking options, the sound of gruff voices stopped them in their tracks.

"Do ya' think it belongs to one of their hunting parties?" one voice asked.

There was the thud of a fist hitting flesh. "Don't be daft. Why would a bunch of human warriors be floatin' around in a boat full of empty sacks? Think they're gonna bag ya' and take ya' home as a pet?"

Niall and Kenna exchanged wide-eyed looks and carefully inched forward to get a better view of their uninvited guests. They stopped just short of the small clearing and crouched behind the fallen trunk of a large tree.

Two hobgoblin scouts were standing by the boat, rummaging through the stack of empty grain sacks. Their greenish-black and gnarled bodies were covered in patches of mud and brambles. What little clothing they wore consisted of furs, with festering bits of flesh still clinging to the leather. Even from this distance, Niall could smell them; the scent was a nauseating musk, like old meat soaking in rancid milk.

Niall leaned close to Kenna and whispered under his breath. "Hobgoblins. There are likely more of them nearby."

"If we can take these two down and get into the boat we might escape before the others join them." Kenna whispered. She reached back to pull an arrow from her quiver and nocked it to the bowstring.

Niall wrapped his hand around the hilt of his sword and prepared to confront the hobgoblins. Kenna's aim was superb and he had little doubt she could dispatch one easily, but if the other charged she might not have time to take it down before it was close enough to cause harm. "Take your shot on the count of three."

Kenna held her bow horizontally until she could rise to launch her attack. Niall rolled his shoulders. He took a deep breath and nearly gagged at the intensity of the hobgoblin's stench. It was stronger now than it had been seconds earlier. A shadow settled across the trunk they crouched behind. Niall turned his head slowly and found a bony, charcoal grey knee, dotted with wiry black hairs obscuring his view.

"And what do we have here?" An enormous hobgoblin sneered at them with malicious intent. The brute reached down and grabbed both Niall and Kenna by the backs of their clothing before either one of them had a chance to react usefully. "Drop your weapons."

Niall's hand tightened on his sword. He started to pull his arm back to swing at the hobgoblin, but another jumped forward to take hold of his wrist and twisted until Niall had no choice but to drop the weapon. Another stepped up to Kenna and yanked her bow from her hands. Niall glanced around, counting four of the monstrous creatures, in addition to the two scouts at the boat.

One of the hobgoblins plucked the squirrel from Kenna and promptly bit the head off with a snap and twist of his jaws. "Not even enough to fill one of our stomachs."

The hobgoblin holding Niall and Kenna grunted and shoved them into the clearing. It was obvious from the behavior of the others that this was the leader of the group. "I don't know, they're a bit scrawny, but I think we can make it work."

Niall pulled Kenna close, wrapping his arms around her protectively. "Oh, gods, I think they mean to eat us."

"I didn't know they did that," Kenna replied, wrapping her arms around him as well.

The brute who dragged them from hiding chuckled with dark mirth. "Not always, humans tend to be a bit too stringy for our tastes. But we're hungry enough to make an exception today."

Niall positioned himself between the hobgoblin and Kenna. He was not going to allow this creature to torment her, even if he had to fight the hobgoblins off with his bare hands. "Stay away from her."

This reaction elicited a chorus of laughter from their captors. The scouts jumped away from the river, and scampered forward to sniff and paw at Niall and Kenna. They snatched at their clothes and tugged on their hair, licking their chops all the while.

"We have gold," Kenna declared. "It's in that pouch on my companion's belt. Take it and we can all go our separate ways without the need for bloodshed."

"And what are we supposed to do with gold?" The leader of the group laughed again, but he snatched the pouch from Niall's belt anyway. "Can't eat it. Can't wear it. It just shines." He drew his arm back and cast the purse into the river in disgust. Niall watched their hope for escape to Arthan disappear beneath the ever-moving water.

One of the scouts pulled on Niall's hair. "This one's head is covered in gold. Maybe after we eat 'em we can use his skull for a cap."

"Oh, think o' what they'd say in Knobnoster if you went waltzin' in with that mop on your head," another scoffed with demented delight. "Cut his head off! Cut his head off!"

"Get your hands off of my husband!" Kenna slapped their hands away. The hobgoblin tugging on Niall hissed at her and bared his spiny teeth but backed away.

Their leader laughed at that. He lifted a finger to drag it along Kenna's cheek. "Don't worry, little one. I'll eat you first, that way you don't have to watch your sweetheart turned into a hat."

Niall's blood boiled. He balled up his fist and slammed it into the hobgoblin's jaw. "I said, leave her alone. Do what you want to me but leave my wife in peace."

The hobgoblin staggered back a step, clutching his jaw. He growled and spit a mouthful of putrid green blood on the ground. Niall lifted his chin defiantly, despite the hopelessness of the predicament. The hobgoblins had his sword and outnumbered them. He didn't offer much of a threat and their captors knew it as well as he did. The other hobgoblins closed in, pulling jagged knives and clubs from their belts. They were growling and drooling in anticipation of their evening feast.

Niall glanced back at Kenna, needing to see her one last time before they fell upon him. It was in that instant that he saw a glimmer of hope. In their eagerness to cause suffering, the hobgoblins left a clear path to the boat. It was still tied to the tree limb, but maybe if they were busy with him, Kenna could get away.

"Kenna, go to the boat," Niall whispered under his breath.

"I'm not leaving you, Niall," she insisted.

"Don't even think of it," the hobgoblin commander pushed through his salivating minions, apparently seeing the possibility as well. He took hold of Kenna's arm and jerked her away from Niall. "Cut the boat loose! There'll be no floating away before we can have our fun."

He drew a long, crooked sword from his waist and pointed it at Niall. "Leave her alone, you say? I think I agree. I'll take my time killing you. When I'm finished pulling your entrails through your nose, your little wife will be left alone; all alone until we finish her off too."

"No!" Kenna jerked her arm free and ran back to Niall's side to grip his hand tightly.

Niall squeezed her fingers and looked at her. "I'm so sorry, Kenna. I wish I could have—"

The hobgoblin lurched forward suddenly. Niall sucked in a breath and jumped back involuntarily, expecting to feel cold steel pierce his abdomen. He heard an odd sound, like a ripe gourd being split with a cleaver. Niall watched in shock as the hobgoblin collapsed on the ground at his feet. The handle of a hatchet was still quivering, held in place by the blade that was embedded in the back of his attacker's skull.

The remaining hobgoblins were scrambling around the clearing in complete disarray. Some brandished their weapons before being cut down by more axes and arrows, while others dashed into the forest shouting in terror. Several figures in brightly colored garb stepped out of the trees and began pulling blades and arrows from the corpses.

"What in the name of a selkie's shiny backside are you two doing out in the middle of the woods so close to nightfall?" A lanky young man with inky black hair and dark brown eyes asked as he yanked the hatchet from the skull of the hobgoblin in front of Niall. "Hobgoblin raiding parties are always on the lookout for easy kills. Have you no sense at all?"

"We were just..." Niall's mind was still trying to unravel the last few seconds.

"Oh, Daris, leave the poor dears alone. A run in with hobgoblins is bad enough without you asking foolish questions," a young woman chided as she drew close. She smiled warmly. "I'm Elize, and the two of you look like these hobgoblins have been the least off your concerns."

CHAPTER 9

The Road to Safety

Their rescuers led Niall and Kenna through the trees to a large meadow running alongside the dusty road that served as the main throughfare for the area. Brightly painted carts and wagons circled half a dozen tents of equally flamboyant canvas. Horses shook their heads lazily as they grazed near the trees in the rosy evening light. Through the spaces between the wagons, Kenna could see the flames of torches, and several small campfires with iron cauldrons hanging over them. Weaving between the caravans ran children of all ages, laughing and squealing with innocent delight as they played.

The hunting party's arrival was heralded by barking dogs before any of the people took notice. The playing children only glanced at them at first but when they spotted Niall and Kenna, they stopped their games and came to stare curiously at the unexpected guests. Elize ruffled the hair of one of the younger boys as she walked past him, then sent the little ones off to alert their parents that there would be company for dinner. The color and life reminded Kenna more of her home in Arthan than the reserved and austere atmosphere of High Lord Edan's estate. It brought both comfort and pain.

It didn't take long for the people of the nomadic community to arrange care for their visitors. A few minutes after arriving, Kenna found herself in the middle of a wagon that served as home for Elize and Daris. It was an impressive example of the ingenious use of space that life on the road must require. There was a bunk at the front of the wagon with a set of drawers built underneath it and cabinets installed above. Vibrantly colored scarves hung from wooden knobs along the ceiling, giving the quaint space a sense of joy and warmth.

Kenna laid the clothes that Elize had provided across the bed and pulled her ragged, stained nightgown over her head. The chemise she'd been given was plain linen, but the blouse was a striking blue, and the woolen skirt a deep emerald. The garments were not the fine silks that Kenna left behind at Britwylde, but they were comfortable and clean. Putting them on gave Kenna a sense of distance from the horror of her memories.

There was a knock at the door. "May I come in?" It was Elize.

Kenna straightened her blouse and turned to address her hostess. "Of course. It is your home after all."

"Well, I didn't wish to open the door and find you half-dressed," Elize said as she closed the door behind her. She examined Kenna for a moment then stepped close to adjust her garments. "Looks a little big on you, but we can fix that with a scarf. The colors suit you though."

"Thank you. I can't tell you how good it feels to be out of that nightdress," Kenna smiled and finished pulling her hair from her collar.

Elize opened one of the compartments built into the ceiling and removed a hairbrush. "Here, let me help with your hair." She began running the brush through Kenna's hair in long, slow sweeps. "One of the men lent your husband some clothes as well. He's changed and waiting by the fire in the center of the camp. We offered him something to eat but he said he preferred to wait for you."

"I should probably hurry up then," Kenna replied quietly. They were safe for now, cleaned up and in the company of kind folk. Yet Kenna felt more alone than she had in weeks. Niall's assurance that he would understand if she wished to end their marriage had created a sort of emptiness in her. It made the massacre on his family real in a different way. Her heart ached for Niall, for Mairi, for the High Lord and Lady. None of them deserved the cruelties they'd faced. *They wouldn't have if I'd been content with a life in Arthan.*

"There you go, all done." Elize had finished brushing, and braided Kenna's hair down her back. She tied the end off with a ribbon and put the brush away. Elize studied Kenna with open curiosity but didn't bring up the circumstances of their meeting. Kenna could tell that there were questions she wished to ask, but the other woman seemed to sense that now wasn't the most opportune time.

"Thank you, again, Elize. I don't know what we would have done if you and your people hadn't shown up," Kenna replied graciously. She shuddered a little. She knew exactly what would have happened if help hadn't come; they would have died. The hobgoblins would have consumed them and left nothing but bones to lay forgotten along the riverbank.

Elize offered her a smile. "I'm just glad we could help. Too often the cruel win the day in this world."

Kenna slumped onto the bed and buried her face in her hands. She didn't want to cry again, but there was no stemming the tide. It felt like she'd cried an ocean of tears in the last few days. Elize's words were just too close to all the loss and violence she'd seen. Ian was dead now because he agreed to marry her, Mairi, her dearest friend, had died in her arms, and the family she was only just beginning to know and to love was gone. Understandably, Niall had retreated somewhere so far within himself that Kenna worried that he might never find his way through this. Niall might not blame her for it, but Kenna couldn't stop blaming herself.

Though still a stranger, Elize moved to Kenna's side quickly. She wrapped her arms around her and rocked back and forth as if they'd known one another for years. No empty words of solace were offered, no promises that all would be well; she simply held Kenna and let her weep.

The tears burst from Kenna's exhausted and strained body with such intensity that it seemed like Elize's arms were the only thing that kept her from blowing apart. She could barely draw a breath between sobs. It felt like she wept for hours, when it could have been no more than minutes before Kenna was able to take a full breath, shaky though it was. She pulled away from the other woman and wiped her face with the backs of her hands.

"Feel any better?" Elize asked gently. "I know a good cry often helps me clear my head."

"I'm not certain there are enough tears to help this, these will not be the last," Kenna sniffled. She took a deep breath and exhaled slowly in an attempt to pull herself together. Falling apart would only make her a greater burden to Niall. "I've made some terrible decisions recently. Decisions that others have paid dearly for. I'm not even sure where to begin picking up the pieces."

"Bad things happen too often in this world. You can't undo them by blaming yourself. I don't know what you and your husband have endured, but you're safe here, and you're together. Hard times are easier to untangle with someone by your side. I know I would be lost if I had to face the trials of life without Daris." Elize rose from the bed and wet a hand towel in the washbasin provided. She held the damp cloth out for Kenna. "Now let's get you something to eat. There's often music after dinner, and we've already made arrangements for your lodging tonight. It won't fix what troubles you, but it certainly won't make it worse."

"Thank you. That would be a relief," Kenna offered her a weak smile and wiped her face, focusing on the sensation of the cool moisture across her skin. It helped her to feel grounded, at least enough to face a group of strangers, and the pain her husband refused to share with her.

The other woman seemed determined to do whatever she could to brighten the evening. To Kenna's surprise, she found that Elize's doting was an effective distraction. The tension in her shoulders eased, and she was able to take a step away from the guilt long enough to finish cleaning herself up for dinner. When they stepped out of the wagon several minutes later, there were no traces of tears on Kenna's face, and the flowered scarf that Elize skillfully tied around her waist made her borrowed clothes look so well-fitted that they could have been made especially for her.

Niall was sitting on a log by the crackling bonfire in the center of the traveler's camp. He wore a billowing shirt of midnight blue with a pair of loose brown trousers that tucked into his boots. It was a far cry from his usual neat-as-a-pin appearance in finely tailored tunics and tight breeches. The colorful and relaxed attire looked utterly at odds with the serious and shuttered expression on Niall's face.

"See, just as I said, perfectly fine," Daris announced when he saw Kenna and Elize approaching.

Niall looked up quickly, and for a second the walls were down. Kenna saw the relief on his face clearly, and it eased her own sense of isolation. Of all the people in this camp, only Niall knew her nightmares. She tried to smile at him but the expression that felt foreign now. It had only been two days since they escaped the bloody attack at Britwylde, and yet, Kenna felt like years had passed.

"You look..." Niall's words drifted off. His face and eyes reddened, and turned away quickly. "You look well."

"Thank you, I'm feeling a bit better. Elize said you were waiting for me to join you before eating," Kenna replied. She tucked an escaped lock of hair behind her ear. "You could have gone ahead without me. I wouldn't have taken offense."

Niall shook his head. "No, I wanted to wait. What's a few more minutes at any rate?" His tone was quiet and careful.

"Right then," Daris said, looking at them skeptically. He clapped his hands together and then gestured to a large, black cauldron sitting near the fire. "Well, you're both here now, and our customs don't allow us to partake before guests. If everyone is done waiting, I'm starving."

Elize passed Kenna and kissed Daris lovingly on the cheek. "You're not a man of subtlety, husband."

"No, I'm a man who's hungry. I'll be subtle when my stomach isn't growling like a bear after its winter nap," he answered, tone more playful than unkind, and his eyes danced merrily in the firelight as he looked down at his wife.

Kenna glanced at her own husband. She felt the distance between them even more keenly in the glow cast by Elize and Daris. "I'm terribly sorry. I didn't realize everyone had to wait on me. I would have changed faster if I'd known."

"Don't listen to Daris, he always grumbles before he's had his dinner," another one of the men chimed in from across the fire. He chucked a twig at Daris. "It's not as if you haven't made all of us wait while you preened for Elize." A chorus of laughter followed the jibe.

"And who can blame me?" Daris grinned with a quick kiss for his wife. "Please, forgive my impatience and get yourselves something to eat."

"No, I shouldn't have dawdled, but thank you," Kenna replied before she made her way to the steaming pot of stew. The smell of it made her mouth water, and the simple luxury of having a bowl was something she never thought to appreciate as deeply as she did right now.

She and Niall both took small portions at first, only to have one of the older women take hold of the ladle and scoop more into each of their bowls. Not satisfied with that, she handed each a sizeable chunk of dark, grainy bread. Then she smiled and shooed them over to a patchwork quilt that was spread out across the grass.

"And when you finish with that, don't be shy about taking a second helping," she called after them, hands on her hips. "The two of you looked like a couple of half-drowned cats when they brought you in." She waited nearby until both Kenna and Niall started eating, then nodded, apparently satisfied, and left them to their dinner.

"She reminds me of Brona," Niall whispered to Kenna.

Kenna chuckled slightly at the memory as she stuffed a spoonful into her mouth. It was delicious, warm and seasoned with savory herbs and spices. The simple hospitality of the caravan had created a sort of shelter against the shadows that encompassed them; but that façade was easily shattered: she couldn't remember Brona without remembering her death as well.

"You laugh, but you've never been on the receiving end of her bedside manner. She makes you eat..." Niall sobered, and again his face turned a mottled red. Kenna suspected his thoughts had taken the same dark turn. "She made me eat to the point of discomfort when I was ill."

Kenna set her spoon down and placed her hand on Niall's wrist. "I'm glad she took such good care of you. It's important to remember those things now."

"I hope she didn't suffer—but it looked like..." Niall shook his head, and Kenna saw unshed tears glistening in his eyes.

"There was nothing you could have done to change what happened. None of them would want you to torture yourself," she said, trying to sound soothing. She left out the fact that she was torturing herself enough for both of them. Her next statement was as much to herself as it was Niall. "All we can do is survive and honor their memories by trying to find purpose as we move forward." Kenna heard herself saying the all-too-common words of comfort given when someone was mourning in Arthan, but they sounded baseless and empty now.

Niall's frown deepened. He looked like he might argue but said nothing. Kenna inhaled slowly and tried to convince herself that there would come a time they could feel something beyond the sadness. With no other words of comfort to give, she returned to her meal.

They continued in silence. What more was there for either of them to say? They were refugees and wholly dependent on the generosity of others. The plan to go to Kenna's family was in dire straits. They had no horses, no food or water, and no money with which to purchase anything to make the long trek to Arthan possible. Kenna wasn't even sure where they were now. They'd spent so many hours on the river, traveling further and further away from the Arthan border.

The sound of footsteps shook Kenna from her endless cycle of worry. She looked up to find Daris and Elize with their own meals in hand. Daris plopped down on the blanket a few feet from Niall, while Elize settled more gracefully at his side.

"Apologies for my behavior earlier. Niall says he was a scribe at the High Lord's estate. Were you in the service of the lady of the house?" Daris took a sizeable bite of his stew and looked at Kenna curiously.

Kenna glanced at Niall. His eyes met hers and held a message of caution. She turned back to Daris. "Yes, I was, but I'm afraid my time at the estate was brief."

"The whole countryside is buzzing with news of what happened. It's a sad turn of events. The townsfolk in this region always spoke of the High Lord with great regard," Daris replied. "How did the two of you manage to get out of there?"

"We weren't in the house at the time," Niall answered quickly. "We were in the stables. When we heard the attack, we made for the river and took one of the boats."

"Which explains why you were dallying on the riverbanks when the hobgoblins found you," Elize finished. She was watching Niall contemplatively. Kenna got the distinct impression that for all her warmth and kindness, Elize was a person of shrewd observations.

"We're lucky that you happened by when you did." Kenna said, hoping to shift the focus from Niall and herself. "What were you doing in the woods?"

Daris shrugged. "We were looking for more to add to the evening meal. Heard the scuffle and thought we'd better see what was going on. I wouldn't leave a mangy dog at the mercy of hobgoblins."

"They were certainly less agreeable than you have been," Niall responded. "Thank you for your help."

"Yes, I've seen quite enough ot the hospitality of the hobgoblins," Kenna added with a shudder.

Quiet settled over the group as each turned their attention to dinner. After a little while, Daris and Elize began chatting about their day, leaving Niall and Kenna to eat in peace. Kenna focused on the food and tried not to think of the circumstances that led them to the traveler's camp; when she looked at her husband's face, it all came flooding back. The lines of grief were there despite his efforts to conceal them.

Another wave of guilt washed over Kenna. *How can I eat when Mairi—when so many of the people I've come to care for are gone?*

It didn't feel right that she should be alive and comfortable. In her homeland they called this the death of the survivor. Kenna had seen others experience it after a trauma, but she'd never understood how surviving something could cause such guilt that they felt unworthy of that survival.

"But today's work is all done and over with," Elize said with careful cheer. She spread her skirts out daintily. "And now we have a chance to get to know one another."

"And when my wife wants to know someone, she finds a way to become fast friends," Daris quickly added.

The idea of a friend almost brought tears to Kenna's eyes again. It was a vicious cycle of relief and then pain. Mairi had been her most trusted confidant. Now she was gone, and Kenna desperately longed for someone whom she could speak to, without navigating the now murky waters she seemed to sail with Niall.

"Where do the two of you plan to go now? Not much call for scribes and lady's maids outside of noble houses," Daris finished his meal and leaned back on his elbows. The man was so far from formal and studied that Niall looked comically rigid sitting next to him.

"I have family in Arthan. Niall and I thought to go to them," Kenna explained. She was careful to leave out details but stayed as close to the truth as possible. She wasn't entirely sure why Niall didn't think it safe to trust their rescuers with their true identities, butshe hadn't been in Venallis long enough to know the spirit of its people and thought it might be prudent to follow Niall's example in this case.

"The border to Arthan is several days' journey from here on horseback, and on foot it would take longer. Our meeting is testament enough to the danger of such a venture without the proper preparation," Elize commented. "How do you plan on making it safely?"

"I don't know," Niall answered. The hopelessness in his tone made the cracks in Kenna's heart deepen.

"The hobgoblins took everything we had. I suppose we'll have to find some way to earn enough coin to arrange passage with someone headed that way,"

Kenna elaborated. It was the only sensible course of action that came to mind. How they would enact such a plan was another matter, and one she was far too tired to contemplate now.

The sound of a fiddle rose up amid the buzz of quiet conversations. Mere seconds later drums and flutes joined in. Daris pulled a pipe from inside his vest and set the instrument to his lips. Several of the people put aside their empty plates and bowls to begin dancing. They leapt, clapped, and hooked arms to spin round in circles with delight. It was a lively spectacle, one untouched by the news of an attack on a noble house. Britwylde's destruction was nothing but a distant reality to the people that surrounded Kenna.

Niall stood up abruptly. "I believe I'll retire for the evening. You said arrangements were made for us?"

"Oh, yes," Elize looked away from the dancing couples and addressed him. "One of the wagons we've been using for storage has a bed in it. We cleared it off for your use tonight. It's there at the edge of camp, the yellow one with a blue door."

"Thank you," Niall nodded. He muttered a quick goodnight and hastily headed in the direction Elize indicated.

Kenna watched him go, wondering whether he'd appreciate her company or would prefer solitude. Until now he'd been insistent on staying together, but he made no indication that he wished her to join him. It felt like all of the closeness they'd gained since their wedding had vanished. She wrapped her arms around herself, helpless to act. *How do I comfort someone who's lost so much? How do I give what I so badly need?* She wanted to go home, but she didn't want to abandon Niall to a desolate existence.

After a few minutes passed without speaking, Elize moved to sit next to Kenna. "I get the impression the

High Lord's estate was more than a place of employment for the two of you."

"We had family and friends there: loved ones who were not able to escape as we were," Kenna admitted quietly. She didn't want to pretend to be anyone but herself. The pain and loss she felt was too heavy a burden to carry alone; but for all the kindness that these people had shown, she didn't know them. She was adrift in the company of strangers. Even her husband was among their numbers.

"I'm terribly sorry to hear that," Elize replied with genuine sympathy in her voice. She waited for a moment, then reached out to wrap her arm around Kenna. "Such losses never leave our hearts. They stay within us and change the paths of our lives. In time, you'll see your new course with greater clarity. Until then, you are both welcome to stay among our caravan."

"Can you speak for all your people?" Kenna asked. She drew a deep and shaking breath. "We have no money—no way to repay the kindness that's been shown. We'd be nothing but a drain on your band."

"Don't let it worry you for another minute," Elize waved a hand dismissively. "I'm sure the two of you can find some way to contribute. But that's a discussion for the morrow. You've been through enough over the past few days. Go to your rest."

At the mention of rest Kenna's entire body seemed to give in to the stress of it all. She'd been holding everything together—crying certainly, feeling the pain of loss and regret, but forcing herself to push through regardless. Knowing that their survival depended on her strength had provided the energy to keep putting one foot in front of the other. Now, there seemed to be nothing but bone-weary exhaustion.

The music died down and Daris put his pipe away. He held both hands out to Elize and Kenna, then pulled them to their feet. "New friends, a hot meal, music, and a comfortable bed for the night. I'd say that's a good way to greet the road ahead."

"It's better than wandering in a stained nightgown and conversing with hobgoblins, at any rate," Kenna answered, trying to put more hope and cheer in her response than she felt. She glanced toward the yellow wagon that would serve as a home for the night. When she looked back, Elize was nuzzling Daris' neck tenderly. Kenna averted her eyes, wondering if she would one day experience that sort of affection for herself. She cleared her throat. Though she didn't want to interrupt, it seemed rude to walk off without another word.

Elize pulled away from her husband with a kiss. "There should be plenty of blankets for the two of you, and one of my younger sisters put a fresh nightdress inside."

"Thank you," Kenna said again. The words had fallen from her lips many times in the past few hours that they were beginning to sound hollow, though she was truly grateful for everything offered. "Goodnight. I hope sleep brings you many happy dreams."

"And you," Daris replied, but his eyes were on Elize. There was need written in the warmth of the looks they exchanged with one another, and Kenna took it as a sign that it was time for her to leave.

She turned away and made the trek across the meadow, feeling colder simply by being out of the presence of what burned between Elize and Daris. Before the attack on Niall's home, Kenna thought there might have been a chance for that in her own marriage. Now it seemed a distant and impossible dream.

She climbed the two narrow steps to the door of the wagon and paused. Not a sound came from inside. She wondered if she ought to knock—if Niall was already asleep she didn't want to wake him. On the other hand, they were married, at least in name, and knocking on the door might lead to questions in the morning. There was nothing for it but to go inside and hope she didn't catch Niall at an inopportune time.

The door opened to a space dimly lit by a single candle. Niall was sitting on the edge of the bed with his head in his hands. He didn't look up when she entered. He didn't speak or even move to indicate he was aware of her presence.

Kenna closed the door but hesitated to move closer. "I'm sorry if you were waiting... or if you'd rather be alone..."

Niall looked up at her slowly, and even in the low, flickering light she could see the tears that trailed down his cheeks. "They're gone. Everything I grew up with— everyone I held dear... is gone." He took a shuddering breath and then his shoulders began shake with a fresh batch of sobs.

Kenna crossed to him in an instant. The hesitation and isolation she'd felt seconds earlier was completely replaced by the need to do whatever she could to soothe the pain Niall was finally expressing. She threw her arms around him protectively as she sat down at his side. "I know, Niall. I know."

He buried his head against her shoulder and clung to her like a man being battered by the currents of a raging river. The sound of his wailing sobs was muffled in the folds of Kenna's blouse. "I can't—I can't survive this. I don't know how to feel this and not be completely destroyed by it."

Kenna rubbed the center of his back just as her father did when he comforted her. She didn't know what to say to Niall. Words were meaningless in the face of such devastating grief. So remained silent and simply offered herself as a grounding point. She held him, stroking his hair and gently rocking as he wept inconsolably. He didn't need to speak; these tears told the details of his anguish accurately enough.

It was nearly an hour before the crying eased and Niall pulled away, still hiccupping for air. He wiped the back of his sleeve across his face and sat quietly staring at the floor. Kenna held one of his hands and continued to stroke his back with her free hand. Her own cheeks were tearstained, and the front of her blouse was more than a little damp from the outpouring of Niall's pain.

"I don't know who I am anymore," Niall whispered. His voice was so small and hopeless that it pierced deep into Kenna's soul and the sound of it lodged there like a barb. "I'm alone."

"You are not alone, Niall," Kenna pulled his hand to her lips and kissed it gently. "I'm with you. You need not face this loss on your own."

His eyes squeezed shut and he nodded. Then pulled his hand from hers and bent to remove his boots. Kenna waited for him to speak again, but no further words followed. She sighed sadly and began loosening the sash around her waist. Niall turned his back so she could change into her nightdress.

When both were ready, he blew out the candle and crawled under the covers next to Kenna. Though they'd slept in each other's arms the past two nights, they'd never shared a bed until now. Kenna longed to scoot closer to him and find comfort in that contact, but she didn't know how he would respond. Instead, she slipped her hand into his and felt his fingers curl around it.

There were no wishes for sweet dreams or pleasant slumber. As Kenna's eyes adjusted to the dark, she could see Niall staring up at the ceiling with tears silently trickling down the sides of his face. The only certainty that lay ahead of them was that this was just the first of many tearstained nights.

.

CHAPTER 10

Lights of Absence

Loud, urgent banging jolted Niall from his sleep. He squeezed his eyes more tightly shut, hoping the sound would stop but it did not. His head throbbed from a night of tears. His body ached from days of tension and sleeping on the ground. In short, he felt awful physically and even worse emotionally.

The knocking continued, growing more forceful. "Niall, Kenna! It's time to wake." Daris' voice was just outside the door.

Niall took a deep breath and opened his eyes to find it was still dark inside the wagon. He tossed aside the blankets and crossed the small space to unlatch the door. "The sun isn't risen yet. Surely we can sleep for a few hours more."

"Sorry, but we're tearing down camp and need this wagon for storage space." Daris was wide awake, without a trace of sleep in his eyes. "Can't waste good travel hours lazing about in bed."

"Very well, we'll be out in a few minutes," Niall sighed. He reached for the shirt hanging from a hook on the wall and pulled it over his head.

"What's going on?" Kenna asked. She sat up rubbing her eyes, hair disheveled.

"They move out early. Our days of leisure are at an end," Niall replied wearily. Their days of leisure ended when his entire family and household were destroyed. He shoved his feet into his boots and turned back to her. "I'll wait outside while you dress."

As soon as they were up and out of the way, their hosts were loading things back into the wagon. Their speed and efficiency were a marvel to behold. In less than thirty minutes the entire camp from the night before was packed up and stowed away, with horses already harnessed and waiting to begin their work. Breakfast was served in the form of flat round cakes, sweetened with honey and warmed by the fire. The simple meal was carried as they began their trek down the road. By the time the sun was fully risen, the caravan was miles away from the campsite.

Still tired, Niall and Kenna were invited to sit atop one of the wagons. They spent their day perched on the roof, with a blanket to sit on. Most of the adults walked alongside the colorful train of carts. Some played lutes and pipes as they made their merry way down the road, others did flips and sang songs. Even the harnesses on the horses were adorned with bells. The air was filled with sounds of cheer from every direction.

As a child, Niall had often watched the progress of the travelers when they passed his father's estate. At the time, life seemed something that only happened outside the windows of his sickroom. He used to dream of what it would have been like to live such a nomadic existence, filled with color and music. The idea seemed like an endless adventure. It never occurred to him that he would find himself in their company without a home to call his own.

Near noon, the caravan stopped alongside a large, glittering pond. The horses were loosed from the wagons for a time to graze and drink while the people pulled trunks from one of the carts and began passing out festive garments of yellow, red, green, blue, and an array of other colors. Their already flamboyant but less embellished clothes were swapped out for the eye-catching garb. Vests with intricate patterns of leaves, bees, birds, stars, and moons were thrown over these new outfits.

Niall and Kenna sat in the shade cast by the wagon they'd slept in the night before. They watched the commotion in quiet contemplation. Niall couldn't help but feel detached from what was happening around him. The reality of the loss of his family was sinking in, and it presented more questions than answers. He felt isolated and not at all a part of the world outside of his own of misery. It was difficult to be among others when all he wanted to do was curl up somewhere on his own and weep himself into oblivion.

Only Kenna's company brought any peace. She had been there and seen everything that happened. In their brief time as husband and wife they'd shared a lifetime of adversity. Even so, Niall was hesitant to rely on her soothing presence. Since their union was born of necessity it was sure to end now that it held no benefits for her Vashirat, and he didn't know how he would be able to walk away once she was safely encompassed in the love of her family.

"One, two, three!" Elize shouted a few yards away. She was balanced on Daris' shoulders, the spring breeze tossing her hair about her face. On three, she jumped and twisted in the air, then landed lightly in her husband's waiting arms. The action made Niall's stomach flip, but Elize didn't show an ounce of fear. Kenna clapped politely and the pair turned to bow at her with a grandiose flourish. The stunt was an impressive feat. Even in his dejected state, Niall had to admit their acrobatic tricks and tumbles were entertaining.

"Do the two of you care to give it a try?" Daris called out. "Kenna, you're a tiny thing. I bet Niall could lift you with one hand."

"I believe we'll leave it to the professionals. Niall might be able to lift me, but I doubt I have the balance your wife does," Kenna replied. She glanced at Niall, who tried to smile, but only managed a pinched lifting of the corner of his mouth.

Elize and Daris locked hands and came to join them in the shade. Niall offered them the waterskin he'd been holding. "You're both quite skilled."

"Half the children born to the troupe learn to do tumbles before they walk," Daris said conversationally. He accepted the water and drank greedily. "Elize and I have been paired since we were old enough to follow instruction."

"Trust between acrobatic partners is vital," Elize explained. "Though, that's true of many of our partnered acts."

"I suppose working closely from a young age helps to establish that trust. No wonder the two of you are so happy together," Kenna commented. Her tone was kind, but Niall knew her well enough to sense the sadness beneath her friendly response.

"It's true, though not all children paired together remain so. Our people allow their children to find their gifts in their own times. Sometimes one child shows a greater aptitude for puppets, others are more inclined to the playing of music or acting out skits. We all have our own set of gifts to bring to the group," Daris cleared his throat and passed the waterskin to his wife. "Which brings me to another matter."

Niall's shoulders tensed. By the change of Daris' tone, it was clear that the attitude of the conversation had shifted from idle to business. "Have we overstayed our welcome?"

"What? No, of course not!" Daris looked at Niall as though he'd said something utterly ridiculous. He leaned back with his palms splayed out on the ground behind him. "Kenna explained your situation last night. Arthan is quite a long way from here."

"We spoke to the elders this morning and they've agreed to allow you to remain with us until you can raise enough coin to travel there safely," Elize explained. She reached out to give Kenna's hand a tender squeeze. "We are not beggars and it is not our custom to force others to become them."

"That being said. You will be expected to earn your keep," Daris added. "Sing for your supper, so to speak. Have the two of you any skills or talents that could be used to entertain an audience?"

The question caught Niall by surprise. Of all the things he'd expected Daris and Elize to suggest, joining the travelers and working as entertainers was numbered among the last. It wasn't the craziest thing he'd ever heard, but he had no sensible notion of what he could possibly contribute as a performer.

"Anything at all? Juggling, um, singing, or playing an instrument?" Elize asked when neither Niall nor Kenna offered their own suggestions.

"I can play the sitar, but I don't think you have one handy," Kenna mused. She looked at Niall thoughtfully for a moment. "Niall can throw knives."

"Oh, I don't think that would be of any use," Niall said quickly.

"No, that works! We used to have a man who tossed knives at one of the lads, but he's getting older and opted to stay in the winter settlement instead of going on the road," Daris said casually. As if the notion of throwing a knife in the direction of a child was perfectly normal.

"You're suggesting I throw knives at children?" Niall gaped. He shook his head, grasping for anything that might turn the focus away from himself. "Kenna is quite remarkable with a bow. Have her shoot apples through rings, or at moving targets."

"Hm, there might be something there." Elize was considering them with dark, clever eyes. She glanced at her husband. "Perhaps a husband and wife, knife tossing and shooting act? I don't think any of the other troupes have that particular combination, and there's room for some comedy in it as well."

"You want me to throw knives at my wife now?" Niall jumped to his feet and began pacing. Kenna was the only person he had left, and he couldn't abide the idea of any harm coming to her. "No, it's too dangerous."

"And Kenna would shoot arrows at you," Daris snapped his fingers and grinned broadly at his wife. "I've married a brilliant woman!"

"I do have my bow. If I can hit a squirrel jumping from one branch to the next, I can miss Niall." Kenna replied slowly, she was looking at Niall speculatively.

Niall stopped his pacing to stare open-mouthed, at the woman he'd married barely a month ago. "I said shoot apples through rings, not shoot at me. I can't believe you're actually considering this."

"Don't dismiss it so quickly, Niall. I've been shooting since I was a small girl, my aim is better than any of my siblings," Kenna was nodding, and Niall could almost see the wheels in her head turning. "We have to make our way to Arthan somehow. I wouldn't think of putting you in danger, and I trust that you wouldn't allow any harm to befall me,"

"Not intentionally, no, but accidents happen. Especially when you're dealing with deadly weapons," Niall argued, still flabbergasted by the direction of this conversation. He couldn't stomach the thought of taking aim at Kenna.

Kenna met his eyes. "I think we should do it."

"You've lost your mind," Niall replied quietly, though he knew he'd already been out-voted by his companions.

Daris laughed. "You worry too much, Niall. There's a village nearby where we always stop to perform. You and Kenna can watch and we'll discuss the idea with the elders after the show."

"And no one is going to ask the two of you to perform an act of that nature without plenty of practice," Elize assured him.

Kenna pushed herself off the ground and took Niall's hand. She met his eyes and spoke with a calm, soothing tone. "Just consider it. If it doesn't look like something we can do safely, we'll find another way to get to Arthan."

* * *

The elders were more measured in their enthusiasm for this new plan than Daris and Elize had been. They insisted on a demonstration of both Kenna and Niall's skills before making a decision one way or the other. So it was that Niall and Kenna stood before the leaders of the traveling band just before sunset, while the rest of the company set up camp for the night. The elders of the troupe consisted of three men, and three women, all in or near their forties or fifties.

Anyone older than that had remained in their winter settlement.

Kenna was given a series of challenging shots to attempt with her bow, all of which she made with unparalleled skill. She hit stationary and moving targets with ease, shot arrows through little rings. Only once did she hesitate at any of the challenges presented to her. After several precise hits, Elize boldly grabbed an apple and balanced it on the palm of her hand. After much reassurance from Elize and Daris, Kenna took the shot. Even Niall cheered when the apple flew off Elize's hand to be pinned to the side of the wagon behind her.

But Niall's applause faded quickly when a set of throwing knives were presented to him. He hefted one, testing the weight and balance of the blade as a target was brought out for him. He put it down and lifted another. They were all the same well-balanced design, with razor-sharp edges. The quality of his tools did nothing to evoke enthusiasm for the task.

"You can do this," Kenna said encouragingly.

His hesitation wasn't a matter of doubt in his abilities. It was quite the contrary; Niall knew he could do it. He knew he'd be able to hit whatever they put in front of him, and that would mean more support for this idea. Hitting a painted target was one thing, throwing a blade at the only person left to him was another prospect entirely. *Kenna is my wife. True, the marriage is little more than a contract at this point, but I promised to protect her. That promise did not include hurling lethal weapons at her.*

A cough from one of the caravan's leaders told Niall that their patience was wearing thin. For a moment, he considered missing intentionally, but one look at Kenna's hopeful expression put that thought straight out of his mind. *She wants this, even if it means we have to engage in this wild and reckless gambit. It's her chance to go home.*

Niall looked at the target, lifted the knife and flung it with as much speed as he could. The blade practically whistled as it flew through the air. It hit the center of the target with a loud thump. The tip of the knife dug deep into the wood, leaving the rest of the blade and the handle shaking with the intensity of the impact.

"Well done," Remmy, the leader of the caravan commented. He was nodding his head with approval. "But can you do that consistently?"

Pleased by the first throw, Niall forgot his earlier reservations and tossed a second knife. This one landed an inch to the left. Niall hefted the third dagger and threw. It found its mark an inch to the right of the first. The three daggers presented a straight and balanced line across the board. This was one of the few things in which Niall had always been able to outshine Ian.

Daris let out an excited yell. "Perfect! And you didn't think it would be a good idea." He clapped Niall on the shoulder. "Between this and Kenna's shooting, you'll pull a crowd at every stop."

Remmy held out a hand to still the younger man's enthusiasm. "A stationary wooden target is one thing. With practice most can hit the center. You'll need to do more than chuck a blade at a painted board if you want to earn your way to Arthan."

Niall's smile faded. He knew what was coming next, and he hated it. Stifling the desire to protest, he approached the target and yanked the knives free. If he wanted to help Kenna get home, he was going to have to accept that the road would not be a simple or straightforward one.

"Do you have the boldness to test your aim when the stakes are higher?" Remmy looked Niall in the eye.

"I'll do what I must," Niall answered through gritted teeth.

"Good. Then Daris and Elize can show the two of you how to add the proper flair to your new act," Remmy replied. He turned to the other elders. "Are the rest of you in agreement?"

"They'll need costumes, and no one is going to believe that boy is one of us," Dana, Remmy's wife, gestured to Niall. "Some already spread rumors that we make off with children when we leave the villages. One look at that mop of curls and they'll claim it gives weight to such nonsense."

"We could shave it off?" Elize suggested.

"No!" Kenna spoke up before Niall could. She glanced at him and blushed. "There are less-extreme options: perhaps a scarf tied around his head. There's no need to cut his hair."

Elize chuckled a little. "I don't blame you. It is rather pretty."

"I will wear a scarf on my head," Niall interjected. Kenna's quick rise to the defense of his hair didn't go unnoticed, though he refrained from commenting on it. The day had been a long one, and it was only the first of what would surely be many more. With the matter of their income settled, he only wanted to escape to a place of privacy. He needed time to be alone with his grief. "Now, if there's nothing else, I should help unload our wagon for the night."

Remmy nodded and the elder members of the troupe left to attend other business as they brought the work of the day to a close. Niall remained behind with Kenna, Daris and Elize. Everything felt like a balancing act for him. He wanted to hide away, but he didn't want to offend the circle of support that was forming around him. He wasn't so lost in his mourning that he didn't recognize the simple acts of caring that were being shown.

"You did well, Niall." Kenna took his hand. "I know you have reservations about this, but I'm even more confident now than I was before. It will work. I'm sure of it."

"Thank you. You were amazing with your bow," Niall managed. Now that the test was past, he felt the grey cloak of despair settling over him again. Making a plan and taking definitive steps to enact it made their situation shift from surreal to the realm of reality in a solid and irrefutable way.

Daris finally picked up on the shift in Niall's mood. He looked around uncomfortably. "But it doesn't make your situation any easier, does it?"

"Kenna told us you lost family in the attack on the High Lord's estate," Elize added. "We truly are sorry for what the two of you have suffered. I can't imagine what such a loss must feel like."

Niall swallowed and blinked back tears. Having others, even people so newly met, acknowledge the passing of his family was comforting. "I can't even give them a proper burial. I feel like I have no way to say goodbye or to honor who they were." The words spilled out as if of their own accord. Ordinarily, he would have kept such thoughts to himself, but there was little point in hiding that from his companions.

"They all deserve better than that. I hate the feeling that the world will simply go on without them," Kenna whispered with a sniffle. Niall pulled her close. He couldn't do anything for his parents, or the people he grew up with, but he could be there for her, and doing so helped him focus through his anguish.

"What if there was something you could do? A way to honor their passing from this life to the next? Would it help make the journey forward more bearable for the two of you?" Daris asked slowly. It was a far cry from the generally confident and blunt demeanor he'd demonstrated thus far.

Niall released Kenna and looked at the other man with a puzzled frown. "What could possibly be done? I don't even know what—" He stopped, unable to finish the statement. He couldn't allow himself to imagine what might have happened to their remains. He didn't want to think of them left unburied for scavengers to desecrate. "They can't be given a proper burial."

"Well, not a burial, no, but our people have a custom that might help provide some peace," Daris explained. He looked at Elize. "I'm sure we could come up with something close at any rate."

"What do you mean?" Niall asked. His interest was piqued now. It wouldn't bring his loved ones back, but at least he wouldn't feel like he'd completely abandoned them.

"Anything would be better than leaving without some sort of farewell," Kenna added quietly, eyes clouding. Niall could imagine where her thoughts dwelled. He too had trouble banishing the visions of that night.

"As you know, our existence is a mobile one," Daris began. "But death comes at all times, and in all places. We lose people along our performance routes, and those we leave behind sometimes pass while we make our way from town to town."

"The Lights of Absence," Elize said, clarifying her husband's roundabout conversation. "I thought that might be where you were going, but Daris, that's only ever performed in our winter village."

"Yes, but that's just to give closure to those who couldn't be present at the burial of a loved one," Daris stated. "There's no rule that it must be performed there. No one back in the village knows Niall and

Kenna or those they lost. We could perform it on the road for them."

Niall and Kenna exchanged looks. It would be something, but Niall had no idea what it involved. After agreeing to participate in an act that included throwing knives at the woman he'd pledged to honor and protect, he was hesitant to agree with so few details.

"Nothing outrageous. It's really quite beautiful," Elize replied, and outlined the details of the custom. "Allow us a day or two to gather supplies and make the preparations. Then we'll give your dear ones the farewell they deserve." Elize turned her focus to the gathering of people in the center of the camp. "But for now, let us look to filling our bellies and then go to our rest. Tomorrow we have even further to travel than we did today."

The conversation ended there and the four of them joined the rest of the band for the evening repast. Niall and Kenna's second night among the traveling folk was spent much as the first. Now that they were out of immediate danger, mourning took the place of fear. They lay in bed, hands clasped once again, and wept together until sleep dried their tears.

It took Daris and Elize only a day to gather everything needed and convince the others to perform the ceremony for Niall and Kenna. The compassion and understanding shown by the traveling folk were astounding. Niall found himself confronted with a new understanding of the people who now surrounded him. Where the nobles tolerated this vibrant and talented group, they never viewed them as anything more than a passing amusement; an oddity to be indulged for a moment of entertainment, but not accepted within so-called polite society. They were indulged at the faires and villages, but not allowed within the walls off the royal city itself.

At the time, Niall had accepted this attitude as the way of things. Now he felt ashamed by what was nothing more than snobbery and disinterest in anything outside the small circle of the elite. The true nature of these people was something deeper, warmer, and more sincere than anything Niall had known before, with the exception of the bond he shared with his family. This was only his third evening among the nomadic band of entertainers, and yet they somberly gathered to pay respects to the memory of people they'd never even met.

The caravan was camped in a pasture with a babbling stream running through it. The evening was as pretty and peaceful as anyone could have asked for. It held a sort of anticipatory stillness. The High Lord and his family had guarded over these lands with skill, and nature itself seemed to hold the proceedings in solemn deference. Niall waited at the water's edge with Kenna. In their hands they each held a small, square lantern of thin twigs and paper, light enough to be caught and carried by the breeze. The community of entertainers stood behind them. Some held instruments, some held small bouquets of flowers, and others simply waited in respectful silence.

The shadows deepened to a violet haze, tinged with gold. A violin began playing. Remmy came forward with a burning candle in his hands. "We gather this evening to bid farewell to those who have passed to their next journey while we continue to travel ours."

Per his instructions, and explanations given by Daris and Elize, both Niall and Kenna remained silent with their heads bowed. Tears welled up in Niall's eyes and began running down his cheeks. This was all he could offer his father, his mother, and so many more who had been a constant presence throughout his childhood.

"We have accepted Niall and Kenna into our midst. They join us in our travels, and must bid farewell to those they could not embrace in departure. Their pain is ours." He gestured for Niall and Kenna to bring their lanterns to him so he could light each one in turn. When both were lit and glowing with tiny flickering flames, he gave Niall and Kenna a nod to indicate that it was time for them to say their goodbyes.

"With the lighting and releasing of this lantern, I send my memories and love with my dear friend, Mairi, and with so many more that I knew for so brief a time," Kenna's voice wobbled, and Niall wondered if she could go on, but after a steadying breath she continued, reciting the words that Daris and Elize had given them before the ceremony. When she finished speaking, she released her lantern. It slowly floated upward. "May the warmth of its glow serve to remind all present of the light the lost cast upon those around them." She bowed her head, and Niall heard her weeping softly.

He swallowed and sniffled as he balanced his own lantern. The hot air from the tiny fire within was already beginning to lift the weight of the paper and wood. It was his turn to speak, but while his own name might not have been enough to suggest his true identity to their new companions, naming his parents certainly would.

This humble band of men and women were good, honest people. When he'd hidden the truth of his birthright it had been due to distrust, borne of trauma and his own sheltered upbringing. Now, he feared that such knowledge could put them in danger. If the soldiers of the Stratham Vashirat were still in Venallis and knew he and Kenna had escaped—if they were looking for them now, the knowledge could put Daris, Elize, and all the others in a terrible position. They might be faced with protecting Niall and Kenna, or with handing them over to bloodthirsty killers in order to preserve their own lives. Even in so short a time together, Niall suspected the caravan would protect them at their own peril.

"With the lighting and releasing of this lantern I send my memories and love with my father and my mother. I send my memories and love with them, and with the members of the High Lord Edan's household, taken too soon from this world." Niall managed to get through the first part, but when he paused to take a breath, it was stolen by a soft sob. This was it, as close to funeral rites as his parents and loved ones would get, and he could not even speak their names. He closed his eyes and bowed his head, trying to find the strength to continue.

Kenna's small, soft fingers settled on Niall's wrist. She stepped closer to him and hooked an arm around his. "Deep breaths, Niall. This goodbye need not happen quickly. They were your family, but you are not alone."

He swallowed and dug deep within himself to continue. "May the warmth of this lantern's glow serve to remind all present of the lights that were extinguished, and the warmth of those no longer with us." Niall recited the words with Kenna's gentle reassurance still ringing in his ears. She was here, and they were surrounded by others who were offering safe harbor and compassion; he wasn't alone. Niall took a deep breath and released his lantern.

The glowing emblems of the people who were taken from him drifted toward the heavens. At first he was able to trace the outline of the paper shades, but as the evening turned to night and the lanterns drifted higher, the flickering lights blended into the stars above. Niall slipped his arm around Kenna's waist and watched the twinkling lanterns float further and further away.

The second part of the Lights of Absence ceremony was similar to Niall's own customs. The evening meal was served, at which time recollections of the departed were shared. At first it was challenging for Niall to navigate the many memories and anecdotes of his childhood. Even beyond his concerns for safety, he was a private person by nature, and his time at court had made him more guarded. Openly discussing times that felt so precious and personal was something that, until now, had been reserved for a select few. His mother was one of them and Ian, and without even realizing when it happened, Kenna had fallen into his circle of trusted confidants. But the traveling folk that surrounded him now were so open and accepting that Niall found himself telling stories he'd only shared with those who'd been present at the actual events. The release was transformative, and uplifting.

Later that evening, after everyone had gone to their own beds for the night, Niall sat out on the steps of the wagon he shared with Kenna. He looked up at the stars, and imagined that some of them were still the lanterns, now hanging among the other glimmering heavenly gems. For a moment he entertained the idea that each star was the memory of one who'd passed before. The thought brought him solace.

The door to the wagon opened and closed. Kenna settled down beside him. She was in her nightdress, with a shawl wrapped tightly around her shoulders. She slipped her arm through the crook of Niall's elbow, and her gaze followed his. Niall laced his fingers through hers. *This feels good, almost normal.*

"You have been remarkably strong through all of this," Niall said quietly. "I doubt I would have fared this well if you weren't at my side. I would have given up before I even made it out of my family's estate."

"We've taken turns being the strong one," she replied in a meditative tone. To Niall's surprise, she laid her head on his shoulder. "I couldn't sleep without you there. Strange, when we've been sleeping next to one another for less than a week."

"It's been a long week," he commented gently. Niall released her fingers and pulled his arm from hers. He wrapped both arms around her and held her close. Then he leaned his cheek on the top of her head. "It feels more like a decade has passed."

"Does that mean we've missed our anniversary?" Kenna asked dryly.

"Only the first ten," he chuckled for the first time since the attack. Without thinking, Niall turned his head slightly and tenderly kissed the crown of her head. He stood up and offered Kenna both his hands to pull her to her feet. They stepped inside their humble sanctuary together.

There was still pain, and Niall didn't think there would ever be a day when the massacre was far from his mind, but being away from the routine of court and life as a High Lord's son made it a little easier to breathe. He felt distance between himself and the tragedy of the estate, and a sense of quiet settled over his heart.

CHAPTER 11

Life Without Roots

Days turned into weeks as Kenna and Niall grew accustomed to the patterns of the traveling community. They rose before the sun and moved through the countryside from one village to the next. During the day, simple fare that could be eaten on the move was passed through the caravan as they progressed from one village to the next. In the evenings, some stayed behind to set up camp, while others were sent out to see what game could be found in the area.

At first, Kenna and Niall shared the evening meal with whoever had a few extra helpings to spare, but once they were settled, they were expected to provide for themselves. Kenna often joined the hunting party, while Niall remained behind to help with the heavy lifting. Even now, he retained his dislike of hunting and had not joined Kenna in the activity since their escape along the river. Kenna understood, and it gave her a chance to practice her archery without putting Niall at risk.

When she returned, the two of them would rehearse their act while the light was still good. Then they would go back to the wagon that was beginning to feel something like a home and prepare a meal with whatever Kenna was able to bag, and a few pieces of bread passed around camp. Some evenings Daris and Elize would walk over with their own meal and the four of them would share what humble fare they had.

For Kenna, acceptance into the ranks of the traveling folk helped soothe the absence of Mairi. It eased the loneliness of being far from the loving presence of brothers and sisters. She felt at home among the entertainers. They took a level of joy in each other's company that reminded her of precious times her own family shared. Simply put, she liked the people of the troupe.

She liked Niall too, more than she could have imagined when they first met. Where Ian had been open and eager to embrace the people in his life, Niall often reminded her of a wary horse. Earning his trust took time and patience, but once obtained, he was loyal to a fault. The quiet evening hours spent alone with Niall brought their walks along the river at Britwylde to mind. It was safe and familiar, despite their new accommodations, and Kenna found that she looked forward to the close of the day and the conversations she shared with her husband.

It was the beginning of a routine that made sifting through the tattered remnants of their lives bearable. Even Niall seemed to be climbing out of the hole of despair from his terrible—at least, when they weren't practicing their knife and archery act. He was still resistant to the concept and voiced his discontent often.

Such was the case after three weeks of travel. The caravan had stopped early that evening. After an hour of perfecting various trick shots, Kenna put her bow away and waited for Niall to fetch the throwing knives and practice his portion of their performance. He had a habit of conveniently forgetting them back at the wagon, something that had caused numerous delays.

Anxiety rippled down Kenna's spine even before Niall took position across from her. She leaned against the vividly painted wood prepared for their act, and carefully placed her hands between two of the little targets that ran up and down each side of the board. Though she trusted Niall, it was impossible not to feel fear when someone was throwing a razor-sharp blade at a space a hair's breadth from your body. It didn't matter that he tended to throw the knives wide, much to the frustration of those helping them prepare.

Niall balanced one of the daggers in his hand and rolled his shoulder. Kenna could see him tensing as he raised his arm to take aim. She'd come to know the subtle clues in the set of his lips, or the tiny crease that would form between his eyebrows. He released the blade, sending it through the air with astonishing speed. It landed toward the edge of the board, as far from Kenna as possible without missing the painted target entirely. Kenna let out a breath even as Daris groaned with disapproval.

"Niall, your aim is better than that. This act will never earn the two of you coin if the audience doesn't believe the danger is real," he grumbled. "It's not just about hitting a target, it's about showmanship."

"The danger is real! I don't have to draw blood to demonstrate that." Niall shot back defensively.

Daris threw his arms in the air and made a small sound of disgust. This was not the first time he'd given these instructions. "I'm not telling you to draw blood, I'm telling you to draw a crowd!"

"Daris is right. There's no point to doing any of this if we don't push ourselves." Kenna added gently. Niall was willing enough when they worked on the archery portion of the act, but his mood invariably soured when it came time for him to take aim at her. It wasn't without justification. They both bore a few small gashes from minor incidents where the aim was slightly too close.

"Oh, there are points. Points that we are repeatedly flinging at one another." Niall countered. "I still do not think I need to throw knives at Kenna at all. Her skill is impressive enough. We could leave the knives out and she can shoot at me until she runs out of arrows."

"An archery act alone won't be impressive enough to get the amount you need to book passage to Arthan. Not if you wish to have enough to do so this season. I don't even know that the knife throwing would be enough on its own, but combine the two and you have something less common. It will hold attention," Elize explained. She demonstrated far more patience than her husband. In fairness, Niall didn't contradict her as often as he did Daris.

"I know this is nerve-wracking. I'd prefer there be less risk as well. But we did agree to this, and we do need to earn our keep." Kenna left her place and moved to stand in front of her husband. She understood his hesitation, though the suggestion that they focus on her archery alone was less rational. Of the two of them, he had received the worst of the injuries. Niall's left forearm had a few stitches due to an unfortunate gust of wind that pushed one of Kenna's arrows off course.

"You're all I have left, Kenna." His tone was intimate as he met her eyes and took a deep breath. "I need you to be safe."

"And that is why I'm willing to allow you to throw weapons in my direction. I know that you won't allow me to suffer any true harm," Kenna answered reassuringly. "Besides, I split your arm open, I owe you a couple scrapes."

"That's not funny," he replied miserably, but from the way his eyes darted to the target board, Kenna could see that she'd talked him past this latest bout of resistance.

"And I'm not laughing," Kenna pointed out. She cupped his cheek. "Now stop letting worry hold you back, and let's finish for the night so we can see about dinner."

Niall nodded and Kenna returned to her place in front of the target. She took a breath and then signaled that she was ready for him to throw. He did, and the knife landed so close to Kenna's neck that she felt a little swoosh of air less than a second before the board shook with the impact. This was usually how their practice sessions panned out. The second the target was against Kenna's back, Niall's resistance slowed progress to a halt, and Kenna was the only one who could get things moving again. Whether it was a matter of the growing trust between them, or something else, it pleased Kenna to know she could reach him.

They rehearsed for another hour without further delays. More than one member of the caravan came by to watch. Some would silently nod with approval, while others stepped forward to offer little bits of advice or ideas. All seemed willing to help. There was an understanding among the troupe, that the failure or success of one was the failure or success of all. It was something Kenna was beginning to love about these people.

She glanced at Niall as he put his daggers away and rolled his sleeves back down. He was still so guarded with most. Where she found it easy to embrace the active and joyful culture of the people they were with, Niall seemed to cling to the old structures of reserve and discipline he'd grown up with. She was sensitive enough to his moods to know that a part of it was his way of holding what he'd lost. In private, he was quite open with her, and she hoped that given time he would grow comfortable with the members of the caravan as well.

They returned to their home on wheels in companionable silence. The earlier tension was all but gone by the time they reached their campsite. Kenna climbed inside the wagon and pulled their dented, fire-stained cooking pot from a cupboard over the bed. It had seen better days, but then, so had she and Niall. When she stepped back outside, her husband was adding kindling and logs to a newly-lit fire.

Kenna set about the task of preparing dinner, adding spices from a small, but treasured collection that Dana graciously gifted them after visiting a market the week before. With little experience in the kitchen, few of the spices were familiar, but Kenna hoped that their smells would offer enough insight into their flavor to produce a more interesting dish than the plain stew they'd been eating.

"I think we're nearly ready," she said, in a carefully conversational tone. Sooner or later the act they were preparing would have to be put before an audience. If Niall continued to resist, they would be ill-prepared for that day.

"Ready?" Niall asked as he dipped his hands in a basin of water and scrubbed away the dirt left behind from tending the fire.

"Our act, I think it's nearly ready. There haven't been any mishaps in almost a week." She smiled at Niall and passed him an onion for chopping when he finished washing his hands. Lacking any experience in cooking, they'd agreed to learn together. The results weren't always palatable, but they were often interesting.

"Ah, the act. I suppose so. It's not how I pictured married life. Though, I have heard the first year can be tricky," Niall replied.

Kenna laughed a little. "You're making jokes. That's promising." She held out the pot for the chopped onions, added the slices of rabbit meat, then sniffed the spices she had on hand. Unsure, she held them out for Niall to consider as well. "Which ones do you think we should use tonight?"

"Maybe that one, with a pinch of salt." He pointed at one of the clay containers. "And yes, jokes. It's easier to laugh at the ridiculousness of where we find ourselves when I'm not being asked to throw weapons in the direction of my dearest friend."

Kenna's hand hovered over the pot. She looked at Niall slowly. "You consider me your dearest friend?"

"I... yes, I do," Niall stammered. He was turning a brilliant pink from his cheeks to his ears. He glanced at her and the shy smile he offered was so sweet that it nearly brought tears to Kenna's eyes. "You are kind and intelligent, and I enjoy being with you. The fact that I can enjoy anything right now speaks volumes of your character. Is it so strange that I might view the person I'm wed to as one of the best I know?"

"Well no. I suppose it's exactly as it should be. I just didn't realize you felt that way," Kenna answered with surprise and delight. From the heat in her own cheeks, she knew she was beginning to blush as deeply as he was. "And I feel the same way about you. I'm glad that you're here with me. I can't imagine facing all of this with anyone else at my side."

Niall studied her face, as if searching for something. Kenna sensed that there was more he might say, but he never gave voice to it. Instead, he took a breath and changed the subject. "We should get that pot over the fire or we'll be waiting all night for it to cook."

"Of course," Kenna replied with quiet resignation. It seemed like they'd been on the cusp of something important. She felt a strange, sad kind of yearning, but didn't know what might satisfy it, only that it kept her up at night and that it eased when Niall smiled at her. She sighed and threw a few sprigs of wild sage into the stew and placed it over the fire. Focusing on the preparation of their meal made it easier to move past the unrest in her spirit.

"Remmy said we'll be approaching the City of the Blessed in a day or two," Niall stated after a few minutes of silence. "I was there with the King once. Are there any magical cities in Arthan?"

"Hm? Oh—um, sort of," Kenna stammered, still distracted. She turned back to Niall. "Arthan isn't united as Venallis is. Each Vashirat has their own group of wizards and Soulbound. They usually choose to live in smaller but separate communities near the estates of a Vashirat's leader."

"Was there one near your home?"

"There was. It was underground, actually. Only those with magic or on official business were allowed inside. I was never permitted entrance," Kenna explained. She paused thoughtfully. "One of the water mages took up residence in my family's palace for a time. My father commissioned a water garden for the anniversary of my mother's ascension as Vashirat leader. He was an interesting sort—quite eccentric."

Niall considered that for a moment. "Why does a water garden require the services of a wizard? Isn't it just water plants and such?"

"Not in Arthan," Kenna laughed, forgetting her earlier consternation. "Arthan is warmer, less verdant. It's not like the rolling hills and babbling brooks here in Venallis." She smiled, thinking of her home. "In some places there are golden oceans of sand, with dunes that look like waves of amber and sunlight. But for all its beauty, Arthan is an arid place. Our homes and cities are built in the oases that form around the water supplies. As such, my people tend to value water and its beauty as greatly as precious stones."

"Ah, so you have water mages to increase the amount available for these gardens," Niall surmised with a nod.

"That is part of it, but not the main reason. The water mages create sculptures by enchanting fountains to shape the water in an array of fanciful designs," Kenna elaborated. She'd spent many happy hours in her family's water garden. It was where her eldest sister was wed, and where she used to imagine tales of adventure and magic with Jaik. She'd spent hours reading poetry at the edge of her favorite pool after childhood fancies were traded for more serious pursuits. "The most magnificent was a sculpture shaped as a great phoenix. I used to imagine that it would come to life, and I'd climb up on its back and fly over the desert."

"That sounds astonishing," Niall commented. "I hope you'll show me when we return to Arthan."

The idea of sharing that place with Niall made Kenna's heart swell. She could almost picture him among the flowering vines and glittering pools—how the color of the water would bring out the blue of his eyes. She envisioned sitting by her favorite sculpture with its tiny flotilla of feathers fashioned from gold floating at the base, listening as Niall read poetry from the book he'd given her when he asked her to marry him. "I'd like that, Niall," she answered softly. "I'd show you that and more if we were there."

Niall was quiet for a time. "I'm sorry I've been complaining so much about the act. Hearing you speak of your home I can see why you're willing to put yourself in harm's way to get back there. I give you my solemn oath that I will do whatever it takes to see you returned."

"Without complaint?" Kenna raised a brow at him in playful disbelief.

"Without complaint. On my honor," Niall placed his hand over his heart and bowed his head toward her. "Though, I might wince now and again."

"Fair enough, especially considering that gash on your wrist." Kenna conceded. "How is it by the way? It seemed to be bothering you earlier today."

Niall rolled up his sleeve and examined the wound for a moment. "It's not too bad. I bumped it when I was helping them water the horses. It soured my mood for a time, but talk of enchanted phoenixes has calmed those troubled waters."

"And if our act impresses the audience you shall see that phoenix for yourself," Kenna smiled at him, feeling a sense of contentment and happiness. For the first time in nearly a month, life felt normal again.

The sun was low on the horizon, and the aroma of their dinner over the fire gave their little corner of the camp a delightful homey feeling. From the smell, it was nearly done, and it wouldn't be a moment too soon. If life on the road had taught Kenna one thing, it was that constant movement created a mighty appetite. Both she and Niall were eating twice what they used to.

By the time they pulled their meal from the fire, Daris and Elize had made their way over with their own contributions to the private feast. The four of them settled comfortably around the fire and passed a jug of ale that Daris had brought. Whatever frustrations he felt with Niall earlier were left behind when the rehearsal ended.

"I spoke to the elders about how the two of you are progressing," Daris said as he filled his plate. "They think, and I agree, that you should debut your act when we perform in the City of the Blessed. The residents there tend to be a bit freer with their money."

"But that's in just a few days," Kenna replied. Her stomach started to knot. Being given an actual time and location for their first performance made the idea more daunting. Suddenly, Kenna didn't feel anywhere near prepared, despite her earlier comments to Niall. "We don't even have costumes yet."

"Oh, that's not a problem. We always have some extra in case something gets torn or ruined in some other fashion," Elize chimed in. "And really, if your first performance goes well, you might be able to get something of your own choosing before we leave the City of the Blessed."

Kenna watched Niall's shoulders tense. She could see that he wanted to protest, but when he spoke it wasn't to offer complaint. "What happens if we don't do well? We've had our share of nicks and cuts over the past weeks. Will people still offer money if we make a mistake?"

"As long as the cut doesn't draw much blood, and neither one of you show that it happened, the audience will be none the wiser," Daris shrugged. "Besides, you still have two days to practice before we get there. You're both skilled, you just have to get over your nerves."

"But... but what if the cut is deep? What if it bleeds too much and is obvious?" Kenna asked. She glanced at Niall's wounded arm, guilt and concern adding to the nervous tangle in her stomach.

"You'll be fine, Kenna. What happened to Niall was the result of nature's interference. It had nothing to do with your aim." Elize reached out and gave her hand a light squeeze before dipping her wooden spoon into her bowl and taking a bite. She chewed for a few seconds and then her nose wrinkled, "Oh, dear. What did the two of you put in this?"

"Just some of those reddish flakes," Niall answered slowly. He took a bite of his own food and quickly spit it back into the bowl before reached for his mug of ale. "Oh, that's potent!"

Daris and Kenna exchanged looks before putting their bowls aside. Kenna retrieved the stores of seasoning and held the spice she used out for Elize to examine. "It was just a few pinches of this."

"Well, a few pinches would definitely add flavor, but paired with onion it goes bitter," Elize managed through a cough. "This is dried pauper's basil."

"I had no idea. There were cooks at the estate," Kenna said, looking down at the innocuous flakes.

"I chose the seasoning and added the onion," Niall's eyes were watering. "A crime for which my tongue is paying the price." He refilled his cup and gulped down half the contents in one go.

Daris snorted, then covered his mouth and tried to play the laugh off as a cough. Kenna caught his eye and felt her own lips curving into a smile, followed by the tiniest squeak of a giggle. Elize and Niall exchanged looks and burst into laughter, faces still red, eyes watering from the onslaught of the stew.

They sat around the fire laughing like fools and garnering curious looks from their closest neighbors. It was the first time since Mairi's death that Kenna felt completely herself. She laughed until her eyes were watering and her sides hurt. It was wonderful, freeing, and enough to make her fears of performing before an audience evaporate entirely.

The noise of their laughter and levity concealed the approaching sound of multiple horses until they were nearly upon the camp. It was the barking of the dogs that caused Kenna, Niall, Daris and Elize to look up from their fire at the band of six riders approaching the camps nearest to the road.

"You there! We seek a place of warmth by the fires for a few minutes, perhaps a cup of ale if it can be spared." The speaker's voice was gruff and he spoke with a thick Arthan accent.

Kenna's smile faded as soon as she caught sight of the newcomers. Even in the flickering glow she could see that the men who approached Remmy and his wife were members of the Stratham Vashirat. Each bore a thick band of fabric around their necks that draped down over the leather armor they wore. The memory of her final night at Britwylde flashed before her eyes and drowned out the tranquility of the evening. The blood drained from Kenna's face and her cheeks went numb. Her hands began to shake.

It was fortunate that their wagon was set on the opposite end of the camp or Niall and Kenna would most certainly have been recognized. It wasn't difficult to guess what business had brought the riders. The conversation and laughter shared seconds earlier was replaced by apprehensive silence. Niall rose quickly and took Kenna's hand as he pulled her away from the fire. They crouched in the shadows on the far side of the wagon.

To their credit, Daris and Elize did a fine job of hiding their surprise. They exchanged quick looks of confusion but remained where they sat, discreetly pushing the plates and cups that Kenna and Niall left behind out of sight.

"Our fires are welcome to all who come without harmful intent," Remmy replied with gracious caution. The traveling man was no fool, and bandits were not unheard of on the roads of Venallis. "You are fellow travelers, no? Your speech and garb are not common in these parts."

"We are indeed far from our homeland, but are carrying out the business of our Vashirat." The rider at the head of the group answered. He swung his leg over the saddle and lowered himself to the ground. The others followed suit as he approached Remmy. "Honor demands that we fulfill our obligations before we return to the golden dunes of Arthan."

Kenna felt a surge of such rage that it made her vision blur. She shook with the tension of forcing herself to stay hidden.

There was no honor in what they did to the people of Britwylde. Kenna's fingers clenched into a fist. She wished she had her bow handy. She'd gladly show them the same honor they offered Mairi.

"It is important to return to one's people with obligations fulfilled," Remmy said carefully.

"Indeed, and among the Vashirats of Arthan, it is law," the soldier replied. The sword at his side reflected the orange flames of Remmy's fire, and in the shifting flash of fiery color Kenna could almost see the burning walls of Britwylde.

Remmy looked around the circle of the caravan's camp. His gaze stopped at the wagon that Kenna and Niall crouched behind. He tilted his head thoughtfully and turned back to the man. "We are but simple minstrels and jugglers. Our only obligation is to bring joy and wonder to those we perform for. And to bring home enough coin to see our people through the winter months."

"You provide for your Vashirat then," the Stratham man replied as he crouched to put his fingers out to the campfire.

Kenna swallowed the curses that threatened to erupt from her lips. She could hear Niall's teeth grinding together at her ear. *He carries on as if the attack was nothing more than an errand to be completed, that the lives lost were of little consequence... No, if I allow myself to lose control it will only cause further bloodshed and endanger the people who've given us succor.*

Elize casually rose from her seat by the fire and moved toward the wagon as if she were tidying up the evening meal. She stopped near the door and spoke without looking at Kenna or Niall. "Do you know them?"

"Not specifically, but the bands they wear at their necks are in the colors of an enemy," Kenna replied through thin lips.

Elize cast a quick look at the Stratham soldiers "Remmy took note of your absence at the fire. It was enough to warn him that they are not friends."

"It was men of this sort who were responsible for the attack on the High Lord's estate," Niall whispered back.

"Do you think they would attack us?" Daris asked, having moved to his wife's side a moment earlier.

"They have no quarrel with your people, but I do not know if that would still their hands," Kenna replied. The Stratham could be vicious, but before the attack on Niall's family, Kenna wouldn't have expected them to attack strangers without provocation. After the savagery she witnessed at Britwylde, she'd put nothing past them.

Daris nodded. "Should I find a way to tell Remmy they should be encouraged to move on?"

"If it can be done without raising suspicion," Niall whispered.

Kenna felt Niall's arm slip around her shoulders. They were a danger to these kind people. As long as they remained here, it put the entire troupe at risk. Fresh hurts widened the cracks in Kenna's already broken heart. The comfort of friendship and home had allowed her to feel safe again. Now she realized it was nothing more than an illusion.

"Perhaps we're the ones who should leave," Kenna said. She didn't know where they would go, but the idea of being the cause of further suffering and death was more than she could bear.

"With men like these wandering the roads and no way to travel in safety? You'd be walking to your deaths," Elize looked at Kenna this time. "We will not abandon you to that."

Daris nodded his agreement. He turned from them and casually walked across the camp to join Remmy. "Will our guests be staying the night?"

Remmy looked from Daris to the Stratham soldiers. "These men are on important business. They merely asked for a moment by the fire and some ale."

"The fire is warm indeed, but my men and I remain thirsty." The Stratham looked over his shoulder at his companions with a laugh. Kenna thought the night seemed to grow a bit colder at the sound of it.

"An unintentional lapse, I assure you," Daris answered. He kept his tone light, but Kenna could see the distrust in her friend's eyes.

"And one we'll see remedied now," Remmy stated quickly. He signaled to Dana, who rose, ignoring the half-emptied bottle closest to them, and made her way to the cart that held their food stores.

"But duty to your Vashirat cannot be delayed by our sad breach in courtesy," Remmy continued as his wife retrieved an unopened jug.

"Of course, it cannot," Dana returned with another jug of ale in hand. Remmy's wife was as astute and composed as her husband. "Take this, enough to provide more than what our manners forgot. It may not stave off the night like our fires, but it will warm your bellies."

The soldier sobered and accepted the jug, inclining his head before passing the offering to one of his subordinates. "Warmth in this country is rare. We all look forward to returning to the sands of our home."

Remmy took a drink from his own cup as his wife moved back to his side. "Then we wish you a safe and speedy return."

Seconds drew out in silence and Kenna began to worry that the encounter was about to turn deadly. The leader of the Stratham party cast a long steady look around the camp and then turned to approach his horse. He climbed back into his saddle and waved, turning his horse without another word exchanged. The rest of the men followed close behind. The band returned to the road and slowly disappeared into the night.

Remmy, Dana, and Daris made no sign of movement. They continued to sip at their ale by the fire until long after the sound of hoof-falls vanished in the distance. Even then, Daris did not move from the campfire. It wasn't until the caravan leader's eldest son approached to whisper something in his father's ear. Kenna guessed it was word that the riders were well away.

When Daris finally returned to the wagon, Remmy was at his side. Kenna and Niall stepped out of hiding slowly. Remmy hadn't revealed their presence, but

Kenna's stomach clenched with fear for the questions that might arise as a result of this encounter. Niall's hand slipped into hers and he held firm. It felt like a rope tossed to her in a sea that was threatening to pull her under.

"They were from Arthan and claimed to be about business for their Vashirat," Remmy began, leveling his eyes on Niall and Kenna. "Would you know anything of what that business might be?"

"I can guess as to their purpose, and I recognize the colors they wore. They were the same as those worn by the attackers of Britwylde," Niall answered carefully.

Remmy looked at them in turn. He drew a deep breath and rubbed at his temples before pacing a few steps. Kenna felt like a criminal awaiting the verdict of a magistrate.

"We will leave and seek to make our own way if that is what must be done," Kenna said when the quiet became too much to bear.

Remmy turned back to them. "No, those men have returned to their business, and we must do the same. We continue to the City of the Blessed and you will perform your act as planned. What the road brings beyond is something to be faced later."

"We would not have our presence bring harm down upon any of you," Niall replied. "Those men were surely loo—"

"No!" Remmy raised a hand to stop Niall.

"But we have not told you—" Niall started to protest.

Remmy silenced him with another gesture. "We have accepted two unfortunate travelers into our company. That is what I know, and that is what I can answer with honesty should anyone ask about the two of you."

"Thank you." Niall replied, resignation in his voice.

"Your kindness will never be forgotten," Kenna added. She shared her husband's concern, but they were in no position to refuse this protection.

"We cannot choose the obstacles placed in the road we walk. It would be wrong of us to abandon you to yours," Remmy rubbed at his temples again. "Now, I suggest we all go to our beds and leave as early as may be possible in the morning. We'll post extra lookouts at night until we reach the City of the Blessed."

"I'll stand watch gladly," Niall volunteered.

"I'll join you." Daris stepped forward. He kissed Elize on the cheek and went to grab a cloak to stave off the night wind. Elize wished them all a goodnight and followed her husband. Remmy returned to his own fire as well, leaving Niall and Kenna alone.

Kenna let out the breath she hadn't even realized she was holding in. Her muscles were rigid with tension. The idea of spending the next few hours alone wasn't a pleasant one. "Perhaps I should join you and let Daris stay with Elize."

Niall shook his head. "There's no reason we should both be exhausted. Besides, your hunting provides for our meals, and it won't do for you to be stumbling through the woods and scaring off all the game. It will only be for a few hours."

"Do you think the Stratham know we escaped?" Kenna asked quietly.

"Possibly. It would be easy enough to tell if they searched the bodies, unless the fire..." Niall's back was to her, his voice heavy with memory. "The attack was well planned and thorough, I doubt they would leave without doing an equally thorough search."

Kenna said nothing in response to that. The fact that there were still enemies so close at hand made her sick with worry. It brought back all the guilt she'd been struggling to overcome. *How long will they remain? How many more will be harmed by this?*

"The Stratham are bold to stay in Venallis so long," Niall commented, revealing that his own thoughts were running in similar circles. "Word must have reached Rosehaven by now. King Fergal will have sent soldiers out."

"How long would it take them to reach your family's home?" she asked.

Niall wiped his hand over his face and Kenna thought she might have detected the glistening of tears on his cheeks. He cleared his throat before answering. "It takes about a week to travel from Britwylde to Rosehaven. Then more time to muster the soldiers and supplies before they can be sent out. I should think they would be close, if they have not already arrived."

"Perhaps we should make our way back, meet with them and seek the aid of King Fergal," Kenna suggested. The prospect of returning to the site of the attack was terrifying, but if their presence put the traveling folk in danger, she would willingly face the nightmare of such a return.

"The Stratham stand between here and there. Even if we didn't have to worry about being caught, it would take weeks to get back on foot. I doubt the King's forces would still be there once we made our way back," Niall sighed heavily. "The City of the Blessed is only a few days away. I think we should continue that far, see what money we can make with our performance, and decide from there."

* * *

The following two days passed without incident, but after seeing the Stratham it no longer felt as safe. Each morning Kenna and Niall climbed out of their bed before dawn, packed up their lives, and moved through the Venallian countryside in a parade of color, song, and laughter, but they both felt anxious and often scanned the countryside for riders in Stratham colors. Most of the group were unaware of the implications of the soldiers' visit. Those who were, covered their concerns well. Even so, there was a level of increased vigilance as they made their way toward the City of the Blessed.

By the end of the second day of travel, an ivory tower glittered in the distance. Despite the heaviness that had tugged at Kenna's heart since the encounter with the Stratham, the sight of the gleaming tower provided a renewed sense of hope. If all went as planned, they would soon have the means to turn their course to Arthan and her family. Getting back might be difficult with the Stratham looking for them, but if they could only make it back to her home, Kenna was certain they would be able to see justice served.

Before the evening's rehearsal, Kenna and Niall were provided with matching sets of sage green and deep, chocolatey brown costumes. The bodice of Kenna's dress was more fitted than the blouses and skirts she'd been wearing for weeks. The skirt was made of multiple layers of light fabric that flared out around her like an open morning glory whenever she turned round. Niall's shirt billowed more at the sleeves, but tucked into a pair of tightly fitted trousers with one green and one brown leg.

Per the instruction of their mentors, they changed into the costumes before beginning practice. to adjust to the fit and range of movement before they performed in them. The flashy garments instilled a sense of showmanship and wonder that couldn't be ignored. Kenna found that she adjusted her movement without even thinking of all the technical applications, swaying her hips more, and turning with greater speed to accentuate the swish and swirl of her skirts. By the end of the practice session, several members of the troupe were gathered round. They cheered and applauded with genuine enthusiasm when Kenna and Niall finished and bowed. The act was ready. The clothes were the final element needed to complete Kenna and Niall's transformation into performers.

It was late in the afternoon the next day when the merrily painted wagons of the caravan rolled through the arched gateway into the fabled City of the Blessed. Already dressed in their costumes, the travelers trekked through the streets, performing little tricks and singing as they went. A drummer pounded the lively rhythm of their procession, fiddlers and pipers played lilting jigs that blended with the strange music that seemed to float through the air from every direction. Kenna and Niall walked side by side in the middle of the group. Niall's hair was already covered by a scarf made from fabric a shade darker than the green of his shirt. To any observing, they were nothing more than traveling entertainers, two in a band of many.

Kenna was astounded by the sights and sounds around her. The City of the Blessed was like its own world. The streets were full of people but never seemed to be crowded. The air itself tingled with magic, and it was no wonder. Faeries flitted above their heads on glittering iridescent wings that sprinkled a fine dust on everything below, where it lingered, shimmering radiantly. Merchants tended booths and storefronts containing an array of strange items: vials with swirling, multi-colored liquids inside, ornate chalices, animals from mysterious corners of the world, and a variety of other oddities that Kenna had never seen and could not name.

"What do you think?" Niall whispered in her ear, so close that the warmth of his breath sent little tingles down Kenna's spine. He was smiling at her, eyes twinkling with delight.

"That if the cities of our mages are as magnificent as this, it's a terrible shame that so few are admitted within their bounds. It's dazzling," Kenna admitted breathlessly. Whether her breathlessness was from the beauty around her or the way her stomach flipped when their eyes met, she wasn't entirely sure. The beauty of the city was astounding, but as wonderful as it was, she felt a touch of regret at having so many others present. She wished that this was an experience shared with Niall, and Niall alone.

His expression grew earnest, but his eyes remained fixed on hers, serious though they were. "It pales in comparison to you." Then he blinked and flinched, as though he was surprised by his own words. He looked away quickly, but Kenna could see his cheeks turning pink.

"Flatterer," she teased, sensing that it would put Niall at ease. And perhaps that was all his comment had been intended as, but it hung in the air between them, like the prismatic faerie dust, drifting down to gently settle on their shoulders.

Niall turned back to her, still blushing, but his smile bright once again. His hand found hers and their fingers laced together. With their free hands they waved at the people who looked up from their work to watch the entertainers as they passed.

The parade ended in an open area, cleared of structures but for the elaborate fountain that frothed and foamed in the center. It showered droplets of water through the air that captured the particles of faerie dust and then hovered above the cobblestone. It was in this enchanted space that the travelers unfolded the wagon that served as a portable stage. They strung up banners and lanterns, and began enticing the denizens of the city to gather round for the show.

Kenna's heart fluttered, and her knees shook with nervous energy as the performances began. She and Niall would follow a pair of brothers, Hagar and Topher, who performed a juggling act with music and bawdy jokes. This act had a tendency to put the crowds in a relaxed and indulgent mood, something Remmy thought would be helpful for Niall and Kenna's debut.

Elize and Daris would follow them as the closing act. Their series of flips and catches were almost always met with cries for an encore. No one wanted to follow such a popular performance. Kenna didn't say anything, but she suspected their placement before Elize and Daris was a precaution should her act with Niall go poorly. As long as the show ended on a thrilling note, the crowds were likely to throw more coins, and return for the second of the travelers' two day stay in the magical metropolis.

Kenna and Niall waited off to the side as the brothers tossed their juggling balls, assorted fruits, and flaming torches in the air, poking fun at one another's wits and manhood as they carried on. The crowd laughed and clapped, gasping when it seemed that one of them caught a torch on the flaming end. Though made to look like an accident, this was a well-rehearsed trick, safely performed by wetting their sleeves and covering their hands in a protective coating. Niall once asked them what it was, but they simply smiled and told him it was a trick of the trade.

The brothers' act continued and built to the climax. They asked for a volunteer from the crowd to stand between them as they juggled torches back and forth. It was a clever trick, the volunteer was never truly chosen at random, nor spontaneously. It was merely their younger sister, or some other member of the troupe with a wig and a clever disguise to blend in with the spectators. Hagar and Topher were skilled at their trade, but the act was far too dangerous to use an untrained stranger.

"Are you ready?" Elize asked, coming up to Kenna and Niall with a bright smile. She had little stars and moons painted on her cheeks and temples. Daris was grinning at her side, equally cheery. Kenna wondered if either of them had felt as nervous as she did when they started performing.

"That depends," Niall began, "on whether feeling like you might vomit the moment you step out onto the stage is the same thing as being ready."

"That sounds about right," Daris laughed.

"Then, yes, we're ready," Niall's voice squeaked ever so slightly.

Daris clapped Niall on the back. "Don't worry. The two of you will be fine."

"Right, and if not, we'll be bleeding and hopefully that will convince the people to give us money out of pity," Kenna replied. She felt a little better knowing that Niall was just as nervous, but the improvement was minor.

The applause grew louder. Hagar and Topher were bowing, waving, and winking at some of the women at the front of the audience as they collected their equipment and hopped off the stage. Remmy took their place. He was in a crimson silk shirt, with a black vest. Beads were twisted into his gray and black beard and the wavy dark hair that hung to his shoulders. He looked out over the crowd with such intensity that the clapping and cheers died down and were replaced by anticipatory silence.

"And now, for the first time, I present an act so dangerous, so thrilling, that few have the courage to engage in the activity. The two individuals I present to you are not born of our ranks, but have traveled from far off lands, exotic places that ignite the imagination and teeter on the realm of dreams," Remmy was pacing the stage, his gestures overblown, and his voice filled with intrigue.

Niall snorted beside Kenna. "I was born in one of the most peaceful and unexotic places in Venallis. I suppose if sheep ignite one's imagination he's spot on."

"Perhaps they're 'exotic' sheep," Kenna returned with a quiet, nervous giggle. "But he's probably referring to my homeland. Many here seem to think Arthan is some sort of mystical wilderness."

"I present to you the blades and bow of Kilian and Cara!" Remmy introduced them using the stage names he'd selected, and gestured with a grandiose sweeping motion.

Kenna's laughter faded, but she managed to keep the smile on her face, despite feeling like her legs had suddenly turned to jelly. Niall's fingers locked around hers, and she could feel his palms sweating. This was it. There would be no do-overs tonight, no second chances with a shot or a throw. The audience was waiting with expressions of curious interest.

The performance started with each of them taking aim at different targets. Niall threw apples and oranges into the air for Kenna to pin against the wooden target with her colorfully fletched arrows. Kenna did the same for him. There were approving claps and the occasional whoop, but this was not the death-defying act they'd been promised at the beginning.

The musicians changed the tone of the music they were playing. The small, round targets were replaced by the door-sized board they would take turns standing in front of.

"I think they'd like to see more, wife," Niall called, holding the final apple out to her. "But we've only the one apple left."

"Oh, I don't think that's a problem. Stand to the side, my darling, and we'll see if we can make things a bit more exciting," Kenna replied. Niall took his place just to the side of the board and held the apple in front of it. Kenna nocked an arrow to her bow and pretended to line up her shot. She stopped and lowered her weapon with feigned exasperation. "We can do better than that, Kilian. Why don't you stand in front of the target instead?"

Niall cocked his head at her and raised a brow as if he didn't know what she had in mind. After a pause, he took his place. "Is the shot more to your liking now?" The audience chuckled.

"Nearly. Put the apple on your head," Kenna instructed.

"My head?" Niall asked. He played at being concerned.

"Oh, don't be so nervous, you rarely use it anyway," Kenna teased. It wasn't her favorite jest, but the others assured her the joke would hit its mark, and it did.

Niall obediently placed the apple on his head. Kenna waited patiently for him to get the glistening piece of ruby red fruit perfectly balanced. He gave her a subtle wink from the eye furthest from the crowd to indicate that he was ready for her to shoot. Kenna lifted her bow, took aim, and fired the second his fingers pulled away. To the outside eye it looked like Kenna had taken the shot well before Niall was prepared. The feigned flinch on his part sealed the illusion. The crowd gasped.

Niall pressed himself against the wooden target and splayed his hands out beside him. Without giving the people time to catch their breath, or question the authenticity of the performance, Kenna shot a series of arrows. Each one hit the wood so close to Niall that when he stepped away from the target his form was sparsely outlined by arrows.

There was a moment of stunned silence, and then the audience burst into a chorus of cheering that filled the area. They were hooked and ready for more. The act progressed with a few more tricks from Kenna. Then Niall took his turn. He tossed his blades at Kenna and the two of them verbally sparred as the performance went on. None of it was spontaneous, but their new friends among the traveling folk had trained them well in making the comments seem new and fresh.

The final trick was one they added a few nights ago, at Dana's insistent urgings. Kenna stepped away from the target and walked to the other side of the stage as Niall pulled his knives from the wood. She picked her bow up casually, keeping an eye on his progress. When Niall took a single backward step to the side Kenna let her final shot fly. It passed so close to Niall's chest that the fabric of his shirt fluttered. The arrow slammed into the board, embedding itself directly in the middle of the cheery pink heart that had been painted there for this final trick.

"I'm told it's wise to aim for the heart," Kenna said with a sweet smile.

Niall turned his head slowly and met her eyes. "As always, you've hit your mark."

The crowd erupted in a cacophony of clapping and cheers, but it sounded like nothing more than a hum compared to the way Kenna's own heart was pounding. Time seemed to slow between the two of them. What felt like several minutes passed, though it couldn't have been more than a second or two. Niall and Kenna came together at the center of the stage to take their bows and then they hurried off so that Daris and Elize could close the night's show.

Kenna and Niall were pulled apart by a wave of their friends' congratulations. Kenna accepted their kind words with smiles but searched the faces for her husband. When she caught sight of his blue eyes, she knew he'd been looking for her as well. In that instant, the shadows of their past felt a world away.

CHAPTER 12

Acceptance

Daris and Elize's performance was half done before Niall was able to make his way back to Kenna's side. He wrapped his arms around her and spun them both in a circle, laughing with delight as he placed her back on the ground. "We did it! We actually did it!"

"You were amazing up there!" Kenna exclaimed. She hugged him, then to Niall's surprise, stood up on tiptoe to kiss his cheek.

"I was amazing? No, my dear, I believe it was you that carried us through the show." Niall couldn't stop smiling. He still felt the warmth of her lips on his cheek and he was practically floating from the sensation. "You had the crowd in the palm your hand, Kenna. Truly, you were... perfect."

Kenna's cheeks turned a dusky rose. She laughed and tucked her hair behind her ears. Niall chuckled: it was ridiculous to him that she should blush at what was such a simple fact in Niall's mind. She was perfect, whether she was on stage or sitting by the fire outside their wagon. He'd known it from the first day they met, when she smiled so warmly at him and spoke of her love of poetry. He fought against acknowledging it then, knowing it would only lead to trouble. He didn't have the will to fight it anymore; nor did he want to.

"Here, Niall, Kenna!" One of the children came running up to them with a cap sagging with the weight of the coins it held. "Your earnings for the night!"

"This is almost half what we'll need to pay for passage to Arthan!" Kenna exclaimed, picking the coins from the hat and placing them in the pouch at her waist. "One more show like this and we can go to my family."

"Then we might have enough by the end of tomorrow's performance." Niall suddenly felt like the wind had been knocked out of him, but he forced his smile to remain firm. Kenna's happiness was obvious, and he would do nothing to dampen it. There was so little else that he could offer her. A way home was not something he would withhold or resent, even if it likely meant the parting of ways. "That's wonderful, you'll be with your family soon."

"Well, we may not make as much tomorrow," Kenna replied, frowning a little. "And it will take time to purchase supplies. Plus, the journey itself isn't a short one."

"Very true," Niall answered quietly. Kenna's reminder that there was still time soothed his spirits enough to take a deep breath and make his smile a genuine one. "At any rate, we just made it through our first performance. I think that's worth celebrating. Perhaps we could delegate a small portion of our earnings to a bottle of wine or some other treat?"

Kenna offered Niall a radiant smile and hugged him again before they moved to a place where they could watch the remainder of Daris and Elize's performance. Their friends were experts at holding the attention of the people. Even their less impressive stunts were met with wild approval from the crowd. It wasn't just their flips and tricks that held one's attention; it was the perfect connection between the two of them. Daris and Elize moved as one graceful entity when they worked their trade. Even Niall, who had seen them practice daily, was captivated by it.

For the finale, Elize stood on Daris' shoulders then lifted a dainty foot and stepped onto the palm of one of his upraised hands. Her balance was so perfect, and Daris' hold on her so secure, that she then lifted her other foot and took a step forward, stepping onto Daris' other hand. They repeated the motion, allowing Elize to walk across his palms as casually as one might stroll down the lane. When the audience quieted, she leapt into a pirouette, spinning rapidly in the air, then fell backwards into Daris' waiting arms. Even the most calloused of hearts couldn't deny the look of absolute adoration that they exchanged before Daris gave Elize a brief, but tender kiss, and set her lightly on the ground.

Without fail, this final series of moves garnered deafening applause wherever the troupe traveled. It was also the reason that the show ended with Daris and Elize. Any mishaps in the other performances were easily forgotten after the spell woven by the two of them.

Remmy jumped onto the platform as Daris and Elize stepped down amidst an uproar of cheers and clapping. He always closed the shows by offering final thanks on behalf of the performers and making a last plea for those present to "show their gratitude," as he put it. Whatever money was tossed forward at this point was put in a collection shared by all for upkeep of property and unforeseen needs during the winter months in their distant settlement.

Though all of the performances were at an end, many of the people who had gathered to watch remained close at hand. The troupe's musicians struck up a lively tune, and local citizens brought out their own instruments to join in the clamor. Faeries played tiny pipes made from hollowed-out willow twigs, whose songs were amplified by magical means. A dark stone elf brought out a harp and began musically dueling with one of the troupe's fiddlers. Dwarves banged on drums of wood and skin, and several people took to dancing in the square. Barrels of ale and wine were brought out by the merchants, who also had a convenient supply of their goods on hand should anyone feel inclined to make impromptu purchases during the festivities. Their time in the City of the Blessed was unlike any of the stops Niall and Kenna had witnessed before. This was not a provincial village filled with people with little more than what they needed to survive. This was a bustling city of magic, merchandise, and art.

Niall hadn't understood the excitement expressed by Daris and Elize in the days drawing nearer to the city. During his previous visit to the City of the Blessed he had been on business with King Fergal. There were official greetings and banquets, but in all the glamour of elite society, nothing compared to the exuberant joy presented now. Fully embracing that sense of exhilaration, Niall took hold off Kenna's hand and pulled her into the midst of the dancing.

A weight lifted from his shoulders as they clasped hands and spun round and round. There was nothing of the perfectly coordinated courtly dances here. People jumped in and out of the wild fray. They locked arms and skipped in circles around one another, kicking up their heels and clapping as they went.

Niall tossed back his head and laughed with delight. Something was different now. He wasn't worried about hiding the fact that he was enjoying himself or that a misspoken word might be used against him. He was no longer the second son of a High Lord or even the person on whom the King leaned, he was simply Niall; and he was genuinely happy.

"Not bad for a scribe!" Daris teased as he pulled Elize past them. He lifted his wife up and spun her around.

"Is that a challenge?" Niall called back.

Daris laughed again. "It absolutely is!"

"I hope you have a plan," Kenna cocked a brow at him. "You did just see him throwing her around as though she weighed nothing, yes?"

"I did, and I haven't even the tiniest start of a plan," Niall replied, grinning from ear to ear. "But it will be fun to improvise." Niall could have laughed at the way Kenna's jaw dropped.

She stared at him in shock. "You want to improvise? You?"

"Unless you don't feel up to the task," Niall shrugged playfully.

"Prepare yourselves!" Kenna shouted over at Daris and Elize, who didn't look concerned in the least. When Kenna turned back to Niall she was grinning from ear to ear. "I've an idea. Do you remember the dance we did at our wedding feast?"

"I do," Niall answered quickly, following her train of thought. He changed the position of his hands. "Shall we?"

Kenna nodded and jumped to action. The dance they performed on their wedding day had been slow and graceful, this was something different. They followed the steps to the letter, but instead of focusing on the symbolism of each move, they increased the speed to match the tempo of the music. The result was an intricate series of lifts, spins, and dips. Where before their hands met gently, precisely, now they were meeting in quick claps that timed out with the beat of the drums.

Daris and Elize were busy with their own dance, obviously confident in their chances of winning the friendly challenge. The space around Niall began to clear as he spun Kenna 'round, and soon their friends stopped their dance to watch instead. They weren't the only ones. Many others were taking note as well. Niall was barely aware of them.

What had started as a playful and good-natured competition between friends, transformed into a moment of partnership and connection between Kenna and himself. Everyone and everything but Kenna faded from his sight. She was a shining beacon, and she was guiding him down the twisting path of their dance. As he tipped her backwards for the final movement, their eyes met and held. They straightened slowly, his arms around her waist, holding her close even after they were upright.

And then the words were there. The simple, undeniable truth that filled Niall's heart and moved him to put her before everyone else, without a thought for his own needs. "Kenna, I—'

The blasting of multiple trumpets, accompanied by the reverberating toll of the city's bell tower, overwhelmed the sound of music and festivity. The clamor silenced Niall's words in an instant. He was jerked back to the present so fast that it almost felt like a physical pull. Kenna slipped from his grip and took a step back. The spell was shattered.

Riders clad in the royal livery trotted into the town square. Uneasy tension replaced the joy of the celebration, and the people grew hushed and anxious. A small contingency of wizards and Soulbound followed in the wake of the riders. Niall only needed to look at their faces to guess the reason behind this interruption. Dread replaced joy.

The head rider pulled his horse to a stop and removed his helmet. Niall didn't recognize his face, but there were many messengers in the employ of the King. The man cleared his throat and unrolled a scroll. "Citizens of the City of the Blessed! It is my unhappy charge to bring tidings of sadness to you this day." Even the birds seemed to cease their songs, and the ethereal music of the city vanished like steam on a windy day. "His Majesty King Fergal has died."

Niall's heart, which a moment earlier had felt lighter than air, sank into the pit of his stomach. He scarcely heard the messenger's praise of the late King, or the hollow assurances of the kingdom's continued prosperity. The message of King Fergal's death destroyed the final vestiges of the life Niall knew before the merciless assault on his family. Until now, a small part of him had been holding on to the faint hope that there would be something for him to return to. Now there was nothing left, and nothing he could provide for Kenna, except a safe return to her home.

"Furthermore, I must relay to you the tidings of a new King. The former High Lord Dempsey has been named the successor to our beloved King Fergal."

Niall's mind managed to focus back in on the words that echoed off the cobblestone streets. He frowned, feeling a sense of strange disquiet at the announcement of Dempsey's accession. King Fergal had been on the throne since before Niall was born. In less than a breath the reign of a good and noble man was ended, and another had risen up to take his place. *I wonder if my family was so quickly dismissed.*

A hand came down on Niall's shoulder. He turned to find Remmy standing behind Kenna and himself. The caravan leader's face was careworn and sad. "Come, it's time to return to the camp. We're less welcome in the towns when ill tidings hang in the air."

Niall nodded and followed him through the throng of stunned and weeping people. The travelers packed up their instruments and folded the stage back into its portable form. They drove out of the gates without fanfare or notice and returned to their camp outside the city walls. The contrast between their arrival and their departure could not have been greater.

Even in the wake of a successful show the mood of the troupe was solemn and subdued. No one played their instruments, nor did they wander from one fire to the other to share stories of the day or tell jokes. Under King Fergal their way of life had been tolerated and even indulged. Though they weren't permitted to perform within the walls of the King's city, they were granted a certain freedom beyond.

The travelers were not officially subjects of the realm and were viewed as outsiders by most. Niall himself had once shared that opinion, despite his childhood fascination with their roving lifestyle. Now that idea seemed like utter nonsense. But whether he agreed or not, a new King could mean new restrictions. A new King would most certainly mean change for everyone within the bounds of Venallis.

The sun wasn't fully set when word came to Niall and Kenna that the next day's performance was cancelled, and the caravan would be moving on in the morning. The magic users had far more freedom to self-govern than the peasantry, but they mourned King Fergal's passing with as much uncertainty. Under the circumstances, it was inappropriate to parade around on stage and make jokes. It would be weeks before such frivolity would be welcomed with cheers and tossed currency. There was little point in remaining. They were on the road again early the next morning.

The caravan continued to make slow progress from village to village. After a few days of travel without stopping, they set up in a pasture just outside one of the larger towns and casually began working their trade. The show was done under the pretense of practicing, but the townsfolk who gathered to watch were not sent away, and the small offerings they tossed were accepted graciously. Niall and Kenna participated as well, though with less flourish than their first, and thus far, only official performance. Even at a time of mourning, a living had to be made. After a few weeks, the pretense was dropped, and they entered towns with the usual gaiety.

Yet, even as life returned to normal for the band of performers, an uncomfortable sense of wrongness settled over Niall. At first, he assumed it was the loss of another person he cared deeply for, but two weeks after hearing the news his agitation only intensified. Though he felt tremendous sadness, it wasn't King Fergal's passing that bothered him. It was the announcement of High Lord Dempsey's accession to the throne. Something about it nagged at Niall relentlessly.

Most nights he lay awake, staring at the ceiling as he contemplated the past months of his life. With distance from the attack on his family, he was able to examine the details with greater objectivity. Things were not adding up as they should have. *How did such a large enemy force make it across the borders and to my family's home without notice? Why would the Stratham Vashirat wait until after Kenna's parents left to launch their attack? Their ranks were that of a* small army, the Rihtall guards wouldn't have tipped the balance and saved the estate.

Then there were the soldiers that stopped at the camp. After such a brutal attack on a family of high-ranking nobility it made no sense for the enemy to linger within Venallis. There seemed to be little concern for any sort of retaliatory response to a deed that should have been considered an act of war.

The lack of response from court created a new fear in Niall's mind. *What if the true enemy isn't the Stratham at all? What if the danger came from someone much closer, someone holding power in Venallis?*

Kenna stirred in her sleep beside him. Niall's heart ached with each beat. He was in love with her. He had come so close to saying that very thing after their performance. If his suspicions were true, his role as her husband put her life at further risk. He could offer her no protection, no status, not even the comfort of a home. There was no reason for her to remain bound to him, and Niall would not ask her to put those she loved in danger for his sake. *If I seek shelter with her family, it could place a target on all their heads.*

That thought made Niall feel like he was suffocating. The confines of their temporary home were too warm, and the walls were closing in on him. He leaned over to place a tentative kiss on Kenna's forehead, then slipped out from under the blankets and carefully crawled out of bed. After pulling a shirt on, he tiptoed through the small space and knelt to open one of the compartments built into the floor. He hadn't opened this hidden cubby since their first week among the travelers.

Only slivers of pale moonlight illuminated their wagon, but even in that dim, silvery glow, Niall could make out the bloodstains on the shirt folded inside the hiding place. He'd considered burning the garment more than once, but could never bring himself to do it. That shirt and the ring that was tucked away inside a hidden pocket, were the only physical remnants he had left of his childhood home and family. He reached inside and pulled the shirt out delicately.

With the shirt in one hand and his boots in the other, Niall stepped out of the wagon. He didn't want to wake Kenna with his fretting, and he needed time in the open air. It was easier to think when he could look up at the stars. Though the circumstances of his existence were dramatically changed, the stars were the same ones that he'd gazed up at as a boy.

The moon was at its zenith and nearly full. It provided enough light that Niall was able to pull his boots on and move through the camp without a lantern. Niall walked past wagons, tents, and the remnants of extinguished campfires, not stopping until he reached the edge of the camp. The night wasn't wholly silent, it never was in the presence of their caravans. Wagons creaked with the movement of their residents, and snores came from the tents of those who preferred to spend the night on pallets laid out on the ground. The sounds were familiar and comforting to Niall now. They were as reassuring as the night noises of Britwylde or the palace had once been.

The wind rustled through the leaves of a nearby grove, and it was here that Niall decided to wrestle with his thoughts. The trees provided a certain level of privacy without fully shielding him from the troupe if trouble should arise. He reached into the folds of the shirt he carried and fumbled to find the secret pocket in the darkness. The weight of his father's ring was heavier than Niall remembered. Were it not for the small square of fabric that was folded around it, the family heirloom likely would have fallen loose when he pulled the shirt out of its hiding place.

When the ring was free of its bonds, Niall laid it out on the palm of his hand and contemplated it solemnly. This ring had belonged to his grandfather, his father; it would have been Ian's. Now it was his. It was a symbol of the power and responsibility that his family had once held. It was also the proof of his identity and the privilege he'd been raised with. It felt like the life of another man, one who was little more than a distant memory now.

On an impulse, Niall took the ring off his palm and slipped it onto the middle finger of his right hand. He stretched his arm out in front of him and examined his hand. The ring glittered in the moonlight, the dark sapphire gem looked almost black in the shadows of the night. By all laws and rights, this was where the ring belonged. It was the ring of the High Lord of Britwylde estate and all that came with that title. Niall was that person, he was the High Lord, the last of his family line. For whatever that was worth without wealth, a home, or the family that went with all of it.

Niall's jaw clenched and he lowered his hand. Even without those things, that title would be worth a great deal to someone who saw it as a threat to their own position and power. The rank of High Lord was closer to the crown than any other, save the Queen and any heirs born to the Royal couple. Before King Fergal's death, only two people held the rank of High Lord; his father and the man who'd just become King, without any challenge or opposition.

The sound of approaching footsteps caught Niall's attention. He jerked the ring off his finger and closed his hand around it. When he looked up, he saw Daris approaching with a lantern in his hand and an expression of concern on his face.

"What are you doing out here at this hour?" Daris asked. He was shirtless and his shoulder-length hair was impressively disheveled. Lifting the lantern higher, he peered at the garment strewn across Niall's lap. "Is that your old shirt?"

"It is," Niall replied simply.

Daris sat on the ground beside him. "So, why are you sitting out here in the middle of the night with it?"

"I was just thinking about the past."

"Does this have anything to do with the King's death?" Daris asked. Niall looked at him sharply, but Daris continued before he could respond. "I saw the expression on your face when the messengers made the announcement. You've been preoccupied since then."

"I knew King Fergal. He was a good man," Niall answered honestly.

"How well could a scribe have known the King of Venallis?" Even in the little light cast by Daris' lantern, Niall could see the incredulous expression on his friend's face.

Niall looked down in shame. Daris and the others had proven to be good and honorable friends. They gave protection and acceptance without question or hesitation. In return, he'd concealed his true identity, and put them in gods knew what kind of danger. *I should have insisted on telling them the truth when the Stratham came to the camp.*

"There's more to your mood than an old bloody shirt or the death of a distant ruler, isn't there?" Daris wasn't looking at Niall. Despite his outspoken nature, he was more sensitive to the moods of those around him than people realized. He was also a keen observer of details most would miss entirely.

Niall frowned thoughtfully. Though he was concerned for the safety of his new friends, he feared revealing the truth, feared the anger it might elicit, or the changes it might force. Yet, there was a measure of relief promised as well. Hiding the truth created a sense of isolation. He had to guard everything he said. Where that had once felt like the natural way of things, it bothered him now. At the Lights of Absence, he wasn't even able to speak the names of his family. *Perhaps it's time to stop running from who and what I am.*

"Daris, I need to tell you something," Niall began. He took a deep breath and searched his mind to find the right words. "I haven't been truthful with you. I was never a scribe in the High Lord's employ."

"What were you then—a groom, some other servant?" He chuckled, but there was tension behind his laugh and in the set of his shoulders.

"I wasn't the High Lord's servant at all." Niall shook his head slowly and looked down at the shirt on his lap. "I was—I am his son."

There was silence for several tense seconds before Daris laughed and gave Niall a nudge. "You almost had me there, *High Lord*. Be serious, I'm worried about you."

"This isn't a joke, Daris." Niall held his hand out to the other man and opened it to show his family's ring. "I am the youngest son of High Lord Edan of Britwylde. The last surviving member of my family."

Daris reached over to pinch the ring between his thumb and forefinger. He lifted it close to his face, frowning before he put it back in Niall's upturned palm. Shaking his head, Daris jumped to his feet and began to pace back and forth in the little circle of light provided by the lantern. He stopped to rub his temples and stare back at Niall. A multitude of emotions scrolled across his features in quick succession; disbelief, confusion, anger, and then a stoic realization.

"I should have told you all from the first day. It shames me that I did not," Niall admitted solemnly.

"Why did you lie?" Daris asked.

Niall looked down and sighed heavily. "I'd just seen my entire family and everyone I grew up with brutally slaughtered. I didn't trust the kindness you offered. I told myself it was because the people who attacked us could still be in the area, and that knowing the truth could endanger you. But in all honesty, I was afraid you'd betray us if the price was high enough."

"Because we're just travelers, right?" Daris voice was steady, but there was an edge of resentment in it.

"Because I was a fool, Daris. You've all proven to be a thousand times more honorable than most of the nobles in the palace." Niall rose and approached his friend. "I was wrong to deceive you. Kenna and I would be dead if it weren't for your intervention, and I repaid you with a lie."

"Why are you telling me all of this now?"

"Because I think I may have been wrong about who murdered my family." Niall made his statement and then took a few steps away from Daris. He hadn't openly voiced his suspicions to Kenna. Doing so would have made them too solid, too dangerous. It was more than he was ready to face at the time. "I have no proof, just a feeling that things aren't as they seemed then."

"Who do you think killed your family, Niall?" It was a friend asking, and not a man who'd just been told he'd been deceived.

Niall looked back at Daris seriously. "To name him could be considered treason."

"Say it, Niall. Tell me who you think killed your family," Daris answered sternly. It was time for truth, and from his tone it was obvious he would accept nothing less.

"I think King Dempsey arranged the massacre. I believe he did it to eliminate any obstacle to his family's accession to the throne."

Daris sat hard on the ground and knit his fingers into his hair. Every tiny noise that sounded in the night added to the tension that emanated from the young performer.

It was Niall's turn to pace now. Having said the words out loud he almost wished he could take them back. The statement felt like a looming predator, stalking them both.

"That is a heavy accusation to level at a King. And the implications are... What makes you even think it?" Daris pulled his hands from his hair and looked up at Niall.

"It was made to look like an attack from enemies of Kenna's family, but there are details that don't make sense." Niall joined Daris on the ground. His friend seemed willing to hear the matter out. "Not the least of which is the fact that the attack came days after Kenna's parents left. They took a small contingent of our fighting men, but not enough for it to have made a difference. Why would the Stratham wait for the leaders of their enemy Vashirat to leave and then attack my home, rather than Kenna's parents? And how did they get a force that size through the countryside without notice?"

"Niall, this is all speculation. Dangerous speculation at that," Daris pointed out,

"I know, and it doesn't make perfect sense. Dempsey's son was at the estate when the attack came. He died there," Niall mused. That was the one thing that made him doubt the possibility. "Why would a man angling for the throne kill one of his heirs?"

Daris was quiet for a few minutes. "Are you certain about that?"

"About what?" Niall looked up at the question.

"King Dempsey's son, did you actually see him die?" Daris asked bluntly.

Niall opened his mouth to confirm Cathal's death, but the words froze on his tongue. He hadn't seen Cathal die. He'd seen Cathal taken hold of and overwhelmed, but he and Kenna fled before the death blow came. Niall's gut twisted. If Dempsey had orchestrated the attack—if Cathal had been privy to those plans, it added a deeper level to the betrayal. Niall's mind flashed back to Ian's death and the scene played out in a new, stark light. "Ian was trying to warn me about something."

"Ian?" Daris asked.

"My brother, Ian. He was the one betrothed to Kenna. He died in a hunting accident a few days before they would have been wed," Niall explained. He was still trying to parse this new implication out. "I married Kenna to preserve the alliance between our families. My father was concerned for my family's security."

"You mean, you and Kenna have an arranged marriage? I would have guessed it was a love match," Daris replied. He seemed almost as surprised about this as he was the revelation of Niall's true identity.

"No, our union was a matter of business between powerful households. At least that's what I've tried to tell myself all this time," Niall said, his train of thought broken. He looked back to the wagon where his wife slept. Kenna, his sweet, intelligent, fiery Kenna. "The truth is that I wanted her from the first words she spoke to me. My brother was heir to the estate, the popular eldest son, and I never once envied anything that he had. Not once. Not until I met Kenna. When Ian died, I was so consumed by guilt over it that I couldn't be a true husband to her."

Daris considered this with an incredulous look on his face. "So, the two of you have never..."

"No, and after my family was destroyed I knew we couldn't. I have nothing. No home, no money. Nothing. That's why we need to get to Arthan, now more than ever," Niall explained. "If my family was killed by the man now crowned King, there's no place she would be safe in Venallis. Even in Arthan her life would be in danger as my wife. Since the marriage has never been consummated it will be a simple matter to dissolve it and release her from any obligations to me."

"That's horseshit, Niall!" Daris snapped. "You may have married her out of some sense of duty, but you just admitted you wanted her from the moment you met her. You love her, and she obviously loves you."

"She was my brother's betrothed," Niall tried to reason.

"And she's your wife, you idiot!" Daris shot him a look that made it clear his words echoed his thoughts on Niall's intelligence at the moment. "She married you, not your brother. Whatever claim he had was dissolved when he died. So what if you thought she was attractive before then? She is. It doesn't mean you're having some clandestine affair with a married woman. You're the one that's married to her! You love her, Niall. That's obvious to anyone with functioning eyes."

"Yes, I love her. I love her so much I can scarcely breath when she's not with me," Niall shot back.

"Then tell her that," Daris argued.

"If I tell her I'm in love with her she'll stay out of a sense of obligation. No." Niall shook his head and felt his heart clenching tight around the idea of putting Kenna in that kind of danger. "She'll stay with me, here, or with her family, and she'll never be safe."

"Tell yourself that if you like, but I don't believe it. I think you're afraid she won't want to stay," Daris countered. "I think deep down you're afraid that she won't return your love, and she'll leave you regardless of how you feel for her."

"You don't understand, Daris," Niall objected, knowing full well that Daris had hit the mark perfectly. He shook his head. "It's not that simple. Nothing about my life is simple anymore."

"It is when you don't cloud things with foolish notions of guilt about something outside your control." Daris gave a disgusted grunt and pushed himself to his feet. "Now stop whining and get your noble ass off the ground. We have business to see to."

Niall obeyed, too surprised by his friend's reaction to offer objections. "What business are you talking about?"

"For starters, you're going to tell the elders the truth about who you and Kenna are. I know Remmy stopped you before, but this is too big to remain secret. Then we're going to figure out how to keep the two of you safe. You're part of our community now, High Lord or not," Daris was speaking over his shoulder, already headed toward the camp. "I can't tell you how to handle your marriage, but I can try to keep you alive long enough to knock some sense into that thick skull of yours."

"You're not angry with me for lying about who I am?" Niall asked, trailing behind, taken aback by the sudden call to action.

Daris stopped and looked him in the eye. "A little, maybe, but I understand why you did it. It was wrong, and stupid, but at least you've come to your senses about that, if not other things."

"You're a good man, Daris," Niall replied earnestly. "Possibly one of the best I've ever known."

"Tell me that again after Remmy and the other elders are through with you," Daris said firmly, but the corners of his mouth were twisting up.

Before they woke the elders Niall stopped at the wagon to wake Kenna and give her the option of speaking to Remmy and the rest of the elders with him. Not surprisingly, she rose from bed to join him without hesitation. She even expressed relief. The leaders of the traveling troupe listened to Niall and Kenna's admission with quiet contemplation. When the entire truth was laid out, Remmy and the others took a few minutes to confer with one another. When they returned their decision was unanimous. Niall and Kenna would be allowed to remain.

The news of their true identities was kept to a small number of the caravan. The elders allowed Daris to tell Elize, but beyond that it was decided that the fewer people who knew, the safer they'd all be. Niall and Kenna continued to perform with the troupe, though masks were added to their act as an extra precaution. It was easy enough to explain the change to the rest of the performers. The masks added to the mystery.

The caravan performed its way through the usual route, going from one village to the next in a circle that turned back toward the lands of Niall's birth. They were on their way to the village of Brittendell, near the very estate where Niall's life had changed forever. There, the traveling folk would help the villagers with the harvest in exchange for a portion of the bounty to take back to the winter village a few miles beyond the Wiettan border.

With the shows along the way, Niall and Kenna were able to save enough to arrange safe transport across the border. When the harvest was complete, they would break ties with the band of traveling entertainers and finally make their way to Arthan.

CHAPTER 13

Standing Still

After months of life in a constant state of movement, Kenna should have felt joy at the prospect of stopping for more than a day or two. Yet, it was a sense of dread that fell over her as the quaint farming village of Brittendell came into sight. They'd collected enough money to make the journey back to her family, and the thought made Kenna's spirit sink lower with each passing day.

She glanced at Niall as he drove their wagon down the dusty road that led into the lush valley. He was not the same man she'd met all those months ago. He was freer with his words, his smiles, and his affection with those around him. He'd shed the stiff shell of decorum that his noble upbringing demanded and seemed at greater ease with himself.

Even so, Kenna knew that there was much still troubling him. Daris, Elize, and the elders knew their true identities now. On one hand it made things easier than it was when they had to carefully monitor every word, but on the other, it presented a danger to those who knew. Kenna could see how much it worried Niall. It worried her too, but her husband seemed determined to bear the weight of it himself, which frustrated her. She would have gladly helped him shoulder the burden as both a friend and a wife.

He wasn't sleeping well at night. Kenna often woke to find Niall sitting up and gazing out the open shutters or turning the High Lord's ring over and over in his hands. She wanted to reach out, to pull him back to her, but she didn't know if he found comfort within her arms as she found in his.

Occasionally, he put it on, but never for more than a minute or two. If he saw that she was awake, he put the ring away and came back to bed, holding her hand until she was asleep again. Even that carried a note of sadness, but Kenna wasn't sure if the sadness was his or hers.

Kenna sighed and looked at the road ahead. Perhaps Niall was not the only one who'd changed. Were such differences visible in her as well? Everything felt so much closer to the surface than it used to. It was almost as if life had once been held at bay by a cloak of duty, and now she could feel the breeze. The sky was a brighter shade of blue, the grass more verdant than before. Even the sound of the bells on the harnesses of the horses jingled with a happier tone. Everything was more intense: happiness and uneasiness.

She missed her family, of course, but she no longer yearned for home or felt isolated in a new land. She loved the humble but cozy wagon she shared with Niall. There was comfort and safety in the sound of his breathing when he slept at her side. She loved the way his golden curls would twist wildly around his forehead when there was rain in the air, or the way her hand fit perfectly into his, as though they were always meant to be linked. In truth, Kenna couldn't imagine her day without Niall's presence. He was as much her family as the one she was born to. She didn't want to think of what life would be like were he not with her.

They pulled their wagon to a stop, and Kenna allowed Niall to help her down from her seat beside him. The business of setting up camp was always a noisy one, but when the caravan stopped in a pasture at the edge of Brittendell, the process was even louder than usual. This was not a quick overnight break for dinner and rest. The troupe would remain on the outskirts of the village for weeks before returning to the road. The residents came out to greet them, not with the usual expectation of entertainment, but with the familiar greeting of old friends and extended family coming together for celebration. Indeed, looking at the villagers, it was clear that some of them were blood relatives of the olive-skinned travelers.

One of these, a young man who bore a striking resemblance to Daris, was the first to greet them. He waved cheerfully at several people, but made a direct line to the wagon shared by Daris and Elize. He barely stopped in his haste to traverse the bustling camp.

"Brother!" Daris exclaimed, all but tackling the newcomer. "So, Brenin, the little woman hasn't tired of you yet?"

Kenna exchanged a glance with Niall. Daris had never mentioned a brother before. Not that either one of them had cause to complain. They'd hidden their full identities for months.

"Not yet, thankfully," was Brenin's playful return. "And I see Elize is still putting up with you."

"He does all the heavy lifting," Elize chuckled as she wrapped her brother-in-law in a warm hug.

Brenin pulled away and looked past Daris to where Kenna and Niall stood. "And who might you two be?"

Daris stepped aside and waved for them to come closer. "This is Niall and his wife Kenna. They joined us on the road and have become quite the favorites with the crowds. Niall, Kenna, this is my younger brother, Brenin."

"Interesting," Brenin replied. He was studying Niall closely with a contemplative expression on his face. "How long have the two of you been traveling with the caravan?"

"Leave them be, Brenin," Elize interrupted. "It's been over a year since you left us to marry your Rowan. Are you enjoying life in one place?"

"I am. There was some concern when the High Lord fell," here his eyes slid back to Niall, "but things have been managed well, and life here is good. In fact, you and Daris have a niece."

"What?" Daris broke into a wide smile. He ruffled the younger man's hair and pulled him into another tight embrace. "Brenin, you rascal! I can hardly believe my baby brother is a father. What have you named her?"

"I can't believe my older brother isn't!" Brenin laughed. "Her name is Ellia, and she has our mother's eyes."

"We have to celebrate tonight, and I must meet my niece as soon as everything is set up," Daris continued. He gestured to the pasture in which the wagons were parked. "You've a beautiful piece of land here. How are your plans for the horses? Have you been able to purchase a good breeding stock yet?"

"Not yet. My plans have been slowed with the arrival of Ellia. I wasn't able to save enough to buy any animals worthwhile at the spring faire," Brenin replied.

"I had hoped to meet with the High Lord to discuss a possible loan of sorts, but well..."

Kenna instinctively slipped her hand into Niall's, knowing that all of this had to be tearing him apart. Her own heart ached for the losses they'd suffered, and for the pain the familiar landscape must be causing Niall. Brittendell was closer to his family's estate than they'd been in quite some time. It even took its name from Britwylde Castle. She leaned close to him to whisper in his ear. "How are you doing?"

"I'm all right," he smiled a little, but the expression was clouded with hints of grief.

"It was lovely to meet you, Brenin, and I look forward to meeting your wife and daughter later," Kenna addressed him politely. The need to free Niall of the burden of polite conversation was overwhelming. Despite his reassurance, Kenna knew he would be more comfortable in the quiet and safety of their wagon. "But Niall and I really should finish preparing our home for the stay here if we're to have any hope of finishing in time to join in the festivities this evening." It didn't occur to Kenna that she'd referred to their wagon as home until she and Niall were away from the others.

She paused on the threshold of the tiny space and stared at it with a new appreciation. It wasn't luxurious, but it was comfortable. It held little trinkets and mementos that they'd collected along the way. Kenna ran her fingers over a little wooden figure of two doves flying with their wings touching. It was carved from pine, smoothed and polished until it shined wherever the light hit it. She remembered the old man who handed it to her after one of their recent performances. His head had barely a wisp of hair on top of it, and his smile was missing several teeth. He was unable to speak, except for a few slurred and indistinct words, but he'd nodded with delight as he pushed it into her hand. Then he gestured between her and Niall, placing his hand over his heart. His daughter explained that he lost his wife the winter before, and that they reminded him of the bond he'd shared with her.

The memory brought tears to Kenna's eyes. She looked at Niall as he bent to lift a crate and carry it outside. Their home; that's what this place was. She wasn't even sure when it changed from a temporary shelter, to the place her heart longed for.

"What's the matter?" Niall asked, catching her eye as he carried the crate past her.

Kenna shook her head and put the birds down. "Nothing. I must be tired."

Niall set his burden down and returned to her. "Then rest, Kenna. I can finish this. The bed is cleared if you'd like to lay down for a bit before supper."

"No, I'm fine," she said and cleared her throat in an attempt to dislodge the lump that seemed embedded there. She looked away quickly, knowing that the expression on her face would make Niall worry more. But that response felt just as transparent. She turned back to him and searched his face, looking for something, but not knowing what it was.

On an impulse, she reached up and cupped his cheek. He was far from the perfectly polished young man she'd met nearly six months ago. His hair was a bit longer, his face now sporting a few days' stubble. Yet, those eyes were the same deep cerulean that caught her attention on the day they met. She smiled softly, remembering how awkward that encounter had been.

"Are you certain everything is all right?" Niall asked gently. He placed his hand over hers and frowned with concern.

Kenna stared up at him and a wave of understanding washed over her. *Home isn't a place at all. It's the people who surround you.* "I am, Niall. I truly am."

"Shall we finish unpacking, then?" He asked. Niall's fingers curled around her hand and he slowly pulled it away from his face. His eyes held hers for a few seconds more before he looked away. "I'm told the welcoming celebration is not to be missed."

Kenna swallowed and blinked a few times. The change in mood was sudden, and she could have sworn there was more Niall wanted to say. She wanted to pursue it, to push him to speak, but there was too much to be done. That was what she told herself at any rate. The truth was that she feared the connection was a figment of her imagination, and she didn't want to destroy the illusion; she needed it.

There was no hunt for their dinner that night. The villagers knew the caravan would arrive soon and had set aside enough food to feed a small army a generous banquet. The atmosphere was always lively and joyful among the travelers, but this evening was even more so. Old friends and distant relations sat around one enormous bonfire, catching up with stories of the past year, exchanging little gifts and trinkets that were saved for this reunion. It was like a holiday that came once a year and was eagerly anticipated when the day drew near. Kenna and Niall were as welcomed as the rest, though there were no gifts waiting for them.

Daris and Elize sat with Brenin and his wife, fawning over the newest member of the family with open delight. Yet, when the two of them were asked about their own plans for parenthood they laughed the question off, and insisted that there was plenty of time for that. It wasn't surprising really, anyone who watched them practice their flips and lifts could see that they loved what they did, and loved the closeness it lent to their marriage. A child would mean more changes than just a mouth to feed.

In an obvious attempt to divert the attention from herself, Elize's eyes fixed on Kenna and lit up. "Kenna, would you like to hold the baby?"

Kenna smiled and nodded, happy to take the focus from her friend if needed. She was fifteen years older than her youngest sister and missed the small cuddles she used to receive from Tia. "Of course, if the little one doesn't object to being passed to all and sundry."

"Oh, she's got a full belly and a clean nappy. I'm sure she won't object," Rowan said. She crossed to Kenna and settled the little bundle in her arms.

Kenna looked down at the baby girl with a smile, imagining what it would be like to hold her own child and wondering what that child would look like. The image of a little face with dark hair that curled at the ends, and blue eyes that sparkled like Niall's flashed through Kenna's mind. She'd known that she would likely bear children one day, but until now she'd never imagined what those children might look like.

"You seem very comfortable with babies," Niall commented quietly. "I'd be terrified to drop it or some other disastrous thing."

"Oh, it's really not that difficult," Kenna replied. She shifted the baby to pass it to her husband. "Here, hold her, and you'll see."

"No, that's not—I shouldn't. I might break it—er—her." Niall's eyes went wide and he shook his head. The look of panic on his face was enough to make Kenna laugh out loud.

"Niall, she's a baby, not a glass vase," Daris teased.

"You won't harm her," Kenna reassured him. She moved closer and slipped the sleeping infant into his arms. "Now, support her head and try to relax. If you're tense, you'll make the baby feel unsafe and she'll cry."

Niall visibly forced his shoulders to relax, but his arms were still rigid. Kenna gently moved them into a more natural position to cradle the baby. She touched Ellia's fuzzy head and smiled at Niall. "See, just like that. She's content and sleeping."

"She is, isn't she?" Niall said with no small amount of wonder in his voice. He shifted a little so that he could tentatively touch the infant's hand with one finger. Ellia sighed and her own tiny fingers wrapped around his. Niall let out a nervous, but obviously delighted chuckle. "I think she likes me."

Something in Kenna broke. Her heart seemed to expand and caused her entire chest to ache with each beat. She took a long draught from her ceramic mug, using it to hide until she could find her center again. By the time she managed it, the vessel was completely drained of ale. Kenna pulled the cup from her lips and smiled just as she would have done if there was a misstep during a performance.

She wanted to be alone, but a sudden departure would garner more attention than she liked. So, Kenna stayed, she listened to the music played, and the stories being shared. She laughed when someone told a joke and pretended for all the world as though everything was completely well and good. It wasn't all an act, and it was impossible not to feel uplifted in the presence of such warmth, but it was a relief when the instruments were put away and people said their farewells for the night.

There were still a few stragglers outside when Niall closed the wagon door behind them. Kenna could hear their neighbors talking and occasionally laughing. She stood in the center of their isolated space with her back to Niall as he lit a lantern filling the room with a soft golden light. Kenna looked around at all the little pieces of the life they'd built together. It was comfortable and perfect.

"I don't want to lose this," Kenna murmured. She wasn't certain whether she was speaking to Niall or to herself. She covered her face with her hands and closed her eyes to block out the sight of all the things she would soon be leaving behind

"What?" Niall was next to her in an instant. He pulled her close and stroked her hair. "What's wrong, Kenna? What do you mean?"

She turned in his arms and looked up at him. "I don't want to walk away from this."

"You want to spend the rest of your life in a rickety old wagon, performing on the streets?" Niall asked, clearly confused. "Don't you want to go home? To let your family know you're alive and safe?"

"I'm not talking about being a performer. It doesn't matter where we are. *You* are my home, Niall! *You're* my family." Kenna replied quickly. "I know you're worried that your presence will endanger these people, but why does going back to Arthan have to be goodbye for us?"

Niall looked down sadly. "You said your parents would push for the marriage to be annulled."

"That's all changed now. They'd never ask me to walk away from a life with the man I love." The words tumbled out of Kenna as though they had a will of their own. "Niall, I don't care where we live, or what we do in this life. I just want to be with you."

Niall stared at her wordlessly. He searched her face, and his fingers flexed slightly where they rested on her back. "Are you saying you love me?"

Kenna suddenly felt nervous. She looked down and started speaking again, afraid he would say he didn't return her feelings. "I'm sorry, I know this isn't what we planned. I know you think—"

Quickly, he moved his hand to lift her chin so she was looking into his eyes, surprising Kenna and interrupting her rambling. He was smiling softly. "I need to hear it again, so that I know it wasn't just my ears playing tricks on my heart."

"I love you, Niall," Kenna replied. She met his eyes and repeated it for a third time. "I love you, and I want to spend the rest of my life with you."

Niall closed his eyes and leaned his forehead against hers. "I love you too, Kenna. I love you with all my soul."

"Then you wish to remain my husband?" Kenna's heart felt like it was beating with such speed that she could have sworn it sprouted wings and was attempting to fly away.

"Until I draw my last breath," Niall replied, opening his eyes. His hands slid down to the small of her back and he pulled her closer still.

They had kissed before, but not since their wedding night, and not without the weight of marital obligations hanging over them. Now, as the little space between them vanished, obligation was replaced by undeniable need. Lips parted, and they tasted one another hungrily. It stole Kenna's breath and sent the room spinning. Her feet no longer felt like they were touching the floor. Months of trust and yearning were set loose in that one embrace. The world narrowed to the taste of Niall's lips, the way her skin tingled wherever he touched, the warmth of his breath against her neck when he kissed beneath her ear.

"Kenna?" Niall's voice held a note of desperation when he pulled back. He looked torn between desire and concern for her. "I won't push you to—"

"I want to be your wife, Niall." Kenna replied. She reached for the ties at the neck of his shirt. "In all ways, my love."

Niall took a shaky breath, then leaned in to kiss her again. He guided her toward the bed, hands exploring the curves of her waist and hips. Their lips continued their exploration as they approached the bed. And yet, Kenna could tell that he was still holding back, giving her time to stop things if she changed her mind. She wouldn't, there was nothing as important to her right now as being with him. She longed for it with an urgency she'd never experienced before, and she was tired of holding back for the sake of duty.

It only took a few steps to reach the bed. They stopped kissing and Niall's hands fell to the sash at her waist, she could feel them shaking as they began to pull the fabric. Kenna began tugging his shirt from the waist of his britches. She needed to be closer to him, to touch without the intrusion of clothing.

Niall fumbled clumsily with the knot that held the sash in place. He let out a nervous, breathy laugh. "I never realized how complicated your clothes are."

Kenna exhaled and forced her mind to focus through the desperate haze. She tore her attention away from her husband and managed to untangle the knot and cast the sash aside. She kissed his palm and placed his hand on the ribbons at the collar of her chemise.

Niall hesitated. He looked down at Kenna with an expression of pure adoration before he slowly loosed the bindings. Kenna closed her eyes when the fabric fell from her shoulders and Niall smoothed his hands over her skin. The touch was light as a feather, but it was filled with such tenderness that it made Kenna's knees wobble. Niall was quiet, his fingers still shaking where they rested. Kenna opened her eyes and looked up at him again

"I love you, Kenna," he whispered with overwhelming sincerity.

Kenna sat on the bed and pulled her husband to her. "I love you too, Niall."

He joined her, but still seemed to hesitate. Kenna lifted her head and pressed her lips to his to reassure him that this was what she wanted. Niall's arms wrapped around her lovingly. With slow, tender care they finally gave into a need that had been building since the day they met. Their bodies fell into a rhythm that thrummed perfectly between them until there was no thought, only sensation, only the touch of the other.

Later, when the immediate need was sated, and they'd recovered enough to pull the blankets over themselves, Kenna lay with her head pillowed on Niall's chest. He had one arm wrapped around her and his fingers gently stroked her side. It was the most content Kenna could recall ever feeling. He was hers, and she was completely his.

"Is it always like that?" She asked as she listened to the steady beat of his heart. "Between a man and woman, I mean. Or is it different when you're in love?"

"What makes you think I know?" Niall huffed out a little laugh.

"Well, I just—your brother told me that he had been with women before. I assumed that being at court, you had..." Kenna let her words trail off.

"It's true, many at court slip in and out of bedchambers without exchanging vows." Niall blushed a little and smiled with endearing shyness. "But I was never comfortable with such casual dalliances."

"Then I'm the only woman you've been with?" Kenna propped herself up to look at her husband. She would have understood if he'd been with another, but it pleased her to think she was the only person he'd shared such an intimate experience with.

"And the only one I'll ever be with," Niall replied sweetly. He lifted his head off the pillow to give her a quick kiss. Then he laughed giddily. "I don't think I've ever been so happy. Why did we wait so long to admit how we feel?"

"I have no idea." Kenna laughed and ran her fingers through the hair at his temple. "But now that we have there's no going back. I fear we're stuck with one another." Niall laughed and pulled her in for a deep and encouraging kiss.

They didn't sleep much that night. Having fully embraced their marriage and the bond between them, it was impossible to resist the urge to touch and be touched. There were months of missed opportunities to make up for, and they set to the task with enthusiasm. When they finally did sleep, it was entwined in one another's arms and skin to skin.

* * *

Whether it was the fact that they were not traveling the next day, or that Kenna and Niall hadn't been as discreet as decorum might have called for, there was no knock at the door to wake them the next morning. Kenna drifted back to consciousness happily wrapped in her husband's arms, just as she had fallen asleep. Niall was already awake, but he was apparently content to remain right where he was for as long as they were allowed to do so.

Eventually, they found the willpower to get out of bed and put clothes on, but it was midmorning before they stepped out of the wagon and into the presence of others. They couldn't keep the smiles from their faces or the twinkle from their eyes. Even surrounded by people, they were unable to resist touching. They had long been physically affectionate with one another, but this was a new level of intimacy, and it demanded more. Discreet kisses were stolen whenever the opportunity arose. Kenna felt like she was glowing with happiness, everything looked more beautiful than the day before.

"My, but the two of you are in good moods. Did you have a restful night?" Elize asked when Kenna and Niall showed up to look into breakfast. "I know I hardly slept a wink. The wildlife was quite vocal last night."

"Indeed, I wondered if things would ever settle down," Daris commented dryly.

"I feel quite refreshed actually," Niall said. He filled a bowl with porridge and passed it to Kenna. He smiled intimately when Kenna's fingers brushed his. "Famished, but refreshed. How about you, my darling?"

"Same," Kenna replied, though she could feel the blush rising to her cheeks. Not that it mattered. She was too happy to be truly embarrassed. "So, what do we do when we're not driving from dawn to dusk?"

"Very well, we'll change the subject." Elize shook her head with a knowing smile. She leaned in close to Kenna and whispered. "But don't think you'll get out of sharing the details later."

Kenna gave her a playful nudge and turned a shade pinker.

"The first day of our stay we usually check all of the wagons and equipment for any repairs or replacements that might need attention," Daris explained. He seemed willing enough to move on to another topic, and Kenna wasn't going to object. "Everything is thoroughly cleaned and made as ready as possible for the return to our winter village after the harvest is complete."

"We'll be here for close to a month before all is said and done," Elize added. "There's a big trading post a few hours' ride from here. You and Niall should be able to make arrangements for your travel plans there. I'm sure there's a merchant or two who trade in Arthan as well. With what you've saved you'll be able to pay for passage with one of them."

"I knew there was a trading post in the area!" Niall stated triumphantly. "It must have been further down the river than I thought."

"Then we're right back to where we started. It's probably the safest way for us to get to Arthan," Kenna replied. The day suddenly seemed a little dimmer. The affection she felt for their new community ran deep and leaving them would be almost as difficult as leaving her brothers and sisters. It had to be done though, her family surely thought she'd perished in the attack, they'd be suffering from that loss, and she couldn't leave them to that grief.

"How soon can we go there?" Niall asked.

"Anytime, but you should see to the cleaning and repair of your wagon," Daris replied. "You could pay for the repairs, but it would make booking passage to Arthan more difficult without the full amount you've raised from your performances."

Niall nodded and looked at Kenna. "I think it's only right to stay long enough to make sure everything is as it was when we arrived. We won't leave until we can do so properly."

"It truly is the least we can do. In fact, it's really only fair that we stay and help with the harvest as well," Kenna commented quickly. They needed to get to Arthan as soon as possible, but they owed much to the travelers. It was easy to justify spending a few more weeks with them. The fact that it delayed a difficult parting was an added bonus; one Kenna was all too happy to embrace.

Niall took a bite of his breakfast and nodded. "I'm going to have to agree with my wife. It would be very poor manners for us to leave before all the work is done."

Daris and Elize exchanged grins. Then Daris shrugged and tried to look casual, though his eyes were gleaming playfully. "Well, if you think you ought to. No one would have said anything, but it likely would have left a bitter taste in the mouth if you departed early."

"Oh, do shut up," Elize laughed and grabbed Kenna and Niall in turn, giving each a sound hugging. "You two can stay as long as you like. Forever, if you choose."

Kenna took a deep and contented breath. With a few more weeks in the company of friends to look forward to, she was able to focus entirely on the blissful change in her relationship with Niall. She glanced at him with an intimate smile. What had started as a union of necessity was now a true binding of souls. Every minute spent together was precious and not to be wasted.

In those first weeks they were barely able to accomplish anything. There were always reasons to sneak off to be alone. If water was needed there was a pond nearby and it would be best if they both went to ensure they could carry enough back to see to all the chores. It only made sense that they should bathe while there. They often made excuses at meal times, claiming to be too tired from the day's work to stay and partake of the shared dinner. They'd grab some bread and cheese then hurry back to their wagon hand-in-hand, grinning like the lovesick fools that they were. Lovemaking was the new and exciting activity, and it was difficult to be apart. For the first time in her life, Kenna was in love.

Three weeks after their arrival in Brittendell the harvest was nearly done. Kenna and Niall were forced to turn their minds toward preparations for the trek over the mountains to the dunes of Arthan. That morning, they rose early to begin work on their wagon before heading to the fields. Kenna finished her breakfast, then turned her attention to begin cleaning their home from top to bottom. She vowed to herself that once she returned to her family, she would see to it that every member of the traveling troupe was gifted with the finest Arthan silk that money could buy. The richness of the colors would make them stand above any of the other troupes and yield greater contributions from the crowds in the larger cities.

She smiled to herself, thinking of the welcome her friends would receive if they approached the City of the Blessed in costumes made from such luxurious cloth. Still pleased by the idea, Kenna pulled Niall's old shirt out of its compartment near the door to pack it safely away for their journey. She understood why he hesitated to get rid of it. If her own home had been destroyed, she would cling to anything that remained.

As she lifted the shirt, something slipped from the pocket and landed on the wooden floor with a muted thud. The High Lord's ring lay on the planks, beside a folded square of blood-stained fabric. Kenna picked the ring up and smoothed the soiled cloth to rewrap the jewelry. She was about to fold it back into place when something caught her eye. Elegant words, which must have been gold once, were woven into the worn silk. One word in particular stood out before all the others: "King."

She poured water into their washbasin and scrubbed at the stained cloth until it was no longer stiff with old, dried blood. Despite the rusty smudges, the words themselves were as bright and clear as if they'd been written that day. They glittered up at Kenna and turned the world upside down.

CHAPTER 14

The Heir

Niall and Daris walked around the wagon, inspecting it for signs of wear and taking an inventory of the repairs that needed to be done. Much of what was required could be found within the village, but Niall wanted to leave everything in pristine condition when they said their goodbyes. In a few days he and Daris would ride to the trading post to arrange passage, and Niall hoped to purchase paint to give the wagon a fresh new coat before he returned it to its owner.

Even with all the concerns that Niall had to contend with he couldn't stop smiling, and didn't think he ever would. Kenna loved him and he loved her. Somehow, in the midst of all the terrible things that had happened over the past four months, their hearts had found one another, had joined and become one heart that beat for both. That, or Kenna had simply taken his. If so, Niall was all too happy to leave it in her tender keeping.

"I swear to the gods, the two of you are worse than Elize and me," Daris said impatiently. "Have you even been listening to a word I've said in the past ten minutes?"

"No one is worse than you and Elize," Niall shot back. His smile broadened. "But I'm certainly willing to challenge your title of most sickeningly sweet couple in the camp."

Daris rolled his eyes. "Well, do you think you can take a break from that long enough to have a look at this wheel? Several of the spokes appear to be cracked."

"It must have been that road outside Thistlewick," Niall said after crouching down for a closer inspection. "It was so washed out after the storm I thought the wagon might come apart before we got over it. I think that wheel is going to need to be replaced entirely." He straightened up and dusted his knees off. "I'll have to take that out of what we've saved for passage to Arthan. I hope it doesn't cut too deeply."

"Rowan's father might be able to help. He replaced a wheel for me last summer in exchange for a day's labor," Daris suggested. "I could look into it if you like.'

"Please do. I didn't anticipate half the costs we've run into with these repairs," Niall admitted. No one was insisting they handle the work, but he didn't want to leave the caravan with any extra burdens, even if some of the damage had happened before they started using the wagon.

"You could just stay with us, you know. Purchase the wagon outright and finish the repairs when we winter over."

"Or I could buy the wagon, and you and Elize could come to Arthan with us. Then we could just pack up and head off together." Niall smiled and clapped his friend on the back before moving to examine the wagon further.

Daris cocked his head to the side and frowned thoughtfully. "What if we did?"

"What if you came to Arthan with us?" Niall turned from the wagon slowly. "I was only joking, Daris. I don't expect you to give up the life you love just so that we don't have to part ways."

"Elize and I like adventure and being on the move. Neither of us have ever been to Arthan. Traveling to new places sounds pretty adventurous to me," Daris said with a shrug.

"And you think Elize would agree to that?" Niall asked. The idea was a happy one, but he didn't want to get his hopes up and be disappointed if Daris was speaking out of turn.

"I can't say for certain until I discuss it with her, but I think she might," Daris answered. He was smiling broadly now, and Niall could tell that there were plans already taking form in his mind.

They finished their inspection quickly. Daris was eager to run the idea past Elize, and Niall was just as anxious to discuss it with Kenna. He considered waiting until after Daris and Elize spoke but decided it would be better to bring it up right away. Kenna would be able to inform the conversation and alert them to any impediment if Daris and Elize did decide to come along.

Excited to share this new possibility, Niall practically hopped up the steps to their home. He closed the door behind him and then turned to Kenna. His smile faded and enthusiasm quickly shifted to concern when he saw her. She was staring down at the unfolded cloth on her lap. When she looked up at Niall, the frown she bore sent chills down his spine.

"Have you read this?" Kenna asked, and held the cloth up. It was wet, as if she'd tried to clean it. Still stained dark with the blood of Niall's father, spidery lines of gold now caught the light.

Niall shook his head, stepping closer. "I didn't know it said anything. I've only ever had it out at night."

"Niall, you need to read it," Kenna said in a tone that carried weight and worry. She held it out to him with such solemnity that Niall felt the ridiculous urge to push it away. She pressed it into his hand gently. "You need to know what it says."

Niall looked down at the damp rag in his upturned palm. Even before he read the message, he could see that the words were imprinted on the fabric by magic. Only a message inscribed by wizard's writ could retain such shine after months of being soiled, and only the King would have conveyed a message in this manner. Niall's hands began to shake as his eyes scanned the extraordinary document. He had to look it over twice, and then read it aloud before the words truly sank in.

"I, King Fergal, first King of Venallis and uniter of the factions, having no heirs of my own, do name Niall, son of the right and High Lord Edan, my heir and successor to the throne of this kingdom so newly formed. It is my final command that upon my death he be crowned the next King of Venallis."

Niall took a couple of steps forward and sank onto the bed beside Kenna. He clung to the proclamation of his ascension with cold, numb fingers that could no longer feel the object they clutched. There were so many thoughts vying for dominance in his mind that it was a senseless and chaotic clamor.

"Niall?" Kenna was staring at him. Her hand was on his, but even the warmth of her touch couldn't break through his shock. "This is a Royal decree. You are the rightful King of Venallis."

Her words jolted Niall out of his stupor. He dropped the cloth and kicked it away, as if doing so could change the command issued. Memories and suspicions locked in place and ordered themselves into a perfect, terrible tapestry of understanding: the arrival of the King's messenger the very night that his family was obliterated. All that death, all the pain and destruction, wasn't the result of a marriage alliance with the Rihtall. *It was my own closeness to King Fergal that destroyed my family.* Niall took a shuddering breath. "This is why my home was attacked. My family is gone because the King named me heir to the throne."

"Don't say that, Niall. Their deaths are on those who executed the attack and no other." Kenna moved to comfort him. She held Niall tightly, and he wondered if her small, delicate arms were all that kept him from flying apart. Her lips were close to his ears when she spoke again. "You would not allow me to put the blame on myself, and I won't allow you to do it either. You had no power over the decisions of the King. You did not bring this on your loved ones."

Niall tried to let her words ease the strangling hold of guilt and panic, but the storm inside was too strong to allow her comfort and reassurances to take root. He'd worked so hard to impress King Fergal, to win his favor and be granted the means to build his own life and fortune. Ian had commented on it once, worrying that Niall was reaching too high, too fast.

But this? The crown was never something I thought to reach for. All I wanted was a way to step out of my place as a second son. I wanted to forge a path for myself.

"No. No, I don't want it." He shook away from Kenna and bent to pick the order up. "We need to destroy this. Now, before anyone else sees it."

"Niall, this holds a King's command," Kenna insisted. "We can't just throw it into the fire and pretend it never existed."

"That is exactly what we must do," Niall replied with urgency verging on panic. "Dempsey has already been crowned King. If anyone else learns of this they could use it to challenge his reign. All it would take is one person discovering I survived, and our lives, along with any children we have, anyone who protected us, could be considered a danger to the current King."

Kenna sat quietly, but Niall could see that his words made an impact. She started to shake her head with a distant expression on her face. "Is it even safe to return to Arthan? If someone discovered you were King Fergal's chosen heir it could put my family at odds with the Venallian throne. To protect us could be considered an act of aggression."

"I'm not certain we have another option. I suspect Dempsey already knows I was named heir. Staying in Venallis would put us in constant danger," Niall stated solemnly. He wrapped his arms around Kenna and held on tightly, needing to have her close. "The details of the attack don't make any sense if the Stratham were the only ones to blame. There should have been some kind of warning. How were they able to enter Venallis undetected, with a host big enough to destroy an entire household?"

"I've wondered that as well," Kenna admitted, nestling closer to him.

Niall bowed his head, resting his cheek against Kenna's hair. His family deserved justice. He had no proof to support his theory, just a feeling that wouldn't go away, and the knowledge of how cutthroat ambition could make those at court behave. *Even with proof that Dempsey had a hand in the attack on Britwylde, who would stand against a King?*

Kenna laid a hand on his back and rubbed in comforting circles. Niall took a deep breath and focused on the sensation of her touch. With each circle, he imagined another one of his disordered thoughts being folded up and placed on a shelf. He'd used this method on the most hectic days of working in King Fergal's service. It always helped him to put the chaos into perspective and prioritize what needed to be done.

"Talk to me, love," Kenna murmured gently. "Let me share this burden with you."

Niall exhaled slowly as one thought solidified and took priority over the others. "I think I need to go back to Britwylde. Whether I'm right, or just paranoid, we need to know the truth before we can decide how to move forward."

"It's been almost half a year. If there was any evidence to point the finger at the King, I doubt it's still there. And what will you do if you find proof of Dempsey's guilt?" Kenna asked.

"Truthfully, I haven't the slightest idea. I just need to know the truth," Niall admitted. "My family's home is half a day's ride from here. If I leave early, I can be there by midday, search the grounds thoroughly, and be back the day after."

Kenna was silent. Her hand stilled for a second, and then started up again, slower. "Niall, what if no one ever came to—to see to the remains?"

Niall answered cautiously. "That's why I think it would be better if I went alone." The thought had occurred to him as well, and he couldn't abide the idea of putting Kenna through something so gruesome. Such sights would plague a person for a lifetime. "If they've been left to the elements, I'll do what I can for them."

"You shouldn't have to face that on your own, Niall," she countered, pulling away. He could hear the trepidation in her voice. "I don't even want to think of what things might be like there, but I won't abandon you now."

Niall took a deep breath and looked at his wife. He kissed her forehead and took both her hands in his. "I know, Kenna. But I'd rather only one of us carry that sort of nightmare through life. I can do this. You need not suffer as well."

"Take Daris, at least," Kenna replied after a time of quiet contemplation. "He knows the truth, and you know he'll do what he can to help."

"I'll speak to him," Niall nodded. Tension settled like a rock in his stomach. *This will not be a happy homecoming. I have to face the past to protect the future.*

A strange conflict warred within him. He hoped that he was wrong about Dempsey, that the new King didn't have anything to do with the massacre, and at least that much of his former life could be undefiled.

However, if Dempsey was guilty, it gave a face and a name to the monster.

Deep in his heart, Niall knew that knowledge would bring a new dilemma. *If I find the answers I seek, what will I to do with that knowledge? Can I walk away and leave the future of the entire kingdom in the hands of someone capable of such heinous deeds?*

Niall wasn't sure he even had a choice, but it was enough to stay his hand when he went to throw the evidence of his claim in the fire.

* * *

There were still stars in the sky, and no more than a hint of the dawn on the eastern horizon when Niall, Daris, and Brenin rode out of Brittendell. There had been no hesitation from Daris when Niall revealed what he'd learned. The traveling man was not familiar with the intricacies of court politics, but he understood the danger without having it explained. Daris also understood the importance of justice and closure, a sentiment shared by his brother. Most importantly, Daris understood the loyalty of friendship.

By the time the sun was fully in the sky, Niall was looking at the familiar landmarks of his childhood. The towers from his family estate could be seen over the trees long before the damaged husk of the rest of it came into view. From afar, those towers looked almost normal. The scorched stone and broken windows were not easily spotted, and aside from the absence of flags bearing the family crest, it was easy to imagine all was well. But as they drew near, any illusions Niall might have entertained were shattered completely.

The fields were overgrown and untended. The road leading to the main gate was void of human life. Baskets, pottery, broken crates, and other items too battered to identify were scattered near the gate, and throughout the courtyard. The castle walls still stood upright, but only blackened beams and rubble remained of the wooden outer buildings. Without looking too closely, Niall could see what appeared to be the charred skeletons of animals in the stable debris. He didn't allow himself to linger on the sight long enough to confirm what a quick glance suggested.

Niall felt bile rising in his throat as he reined his borrowed horse to a halt in the middle of the ruined courtyard. Though bereft of human life, the echoes of existence reverberated in Niall's ears. Even on the quietest days in his memory, this space had been full of activity and noise. Horses would whinny as they turned circles in their stalls, dogs barked, and servants chattered back and forth as they went about their daily duties. He could almost hear Brona scolding one of the kitchen boys for stealing sweets or spilling a pail of milk.

Pain and grief rolled over Niall like an avalanche. There'd been a level of blissful deniability while he and Kenna were with the caravan. Reality came crashing back down on him now. This was all that remained of a home that was once filled with warmth, love, and life. Niall had taken this once beautiful place for granted. He'd longed for the freedom to strike out in the world and discover all the possibilities of the people and places around him. Now he would give anything for one more hour in the sweet comfort of his childhood home.

"Do you need a moment?" Daris asked, putting a hand on Niall's shoulder. "Brenin and I can take a look around if you'd like to be alone."

Niall closed his eyes and shook his head. He took a few deep breaths and swallowed against the sickness and the choking lump in his throat before he could form words. "I just want to get this over with, but thank you for offering."

"Brenin said some of the villagers were brought in to help with the burials," Daris replied. "At least you know they weren't left unattended."

"Do you know where my parents were buried?" Niall's voice was rough, though he was trying to keep it steady. Maintaining even the smallest semblance of composure felt critical if he was to get through the task that lay before him.

"Most of the bodies were too badly—" Brenin gave him an apologetic look. "I'm sorry. Those left after the fires finished burning were too damaged to put names to. We buried the few bearing signs of possible nobility in the family burial grounds with unnamed markers. It was the best we could do for them."

"Thank you for that," Niall sniffed. "It was a kindness, and more than anyone should have to carry out."

"The High Lord was loved and respected by his tenants. We wanted to honor him, and the rest of those who were lost that day," Brenin inclined his head. He looked almost as uncomfortable to be there as Niall felt. When they'd revealed Niall's identity to Daris' brother, the younger man had admitted to having pieced it together the evening of the caravan's arrival. "If High Lord—King Dempsey had allowed, we would have held a proper memorial, but he was eager to be away after paying for the release of his son."

"Cathal survived?" Niall felt a cold chill run through his veins. He caught Daris' eye, remembering their conversation the night he revealed his identity. It wasn't hard evidence, but Cathal's possible death was one of the few things that kept doubt in Niall's mind. "And Dempsey himself came to negotiate the terms? He didn't send a representative?"

"Yes, he arrived a few days after we saw the beacon," Brenin answered slowly. "He was quite distraught and used the gold he'd intended as a wedding gift for you and your wife to buy the freedom of his son."

"Were there any others taken captive?" Niall's contemplation of Dempsey's guilt was stalled by this new information.

Brenin lifted his shoulders in helpless confusion. "He didn't say, and he left as soon as he charged us with seeing to the burials. We're not members of the nobility. It wasn't our place to ask questions of a High Lord. They give us orders, and we follow them."

Niall nodded, and the little glimmer of hope that had started to ignite in his heart sputtered back into darkness.

He stifled the fresh bout of grief and focused on the doors leading into the castle. One was twisted off the top hinge. It leaned awkwardly into the dark entryway, corners burned to a rounded edge and seared black.

The other door was missing entirely. Niall's jaw clenched tight. Dissipating hope turned to anger and resolve.

The sanctuary of his youth was now a bleak and silent tomb. It took every ounce of strength for Niall to cling to that resolve as he climbed the steps and maneuvered around the broken door. To his relief, there was some semblance of care given by the villagers when they searched for the victims of the attack. Much of the floor was cleared, and rubble was ordered in piles rather than strewn haphazardly through the damaged rooms. Despite the orderly efforts, there was evidence that animal and human scavengers had gone through the place as well.

At first Niall took mental stock of the devastation and insult, but he soon abandoned the tally. There was too much, and he'd seen enough of the poor during his travels to know that many were desperate. He couldn't blame those dwelling in poverty for seeking something to aid in their survival. He deliberately avoided the possibility that some might have simply sought riches out of greed. There was enough pain within these walls without adding such heartless contemplation.

The work was slow. Many of the corridors were piled with debris and impossible to pass through. They searched all the rooms that were stable enough to enter and found nothing. Niall's father's study was reduced to a collapsed pit of charcoal and broken stone. Brenin told Niall that they had tried to enter during the initial sweep, but the destruction was too great, and they were forced to abandon their efforts for fear that what little remained of the ceiling would collapse in on them.

Niall broke at last. Tears slid down his cheeks, leaving clean paths through the soot and dust that coated his face. He sank to his knees and dug his fingers into the compacted ash and dirt. "My parents sacrificed themselves here so that Kenna and I could escape."

"As any parent would." It was Brenin who offered comfort, speaking with the voice of a father. "Do not hold yourself to blame. Were I faced with the choice of my life for Ellia's, I would not hesitate to offer myself. They would not wish you to carry guilt for that."

Niall drew a ragged breath and wiped the back of his sleeve across his face. Brenin was a year his junior, but the steady authority and earnestness of his response helped Niall to find enough composure to continue. He pushed himself off the ground and reached for the dagger in his boot. A proper grave was beyond his ability to provide, but he would not let their final resting place remain nameless. He put the blade to the singed walls and painstakingly etched his parents' names into the stone. Under that, he added a verse from a song his father used to sing to his mother.

I float on the breeze
Hapless, asunder
'Til love grounded me
Rooted, yet tender

Time seemed to stand still as Niall worked to honor his parents. It didn't matter to him, that his hand ached with the effort of carving the words into the stone. His parents had died for him and this was the least he could do. When he was done, the three of them stood in silent reverence for the dead. Neither Daris nor Brenin spoke or moved until Niall did. With a final thought of farewell, Niall turned and walked down the hall. There was one more room he wished to see before he left this place and never returned.

The chambers that he'd shared with Kenna so briefly were in better shape than many of the other rooms. Most of the furniture was broken and everything was covered in layers of soot and dirt, but a few small corners remained reasonably unscathed.

Niall sifted through the rubble for anything of Kenna's old life; any small piece that he could bring back to her. He found torn dresses, black and stained from the smoke, crumpled in a trunk that had been ransacked. There were two chalices under the bed that must have been missed by the looters. Niall used a board to draw them out and pushed them into Daris' and Brenin's hands, despite their initial protests. After a thorough cleaning, the chalices would fetch a good price. Niall insisted on offering them this much for their company in carrying out such a sad task.

To Niall's disappointment, he saw nothing that he felt Kenna would wish to have. He was about to leave when something caught his eyes. In the far corner, amidst a pile of debris set aside by the villagers, or piled up by thieves, Niall spied a slip of leather and paper. He hurried across the room and shoved the broken pieces of porcelain and fragments of furniture away. A deep sense of satisfaction and relief replaced the despair that hung over him like a cloud. Laying open on the floor, in miraculously good condition, was the book of poetry Niall gave to Kenna the night he agreed to their betrothal.

Niall picked the book up and gingerly dusted it off. He smoothed the pages down and closed the cover, silently offering thanks to whatever being had spared the little treasure. Without giving an explanation to his companions, Niall tucked the book into the pouch on his belt and left the room. There was nothing more the broken house could offer, but this one small gift represented the most precious part of his life.

They didn't dally in the house much after that. If there had been any evidence to implicate King

Dempsey, it was long gone. It had either been destroyed by the fire or removed by Dempsey himself. The lack of success was disappointing, but finding anything in the wreckage after so many months of neglect was a long shot at best.

It was late afternoon when they stepped out of the castle. Niall placed the book in the safety of one of his saddle packs and then turned to lead his companions around to the back of the estate to wash up and water the horses at the river's edge. It was surprisingly peaceful at the dock. The fire hadn't made it to the pier, and it offered a quiet place to rest and collect themselves after the trials of searching the ruins.

Niall took his boots off and dangled his feet in the water as he'd done with Ian when they were children. He closed his eyes and let the cool, rushing liquid ease away some of the tension of their work. The sunlight filtered through the leaves of a nearby tree, and the birds were singing as sweetly as ever. It seemed as if they were lending their voices to his memories and trying to remind him that all was not sadness.

"Rowan sent a basket of food for our dinner," Brenin was telling Daris. "I'd rather not camp in the shadow of the estate. I swear I can feel the spirits of those who perished. Perhaps we could follow the river and set up camp along the bank. It would make for a nice picnic."

The wind shifted ominously. The shadows of the trees took on a chill, and a song started to echo in Niall's ears. He knew the banshee wasn't there, that the song he heard was only a memory, but it shook something loose in his mind. His eyes snapped open. He reached for his boots and shoved his feet into them regardless of the difficulty wet skin presented.

"A crown of bones! Ian heard the banshee sing of a crown of bones!" Niall stumbled past the other two, ignoring the confused looks on their faces. His mind was racing, flipping through images of a bloody clearing in the woods. "The squire! Cathal's squire was near the bushes!"

"What are you raving about?" Daris asked, chasing after Niall. "Slow down. You're not making any sense."

Niall grabbed his horse's reins and climbed into the saddle. He looked down at his companion. "Ian was trying to tell me something before he died. I thought he was saying that the stag attacked from the bushes, but I think he was trying to warn me that it wasn't the stag at all."

Daris was giving Niall a look that indicated concern for his sanity. He put a hand on Niall's wrist. "I think you should get off the horse and have some water Niall. It's been a difficult day."

"I'm not mad, Daris. Well, I am, but not crazy—angry," Niall shook Daris off. "I think there was more to Ian's death, and he was trying to tell me what happened. I have to go back to where he was attacked. I need to know."

Daris gave Niall a long, hard look before he let out a resigned sigh. He called back to his brother. "Get on your horse, Brenin. There's something else we need to do."

"Thank you," Niall whispered. He relaxed in the saddle and waited for the other two to mount before spurring his horse to a canter.

The site of Ian's accident was less than an hour from the house at a gallop. Aside from Britwylde castle, this small, unassuming clearing at the edge of the woods was the last place Niall had ever planned to revisit. It held too much trauma and had been the first bend in the twisted path he found himself on now. In his heart, broken though it was, he knew that the evidence he was searching for waited there.

Niall urged his horse to a faster gallop when he saw the tree line. He rode as hard as he had when he heard Ian's cry the day of the hunt. The beast that he sat astride now was not as well-bred or as fast as the fine horse that carried him then, but it crossed the grassy field and plunged into the trees as if its tail was on fire. The animal was still legging to a stop when Niall jumped out of the saddle and stumbled to the brambles and shrubbery across the clearing.

It was nearing dusk and the faeries were flitting from branch to branch as Niall burst through the undergrowth. He stopped, looking around the forest and panting. Now that he was here, he realized he had no idea what he was looking for. The fire that pushed him to such haste was beginning to cool.

If there's any hope of finding something, it requires a more methodical approach than tearing through the woods with night approaching.

"The youngest son returns," a strange, musical voice lilted on the wind. A chorus of bell-like laugher jingled through the tree branches surrounding Niall.

A faerie fluttered forward and hovered inches from Niall's face. It was a tiny creature of gold and green light that looked neither male nor female. "Silly boy hasn't even noticed he's disturbed one of our rings."

Niall looked down but saw no indication of a ring. The ground was free of forget-me-nots or toadstools. He gently nudged the little creature away from his face, not foolish enough to risk harming it and bringing the wrath of the forest fae down upon himself. "Stop playing around. I've important business here."

"Of course you do, little King." Yet another faerie approached. It floated by his ear, and whispered in a voice that echoed as if the words were uttered in the deep and hidden caverns of the earth. "You're looking for a crown."

Niall gasped. "What makes you think I seek a crown?"

"Because that is what a King wears." There was a brilliant flash and a million prismatic rainbows arranged themselves into a tall, golden-skinned woman with large wild eyes whose grey irises shifted like moving water. Her sparkling, emerald hair fell past her thighs, unbound and floating in the evening breeze. She was beautiful and terrifying all at once. "It was scrolled in wizard's writ, and only the dust of our kind can seal such words. We are the spirits of nature itself. Whatever our magic touches is known to us and written in the earth. Such truths cannot be denied."

"I don't want the crown," Niall croaked. His mouth was too dry for anything else. He cleared his throat and tried to sound less petrified. "And I don't have time for faerie games."

There was another peel of laughter. "You have all the time we gift to you. This place was defiled by the greed of your kind, stained by the same blood that flows through your veins. We have cleansed it, and in doing so, claimed it."

"I see no signs of your claim," Niall replied.

"Are you certain of that?" The ethereal woman cocked a brow at him. "Look again."

Niall turned slowly, scanning the area with a growing sense of dreadful realization. There was no tiny circle of flowers on the ground, but the trunk of every tree surrounding the clearing was covered in glowing purple mushrooms. Most frightening of all, was the sight of Daris and Brenin standing outside the ring, frozen place.

"Free them!" Niall demanded, turning back to the faerie. "They've done nothing to harm you. They have families waiting for them!"

"We cannot free what is not captive. They have not stepped inside the ring," she responded. "'Tis you who stand within our realm."

Niall felt the blood drain from his face. All of his childhood he'd been warned of the dangers of the wild places of the faeries. He'd always looked before he stepped off the path, always been careful to honor their borders. Now, in his desire for truth, he'd run headlong into one of their gateways.

"Please, don't keep me here. I didn't mean to trespass. I only wish to learn the truth of my brother's death," Niall's tone lost all defiance. The situation was a delicate and dangerous one. "My wife is waiting for me to return. There has been so much loss already, and we only just found one another."

The look the faerie fixed on Niall was surprisingly compassionate, despite the wild power that pulsed from her. "You do not need to fear us, Niall of Britwylde. The blood of your family is in this ground, and the crown of bones must be found." Her eyes darted to a bare patch of earth near Niall's feet. "You will find the answer you seek there."

Niall glanced at the cleared earth, and when he looked up again the woman was gone. The faeries around him had vanished as well, and all that remained was the strange, ghostly sound of their laughter. Niall took a few steadying breaths and willed his legs to stop shaking.

He knelt and started scraping away at the dirt with his bare hands. The hole was no more than an inch or so deep when he caught sight of something dark and unnatural. Niall increased his efforts, pushing soil aside until he saw what was unmistakably a hilt.

"Niall? Dammit, man, where are you?" Daris called out.

"He was here one moment and then vanished," Brenin replied.

Niall ignored them, too intent on his task to bother with an answer. He dug a little deeper, until he could take hold of the hilt and pull it free. The ground gave up its secret with unnatural ease. Niall stood slowly, examining the object in his hand.

"Thank the gods!" Daris ran to him. "Why didn't you answer when we called?"

"My brother was murdered." Niall lifted his hand and held the weapon out for Daris to see. It was a single antler, fitted to a hilt, and sharpened to several deadly points. Daris stared at it speechlessly, and Niall didn't have the heart to offer further explanation. "Let's go. I've found what I was looking for."

CHAPTER 15

The Life We Choose

The wagon felt terribly empty without Niall there to share the space. It wasn't that Kenna was afraid to be alone, she'd just grown used to his quiet presence as she settled in for the night. They'd slept in the same room since their wedding, and in the same bed since joining the caravan. She missed him, and she worried about how seeing the battered remnants of Britwylde would affect him. Just the idea of going back there brought all the pain and fear of that night to the surface.

The sounds of weapons and screams were so vivid in her mind that Kenna could almost swear she was hearing them again. She had to clench her hands into fists to keep them from shaking. After an hour of tossing and turning, Kenna flung the blanket aside and lit a candle.

It's silly that I should be so disturbed just because Niall isn't here. Worry isn't going to help him, and I'll regret the lack of sleep in the morning. What I need is a distraction. Sleep certainly isn't going to happen anytime. I need to work some of this tension off. Lecturing herself seemed to make it easier to push her anxiety aside.

It was well into the night, eliminating archery practice as an option. If the moon were full and the sky unclouded things might have been different, but what little moonlight managed to pierce the cloud cover was sickly, too dim for anything with the bow. All the same, outside seemed more appealing than a wagon that felt uncomfortably empty. Missing Niall brought back the faces of the others she longed to see. Her parents, her siblings, Mairi, even Niall's parents came to mind. The cycle was vicious and not something Kenna wished to indulge.

With a candle in hand, Kenna stepped out into the night. The air was cool but still comfortable, with a slight breeze that carried the earthy musk of nearby rain. Kenna loved the scent. It rarely rained in Arthan, and the smell was different when it did. She couldn't put her finger on what the difference was, but preferred this smell. Perhaps it was the lush foliage that sprang up everywhere. If Arthan was a world of gold and amber, Venallis was made of emerald and sapphire. Both were precious and beautiful, both had a place in her heart, but her heart now belonged to Niall. He was a creature of green fields and sparkling brooks, and she reveled in his world.

She walked barefoot through the pasture, her unshod feet barely making a sound on the soft, moist grass. Even if someone heard her passage, it wouldn't raise any alarms. There was always some measure of activity among the travelers. She loved the lively band of performers, but there were times when she longed for stillness and peace.

A short distance away she could see the shadows of the village houses. Not a single light shone from the windows. The only signs of life came from the few animals that prowled from house to house. A cat crept around a woodpile, and a pair of dogs trotted down the lane. It was comfortable and homey, but the peace did nothing to soothe Kenna's spirits. If anything, it aggravated her disquiet and loneliness. Niall was her home, and he was away looking for evidence to support his theories about the new King of Venallis.

Though she wasn't born to this country, Kenna cared what happened to it. She cared for the well-being of its people. *I never expected to love Venallis as much as Arthan, but I do. Even in my darkest hours this place and its people have provided shelter. What will happen to them if King Dempsey is the killer Niall suspects?*

What bothered Kenna the most was that even in the absence of evidence, the logic was sound. It would have been impossible for the Stratham Vashirat to move a large force through Venallis without detection. Even if there wasn't time for help to come, Britwylde would have had warning of the attack. Kenna didn't know a great deal about the politics of Venallis. She knew the workings of its governing body, and the names of the highest-ranking nobles, but not the moods and attitudes of those in power. *If the man on the throne in Rosehaven was allied with her family's enemies...*

The Stratham sought power and would stop at nothing in their pursuit of it. Any ruler who would ally himself with the likes of them was not to be trusted. She hoped her husband's fears were unfounded.

If Dempsey was a good man, he would likely accept Niall's assurances that he had no interest in the throne. Niall could publicly renounce his claim and, in theory, all would be well. There might be talk when the King made an unpopular decision, but surely that would be as far as it went. However, Kenna had never met the man. She only had Niall's impressions of him to go on, and those seemed to indicate this would not be how King Dempsey would respond.

"Ouch!" A sudden, sharp prick in her right foot forced Kenna to focus. She sat on the ground with a curse and lifted her foot to check the stinging appendage. Upon close inspection she found a nasty-looking thorn embedded in her heel. She'd been foolish to forego shoes. These were not the tiled patios and sandy paths of Arthan, and her feet were not accustomed to going bare.

She pulled the thorn from her flesh with a little wince. The wound wasn't a serious one, but it bled freely. Kenna huffed an infuriated sigh. It would be unwise to continue to wander around with it bare and unbandaged. There was nothing for it but to return to her wagon and tend to the wound, minor though it was. If she wanted to continue her walk it would have to wait until she had shoes on.

Kenna hobbled back through the camp, grumbling to herself as she went. The return to her wagon was a slow trek. Walking while trying to keep the injured part of her foot from touching the ground, and straining to look out for more thorns was a frustrating process. Despite the annoyance, it did give her something practical to focus her worries on. *Gratitude for small blessings, I suppose.*

Walking as awkwardly as she was, Kenna had difficulty shielding her candle from the wind. It wasn't a violent gale, but there was enough power to the gusts that by the time she reached the outer ring of wagons, her candle had sputtered out and she was forced to continue in the dark.

"Is that a dance step among the nobles?" Elize's voice drifted from a small square of illumination shining through the open window of her wagon.

"I stepped on a thorn," Kenna explained. She limped toward her friend's home and met Elize at the door. "I suppose that's what I get for taking a midnight stroll in bare feet." She didn't mention her difficulty sleeping without Niall there. Daris' absence was likely the reason for Elize being awake at such a late hour.

"Well, we can't always take the safest course. Life would lack any excitement if we did," Elize mused as she offered Kenna a hand up the steps and ushered her inside. She directed Kenna to sit on the bed and poured water from the pitcher at the bedside into a shallow bowl.

"I believe I've seen enough excitement over the last few months to fill the rest of my days," Kenna said, accepting the water and a square of clean, cream-colored linen. "I'd be quite content to spend my remaining years in complete boredom."

Elize laughed at that. She seemed as relieved to have company as Kenna felt. "Oh, come now. I've seen your eyes light up on stage. You enjoy a good thrill as much as any person born to a band of travelers."

"No, I'd give it all up for an existence of mundane afternoons and total anonymity," Kenna replied, knowing full well that she'd never last in a world like that. She offered her friend a playful smile. "Well, a few afternoons of boredom at any rate."

"If you even survived that much," Elize teased, then blanched. She shook her head. "I'm sorry, I was only speaking of your impatience with idleness. I know you're in a precarious position, and now I've gone and reminded you of the whole mess."

Kenna reached out to touch her friend's hand reassuringly. "I know, Elize. You needn't worry about it. I'm made of tougher stuff than can be shattered by a few words meant innocently. Besides, we're friends."

"I wish it could stay like this forever. Traveling the countryside and putting on shows together." Elize plopped down onto the bed beside Kenna and tucked one of her feet under her. "This life suits you, and having you around suits me."

"There is something exhilarating about holding an audience in the palm of one's hand," Kenna admitted. She liked performing, she liked moving from place to place and seeing life beyond the confines of the station she was born to. Even though her homeland was less reserved than Venallis, there were still expectations on the behavior and achievements of a daughter of the Vashirat leader.

"Why don't you stay?" Elize asked. "As far as anyone knows, the two of you died in the attack. Surely after all this time it's assumed you're dead. No one would be looking for you, and even if they were, who would think to look for you with us?"

Kenna turned away and pretended to focus on her foot. Despite the initial bleeding, the tiny puncture was hardly more than a pinprick. She set aside the cloth and water with a sigh. "I wish it were that simple. Even if it were, I can't let my family live on thinking I've been killed. It would be cruel, and I won't prolong that suffering."

"I understand, I do. I just—I hate goodbyes," Elize admitted. She stood up and paced steps before turning back. "No matter how things move forward, Daris and I will have to face parting with people we care about. If we stay here and continue on as we were before, then we have to bid the two of you farewell. If we follow you to Arthan, we'll be saying goodbye to everyone here."

"You don't have to do that. I'd love to take you to Arthan and show you all the wonders it offers, but I understand what it's like to leave everything you know behind. I've done it twice already, and when we leave the caravan, I will have done it a third time," Kenna sighed sadly. She was dreading that parting; it made her chest ache to even think of it.

"Still, there is a certain appeal to the idea of leaving everything behind and going to Arthan. I think it was brave of you to embrace all of those changes," Elize looked at Kenna thoughtfully. "And now you've experienced life from so many different perspectives. It's a gift in some ways, though you've paid a steep price for it."

"It's changed how I view things. I feel like a different person than the girl who left her family and moved her life to an entirely new country," Kenna frowned contemplatively. "I wonder if going back to Arthan will be as simple as returning home from a long journey. Will it even feel like home after experiencing so much of the world?"

"It might take a little time, but I think it will. It always takes a few weeks to feel settled when we return to the winter village," Elize reasoned. "Although if I really wanted to give you an informed answer, I'd probably have to broaden my perspective as well."

Kenna smiled, sensing where this was going. "Perhaps an extended stay in a realm you've never been to before? You know, I've always wanted to visit the elves who live on the fire plains of Arthan."

"Fire plains?" The look on Elize's face was comically incredulous. "Are they actually alight with fire?"

"I don't think so," Kenna laughed. "But we'd have to visit them to know for sure." A yawn broke her smile.

It was contagious apparently, for Elize had to hide a yawn of her own behind her hand. "I think we may have to sleep on this, and judging by the name, the place sounds perilous. We should probably let our husbands think they have a voice in the discussion, before we make up our minds and go regardless."

Kenna laughed again. Her conversation with Elize had done much to break the cycle of anxiety that was keeping her awake. She thanked her friend for the water and the conversation, and made for the door. After Kenna accepted a pair of slippers from Elize, they bid each other pleasant dreams and parted ways for the night.

* * *

Kenna and the others were working in the orchards, plucking apples from the trees to be preserved and set aside for the winter. The distant whinny of an approaching horse pulled Kenna's attention from her task. She shielded her eyes from the glare of the sun and exclaimed with relief when she saw the sunlight glinting off her husband's flaxen hair. Delighted, she practically threw her basket of apples to the ground, and picked up her skirts to run down the road to greet her beloved.

"Niall!" She called out as she rushed toward him. It was not yet noon, but the separation of a single night was more than enough for Kenna's taste.

Niall spurred his horse to a canter and spanned the last stretch of road urgently. A few feet remained between them when he stopped the animal to jump from the saddle and wrap Kenna in his arms. He held her tightly, whispering her name and how desperately he'd missed her.

Kenna pulled back and smiled before kissing him enthusiastically. She didn't give a fig for those who might be looking. Niall had returned from what must have been a nightmare to endure. Her night was filled with worry and regret, but it could not compare to what he experienced returning to the ruins of Britwylde. Having him safely returned to her now put the world back in order.

"Gods, I missed you, Kenna," he reiterated, resting his forehead against hers. He closed his eyes and stroked her cheeks gently. "I've lived most of my life without you in it, and now the span of a day and a night apart feels like an eternity."

"I worried for you the entire time. I should have gone along." Kenna laid her head on his shoulder and allowed the familiar scent to fill her nose.

"No, I wouldn't wish that on you. Though it was not as bad as it could have been." Niall stepped back and wrapped his hand around hers, leading her to the side of the horse. He lifted her into the saddle and then climbed up behind her. "The villagers had already buried the bodies they were able to recover. The graves were unmarked, but I placed flowers for Mairi and my parents before we left."

Kenna leaned back against his chest and closed her eyes. She hated to think of their loved ones laying in the cold, hard earth with not even a name to mark the place of their repose. The only solace was that they were not left to the elements and appetites of the wild creatures. She opened her eyes again and turned to look at his face. "And did you find anything to confirm your fears?" She was hoping the answer would be in the negative, but knew from the way his arms tightened around her that Niall had found something.

"Not to implicate the King specifically, but," he paused and drew a shaky breath. "I did find evidence that Ian's death was not the accident it appeared to be. Cathal and his squire were the only people present when my brother was injured. It leaves little room for doubt."

"What do you mean?" Kenna tensed, sitting straighter. She thought back on the day of the hunt, swallowing against the churning tightness in her stomach. "Ian was obviously attacked by the stag. I saw the wounds and the animal that inflicted them myself." She shuddered. Prior to that she'd never witnessed death of that nature, and the damage to Ian's body was horrific.

Niall glanced pointedly at the people bending over their work in the nearby fields. "I think it would be better to discuss this alone in our home. I'd rather not be overheard. There are laws against torturing the nobility, but nothing to protect these people from being pressed for information."

Kenna's uneasiness intensified, but she smiled at the people who came to greet Niall and ask if his business had gone well. It was a perfectly normal day to all of them, with no looming sense of danger to cloud their moods. If she could have traded places with any of them, Kenna would have done so, gladly.

They returned to their wagon and dismounted. Niall removed the saddlebags and set them just inside the door before unsaddling the horse and turning it loose with the others in a fenced swath of grazing land. When the animal was cared for, Niall returned to Kenna and led her inside, closing and locking the door behind them.

"I didn't find anything at the house," he began. "After we finished there, I remembered something Ian tried to tell me when he was injured. I went back to the site and found this."

He reached into his saddlebag and pulled forth a stag's horn fitted to a hilt. The points of the antlers were discolored by deep brownish strains. To Kenna's abject horror, there were still threads from the tunic Ian was wearing the day he died. She gasped and put her hand over her mouth to hold back a scream or illness, she wasn't sure which. Her knees wobbled a little, and she quickly moved to sit on the bed.

"The faeries claimed the area, which I expect is the reason it looks so... fresh," Niall grabbed a rag and wrapped the wretched thing up before stuffing it in the same compartment where he stored his old shirt. "I found it buried in the underbrush near where Cathal's squire was standing. I assume the dying stag we saw that day was felled before Ian ever entered the clearing."

Kenna pulled her hand from her mouth, still shaking with revulsion. "But why would Cathal kill your brother? You were the one named heir. Ian was to inherit the title of High Lord from your father."

"I don't know. Perhaps killing me would have been too obvious. If my father only had one heir it might have swayed King Fergal toward Dempsey's family. Even if Cathal wasn't the one to strike the actual blow, he had to have been there when it happened. He was only a pace or two behind Ian. He knew it was no accident." Niall filled the washbasin and splashed water over his face and hair. When he was finished, he pulled off his shirt and replaced it with a clean one. "Perhaps he thought Ian was the one who would be named by King Fergal. For all I know he would have been, if not for his death."

"I doubt that, Niall. Your brother had no fondness for the court and no interest in pursuing anything beyond his inheritance. I may not have known him long, but that much was obvious. He expressed relief that I had more patience for political matters," Kenna answered thoughtfully. Trying to focus past the emotion helped to steady her nerves. "To be honest, I don't know what to make of this. It does seem Cathal had to have been a part of the whole thing. It lends weight to the idea of King Dempsey's involvement, but it's not proof enough to bring an accusation against a King."

"I'm not going to accuse the King," Niall said firmly. "As you said, it's not enough to bring such charges, and even if it were, no one would back me. I have nothing of value to offer any of the nobles in exchange for support. My family's lands will have been divided among them by now. My return would hardly be welcome. Technically, I'm still a High Lord, but High Lord of nothing more than a burned castle."

"You're the rightful heir to the throne, Niall," Kenna pointed out. She was torn between fear for their safety and concern for the people of Venallis.

Niall laughed mirthlessly. "Yes, but the wishes of a dead King mean little to those who risk the wrath of a living King."

Kenna nibbled her lower lip. While the weapon used against Ian might not be solid evidence of King Dempsey's involvement, it was enough to convince her that they had enemies among the people in power here. She moved to Niall's side, wrapped her arms around her husband's waist to lay her head on his shoulder. "We can't go back to my family. What happened at Britwylde is evidence could happen there if we do."

"I'm sorry. You came to my family in the hopes of preserving yours and it's only created a new threat," he replied, returning the embrace.

"No one could have known this would happen," Kenna said as she tried to keep her tears at bay, not wishing to add them to Niall's burdens. The idea of never seeing her parents or siblings again was unbearable. "I have to find a way to let them know I'm safe, and then we have to go where no one will think to look for us."

Niall didn't provide any empty promises; he didn't point out the risk of sending a letter to her family. Kenna preferred it that way. She knew they faced difficult decisions, but right now she needed to cling to something, and letting her family know she was alive was that last thread that tied her to them. If Niall were not here with her, Kenna knew she'd give up entirely. She nestled closer to him.

They held each other in silence for several minutes before Niall kissed the top of her head and pulled back. His mood seemed to lighten a little. "There was one other thing I found."

"If it's as terrible as that *thing*," she gestured at the direction of the hidden weapon, "I think I'd rather not hear about it until tomorrow."

"Actually, it's something that I hope will please you," Niall replied with a gentle smile. He returned to the saddlebag and opened the other pouch, then turned and pushed something into Kenna's hands.

It took a few seconds for her to realize what she was holding. When she did, it felt like a ray of sunshine had pierced the gloom that clouded her mind. "The book of poetry you gave me! I thought this was lost forever. I was certain it was destroyed by the fires for sure."

"Our bedroom was remarkably unscathed. A few of the pages are torn, and the leather binding is stained by the smoke, unfortunately," he replied, obviously saddened by the damage. "It was one of the few things intact. I looked for any of your jewels or belongings from Arthan, but there was nothing of that nature. I suspect that either the men who attacked took them, or looters got them when they went through the rubble."

"It's perfect, Niall. The first gift you ever gave me." Kenna held the book close to her heart and leaned over to give him a kiss. "Thank you for returning it to me. Now, at least I'll have this, wherever we go from here."

"I love you," Niall whispered to her. He kissed her and then pulled back. Though his happy expression didn't change, there was a downturn at the corner of his lips and a sadness in his eyes that revealed the strain of his return to Britwylde.

Kenna ran her fingers through the hair at his temple. She could see the toll the last day had taken on him, and she hated it. She guided him back to the bed and gently, but firmly, pushed him down onto it. "You should rest. They made do in the fields without you yesterday, they can survive the rest of this day too."

"I wish I could, but there's so much to figure out, and we'll need our portion of the harvest when we leave here." Niall started to get back to his feet. "And I still have to make the journey to the outpost to get everything we need to repair the wag—"

"Niall, you've just returned from the ruins of the home and family you loved. If you will not take the remainder of the day to recover, you should allow yourself a nap at least," Kenna used the same commanding tone her mother did when she would not be dissuaded but preferred her words not become a command. "The midday meal is only an hour away. I'll return to the orchards and come wake you when it's time to eat. You can join the work after, if you feel you must."

He leaned back on the bed, but pulled her toward him. "Or you could stay here, and help me recover in other ways."

"Later, my love, after you've had a nap, and finished the work you're so determined to help with." She gave him what she hoped was a sultry smile and a promise of things to come.

Niall kissed her hand, settling back on the bed. "As my lady commands."

Kenna was tempted to give in then and there, but she exercised restraint for the sake of her husband's rest and bid him pleasant dreams. Even though Niall wasn't at her side when she returned to the orchard, she was able to focus on her task, knowing he was tucked in their bed only a short walk away.

The passage of time stopped dragging, now that Niall was home again. At noon Kenna woke him, and was pleased to see that the brief nap did much to refresh her husband. He was still understandably disquieted by the experience at the estate, but the shadows under his eyes were less pronounced and there was more energy in his gait. After the meal, he joined the other men who toiled in the barley fields, laughing and carrying on as if nothing in the world were wrong.

Kenna could see why King Fergal had chosen Niall to follow in his stead. Despite the pressures he faced, he was able to carry forward and do the work that needed to be done. She felt a surge of pride wash over her as she watched him with the others. *If things hadn't gone so terribly awry, he would have made an excellent King.*

It was already dark by the time the chores were complete and they were able to return to their fires to settle in for the night. Kenna and Niall joined Daris and Elize for the evening repast. Of all the people in their new community, these two were the only ones who knew every complicated detail of the difficulties they faced. It was a relief to have friends they could trust completely. Both Kenna and Niall wanted to enjoy their company for as long as circumstances allowed.

Upon their arrival at the campfire, Daris greeted them with his usual teasing. "By the blessed court of the faeries, they actually showed up on time! I thought after a night apart we'd be waiting at least an hour before we saw the two of you outside of your wagon."

"Pot, meet kettle," Niall shot back laughing. "I can think of at least a dozen occasions over the past months when we were forced to wait on the two of you."

Kenna watched the exchange thoughtfully. She still felt the sadness of their situation, but after so many months of grief she didn't want to feel miserable anymore. She wanted to laugh and connect with their friends, and feel like a person again. *Let sadness have its time when we leave.*

With a resolute nod of the head, Kenna hurried over to join Elize over the cooking pot. "Is there anything you need help with?"

"No, I think I have everything under control." Elize replied, her hands on her hips as she surveyed the small banquet of treats that were awaiting them, or bubbling in the cauldron over the fire. "Besides, Daris and I have something special to announce."

"Oh?" Kenna asked. "Is there a new little acrobat joining your act?"

"No, not that. Daris and I are diligent in ensuring the act remains a duo. There'll be plenty of time for that later," Elize shot her a look of playful reproach.

"Forgive me for suggesting such a thing," Kenna chuckled as she pushed a jug of apple cider into her friend's hands. "Here, a peace offering. The orchard keeper gave it to me in thanks for my help with the picking today." She leaned in close. "I thought it would mix well with that whiskey Daris keeps hidden under the bed."

"How do you know about my whiskey?" Daris asked from across the fire.

Niall put a hand on his friend's shoulder. "Daris, everyone knows about the whiskey. It's the worst kept secret in the entire camp."

"Really darling, under the bed is the most obvious place for something like that," Elize added. "And I agree with Kenna. I think it would go wonderfully with the cider, and be the perfect drink to toast with."

Kenna settled next to her husband, who wrapped an arm around her. It was such a casual gesture, yet so comforting that it warmed Kenna and made her tear up. They'd come so far from the days of their unexpected betrothal. Niall wasn't the husband she'd expected, but he was the man she would have chosen to spend her life with, no matter their current circumstances.

"What are we toasting?" Niall asked.

Daris smiled broadly. "Elize and I have come to a decision." He glanced at his wife with an air of conspiracy. "Do you want to tell them or shall I?"

"Tell us what?" Kenna suspected what the announcement might be, but she was afraid to give it conscious thought.

"We're coming with you to Arthan," Elize blurted out with unabashed glee. "We talked it over—and then talked it over again, and it's what we both want."

Niall and Kenna exchanged a quick look. They hadn't decided where to go specifically, but Arthan was no longer an option. Kenna's heart clenched with regret. Their friends were so excited, and now they would have to be disappointed.

"That's very touching, but we won't be going to Arthan," Niall explained. Then he quickly added. "We aren't staying here either."

"Then where are you going to go?" Daris asked, his enthusiasm visibly deflated.

"We aren't certain of that yet. Probably, to the coast to book passage on one of the trade vessels," Kenna answered. She hated that they had to dampen what their friends expected to be a happy occasion.

"That's a terrible idea," Daris stated bluntly.

"I beg your pardon?" Niall frowned. "What about it is so terrible?"

"Well, for one thing, you'll have to pass Rosehaven to get to a port," Daris pointed out. "And if this King Dempsey is as devious and paranoid as you say he is, don't you think he'll be keeping an eye on every ship that comes in or out of Venallis?"

"I agree with Daris. I don't think you'd be any safer getting out of Venallis that way than you would be going to Arthan." Elize said, quickly supporting her husband's statement.

"Then what do the two of you suggest? You know we can't just stay here," Kenna said. She understood how they must be feeling, but there were only so many options available.

"Of course not, but if you're determined to go across the sea there are better and safer ways to set about doing it," Elize answered matter-of-factly.

Niall looked dubious. "Such as?"

"Well, travel through Venallis would be much safer if you weren't alone, or even with one or two companions," Daris began. Kenna could practically see the thoughts twisting into existence as he spoke. "I believe you when you say Arthan isn't a safe place for you, but it's not the only country that borders Venallis. Why not come with us to the winter village in Wiettan?"

"Because we'd be putting all of you at risk. A small village just inside the Wiettan border isn't much safer than staying here," Niall argued. "We won't bring any more danger down on the people of the caravan than we already have."

"Of course not," Daris replied, as if Niall had misunderstood him entirely. "But no one will be looking for you in a band of traveling entertainers. Our group crosses that border every fall. It won't raise any eyebrows. You can hide inside one of the wagons if we encounter anyone who might cause problems. Once we're over the border the four of us can travel to one of the ports in Wiettan."

"That's perfect," Elize agreed. "The caravan will be leaving here in a little over a week. We always stay to help finish the harvest, and we don't stop for any more performances on the way home. We can use the time to plan, and no one will be the wiser."

Kenna looked at Niall as she balanced out their options. "It does make a certain amount of sense. We'd be safer traveling with them."

"And I can trade that goblet you gave me to buy passage for Elize and myself," Daris chimed in.

"It could be even more of an adventure than going to Arthan," Elize said with a resolute nod. "I've heard the lands across the seas are still governed by the elves. The king of a human realm like Venallis holds no sway there."

"And you're both certain you want to do this? There might not ever be a return trip," Niall's voice was hopeful, despite his words of caution.

"We've already decided that we're throwing our lot in with the two of you. The destination is nothing but a small detail," Elize waved her hand as though they were speaking of something trivial, rather than a life-altering decision.

Daris stood up and offered his hand to Niall. "Besides, a King needs a bodyguard."

Niall jumped to his feet and clamped his hand down on Daris' mouth. "Don't call me that, not even in jest. I want nothing to do with it."

"If you want nothing to do with it, why do you carry the decree with you?" Daris asked after Niall removed his hand. "You could have destroyed it, but you haven't.

Why keep it unless there's some part of you that wants to be King?"

Niall sank back onto the log he'd been sharing with Kenna. When he finally spoke, it was in a steady, but quiet voice. "Fine. I admit there is a part of me that wants it. I worked for years to claim some small portion of the kingdom for myself. I was favored by King Fergal and knew it, but I never dreamed he'd name me his heir."

"Then why not fight for it, Niall?" Elize asked. "Why not claim power for yourself. We live our lives subject to the whims of nobles who are untouched by the struggles we face. You have the opportunity to step outside of that. If you took power for yourself, you could make life better for everyone. You could change the world for the better with a crown on your head."

"That decree cost my family, our servants and their families their lives. It paints a target on my back, on Kenna's back, on anyone who helps us." Niall shook his head vehemently. "No, I will not touch a crown that is formed from the bones of my loved ones."

"The price of such power is too high." Kenna wrapped her arms around Niall. As much as she could see the truth in Elize's words, she knew trying to win Niall the throne would lead to more bloodshed and heartache. "We'll go to Wiettan, and from there we'll make our way across the sea. No one else will suffer for it, Niall."

"If you really think that's the best course," Elize replied. She shook her head, but didn't press her argument further. The mood around the fire grew tense and quiet.

"If that's settled maybe it's time we break into my not-so-secret stash of whiskey," Daris said, his tone carefully cheerful. He rubbed his hands together. "A good drink and a meal among friends is the perfect way to end a long day, don't you think? We've all but spoiled our dinner with doom and gloom, but whiskey is the solution."

"You always think food and whiskey are the solution," Elize laughed. She gave her husband a quick kiss on the cheek and turned to check the pot on the fire. The sense of tension was eased by the time Daris returned with his prized jug of whiskey, and after a few rounds of spiked cider they were beyond the matter entirely and happily discussing the prospect of a sea voyage.

* * *

The next morning Kenna regretted the third mug of cider she'd indulged in. Despite having a full night of deep sleep, she felt drained and a little queasy. Niall wasn't fairing much better, having polished off both the cider and the whiskey with Daris before they ended the evening.

"I don't think I'll ever be able to look at a cup of cider again," he moaned. He pulled on his boots and then let himself fall back onto the bed, his legs still hanging over the edge.

Kenna filled two cups with water and passed one to Niall. She slowly drank the entire cup, hoping it would settle her stomach. "Agreed. In fact, right now I don't think I'll ever want to look at food again either."

"Ugh, don't even mention the stuff," Niall sat back up. He drank his water and then stood, looking a bit green and wobbly on his feet. "Never again. Never—never again."

If she didn't feel so terrible, Kenna would have laughed. As it was, the only thing that held any appeal was going back to bed and sleeping for a week. *Even if*

I did, I think I'd still need a nap afterward. "Come on. Hopefully the fresh air will help."

It was a blessing that the morning was a little cooler than the previous days. The breeze that came up from the river did help alleviate some of Kenna's misery, enough to keep the world from spinning and her stomach from heaving. To her profound annoyance, Daris and Elize seemed perfectly fit when they joined them for the walk to the fields.

"What happened to the two you?" Daris asked, obviously holding back his laughter. "Do they not have whiskey in your fine halls?"

"Oh, you poor dears," Elize hooked her arm through Kenna's. "Don't worry, Dana has a foolproof remedy for this. It tastes horrible, but you'll feel better in no time."

"I feel perfectly fine," Daris chimed in. He had a spring in his step and a bright smile on his face. "I could run back and forth, jump up and down, even swing from limb to limb in a tree."

"Good. Go jump out of a tree and leave us alone." Niall glared at Daris. He leaned over to Kenna, "Remind me never to drink with him again. Ever."

Daris laughed and handed Niall a water flask. "You'll be fine. You didn't have that much to drink last night."

"One day, you will be the one who 'didn't drink that much' and on that day, I'm going to show you the same care and pity you're showing now," Niall grumbled as he took the water from Daris.

"I'll make sure Dana mixes a large batch of her special brew," Elize said, shaking her head.

Their conversation died down as they approached the village. By this hour the men and women of the town were usually hard at work. Today they were gathered round the stone well that stood in the center of the town. Everyone's backs were turned, their focus on something or someone obscured by one of the houses.

Kenna exchanged a puzzled look with Elize. Her curiosity enough to cast aside the physical discomfort. "What do you suppose is going on?" Elize lifted her shoulders in a gesture of bewilderment.

"Let's go around the other side of the house," Daris suggested. "We'll never see anything standing at the back of that crowd."

They picked up their pace, nausea and headaches forgotten for the time being. Kenna could hear someone speaking, but the words were lost on the morning breeze. Yet, there was something about the voice that seemed familiar. The sound filled her with unrest. They'd been with the villagers for nearly a month, and there was something out of place about the manner and tone of the speaker.

The second the four of them rounded the corner everything seemed to slow. They were mere feet from the speaker. He glanced down, suddenly stopped his oration, and gawked at Niall and Kenna in stunned silence. Kenna's eyes shot to her husband's face. It was utterly void of color.

"Lord Niall?" Sir Liam sat atop his horse, staring at them as though he'd seen a pair of ghosts appear out of thin air. "Gods' breath, man! We thought you were dead."

CHAPTER 16

Viper's Nest

With one seemingly innocuous decision, all Niall's hopes for a safe escape were as easily obliterated as his old home. *If we'd only been content to stand at the back of the crowd, Sir Liam would never have seen us. We could have slipped away unnoticed and stayed at the camp until he was gone.*

But face to face with the lesser noble, Niall could do nothing but stare back at him as every eye turned in his direction. The faces of those he'd lived and worked beside over the past months now looked at him with confusion, and in some cases, distrust.

Sir Liam dismounted and took a few steps toward Niall. "There were rumors of sightings, but to be honest, I gave them no credence. Why have you stayed away for so long?"

"I—I was trying to find my way back," Niall lied. His heart was racing. He attempted a smile but couldn't force the numbed muscles in his face to obey.

"You should have sent word to the palace. The King would have arranged for your safe return." Sir Liam studied him, eyes raking over the rough clothing that Niall wore, the garb of a peasant. "You're the High Lord of this region. King Dempsey would have seen that you were afforded all the honor and respect that comes with your title."

"Surely His Majesty has distributed the holdings of that office by now," Niall replied, puzzled. "It's been half a year."

"Yes, but your mother has been managing the estate since your father's tragic death," Sir Liam stated slowly. "That's the reason for my presence. Since my lands border yours, I've been collecting from the tenants on your mother's behalf."

Niall's trepidation was replaced by shock, relief, and a joy so profound that it brought tears to his eyes. His family wasn't as lost as he thought. "My mother is alive?"

"She is, High Lord, and will be as overjoyed as I am to learn of your survival," Sir Liam put a hand on Niall's shoulder. "King Fergal invited her to court after the attack. When he died, King Dempsey insisted that she remain. He feared for her safety anywhere else."

The happiness Niall felt upon hearing of his mother's survival quickly twisted into fear. She was alive, but far from safe. She was in Rosehaven, at the mercy of the very man who he suspected was responsible for all their suffering.

"High Lady Carene is with King Dempsey?" Kenna asked, her voice shaking. She glanced at Niall and gripped his hand tightly. In his shock, Niall barely felt her touch.

"You said there were rumors of my being sighted?" Niall managed to ask, though his throat was starting to feel like it was being squeezed shut. Every word Sir

Liam spoke added another brick to the wall that was closing in around Niall. "Does King Dempsey believe them to be true?"

"His Majesty took great interest whenever the whispers reached court. I believe he hoped they were true. He sent representatives to investigate them," Sir Liam explained. "You must remember that King Fergal and your father were our new King's greatest friends. Losing them both in such a short span of time saddened him greatly. It was only natural that he clung to the idea you might be alive."

Niall's grip on Kenna's hand felt like the only thing keeping the world from falling apart. Dread settled over him like a heavy blanket. Even if they managed to leave Venallis safely, his mother was in the King's grasp. Dempsey may claim that the extended visit was for her safety, but nothing could be further from the truth. She knew who King Fergal named as his heir. That alone put her in danger.

She's bait to bring me in, and a threat he can wield over me if I dare to move against him. She'll be his prisoner for the rest of her life, or until Dempsey's certain I'm no longer a challenge to his power.

There was no choice. Niall had to return to Rosehaven. He would not risk losing his mother a second time, not when he could stop it. There was a slight chance Dempsey could be convinced that he had no designs on the throne and they might be allowed to leave. That outcome was an unlikely one, but attempting it could give him enough time to rescue his mother and slip away from the palace, with or without the King's permission. It was a risk that had to be taken. Niall would not condemn his mother to life as a hostage.

"You and your wife have been through a terrible ordeal," Sir Liam continued, clearly mistaking Niall's silence for continued trauma. He wrapped an arm around Niall's shoulders. "I'll finish collections here, and then we'll make all haste to return you to your proper place. You're safe now, High Lord."

Proper place? Niall wasn't even sure what that meant anymore. The only thing that was certain now was that he was anything but safe. A single, joyless laugh pushed past Niall's lips. "Yes, of course. My family is held in the King's mercy."

"Indeed, they are," Sir Liam replied with a smile that Niall could not quite read. "Now, we must get the two of you out of those ridiculous clothes and into something befitting your stations." He looked Niall over thoughtfully. "You've put a bit of muscle on since last we met, a testament to all you've been forced to endure, no doubt. I have a fresh tunic and cape in my trunk in the carriage. They might still be a little large on you, but better than those rags."

Out of the corner of his eye, Niall could see Daris and Elize silently bristling at Sir Liam's comments. They stood side by side, with their heads bowed, as was expected when in the presence of nobility, but Daris' hands were clenched so tightly that his knuckles were white. Elize's shoulders were rigid. Niall shook off Sir Liam's arm, disgusted by the display of clueless snobbery. The man barely noticed Daris and Elize, but if they'd dared to show anything outside of humble deference it would have cost them dearly.

"Sir Liam, the people here have been nothing but kind to us. They've offered the best of what they have," Kenna responded before Niall could. Her tone was regal and commanding. She lifted her chin and held herself as though she wore the finest silks and jewels money could buy. "As such, these 'rags' carry greater value than any finery wealth can offer."

"Of course, my Lady," Sir Liam bowed to her. "You are truly gracious in your acceptance of such things. Luckily, I purchased a gown for my daughter from a rather talented seamstress several towns back. The two of you are close enough in build, and I know my Lisbeth would not object. Like you, she is the very spirit of kindness and generosity."

"Go fetch the garments," Niall commanded, disgusted by Sir Liam's obtuse behavior. He raised his chin and looked down his nose at the other man. If Sir Liam would treat Daris and Elize with so little regard than Niall would remind him who held greater rank. "I am High Lord here, and I will see to the business of my tenants."

Sir Liam bowed quickly. "Of course, High Lord." He started to hurry back to the carriage.

"And Sir Liam," Niall called after him. When the older man turned, Niall took a few steps toward him. "I would have these people rewarded for the kindness they've shown my wife and me. Your soldiers will treat them with the same respect they would show me."

"But surely— As you command, High Lord," Sir Liam bowed again and scurried off.

Niall felt like his knees might give out. He exhaled slowly and stumbled to the back of the house, away from the eyes of the crowd. The second he was hidden from view, Niall threw a hand out and leaned against the wall. The world was spinning. He stood there, looking down at the ground, taking deep, slow breaths. Whether it was the result of his overindulgence the night before, the meeting with Sir Liam, or a combination of the two was of little consequence. His mother was alive and in the hands of the man Niall suspected was responsible for the utter annihilation of their home. There would be no sneaking out of Venallis now. For good or ill, Niall was returning to a life that he had thought burned to the ground months ago.

Niall felt Kenna's hand on his back. "Your mother is alive. That is what's important. We will do whatever we must to keep her safe. We'll figure this out together, Niall." Her words were meant to be soothing, but it only heightened Niall's distress.

"I have to go to her," he said. Niall drew another deep breath and turned around to face his wife. He knew she wasn't going to like what he had to say next. "But you should stay here. I'll go to court and once I have my mother, we'll meet up again and leave Venallis together." The suggestion was a vain hope at best. Niall doubted he would ever be allowed to leave Rosehaven once he was there.

"I'm not as naive as that, Niall. I won't stay here while you exchange your life for hers. We've survived all of this by working together," Kenna crossed her arms. "I'm your wife. Where you go, I go."

Niall knew there was no point in arguing with her. As much as he feared for Kenna's safety, she was right; they were stronger together. "We can't let our guard down for a second. They'll exploit any weakness they can find, no matter how trifling it may seem to you and me," Niall cautioned as their friends came around the corner to join them.

"Are the two of you mad?" Daris hissed under his breath. "You've said yourself that this man wants you dead. This is obviously a trap that was set up the moment he caught a hint that you might still be alive."

"They have his mother, Daris," Elize whispered. "Would you do any differently if it were a member of your family?"

Daris looked at each of them in turn, and began to pace. "Then we'll go to Rosehaven as well. You'll need people you can trust to watch your back."

"It isn't that simple, Daris. You'd be treated like the lowest servants. You wouldn't be at our sides; you'd be relegated to the stables or the kitchens or sent straight to the dungeons." Niall shook his head, glancing around the corner to check on Sir Liam's progress. He'd collected the clothing and was walking toward them. "Having you and Elize there would just make you targets. King Dempsey would use you against me."

"But we can't just allow you and Kenna to walk into something like that," Daris argued.

"You don't have a choice," Niall stated flatly. "None of us do." He composed his features and stepped back into view of the people as Sir Liam returned. "Thank you for the clothing. My wife and I will change and make ready for our departure."

"But what of the taxes, my Lord?" Sir Liam looked back at the villagers. "Your estate needs such things now more than ever."

"I will take nothing else from this village. They've more than covered their offerings in the shelter they provided," Niall replied. "Their tithes are paid."

A collective buzz of astonished whispers rose up from the men and women who stood nearby. A few called out their blessings and thanks to Niall. He inclined his head toward them, then took the clothing offered by his fellow nobleman. Without a word of explanation, he turned toward the travelers' camp. Kenna fell into step beside him. They walked back to their home together. With each step, Niall could feel parts of himself being shuttered behind a facade that had once provided a sense of control and safety. Now that façade felt like iron bars, caging him in.

Niall and Kenna packed up the few belongings they'd collected during their travels. Niall rolled his throwing knives into their leather binding and started to put them into a canvas bag before he remembered that they were not his at all, but lent by a member of the caravan. He folded the scarf he wore on his head anytime they were in a town and laid it on top of the bundle, it was borrowed as well. Kenna took her bow, the book Niall gave her, and the pair of wooden doves. There was so little to take, so little that actually belonged to them... and yet even with so little, they'd been rich in so many ways. It was a stark contrast to life among the nobility, where a person's worth was measure by material possessions.

Finished packing, Niall and Kenna turned their attention to the clothing provided by Sir Liam. After months in the comfortable, simple garb of the traveling entertainers, the stiff and tightly fitted brocades and velvet were heavy and constricting. To Niall, it felt like the noose was already starting to tighten around his neck.

He looked around the wagon that had offered sanctuary and wished for nothing more than to hitch the horses and take off down the road again. This felt like home. This was where he felt like himself. The life he led before this felt foreign now. The only physical remnants of that existence were his sword, the ring of the High Lord, and a bloodstained shirt. Niall knelt to retrieve his sword from its place under the bed. He partially pulled the blade from its sheath for a moment before sliding it back in place and buckling the belt around his waist.

"Could you help me with my laces?" Kenna asked. She turned to present her back, and pulled her long, dark hair out of the way.

"And I thought the sash you wore around your waist was complicated," Niall tried to lighten the mood as he fumbled through the process of tightening Kenna's corset. He'd never laced, or even unlaced, one before. The women of the troupe didn't wear them, and Kenna hadn't since their last day in Britwylde and Mairi had been there to help her then.

It took a little trial and error, but he managed with some guidance from Kenna. When Niall finished lacing the back of her dress as well, he wrapped his arms around Kenna's waist and placed a soft kiss on her neck. Her warmth and the scent of her hair offered a small measure of peace. As much as it might have been better for her to remain away from the court, Niall was grateful for the strength her presence provided.

"I have not given up hope, my darling," she whispered, turning in his arms. She stroked the side of his face. "King Dempsey couldn't stop us before, and we were little more than friends. How can he hope to keep us from achieving our goals now that our hearts beat as one?"

Niall smiled down at his wife. "You make it seem as though we could take on one of the great dragons from the tales of old."

"I've always viewed the dragons in those legends as metaphors for the challenges life presents. I know we'll find a way to defeat this one," Kenna replied solemnly. She stepped away and knelt to pull his shirt from the cubby that hid it. When she rose again, she held her hand out to Niall. The ring of the High Lord of Britwylde was glittering on her upturned palm. "I think it's time for you to wear this in the light of day."

Niall exhaled slowly. It wouldn't be the first time he wore the ring, but it would be the first time in public. He wasn't just wearing a random piece of jewelry; he was accepting the title it represented. Once he put it on and stepped out of the wagon, he would be a High Lord of Venallis. "I'm not ready, Kenna. I was prepared to walk away from this. I never wanted it in the first place."

"Niall, you may not have expected to become the High Lord, but you were ready for this long before your father died," Kenna stepped closer to him and She reached for Niall's right hand. She looked him in the eyes as she slid the ring onto his middle finger. "You can do this. You are more than a match for the challenges we face."

"Thank you," Niall whispered. He closed his eyes and leaned his forehead against hers. "Thank you for being my Kenna, for loving me. I'd be lost if you weren't here."

"I'll always be here, Niall," Kenna answered. She kissed him and then slid her hand into his. They paused at the door, taking a few seconds to prepare themselves before they stepped out of the wagon and became a High Lord and High Lady of Venallis.

When they cleared the door and turned to make their way back to Sir Liam's carriage, they found themselves facing every member of the caravan. Daris and Elize were standing a few feet in front of the others with Remmy and Dana. Each person held some symbol of their act, an instrument, a ball for juggling, a puppet, or even pieces of their costumes. They bowed low, then straightened with the tools of their trades held over their hearts. It was not the deference of a peasant to members of the nobility, but a show of respect and farewell from one performer to another.

It took Niall a moment to find his voice. When he did it was choked by the intensity of gratitude, affection, and sadness coursing through him. "Thank you, all of you. You saved our lives, and then helped us rebuild them."

"We won't ever forget our time with you," Kenna added. She was weeping as Elize wrapped her arms around her.

"You're both part of our troupe now. You'll always be welcome with us," Elize sniffled. She reached over to hug Niall firmly. "Take care of each other."

Niall nodded as she stepped away and Daris moved in to take her place. The look on the other man's face was one of utter misery. "I never would have imagined I'd count a High Lord as one of my closest friends, as another brother."

"You and Elize became our family," Niall gripped Daris' arm. "I wish we could have gone on that sea voyage together. I was looking forward to seeing where those waves would take us."

"We have a saying among the caravans: 'Though our paths may diverge, we still travel together.'" Daris smiled ruefully. "Who knows? Maybe we'll find ourselves on the same stretch of road again someday."

Niall nodded sadly, not giving voice to his fears that the road he took now had but one destination. "I hope so, Daris. I truly do."

Daris blinked a few times and then pulled Niall into a hug. He turned to Kenna and squeezed her just as tightly. "Try to keep him out of trouble, hm?"

"I'll do my best," Kenna laughed, through sad sniffles.

Remmy cleared his throat, causing Daris and Elize to take a step back. The leader of the caravan presented a basket to Niall and Kenna. It was filled with small gifts, a bottle of mead given to one of the elders after a performance, a humble, but precious round of goat cheese, apples from the orchards of Brittendell, a bouquet of tiny paper flowers made by one of his daughters, and other various tokens from the people of the caravan.

Niall accepted the gifts and held his knives out to Remmy. "See that these get back to their owner, please."

"You may be the High Lord and Lady, but you've performed with us. You've helped haul mired wagons out of the mud during rainstorms. You laughed and cried with us." He pushed the bundle of knives back toward Niall. "You are members of our troupe now and always. We will retire your costumes in honor of your time with us. The knives are yours, no other will use them again."

The gesture was an overwhelming one. Niall and Kenna exchanged teary looks and then bowed to their chosen family, returning the respect that was afforded them. Niall held the bundle close. It didn't matter that he would never use them for another performance. The knives were a part of the man he was now, and keeping them made leaving this life behind a little easier. Niall was still dashing tears from his cheeks as he bid the rest of traveling folk farewell, receiving hugs and well-wishes from one person after another.

Each step they took toward Sir Liam's carriage felt heavier than the last. Niall clung tightly to the hand that Kenna had looped through his elbow. The royal city used to fill him with excitement and an air of pride. He was barely fifteen when he'd left his family to take a position within King Fergal's household, full of youthful expectations. Today it was another prospect entirely. It would take everything Niall knew about the inner workings of the court to find a way out of that den of snakes and ambition.

Sir Liam bent in a low, elegant bow when they finally approached the side of his carriage. "My Lord and Lady, I offer my service and wish to express my deep joy at being able to aid in your triumphant return to home and safety." He straightened and opened the carriage door. "I will defer to riding my horse, so that the two of you may travel in greater comfort. I promise we'll make all haste in our return."

"Thank you," Niall replied with little enthusiasm as he assisted Kenna into the carriage. He passed her their meager bundle of belongings and climbed in after her. Having the carriage to themselves was a blessing on a difficult day. They didn't have to smile and carry on as though this journey was a happy one.

The door closed and Niall heard the driver cluck to the horses a second before the carriage heaved forward. It bumped and creaked along the packed earth that served as a road. As they reached the edge of Brittendell, Niall heard the sound of a single pipe rise in the air. It played a sad and haunting tune. He looked at Kenna and then they both craned their necks to peer out the carriage window.

Daris stood in the middle of the road behind them. He held his flute to his lips and played a final farewell. The music continued until they rounded the bend and lost sight of the provincial village. Whether Daris ended the song, or they were too far away to hear it, was unclear.

Niall and Kenna sat in silence. Both were still feeling the effects of their final night with Daris and Elize, and the movement of the carriage did little to ease that discomfort. After an hour of bumping along the country roads they fell asleep, holding one another. It was a gentle reprieve from the grief and tension of the morning.

Sir Liam woke them hours later to stop for a late lunch at a tavern along the way. Niall was in better sorts after the nap and thanked Sir Liam more graciously for the use of his carriage. The poor man was hardly to blame for the danger Niall and Kenna now faced, and he seemed genuinely pleased to have found them alive and well.

Though it no longer came with the same effortlessness as before, Niall slipped back into his old habit of hiding his feelings behind a mask of propriety. He didn't detect any malice from Sir Liam, but if Niall was to conceal his resentment for Cathal and the King, he needed to relearn the art of careful conversation.

Despite Sir Liam's assurance that they would make all haste in their journey to Rosehaven, the trip took longer than usual. Sir Liam was not a man who enjoyed long hours on horseback. As a result, he called for frequent stops along the way. After several of these delays, Niall offered to ride the horse so the older man could rest without having to slow their progress further. Despite everything, Niall was eager to be reunited with his mother, whether or not he had to endanger his life to do it.

It was strange how different travel through the countryside felt when in the trappings of the ruling class. As members of the traveling troupe, the people greeted them with excitement and vigor. Some were disdainful, but most were delighted by the break from their daily toils. The people who came out as the carriage passed kept their distance, and Niall could see that their curiosity and admiration were tinged with a small measure of fear. He saw it in the eyes of every person they passed on the streets, and the faces of those who worked at the inns where they took rooms at night. The fear grew more palpable in each town as they drew nearer to Rosehaven.

A week and four days after they left Brittendell, the walls of Rosehaven and the castle towers loomed beyond. The city was as magnificent as Niall remembered. The flags of the Venallian monarchy fluttered in the air, bright against the backdrop of the purple mountains that stood behind them, shrouded in mist. Six months ago, the sight would have been a joyful one. Now, Niall imagined threatening eyes staring out from every visible window.

Their entrance into Rosehaven was not a quiet, unnoticed affair. Sir Liam had sent one of his pages ahead the night before to alert the King and Niall's mother of their return. At Sir Liam's insistence Niall sat in the carriage with Kenna as they progressed through the streets. People stood out in front of their shops and houses to cheer as they drove by. High Lord Edan had been a loved and respected member of the nobility, despite his irregular visits to court. The news of his death had shocked and saddened the people of Rosehaven. The joy they showed at the return of the new High Lord was heartfelt and unabashed.

"Do you think we'll receive so warm a welcome at the palace?" Kenna asked, peeking out of the curtains.

"From my mother, yes; but I'm not sure how many others will be pleased to see me return from the dead," Niall muttered. He looked at the people outside, smiled stiffly and waved at a family who tossed flower petals on the road.

Kenna pulled the curtain closed and leaned back in her seat. "What of your friends? You must have made a few in the five years you were here."

"Friendship at court is less about genuine affection and more a matter of what can be gained by association," Niall admitted. "I'm sure many have offered my mother friendship in the hope of being granted a portion of my family's property when she dies. Now I'm High Lord, and I'm married. The nobles will see fortune slipping away with every step I take in the palace. They will smile to my face, but there will be no truth in it."

"And you enjoyed your time here before?" Kenna asked. She looked at him incredulously.

"Enjoyed is a strong word," Niall admitted. "There's a certain artistry in navigating the currents of court. I found the challenge exhilarating. At least I did when I was here as the godson and favorite of a King. There was safety in that position."

Kenna wrapped her arms around herself as if doing so provided some shield from the troubles they faced. "And now we may be viewed as enemies to the new King."

"We won't be set upon and thrown into a dungeon the moment we walk through the doors," Niall reassured her. He slipped an arm around Kenna's shoulders and pulled her close. "My rank is high enough that the King will have to find a reason to act against me. I don't intend to give him one, and with a little luck we should be able to find a way to leave before he comes up with something on his own."

"It's ironic," Kenna laid her head on Niall's shoulder.

Niall kissed her temple. "What is, my love?"

"I felt safer when you were throwing knives at me," Kenna replied dryly.

"Ironic indeed. You had far more trust in my aim than anyone ever should," Niall laughed. It was a precious moment of levity, and he didn't take it for granted.

The carriage turned onto the wide cobblestone street that led to the palace. Niall had gone down this lane so many times before that he didn't need to look out the window to know when they approached the castle. He heard the whine of the great iron gates swinging open and felt his stomach knotting. He clung to his wife and prayed they would one day be allowed to pass back out of those gates safely.

The carriage lurched to a stop, and a few seconds later Sir Liam flung the door wide. He was grinning from ear to ear. "High Lord Niall, High Lady Kenna, it is my unequaled pleasure to welcome you to the court of King Dempsey and Queen Elanor."

Niall carefully schooled his expression to one of control and calm. He carefully climbed out of the carriage, hoping that his shaking knees wouldn't betray the depth of his anxiety. Kenna took his hand and stepped out behind him. They ascended the stairs and approached the magnificent marble entrance. The ornately carved and polished wooden doors swung open in unison. Niall paused on the threshold and looked at Kenna with unease.

"One step and then another," she whispered, and her grip on his hand tightened. Niall took a slow, calming breath. He straightened his shoulders and stepped into the viper's nest.

They were met by a host of guards, and for an instant, Niall feared he was about to be arrested and cast into a cell, despite the assurances he'd offered Kenna. He went rigid and braced himself for a fight. They were close enough to the doors that there was hope for escape. However, his fears appeared to be unwarranted. Instead of striking, the guards bowed. A valet stepped past them and asked Niall and Kenna to follow him to the great hall to be welcomed by the court.

Niall's heart was still racing when they drew to a stop outside the hall. The hum of many voices drifted past the thick oak doors that shielded them from viewing the crowd that awaited. Without a word of warning, their escort flung the doors wide. The conversations stuttered to a stop, and the eyes of every noble at court turned in unison to focus on Niall and Kenna.

"The esteemed High Lord, Niall of Britwylde, and his wife, the High Lady Kenna," the valet announced with precise pronunciation and a voice that carried from one end of the hall to the other.

Niall took one step inside and a round of applause broke out. Cheers and greetings bounced off the stone walls and echoed through the air. Lords and Ladies stepped aside and dipped in perfectly practiced bows and curtsies. It was a pageantry of false joy and friendship. Niall smiled, and hated the sickeningly sweet poison of it all.

The center of the room cleared, creating a sort of corridor in the crowd. When the last of the courtiers moved aside Niall's eyes fell upon the familiar and beloved face of his mother. In an instant, he cast aside any pretense of being dignified and aloof. Niall ran the breadth of the room, pulling Kenna along behind him.

"Mother!" he exclaimed, releasing his wife's hand to throw both arms around his mother. He clung to her with tears of joy spilling down his cheeks.

"My boy, my precious boy. You've come back to me, Niall." She returned his embrace with a fierceness that made Niall's sides ache. She was weeping as fervently as he was.

Niall didn't care that her hold on him was physically painful. His mother could have squeezed him tightly enough to break his ribs and he still wouldn't have broken that hug. "I'm so sorry I didn't come sooner. I thought you were dead, Mama," he fell back on his childhood name for her.

"None of that, no apologies," she replied, and pulled back to cup Niall's face in her hands. She stroked his cheeks and gazed up at him as if he were the most beautiful thing she'd ever seen. Yet, there was fear behind her joy. "Oh, my sweet baby. I have longed to see your face and thought I never would."

"I'm so happy to see you alive," Kenna said, only making it halfway to a curtsy before Niall's mother pulled her into the embrace as well. "You are my daughter now, dear. I am as happy to see you as I am to see my son."

Niall wrapped his arms around them both and held on tightly. The broken pieces of his life melding together again gave him a sense of renewed hope; one that was quickly tainted by the reality of their situation. He turned his head close to his mother's ear and whispered. "It is not safe here. We need to leave as soon as possible."

Her arms tightened around Niall and Kenna, fingers digging into the fabric of Niall's tunic, but she said nothing, practiced enough in the intrigues of power to refrain from providing any reaction that might be commented on. She released them and smiled up at him. "We have a great deal of lost time to make up for, and many important matters to discuss, my darlings."

They were still standing close to one another when the fanfare started playing. Niall stepped away from his mother but didn't immediately turn to look at the source of the interruption. His hands tightened into fists that he hid in the folds of the cape he wore over his tunic. The sound of booted feet marching across the marble tiles filled the room and stopped with the music.

"Their Royal Majesties, the high and mighty King Dempsey and Queen Elanor!" The King's herald declared loudly. The sound of shuffling feet and shifting silk filled the air as the men and women in the room lowered themselves before their monarch.

"Master Niall," King Dempsey called out. His voice was as slick as goose grease.

The use of his former title was a calculated insult, and one that was not lost on Niall. He looked over his shoulder, then turned around slowly to face the new King of Venallis. He met and held the man's eyes for a second, knowing that despite his efforts, he wasn't able to fully hide the contempt he felt.

"Or rather, High Lord," the King purred, reminding Niall of a cat toying with a mouse. "From second son to the heir of all your father held. My, but our lots have changed."

"Your Majesty," Niall managed to make his words sound mild. He bowed, then stood up again to meet the King's gaze.

King Dempsey smiled at Niall and opened his arms wide. "Come, come, my boy! Your father was like a brother to me. We are practically family. It warms my heart to see you back at court, safe and sound within these walls."

Niall wanted to spit in Dempsey's face. The idea of embracing the man was anathema. He glanced at Kenna and his mother, and found the strength he needed to approach the villain with a smile. "The magnitude of emotion this reunion brings is truly beyond description."

"Indeed, it is," King Dempsey folded his arms around Niall, but there was no warmth in the gesture. He pulled back, patting Niall's shoulders. Niall tried to take a step away, but the King's hands tightened and held him in place. "Such haste, when there is business to be seen to."

"Your Majesty?" Niall met Dempsey's eyes. "What business do you wish for me to attend so soon after returning?"

"It's a technicality really, but tradition must be respected," King Dempsey replied. "All the nobles have publicly taken the knee and sworn fealty. All but you, that is."

Niall inhaled sharply. "It was not by design. Circumstances beyond my power have kept me away from court, Your Majesty."

"Yes, of course, but you are the only remaining High Lord of Venallis. A rank exceeded by none at court save myself and my family," King Dempsey stated. "If I make an exception for you, others might think you do not fall under the same laws as they do."

The threat was obvious, Niall knew he had no choice but to do as the King commanded. He slowly lowered himself to one knee and bowed his head. The gesture looked like respect, but Niall did it to hide the loathing on his face. The words of loyalty sickened him, but he forced them past his lips. "I, Niall, High Lord of Venallis, do humbly swear my allegiance to your rule and that of your line."

"I accept your fealty, High Lord," King Dempsey offered his hand to Niall.

Niall's jaw clenched. He took the King's hand and kissed the ring on his finger. Doing so made his skin crawl, but he knew he had to play the part of the loyal servant long enough to find a way out of Rosehaven. Having made a demonstration of his allegiance, Niall started to get to his feet, but King Dempsey stopped him.

"I did not give you leave to rise, Niall." The King's fingers tightened.

Niall's eyes shot to Dempsey's face. A chorus of whispers filled the room. He glanced at the onlookers nervously. His heart was thundering against his ribcage. Niall bowed his head again, hands trembling with the attempt to stifle the anger he felt welling up inside. *He's avoiding my title on purpose, keeping me beneath him in every way he can.*

The span of several heartbeats passed and the tension in the room was revealed by the nervous shifting of those present. What should have been a reunion was beginning to feel like a trial. Niall could sense every pair of eyes boring into his back. He had to work to lock away the angry words that burned behind his lips.

"You may rise now," King Dempsey pulled Niall to his feet and kissed him coolly on each cheek. "Welcome home, High Lord."

Niall kept his eyes downcast and twisted his lips into a smile that he hoped would appear gracious. The King released him and waved to the court. Niall slowly and calmly walked back to Kenna and his mother. He pulled his wife into an embrace and clung to her, heedless of the reactions of those nearby. There was no denying the truth; they were already prisoners.

CHAPTER 17

Wicked Games

Kenna's vision was tinged with red, her lips numb from the effort of biting back her words. King Dempsey's display was a public demonstration intended to humiliate and lower Niall. Everyone in the room knew it. Those same people who cheered and applauded his safe return stood by and watched the King force her husband to his knees. The court was like a glittering apple with a rotten, worm-infested core, and Kenna already longed to be far from it.

The King utterly ignored Kenna. The snub suited her just fine, whether or not it was a breach in protocol. Everything about Dempsey disgusted her, and her fingers itched with the urge to slap the self-satisfied sneer off his face. She ground her teeth and counted to ten, then exhaled slowly before she lost all sense and told the pathetic excuse for a leader exactly what she thought of him. A miniscule sense of calm bridled her anger when the King and Queen stepped out of the hall.

The rest of the court was not as dismissive of Kenna as the Royal couple were. As soon as the monarchs left, all eyes shifted to her. She was a novelty here, and the sudden attention made that uncomfortably clear. They all wanted a look at the unexpected and foreign wife of the former King's favorite. Even the kindest faces bore expressions of aloof interest; the worst seemed to be sizing her up. In seconds, Kenna understood that there were two stories being told at court: the one in public and another, far deadlier tale that was whispered behind closed doors.

They weren't left standing in the midst of the crowd for long before a servant arrived to lead them to the residential wing. Lady Carene remained close as Kenna and Niall were shown to quarters that were obviously designed for an unmarried man of low rank. Kenna could have laughed at the intended insult. Compared to their living arrangement over the past months, this room was the epitome of space and luxury. The bed was twice as large as the one in their wagon. There was an enormous, ornate wardrobe near the single, paned window, and a small, round table of dark, polished wood with three matching chairs. It was a poorly aimed barb, dulled by King Dempsey's ignorant snobbery.

Kenna crossed the room to stare out the window as she sifted through their meeting with the King. *If anything, it shows just how small and pathetic the man actually is. A true leader doesn't need to tear down the people below him or her. A leader lifts up those around him. Dempsey is nothing but a power-hungry killer and a thief.*

"What are you doing here?" Lady Carene asked as soon as the door closed behind the servant and the footsteps in the hall grew distant. "Why didn't you go to Arthan as your father instructed?"

"We tried, but were set upon by a band of hobgoblins," Kenna explained, turning away from the window. She was speaking to her mother-in-law, but her eyes settled on Niall. He was bracing himself on the table, his face white, gaze distant and shadowed. Worry knotted in Kenna's shoulders. "They cast our gold into the river. We would have been killed were it not for the intervention of the band of travelers that took us in."

Niall looked up slowly and set those haunted eyes on his mother. "Why didn't you tell me?"

Lady Carene held his gaze before answering. "King Fergal commanded your father and I to keep our silence until his decision was final," she sighed heavily. His mother crossed the small room and placed a hand on his cheek. "The choice for the succession fell between you and Cathal. The King wished to see the true measure of you both, to see how you conducted yourselves without promise of such an immense reward."

"Not that it mattered in the end." Niall pulled away from his mother and sank into a chair, sliding his hands into his hair. Kenna could see that he was shaking. "Dempsey didn't even allow his son to take the throne, and I'd say his greeting makes it obvious that he knows King Fergal chose me over Cathal."

"Which is why you and Kenna must leave here as soon as possible," his mother replied. She frowned and seemed to be ordering her thoughts as she pulled one of the other chairs closer to his and settled in it. She took hold of Niall's hands. "I cannot express properly the joy that seeing you has brought me, but you never should have come."

Kenna moved to join her husband and his mother. "We were not going to, not until we learned of your survival. There was no choice after that. We couldn't leave you in the hands of a murderer and usurper."

"The current King may not be the man that was intended for the throne, but that is not evidence that he committed murder," Lady Carene answered slowly. "Even so, he is intelligent enough to know your presence could threaten his reign."

Niall's hands slipped from his mother's. "Cathal killed Ian. I went back to Britwylde. I went back to the site of the *accident*. I found a sharpened stag's horn, fixed to a hilt. Cathal and his squire were the only ones with Ian. I do not believe for a second that he would take such actions without the command and support of his father."

Lady Carene's face turned red, then went ashen. She leaned back and gripped the arms of her chair so tightly that the knuckles of her fingers turned white. Tears flowed silently and freely down her pale cheeks. Kenna knelt at her knees and placed her hand over one of Lady Carene's, desperate to offer some kind of comfort. To lose a child was a terrible thing. To learn that her child had been betrayed and murdered must add new layers to her agony.

"I'm sorry to bear such tidings, mother. Ian tried to tell me that day, but I didn't understand what he was getting at," Niall continued softly. He shook his head and looked up at his mother. "I still don't understand why Ian was targeted though. If I was the one King Fergal was considering, why not simply poison me before I left court for the wedding? It would have been a simple enough thing to manage."

"The betrothal," Lady Carene looked from Niall to Kenna. "Even before Kenna's family approached us, we were seeking a way to strengthen your chances of being declared heir. The trade routes that opened with an alliance to Kenna's Vashirat provided access to Arthan iron. It's lighter and far stronger than anything forged in Venallis. Not only that, it connected our family to one of the most powerful houses in Arthan. It was a far greater match than anything we might have hoped for."

"And by marrying Ian to me you gained all of that, while leaving Niall available for another political match if he was named heir," Kenna finished, seeing the lines connecting. It was exactly what her own parents would have done if they were faced with such a decision. She suddenly felt like a fly caught in a web far more intricate and complex than anything she'd imagined.

"Did you already have someone in mind for me?" Niall asked. He reached out and placed a hand on Kenna's shoulder, as if an answer to his question would somehow tear her from him. "Why have Kenna and I marry if you thought to secure another alliance?"

His mother drew a shaky breath. She closed her eyes and turned her face away. Tears continued to flow down her face and dripped from her jaw. Kenna noticed how haggard the woman looked. Her face bore lines that had not been present before, her hair had streaks of white at the temples, and the shadows under her eyes told a tale of many sleepless, tear-stained nights.

"You were trying to protect Niall, weren't you?" Kenna gently replied, squeezing the older woman's hand. "You hoped my family's influence would offer some security if King Fergal chose him."

"I'd already lost one child, I could not bear to suffer that again," Lady Carene held a hand out to her son. Niall took it, scooting his chair closer. She returned her regard to Kenna. "Niall heard the banshee sing of poison. I knew Niall's closeness to King Fergal made him a target. It's rumored our new Queen is an expert in such arts. I feared if Niall returned to Rosehaven she would find a way to eliminate any threat to her son's chances of ascending the throne. Cathal is a fool. It was obvious to anyone with even a little sense that Niall was the stronger candidate."

"My Vashirat is one of the oldest and most powerful in Arthan. The connection between our families strengthened Niall's prospects, regardless of which son I married," Kenna felt a wave of exhaustion. After less than an hour at court, she already ached from the relentless tension that coiled through her. All she wanted to do was curl up in bed with Niall and imagine they were back in the peace of their home among the traveling folk.

Lady Carene sat up, rigid. "Niall, tell me you did not bring the weapon here. If the King and Queen know you have proof of their betrayal they will act swiftly and without mercy."

"No, not here. It's a few hours' ride from Rosehaven, at an inn where we stopped to water the horses," Niall replied. "I buried it under some bushes just past their hen house. I should have destroyed it entirely, but—"

A knock at the door sent a pulse of adrenaline through Kenna. She jumped, all thoughts of sleep vanishing in an instant. Niall's eyes met hers. If their words had been overheard it could spell disaster for them all. King Dempsey could declare it treason, send someone to take the evidence from its hiding place, and any hope of escape would be lost.

Lady Carene wiped her face and rushed to pour three chalices of wine. She put them around the table and silently urged Kenna into the remaining seat. Another knock sounded. Kenna lifted her wine to her lips and drank deeply, hoping to still her nerves and slow her racing heartbeat. They must give the impression that all was well; looking as though she might faint with fear would hardly be convincing.

"Yes, enter," Niall called out. He leaned back in his chair and managed to present a reasonable display of relaxation. Kenna could see the subtle signs of strain in how he gripped the stem of his goblet, and the way the corners of his mouth were turned slightly downward.

One of the palace stewards entered and bowed. "Forgive the intrusion, High Lord, but Her Majesty Queen Elanor has sent garments for you and your lady wife. She has arranged a banquet in your honor this evening, and said the clothes were to be worn while you're in attendance."

Two more servants entered, each carried a set of clothing in their arms. A tunic and overcoat for Niall, and a lavish gown for Kenna. Even from across the room, she could see that the pale grey and white silks and brocades were of the highest quality. At a different time and place she would have been pleased and flattered by such extravagant gifts. In this castle, they were yet another means of ensuring that she and Niall understood exactly who was in control. It was all a production, and they were being dressed like puppets in a skit.

"When is this feast to take place?" Niall asked.

"The Queen has commanded that the festivities begin as soon as you have washed and changed," the steward bowed and took a step toward the door. "She is most eager to hear of your adventures away from the palace."

"My son and his wife have only just returned. They're weary from travel," Niall's mother stated. "It's not yet evening. Surely, they can be afforded time to recover from such a long ordeal."

The steward signaled for his companions to place the clothing on the bed. "I do but convey the Queen's commands, my Lady."

"Of course. Queen Elanor's gifts are generous, and her thoughtfulness is most touching," Kenna smiled warmly at the man. He was only the messenger, and she wouldn't vent her frustrations on the poor fellow. Nor would she give Queen Elanor the satisfaction of thinking they could be easily rattled. The timing was a ploy to prevent them from settling. It had, but Kenna wasn't going to make that apparent. "Please, convey our gratitude to Her Majesty, and assure her that we will ready ourselves with all haste."

The man looked uncomfortable. Kenna suspected he'd been told to report any hint of displeasure on their part. After another second, he bowed and left to return to his mistress. When the door closed Kenna, Niall, and Lady Carene let out a collective sigh of relief. Nothing in the steward's demeanor, or that of his companions, indicated that they'd overheard any of the conversation going on prior to their arrival. It could be a façade, but Kenna thought not. The doors and walls of the palace were thick, and they'd been speaking quietly.

Lady Carene pushed herself out of her chair and looked at the two of them. "Be careful, my darlings. I would not have you returned to me now only to lose you again."

"We'll all be careful and get out of here as soon as can be arranged," Niall replied. He rose to wrap her in a tight hug. They held one another for a minute before Lady Carene released her son. She pulled Kenna close and held her for a moment before she left to prepare for dinner.

Kenna grabbed her cup and gulped down every drop of wine it held. The rich, semi-sweet liquid slid down her throat and settled warmly in her stomach. It was a small comfort that gave her the courage to examine the clothes in greater detail. The gown was elegant, and she wished she could believe the clothes were sent in genuine welcome. Kenna took a deep breath and tried to summon the energy needed to face the evening's activities. Strong, familiar hands settled on her shoulders, then slid down her arms and pulled her close.

Niall kissed her temple but said nothing. Kenna turned to rest her cheek on his chest. Alone with her husband, the weariness returned in full force. The thought of going back into the presence of so many strangers made her want to weep. Every muscle in her body felt heavy and burdened, as if she'd spent hours performing hard labor.

Until coming to this palace, she'd never felt out of place in Venallis, but nothing about the court felt comfortable; it put her on edge. Being in Niall's arms was the only thing that felt safe now. It offered a sense of balance, and hope that, somehow, all would be made right again. Even without words, Kenna could tell that their closeness brought the same peace to him.

But the "welcome" of a Queen could not be ignored for long, and they were forced to release their hold on one another. There was no time to rest, or even unpack the few belongings they carried with them. They changed out of the clothing that Sir Liam provided and put it aside to be washed and returned to him as soon as possible.

Kenna hated the feel of her new dress. It was stiff and seemed ill-fitted. It pinched uncomfortably in the bust, and the sleeves were a touch too long. It would have been easy to see such things as another slight, but the gown couldn't have been made for her specifically. *I must not let my fears and weariness get the better of me. It serves no purpose to see insults in such small details. Certainly not with so many real ones to endure. I must keep a clear head.*

Over an hour passed before Kenna returned to the great hall on Niall's arm. In the time since their initial arrival, the room was transformed. Tables were moved in, blanketed in silver satin cloth. Each was adorned with several crystal vases, brimming with crimson roses. Banners the same shade of red hung from the ceiling and along the walls. Kenna's fingers dug into Niall's sleeve. The colors were those of the Stratham Vashirat.

"Niall," Kenna kept the expression on her face pleasant, and her voice quiet enough for only her husband's ears. "They've decorated in the colors of my family's enemies."

He placed his left hand over Kenna's fingers. "I know. I believe the King and Queen do as well."

"It seems a bold move to publicly display the colors of those responsible for the death of a high-ranking noble and his household." Kenna replied, stomach churning, and head throbbing. She remembered the look on Mairi's face as the light in her eyes faded, the sounds of weapons clashing, and the screams that echoed down the corridors. The music that filled the banquet hall was no longer a cheerful melody, but a mockery of the pain and terror of that night. "They're practically admitting their involvement in the attack."

"It's not likely anyone else in this room is aware of the customs and details of the Arthan Vashirats. This is aimed at us." Niall's jaw tightened. "At you specifically."

Kenna lifted her chin defiantly. "They'll have to do better than petty insults and games if they wish to break me."

"You are a force they have yet to reckon with, my love," Niall replied. He looked down at her and smiled. It was the sweet, warm smile that had lodged itself firmly in Kenna's heart. "They'll never be able to match your strength, and as long as I have you by my side, I can face anything."

Kenna loosened her grip on his arm and returned the smile with an equally warm one of her own. If King Dempsey and Queen Elanor needed to play such childish games to demonstrate their power, then Kenna would show them the steel of a daughter of the Rihtall Vashirat. She wouldn't sink to their level or give them even a second of victory by allowing them to see the impact of their barbs. Resilience and composure would be her weapons in this battle. *But I will not hesitate to do what I must to protect the people I hold dear.*

Kenna looked to the far end of the hall. The King and Queen were seated behind a table set upon a dais, staring back at her from gilded thrones. She met the eyes of Queen Elanor and held steady as she walked down the length of the room with Niall. Kenna lowered her gaze long enough to dip her head slightly to curtsy before the monarchs. When she lifted her eyes again, the smile she fixed on the Queen was as cool and confident as the one returned by the other woman.

"Your Majesties, I must thank you for the tremendous hospitality you've shown. I can see that you took great care in arranging this celebration." Kenna's smile grew wider as she gestured at one of the banners hanging nearby. "And your taste is remarkable. Such color makes an interesting statement."

Queen Elanor's eyes narrowed slightly. The change was almost imperceptible, but Kenna caught it. This was clearly not the reaction hoped for. Kenna took a small amount of satisfaction in knowing she'd spoiled this snake of a woman's sport. The Queen fixed an intelligent assessing gaze on them. She was a stunning woman: tall and willowy, with porcelain skin that bore few signs of age. Her golden-brown hair was piled on her head in an intricate array of twists and jeweled adornments. But it was the clever and probing intensity of her amber eyes that struck the deepest. Kenna could see in an instant that this was not an adversary to be underestimated.

"You are as gracious and as lovely a creature as I've heard, my dear." Queen Elanor spoke with the most perfect and polished accent Kenna had encountered in Venallis. "I can see why your husband *values* you so. You are a precious commodity, to be certain."

"As I value him, Your Majesty," Kenna replied. She looked up at Niall with adoration. Her love for him was the one thing Kenna didn't have to pretend at. It made hiding the insult of the décor easier. "We are true partners, in all things."

"She is most precious to me, indeed." Niall slipped his arm around her waist and held her protectively. "I'm honored to spend my life in proving *my* worth to her." He looked at the King and offered a bow. "And now, Your Majesties, I beg leave to enjoy the feast that you've laid out for us. My wife and I are quite famished and worn from our recent adventures."

"Of course, Niall," King Dempsey replied, blatantly disregarding Niall's title yet again, Kenna noted. He gestured to one of the tables. "Places have been prepared for you." He then shifted attention to his wife and began conversing with her as though he'd dismissed a servant.

They turned and made slow progress to the table indicated by the King. For the entirety of the short walk from the thrones to their own seats, Kenna half-expected the King or Queen to summon them back and complain that they'd made some ludicrously minute protocol error or courtly *faux pas*. It was the sort of manipulation in which they obviously reveled. To her immense relief, no summons or admonishment came.

Kenna let out a long, measured sigh of relief when they finally settled in their seats. For the time being, the King and Queen were focused on other matters—or were pretending to be. It was a brief respite that would not be squandered. She reached for the goblet to the right of her plate and pulled it toward her lips, then paused and looked down at the silver cup with suspicion. Lady Carene's mention of poison flashed through Kenna's mind. Her mouth was as dry as chalk, but the idea of drinking from that cup made her skin crawl.

Niall leaned close to her, pitching his voice beneath the clatter of dishes and noisy hum of the other conversation around them. "They won't strike in front of so many and so soon after we've arrived. It would draw the wrong kind of attention."

"I'm sure you're correct. They wouldn't want to spoil the evening by showing their true faces," Kenna replied behind her glass. She took a sip, still fearing to feel her throat constrict as soon as the wine passed her tongue. She held her breath for a few seconds in anxious anticipation. Then leaned toward her husband to whisper in his ear, "I believe they wish to find a way to get you to incriminate yourself."

"Oh yes, how gracious of them to allow me to see to my own damnation," Niall answered dryly, and in an equally hushed tone. "I don't know why I ever dreaded coming back."

Kenna allowed a slight laugh, which seemed to have been what Niall was aiming for. He wrapped his arm around her shoulders and kissed her temple. The action was something that wouldn't have been noted among the travelers, but here it drew disapproving glances. Niall didn't seem to care, and Kenna found the display of affection reassuring. *Let these people sit cold and rigid next to their spouses. I love Niall and don't give a fig what they think of that.*

The gathering continued without interruption for several minutes. People came to greet Niall and welcome Kenna. Some Kenna remembered seeing at the wedding, others were strangers. They all claimed delight and relief at learning of Niall's survival. Invitations to picnics and other social engagements were issued by half the court before the second course was complete. The food was delicious and the wine flowed liberally from countless bottles. But even with all the finery, Kenna wished she were sitting by a campfire and sharing a simple meal with Elize and Daris.

The servants were just clearing away the dishes from the second course when the main doors swung open. That alone would not have been enough to draw Kenna's attention, but as soon as they did there was a dissonant clamor of metal platters crashing to the tiled floor. All conversation stopped and the entire court turned toward the spectacle.

Cathal was stumbling away from one of the serving lads, who was kneeling on the floor and frantically trying to clean up the chaos spread across the marble. An unsteady gate and bleary eyes made it readily apparent that Cathal was inebriated and had been for some time. Niall's hand gripped Kenna's under the table.

"Forgive my t—tardiness, father. I mean, Your Majesty," Cathal's words were slurred and sluggish as he approached his parents. "I was quite delayed by important business." He caught sight of Niall before the King or Queen could respond. "Niall! My old friend! You're alive! And Kenna as well. But... but not Mairi. I couldn't save her."

Kenna would have blanched at the mention of Mairi's murder, but she was too shocked by the state Cathal was in. The man looked like he hadn't shaved in days. His eyes were red-rimmed and seemed to have difficulty focusing on any one point for more than a minute or two. The clothing he wore looked like it had been slept in at least once, and his hair was in complete disarray. This was not the same man that she met at Britwylde castle. This man looked like the only thing he was capable of managing was a bottle of spirits, and it was obvious he'd managed more than one of those in recent hours.

King Dempsey leapt to his feet and crossed the room to grab his son by the elbow. His voice was lowered, but the intensity of it echoed through the high-ceilinged room. "You were told to arrive on time and in a respectable state."

Kenna tore her eyes away from the spectacle to look at her husband. Niall bore a disgusted frown and was doing nothing to hide it. She imagined her own disapproval was equally plain to see. Kenna leaned close to Niall, and covered her mouth with a napkin. "This is the same man that King Fergal was considering as his successor? He never seemed as serious as you or your brother, but he wasn't a drunkard."

"I—I'm sorry, father," Cathal said. He looked around the room, swaying slightly as he did. He patted his father's chest clumsily. "I swear to you, it will not happen again."

"See that it does not," King Dempsey snarled through gritted teeth. He pushed his son's hand away and looked around the room with a forced smile. "Our Prince is overwhelmed with the joy of his friend's return, as anyone might expect after having seen the violence that the Arthan savages rained down upon one of our own."

"The Stratham, Your Majesty," Niall spoke up. His tone and expression were mild. He rose from his seat to approach Cathal and the King.

"What?" King Dempsey glared openly at Niall. Kenna could see that Cathal's public display had soured Dempsey's evening. If the mood of the room weren't so dangerous, she would have taken satisfaction in that knowledge, but the situation was too precarious to allow herself that.

"The Arthan people are divided into Vashirats, similar to the clans that used to control Venallis. It was Vashirat Stratham who attacked my family, not the Arthan people in general." Niall bowed his head.

King Dempsey studied Niall coldly. The differences between Cathal and Niall were stark, and at the moment they were on display for everyone in the room. Cathal was grinning like a fool and barely able to stay upright. Niall stood tall and composed.

He looks like a king, Kenna thought to herself. It filled her with a sense of pride and with fear.

"Are you contradicting me, *High Lord*?" King Dempsey asked in a dangerously quiet and steady voice. He was obviously preparing for a fight, hoping that Niall would give him exactly that. The focus of the entire room was narrowed to the three men standing in front of the throne.

"No, Your Majesty," Niall finally said. "It is not the place of a High Lord to contradict a King."

Kenna's stomach flipped. *Niall's treading a dangerous line.* She pushed up from her seat and approached them, stopping to offer a practiced and graceful curtsy before King Dempsey. "Your Majesty, may I have leave to speak?"

The question seemed to dissipate the storm that was building around the King. He looked down at

Kenna as though he hadn't noticed her approach. "You may."

"My husband only seeks to inform Your Majesty, for the good of the realm." Kenna offered him her most charming smile: it was one Mairi used to say could enchant a spitting cobra. "There are some Vashirats within Arthan who would take such a mix-up as a great insult to their honor. My own, the Rihtall, would understand the honest confusion, but I'm afraid the Stratham and their ilk can be most savage when they feel insulted."

King Dempsey drew a slow breath. His eyes shifted between Kenna and Niall. The action created the sensation of a thousand insects crawling across Kenna's skin. She had the terrible feeling that he'd spotted a point of vulnerability and was already working out how to exploit it.

"My wife speaks the truth," Niall agreed. He looked as uncomfortable as Kenna felt.

"Of course, she does. I can see the two of you share a deep trust and understanding." King Dempsey looked back at his wife and smiled. "It's something that takes some couples years to develop; how fortunate that the two of you have come to it so quickly. No doubt it's been a source of strength and comfort during your trials abroad. I appreciate the insight you've provided, High Lady Kenna. Now we can all return to the festivities with a greater understanding of your culture."

Cathal threw an arm around Niall. "I am so glad you made it out of there alive."

Out of the corner of her eye, Kenna could see Niall flinch at Cathal's touch. She tugged on his arm and began moving back to their seats. The King pulled his son away from Niall and took his place on the throne once more. The hairs on the back of Kenna's neck stood on end as they returned to the table. She knew the King's gaze followed them every step of the way.

He continued to stare for the remainder of the meal, but whenever Kenna met his eyes, King Dempsey simply smiled and bowed his head in slight acknowledgment. It was like being stalked by a predator. Kenna had the terrible sense that he was already plotting the next assault.

It was no small relief when the plates for the final course were cleared away. The hour was late, and Kenna had never been more ready to climb into bed. Her shoulders and neck felt pinched and knotted from the stress, and her eyes burned to close. The dress, which had simply been uncomfortable before, was painfully tight after the enormous meal. She watched the doors anxiously, praying that there wasn't some fresh torture planned under the guise of entertainment.

As if in response to her silent pleas, the King and Queen stood and addressed the nobility. "As delightful as this evening has been, I believe it is time the Queen and I retire."

Everyone at the tables rose as the Royal couple stepped away from their seats. Kenna allowed herself a sigh of relief. She was already anticipating the joy of being unlaced. Niall looked just as fatigued. Even if it weren't for the travel of the past week, the strain of maintaining a careful facade was enough to make time pass at a snail's pace, and each minute felt like a lead ingot being placed on their shoulders.

"High Lady Kenna," Queen Elanor called, stopping as she passed Niall and Kenna's table.

Kenna's teeth grit behind a mask of respect. "Yes, Your Majesty?"

"I should like your company in the morning. After all, your station dictates that you should be in attendance with the other ladies of court," she said. Her tone was like over-sweet honey. "Your husband will be in service to the King, of course. It would not be appropriate for you to be at his side."

Kenna wanted to throw what little wine was left in her goblet in the Queen's face. She was tired and cross, and loathed the idea of spending the entire day verbally sparring with the Queen. But such a display would be deadly, and all Kenna could do was return the other woman's gaze steadily and force her lips to curve upwards as she curtsied in acceptance. She couldn't muster the energy nor the heart for words. Queen Elanor didn't seem to care if Kenna spoke or not. She simply wished them a pleasant night and arrogantly paraded out of the room with her husband.

"Shall we retire as well, my Lady?" Niall offered his hand to Kenna.

"Of course. This day's been a long one," Kenna replied. She took hold of his frigid fingers and allowed him to lead her from the table

They exchanged a few hasty goodbyes with those who were also taking their leave for the night. Niall stopped when they met his mother, kissing her dutifully on the cheek and offering to escort her to her apartments. She took one look at his face and declined, insisting that they go straight to their chambers and see to their own rest.

After that they said nothing more until they were back in the peace of their own room. As soon as the door was shut and bolted, Niall sank onto the bed. He looked utterly lost. Kenna forgot the discomfort of her gown and joined him. She held him tightly, taking as much strength from the contact as she tried to give.

"They're separating us, Kenna. We've survived all this time by staying together, and in less than a day they've taken that safety from us."

"All they can do is keep us busy in different places. Our marriage is stronger than that. *We* are stronger than that." She took his face in her hands and turned him to her. "It does not matter where I am, whether it's by your side or an ocean apart, they cannot break the bond we share. I am yours, and you are mine."

Niall took a shuddering breath and kissed her. It was a deep, desperate plea for closeness and comfort that Kenna answered willingly. Niall's hands drifted to the laces of Kenna's gown. He tugged and the sudden release of the tightly fitted fabric caused her to exhale with relief and satisfaction.

"Better?" Niall asked, nuzzling her neck.

Kenna smiled. "There are not words to describe how much so."

They took solace in one another's arms that night. The physical intimacy eased the torment of the last few hours. The fears and concerns were still waiting for them, but the connection they shared soothed the sharp edges of their situation. Afterwards, Kenna lay with her head pillowed by Niall's chest. She listened to the steady rhythm of his heartbeats. *If I just keep my eyes closed, I can almost imagine we're back there. Safe and sound, in our home.*

* * *

Kenna and Niall were awake long before the servant came knocking on their door. They exchanged a moment of slight satisfaction. It was early by the standards of court, but not so for those who were used to being on the road before the sun rose. Fully dressed, Niall flung the door open, startling the poor man who'd been sent to wake them.

"The King has need of me, I take it?" he asked, smiling broadly at the servant, who nodded with mute surprise. Niall pulled Kenna into a lingering kiss. "I shall try to meet you for lunch, my darling." He turned back to the servant. "Come then, mustn't keep His Majesty waiting."

Kenna watched until he turned a corner before she shut the door and finished pinning her hair up. No maid had been provided to see to her needs, leaving Kenna to rely on Niall to help her lace the gown that was placed outside their door the night before. It fit better than her dinner dress, but the pale yellowish-brown velvet looked terrible on Kenna. It was plain, with tightly fitted sleeves and a low bodice. The only adornment present was a line of tiny pearls sewn along the collar. Kenna hated the drab frock, as much for the bland color and simplicity, as for what it represented.

Another hour passed before she was summoned to join the Queen and her ladies. Kenna followed the lady's maid through the corridors of the palace with her eyes fixed ahead of her and what she hoped was a fearless expression on her face. At last, they stopped outside a beautiful door, stained dark and embellished with intricate, swirling patterns of gold. Kenna was announced and ushered inside without pomp. To her profound relief, Lady Carene was among those in Queen Elanor's entourage.

"I knew that gown would suit you," Queen Elanor purred from the easel she was seated at. She put aside her paintbrush and approached with her hands outstretched, as if they were the oldest and dearest friends. She examined Kenna with a chilling smile that came nowhere near her eyes. "Your looks are so very... exotic. You're far more flattered by gowns of simplicity."

"Thank you, Your Majesty," Kenna replied. She wanted to turn her back on the woman and leave the room. The Queen's back-handed compliment stung more than expected. It made Kenna feel singled out as different. Less. Her eyes burned, despite her determination not to be disquieted by the Queen. She was in the lair of the enemy.

"My daughter-in-law is a rare beauty, inside and out. Some women shine with their own light, making any extra adornments unnecessary," Lady Carene walked across the room and embraced Kenna warmly. She held her close and rubbed her back. It was the touch of a mother, and Kenna felt like she was wrapped in a blanket of protection. "Did you sleep well, my dear?"

Kenna nodded. "Yes, thank you. Niall asked me to send his love."

"Do not eat or drink anything unless you have seen it tested," she whispered, still holding Kenna tightly. Lady Carene pulled away and smoothed Kenna's hair from her face. "Now come, take a seat next to me. We've lost far too much time. I won't miss another moment."

She gripped Kenna's hand firmly and guided her over to the cushioned ottoman next to her own chair. The Queen returned to the painting she'd been working on. Kenna clung to her mother-in-law's hand for as long as she could.

The hours until lunch passed slowly. Every word from Queen Elanor was fraught with insults and double-meaning. Even questions about the weather could contain thorns. Kenna was sent out for any task that could be asked of her without being too far below her station as wife to a High Lord. It was a slow, painful game of cat and mouse. Queen Elanor possessed an uncanny talent for finding the weaknesses in those around her, and though Kenna was her obvious favorite target, she was by no means the only one, and Queen Elanor made no effort to hide her gratification whenever a comment had its desired effect.

It was not all terrible though. As the days passed, Kenna came to know some of the other young women in the service of the Queen. Sir Liam's daughter, Lisbeth, became a surprising ally. They'd spent a little time together at Britwylde, but not enough for Kenna to get her true measure. Lisbeth was a sweet girl who possessed great sensitivity to the moods of those around her. Where Sir Liam had a tendency to utterly misread a situation, his daughter had a clarity of mind that Kenna found admirable.

After spending a week in friendly conversation, Lisbeth admitted that she'd had a special affection for Niall, but assured Kenna that he'd never shown any interest. Her father's attempts at securing a betrothal had not been at her request. With a smile, she revealed that until now, she'd never seen Niall show much interest in any of the women around the palace.

Unfortunately, for Kenna, Queen Elanor walked by as this sentiment was expressed. Her eyes sharpened with the savage delight that always accompanied a chance at cruelty. "Yes, it seems our Lady Kenna is quite skilled at charming the sons of Britwylde. From all accounts Niall's brother, Ian, was equally enamored by her."

"Ian was a kind man, and he honored our betrothal," Kenna replied calmly. She wished Lady Carene were here. The Queen's tongue was never as sharp when Niall's mother was present, though whether it was due to some small sense of guilt or simply because Lady Carene was not easily shaken by such games, Kenna couldn't say. But her mother-in-law had been overtired and begged leave to rest for the day.

"I've heard he was quite popular among the young ladies when he visited court a few years ago." Queen Elanor leaned in. "Both such handsome young men. Tell me, Kenna, how do the brothers compare? After all, you know both so much more intimately than any of us here."

"Surely any who knew them both can speak to the differences in their personalities," Kenna replied. Her mouth was dry, her hands shaking with anger at the Queen's implication. "Beyond their obvious differences, I can make no other comparisons."

"But surely you've taken greater measure of them than any here," Queen Elanor laughed. She squinted down at Kenna. "Are you feeling quite all right, my dear? You look shockingly pale for one with your complexion."

"I'm well enough," Kenna answered quickly. She wanted to spit in the face of the petty hag. She could imagine the shocked expression it would cause. If Kenna were free to do as she willed, she would have charged from the room, grabbed her bow, and worked out her anger with a lengthy turn on the practice range. But such escapes were beyond her, so she offered a lame explanation instead. "I'm only a little thirsty."

The Queen signaled to one of the serving girls. "Fetch High Lady Kenna some wine and perhaps a bit of bread. She looks rather unsettled."

Kenna gripped the arm of her chair and watched the girl pour wine from a pitcher and slice a small portion of sweet bread from the tray nearby. She was so upset that focusing on the mundane was the only way to keep herself from telling Queen Elanor exactly what she thought of a woman who had to tear down those around her to feel equal to them.

The maid pushed the goblet and bread into Kenna's hands. Kenna took a long, deep drink, draining over half the contents before she pulled the cup from her lips and took a bite of the spongey bread. As she chewed, the sweetness began to sour, and it felt heavy on her tongue. Her chewing slowed. Something felt off, but she couldn't simply spit the bread out. She swallowed, and immediately regretted it. Kenna's stomach churned angrily, the muscles in her abdomen tensed, and a curdled taste rose up from her throat.

"Excuse me," Kenna slapped her hand over her mouth, jumped out of her seat and pushed past the Queen. She made a wild dash for a nearby vase and then doubled over it to immediately expel the contents of her stomach. Behind her, the other ladies in the room squealed with disgust and scurried away. Kenna could only cling to the edges of the vase and yield herself to the violent upheaval her body was enduring.

Lisbeth came to her side and held Kenna's hair back until the spasms ceased. She kindly sent for some ginger tea and escorted Kenna to a nearby chair, before turning to curtsy to the Queen. "Your Majesty, may I have leave to take the High Lady Kenna back to her rooms?"

"Of course; she's clearly unwell." Queen Elanor studied Kenna closely, the faintest hint of a smile on her face. There was nothing of surprise or compassion in the woman's eyes.

Kenna felt her stomach beginning to twist again. She swallowed hard, and leaned against Lisbeth as they made for the door. A terrible possibility entered her mind, one that she could not give voice to. She clamped her mouth shut and walked through the halls of the palace in a daze.

"Will you please send for my husband, Lisbeth?" Kenna asked once they were well away from the Queen's chambers.

"Of course, but let me see you to you room, and help you into bed first."

Kenna nodded and said nothing more. She remained quiet even after they were alone in the safety of her chamber. Lisbeth helped her change into a nightgown and tucked her into bed with gentle efficiency. She refused to leave Kenna's side until a maid arrived with the kettle of ginger tea ordered earlier. When Kenna was settled with the tea in hand, Lisbeth left her alone to wait for Niall's arrival.

Kenna barely touched the tea. She stared up at the ceiling and tried to keep from jumping to conclusions as to the cause of her fit of nausea. She didn't want to examine it, didn't want to think of the possibilities. She only wanted to see Niall, and get as far from Rosehaven as they could.

Though her mind was spinning with possibilities, the physical toll of stress caught up with her. Kenna forced down a single cup of tea, and then curled into a tight ball under the covers. She wrapped her arms around herself, closed her eyes and waited for Niall to come. After a few minutes she pulled his pillow close and inhaled deeply, taking comfort in her husband's familiar scent, and fell asleep clinging to his pillow.

It was hours before Niall finally arrived, frantic and furious, though not with her. "Are you all right? What happened? I was told you became violently ill."

Kenna sat up, rubbing her eyes. "I'm well enough now."

"I'm sorry it took me so long to come to you. The King refused to allow me to leave." Niall sat on the edge of the bed and stroked her hair. "What happened?"

"I don't know," Kenna replied. "I took a bite of sweet bread and all of a sudden my stomach turned."

Niall was quiet for a long time. "Do you think . . . you think you were poisoned?"

Kenna didn't respond. She couldn't be certain why her body had reacted so violently. Niall pulled her into his arms, and Kenna nestled closer. "Just hold me, please. Hold me and tell me everything is going to be all right."

"It will be. I'll make certain of that," Niall stated with grim determination. He rocked her back and forth and continued to hold her for several minutes before speaking again. "I'll go to the King and ask permission to return to Britwylde as soon as you're feeling well enough to travel. I can't allow this to continue."

Kenna buried her face in the fabric of his shirt front. Everything felt so much bigger than it did when she woke up this morning. Britwylde was hardly a home, but anything would be better than dwelling in the shadow of the King and Queen's malice.

CHAPTER 18

The Trap is Sprung

Niall didn't leave the room for the rest of the evening. He called for dinner to be sent up and tasted everything himself before passing a plate to Kenna. Whatever she'd ingested before continued to sour her stomach, and she was exhausted from the experience. She tried to eat but even the smell of the food was enough to cause her to retch again. Niall could do nothing but hold her hair away from her face and wipe her brow with a cool, damp cloth when she finished.

That night, he lay awake in bed, staring at the ceiling and listening to his wife's breathing. He needed to get Kenna away from court, but had little hope that the King would grant a request to leave. *I have to try. It's one thing to subject myself to Dempsey's daily humiliations, it's another thing entirely to have Kenna physically threatened.*

The still, small hours of the night were full of sounds that Niall used to find safe and familiar. The shuffling of servants' footsteps in the halls used to provide a sense of order. Now he saw danger in every shadow. He knew that not everyone was as duplicitous as King Dempsey, but the lives of the nobles depended on the King's favor. Niall wasn't sure who could be trusted. Even those who showed kindness only did so when Dempsey was out of sight. It was hardly a secret that Niall was not in the favored position he'd enjoyed when King Fergal was alive.

Kenna stirred in her sleep and nestled closer to Niall. He would carry her straight out of this castle and disappear into the night if he thought they'd make it past the doors. There were too many eyes watching for there to be any hope of a stealthy exit. *And what of my mother? Is she willing to live the rest of her life on the run? No, the only option with any chance of succeeding is to throw myself on what little mercy King Dempsey possesses. If he won't listen, drastic steps will have to be considered.* What those steps might be, Niall could not say.

It took hours for exhaustion to overcome anxiety, but his sleep was hardly restful. Nightmares that hadn't plagued Niall since the days directly following the attack on Britwylde returned with renewed intensity. He dreamed of being held down and forced to watch as Stratham soldiers without faces tormented Kenna. Then the dream changed and he heard her screaming his name, but no matter how fast he ran, Niall never drew closer to the sound of her cries.

When he woke in the morning, Kenna was wiping tears from his cheeks and whispering his name. Niall wrapped his arms around her and clung tightly to reassure himself that she was alive. It took several minutes for the nightmares to fade enough for him to release her. She was everything to him now, and it was horrifically obvious that King Dempsey and Queen

Elanor saw how he depended on her. They were aware—and would use it without hesitation.

"How are you feeling today?" Niall asked when his heart stopped pounding.

Kenna smiled sweetly. "A bit better. I'm hungry, which I take as a sign of improvement."

"I'll have breakfast brought up to you," Niall climbed out of bed. "I think it may be better for you to claim indisposition and avoid joining the Queen's ladies for as long as the excuse holds."

"Do you suppose Queen Elanor would believe I'm still ill?" Kenna asked. She was out of bed now, pouring herself a cup of water before she looked in the mirror and frowned at her reflection. "Oh dear. I certainly look convincingly terrible."

Niall stopped what he was doing to stand behind her, placing his hands on her shoulders. "You look beautiful, as always. Claiming you're ill is hardly a lie. You weren't able to eat without becoming sick last night. You need to rest and regain your strength."

"I do feel rather drained," Kenna admitted with a rueful smile. She placed a hand over his, where it rested on her shoulder. "You need rest as much as I do, perhaps more. King Dempsey seems determined to run you to the point of collapse."

"I'll be fine. It's not the first time I've served at the hand of a King," Niall sighed. He released her and focused on dressing. Kenna's concern was justified. Even during the most hectic days in King Fergal's service, he'd never experienced this level of fatigue. But then, he'd never worried that King Fergal was waiting to strike him down. There was nothing to be done about it, he had to tread carefully as long as Kenna and his mother were within the King and Queen's reach.

"Yes, but the last time you served a King, the man actually cared about your well-being." Kenna pointed out. She was as accurate in her observations as she was with her bow.

"Well, now I have you here to care about me instead," Niall answered, pulling a shirt over his head. He turned and smiled with confidence he didn't feel. "Rest while you can. I'm sure Queen Elanor will give you this day, but anything more is unlikely. I intend to speak with King Dempsey about giving us leave to return to Britwylde. If he agrees to let us go it will take a little time to make all the arrangements. We'll need to look into appropriate lodging until my family's home can be restored. I doubt my mother would be comfortable living out of a wagon as we did. In the meantime, I'll ask my mother to stay with you today. I'll feel safer knowing she's here."

Niall hurried to the door without delay, He called out to a nearby maid and bid her to his mother's chambers to relay his request. With word sent, Niall returned to his wife's side.

Kenna quietly twisted the edge of her sleeve and stared pensively into the flame of the candle nearest her. "I don't know if I'll ever be able to feel safe in Britwylde after what happened."

"I know. It wasn't easy going back there with Daris and Brenin. I'm not looking forward to facing it again," Niall didn't relish the idea of taking his family back to that place either, but their options were limited. With time, he hoped the horror of their final night in Britwylde could fade, just as his nightmares had done with Kenna's soothing presence.

"Perhaps we could look into building a new home instead of repairing the old one. A place that we could make our own," she sighed and sat back onto the bed. "A place that doesn't echo with the threats of an insecure King or the ghosts of those taken from us."

"Sounds like a perfect way to begin our lives anew," Niall said, straightening his tunic. He could almost picture it. He didn't see a castle or a brightly colored wagon. It was something simpler, more common. A house with a green yard, and children playing among the flowers. It was a pretty dream, and one he hoped could be made into reality. "Try to rest. I'll speak to the King straight away."

"If he'll allow you an audience," Kenna muttered as she climbed back into bed.

"He will." Niall moved to the bedside to tuck the blankets in around his wife. "I'll be persistent. Beg, if need be."

Kenna took hold of his hand and squeezed it gently. "I hate to think of you begging that monster for anything. He should be begging for your mercy and he knows it."

"I believe that's the cause of all of this," said Niall as he kissed her cheek. Kenna had been his strength since the attack. Now he was determined to be hers.

A tapping at the door heralded the return of the maid, and to Niall's relief, his mother. Niall turned back to Kenna and smiled reassuringly. "I'll come back to you as soon as I can. In the meantime, my mother has agreed to come keep you company."

Niall gave Kenna one last kiss and then braced himself to face the King. He decided against asking for a formal audience, as propriety demanded, knowing that it would only give Dempsey the means to delay the matter. In this he would not be put aside. *Protocol be damned, I'm speaking to him today.*

After five years at King Fergal's side, Niall had learned how the intrigues of court were carried out. He knew when to observe the formalities and how to find a way around them. This time it wasn't a matter of winning or losing, he was intent on leaving the playing field entirely.

As usual, there were few people in the King's chambers at this early hour. King Dempsey was rarely even awake at the time he demanded Niall arrive. Today, to Niall's surprise, the King was already out of bed and dressed. After two weeks of being toyed with, Niall's first instinct was to brace himself for some new attack. He stopped short and stared at King Dempsey for a moment, before offering a deceptively respectful bow. "Your Majesty. I trust you slept well."

"Quite well, High Lord." The King flicked a finger upward, indicating that Niall could rise. "And yourself?"

"Not well at all, I'm sorry to say." Niall swallowed back any note of resentment or disdain, though even being in Dempsey's presence made his skin crawl with disgust. "Which brings me to an urgent matter I must discuss with Your Majesty without delay."

King Dempsey's eyes sparked with interest. "Ah yes, your wife's illness. Queen Elanor spoke at length on the matter yesterday evening. I do hope Kenna's recovered."

"I fear she is still suffering, my King. Even the smell of food causes her to become violently ill," Niall explained. The King's expression and tone of feigned concern made him feel a touch nauseous himself. "In light of her ailment, I must ask permission to take Kenna and my mother away from court. My family's home needs restoration, and fresh air away from the city would do the High Lady a world of good."

"But you're so recently returned to us," King Dempsey replied. The lack of an outright refusal gave Niall hope.

"Yes, but only because I learned of my mother's survival. Were it not for that, I would have remained in my family's lands and found a way to rebuild what was destroyed," Niall answered carefully. He dropped to his knees, knowing the demonstration would keep Dempsey from going on the defensive. It would have been more effective if others were present to witness this submission, but Niall wasn't willing to wait just to satisfy the man's ego. "Please, Your Majesty, I have so little left. I only wish to take my family and return to a quiet life away from courtly politics and anything but the business of my own estate."

"Away from courtly politics? As I recall, you used to be quite the avid participant in such things. Always at King Fergal's side, always eager to promote your family's interests. You were his little pet." King Dempsey's eyes were full of thinly veiled contempt. "In fact, he seemed barely capable of noting the accomplishments of anyone else."

Niall's eyes locked with Dempsey's. This was the closest they'd ever come to openly discussing King Fergal's favoritism or who the crown was intended for. "King Fergal is dead. My father and brother are dead. My only desire is to see to the well-being and safety of those remaining to me. A dead King can offer nothing to me now. It is the blessing of a living King that I seek."

"It is true, the wishes of a dead man—even a King— are of little use when the world continues without them," Dempsey contemplated Niall coolly.

"Please, Your Majesty. For the love you once bore my father and the late King," Niall pressed his palms together in supplication. Pride meant nothing compared to Kenna's needs. "I beg you, please, let us go. Let us be forgotten in the countryside."

King Dempsey remained silent, but his demeanor shifted and almost seemed to soften. Niall thought there might even be a hint of compassion in his eyes. He took a breath and nodded. "Very well, then, High

Lord Niall. You have my blessing to take your family and leave Rosehaven. You are more suited to the managing of sheep than the duties of court."

Niall almost fell over with the surprise. He'd hoped for this outcome, but never actually believed he could reach the older man's sense of fairness with so few words. He closed his eyes and let out a breath of relief. "Thank you, Your Majesty. Truly, thank you."

"Of course, Niall. I only seek what is best for my subjects, and you are counted among them, after all," King Dempsey replied. "I trust that you will continue to serve me loyally if, and when, I should call on you to do so."

"Of course," Niall answered quietly. He would not risk losing this small victory by allowing Dempsey's displays of superiority to bait him into a rash response. *Let the man have his court games. Soon enough I'll take Kenna and my mother far from this place. With any luck, we'll be utterly forgotten in the simplicity of country life.* "May I go to tell my wife and my mother that they should begin preparing for our departure?"

"The matter can wait until your day's work is done. You are still expected to perform your duties while you're in residence. As High Lord, others look to your example." Any glimmer of kindness in King Dempsey's countenance vanished. "If you have so little patience, you may send a servant to tell them."

Niall rose, bowed a final time, and backed out of the room. He quickly charged a servant with the task of delivering the King's decision to his family. He would have preferred to share the news himself, but such tidings could not wait until the end of the day. There was little time to celebrate, and most of the work to make ready for their return would fall to Kenna and his mother; but there was a light at the end of the tunnel now. Freedom was so close he could almost see the bright future it promised.

Though Dempsey had agreed to let them leave, it seemed he was determined to run Niall ragged in the meantime. As suspected, arranging the details of their departure fell to Kenna, giving her an excuse to avoid the Queen. It was a blessing that neither of them took for granted. There was much to consider before they returned to Britwylde, and Kenna's stomach remained sensitive. Niall watched over her with apprehension whenever he could steal time away from the King.

Even with so much to do, life seemed to ease as their return to Britwylde drew nearer. Kenna made arrangements for them to take up residence at the family's hunting lodge a few miles from Britwylde castle until repairs were complete. The lodge wasn't a luxurious home, but it had room for the three of them, and would provide comfortable accommodations until a more suitable place was built.

In a matter of days, all the details of their new life were made, and their few collected possessions were packed for the journey. On the evening before their departure, the court was gathered for dinner in the great hall. After a long day In King Dempsey's company, Niall was relieved to join Kenna for their farewell banquet.

Sir Liam sat across from them, his wife Aileen on one side and his daughter on the other. Considering his near-betrothal to Lisbeth, Niall was surprised by the friendship that had developed between her and Kenna. He'd never paid much attention to Lisbeth during his earlier life at court, but the kindness she had been showing to Kenna made Niall regret that aloofness. Over the past weeks, Sir Liam's entire family had proven to be of greater character and kindness than Niall expected.

"We must plan a visit once you've seen the castle restored," Lady Aileen said as she sipped her wine.

"Actually, Niall and Kenna intend to build a new home," Lisbeth said to her mother. "I can't say that I blame them. I think the prospect of starting over is a rather exciting one."

Niall smiled at them all. "Rest assured, as soon as we have lodgings with appropriate guest quarters, you'll all be welcome any time you'd like."

"In fact, I insist on it," Kenna added. She'd been feeling better today, though it didn't keep Niall from fretting over her. She tired easily, and continued to vomit on occasion. Kenna reached across the table to take Lisbeth's hand. "After all, you were almost betrothed to my husband."

"As I explained before, I was not myself when the union was put to me," Niall grumbled. Kenna and Lisbeth frequently made jokes about the matter. It was innocent enough, even if it made Niall blush. "But I would never deprive my wife of the company of a friend." A little pang of sadness pricked at Niall's mind. He missed Daris and Elize. Though freedom was near at hand, it would never be the same level that they experienced during their time with the travelers.

Sir Liam smiled indulgently, an expression muddled by the amount of wine he'd enjoyed over the course of the meal. "You really have changed from the young, ambitious man at King Fergal's side. High Lord now, married, and the man Fergal wished to follow him to the throne."

Niall choked on his wine. He looked around their table, catching the curious eyes of those nearest. Clearing his throat, he swallowed and put his goblet back on the table. "I highly doubt that, Sir Liam. And it is not an idea to be whispered idly, nor of interest to me."

"Pfff, it's more than an idea. King Fergal obviously intended to name you his heir," Sir Liam waved his hand in Niall's direction. "Not surprising in the least when you look at the man who will follow King Dempsey."

"Sir Liam, you should mind your words," Niall grabbed the other man's wine. "Perhaps you would benefit from a little water."

The atmosphere in the room was already shifting. Niall could sense more and more attention focusing on the conversation. He looked to Kenna, whose face had gone remarkably pale. Then he chanced a glance in the direction of the King.

Dempsey's eyes were locked on their table. He held his own goblet, but any sense of mirth or merrymaking was absent from his face. Niall couldn't say if King Dempsey had been keeping an eye on what was happening, or if some loyal courtier had already reported the conversation. It didn't matter: the one thing that was clear was that the King knew what had been said.

"A toast," Niall stood up and raised his cup in Dempsey's direction. "To our new rulers, King Dempsey and Queen Elanor. Long may they reign over us, and may their dynasty flourish in the years to come." It was the only thing he could think to do to defuse the situation and demonstrate his disinterest in ruling.

Dempsey stared at Niall for a few seconds before he smiled, an expression that was chilling and void of joy. Others lifted their goblets and drank with cheers and statements of agreement. Niall took a slow sip of his wine and then bowed slightly. The King nodded at him in return and lifted his cup to drink, but his vengeful eyes never left Niall's face.

The toast did serve its purpose on one front. The commotion ended the dangerous conversation around Niall and returned it to the mundane. People wished Niall and Kenna safe travels, and made empty invitations for lodgings when the two of them visited court. Lisbeth and her mother ushered Sir Liam out of the banquet, quietly making excuses as they took their leave.

"Sir Liam has a gift for saying and doing the exact opposite of what the occasion calls for," Kenna whispered to Niall as Lisbeth waved to her from the door. "It's a good thing we're leaving in the morning. I'd hate to see how you'd be made to pay for those comments in the weeks to come."

Niall looked at the King surreptitiously. The man was no longer focused on them. He seemed to be engaged in pleasant conversation with Cathal, who for once, was not utterly besotted by wine. Cathal caught Niall's eye and looked away quickly. The action made Niall feel as if his stomach had suddenly filled with rocks.

"I think we should consider making an early exit as well," Niall muttered. He downed the last of his wine and stood to offer his hand to Kenna. "Come, wife, we depart early, and you are only recently recovered from your infirmity."

They were nearly at the door when King Dempsey called out. Niall exhaled slowly. He exchanged a quick and fearful look with Kenna before turning to face the King. "Yes, Your Majesty?"

"The hour is still early. Surely you would not deprive us of your company before the evening is up?" King Dempsey stood and gestured for the servants to bring the dessert. "Not when you and your lovely wife will be departing Rosehaven entirely in the morning."

"I was beginning to feel ill again, Your Majesty," Kenna piped in. She curtsied demurely and then put a hand over her stomach, as if it were unsettled. The performance was a convincing one. Even Niall found himself worrying.

"Such a pity, High Lady. You may go to your rest if you feel too unwell to remain, but I must insist that your husband stay. I thought we might engage in a bit of entertainment," the King replied. Dempsey looked around the room. "What say all of you?"

"May I at least escort my wife back to our room?" Niall asked, once the cheers for sport died down. He didn't know what fresh torment the King had planned, but it was sure to be something constructed to humiliate and bring misery to them both.

"Actually, love, I am already feeling a bit recovered. I'll stay. I'm curious to see what the King has in mind." Kenna gave his hand a reassuring pat. "Truly, I would not miss our final evening in such robust company."

"How marvelous," it was Queen Elanor who spoke now. She smiled at Kenna and Niall, then looked to her husband. "Darling, what manner of revelry do you have planned for us?"

King Dempsey gestured to his son. "Actually, it was Cathal who put me in mind of it. He and I were commenting on how High Lord Niall looks so much less scholarly than he did before he left court. His time in the wilds has obviously made him more sporting."

Niall clutched Kenna's hand tightly as he escorted her back to their seats. He pulled the chair out for his wife and went to sit down beside her.

"Don't bother sitting, High Lord," King Dempsey called out. "Your participation is crucial. After all, did you not spend time on stage while you were away?"

"I did what circumstances required." Niall had to work to keep from grinding his teeth. "What sort of entertainment would please my King?"

"A test of strength between Prince Cathal and yourself," King Dempsey purred. "It has been quite some time since my son had to prove his competence in combat. As I recall, you never were much for such endeavors, were you, High Lord? But surely you've gained greater skill during your time away."

Niall's pulse was racing. This was undoubtedly the result of Sir Liam's drunken comments. The King was determined to prove to all assembled that his son was the better man, and that Niall was weak in comparison. It didn't matter what King Fergal might have thought before his death.

"I fear I would not be up to the task, Your Majesty," Niall glanced down at Kenna miserably.

Cathal looked as if he wanted to leave as badly as Niall did. "Father, I don't think—"

"Nonsense," King Dempsey cut his son's words short. "I insist upon it." He pointed to one of the guards at the end of the table. "Go fetch a pair of blunted swords. We will have a contest of skill to entertain us over dessert."

Niall swallowed back his own protests as he watched the guard leave the room. There was no way for him to get out of this, and no way that he could allow Cathal to do anything but win. King Dempsey wouldn't allow the evening to come to a close until his son was proven the better man. Or at least, until Niall was forced to publicly concede to the idea. *I can barely stomach being in the same room with Cathal. Now I have to let the deceitful, murdering drunkard triumph in front of the entire court.*

"Very well, Your Majesty," Niall bit out through clenched teeth. He unfastened his tunic and gave it to

Kenna to hold before he marched to the open space between the tables. Cathal approached, looking equally miserable by the proposed entertainment. He offered a hand to Niall to shake. Niall stared down at it for several seconds before he was able to dismiss his revulsion. He shook Cathal's hand quickly then jerked his hand away.

He caught Kenna's gaze as the guard returned with the practice blades. She looked worried and strained, and the pallor of her skin was pale. Anger welled up inside Niall. This was as torturous for her as it was for him: no doubt King Dempsey and Queen Elanor had intended it to be. Niall accepted one of the swords and turned back to Cathal. The image of Ian's final agonizing moments flashed through his mind. The memory was followed in quick succession by the nightmare of the attack on Britwylde.

Cathal hefted his weapon and began to circle. Niall's grip on the hilt of his sword tightened. His knuckles were white with tension. The culmination of everything these people had taken from him, his mother, and everything that they'd done to Kenna, swirled in Niall's mind. It coalesced into resolve fueled by rage.

Niall charged first. He swung his sword down and to the left. Cathal barely had time to block the blow. The sound of metal clanging against metal echoed off the marble walls of the otherwise silent room.

Cathal stumbled backward and twisted away. As one attack followed the next, he was forced to remain on the defensive. It was obvious that the High Lord was in far better physical condition than the Prince. Niall was fast, he was precise, and he wasn't holding back. Cathal's movements were slow and clumsy by comparison.

Niall swung again and again, driving Cathal through the room. He hated these people and the ridiculous, vengeful ways in which they toyed with him. King Dempsey and his family had taken everything that was precious and now they had the audacity to ask for more. It was all Niall could do to keep his weapon from actually striking Cathal.

Their swords met and clashed several times. Cathal blocked the onslaught but never launched an attack of his own. The display would have continued if it weren't for a little puddle of wine on one of the tiles. Niall's foot hit the burgundy liquid and slipped slightly. It wasn't enough to cost him his balance, or the upper hand, but it did cool the white-hot rage that fueled his attacks. Niall looked at Cathal, seeing the pathetic, weak fool that he was. The man was terrified.

No, it isn't terror, it's something else. He isn't even trying to fight back. Niall slowed his assault as clarity took the place of anger. *Cathal doesn't want this. He wants me to beat him.* Panting, Niall lowered his sword. The two of them stared at one another in silent understanding. Cathal shook his head and started to walk back to his seat at the King's side.

"The match is not complete until one of you yields to the other," King Dempsey declared. His face was practically purple with ill-concealed wrath.

Cathal stopped in his tracks. Niall couldn't see his face, but from the set of his shoulders, and the way King Dempsey's upper lip curled in disgust, he guessed Cathal was about to concede the match.

"Come then, Your Highness," Niall called out. "The King has spoken. We cannot deprive these people of their sport."

Cathal turned back slowly. He approached Niall and leaned toward him, lowering his voice to a whisper. "There's nothing sporting about this. We already know who the better man is."

"Maybe, but you chose your path," Niall shoved him a little. "Now see it through so I can be done with this charade."

Cathal shook his head again and for a moment Niall thought he would refuse to carry the bout further. He was on the verge of shoving Cathal a second time, when the other man hauled off and struck Niall in the face with the pommel of his sword.

Niall dropped his weapon and it spiraled away, as he staggered back in surprise. Blood spurted from his nose. He heard Kenna gasp. Cathal was stalking toward him now, weapon poised.

Clutching his bleeding nose with one hand, Niall side-stepped the attack and hurried to retrieve his sword. The two of them circled one another, exchanging blows on occasion. They both knew that it wouldn't be enough for King Dempsey to see Niall yield without a fight. This had to look real. Niall went on the offensive again, forcing Cathal to engage.

No one cheered or offered applause. They watched in complete silence. This wasn't a friendly display, and everyone present knew it. The combatants parried and turned 'round the room. Niall pushed Cathal back a step at a time, almost taking him down more than once.

Suddenly Cathal charged at full speed. He ducked down and crashed into Niall, lifting him off the ground entirely before slamming him onto the stone floor. The force of the attack was enough to knock the air from Niall's lungs. His head hit the marble tiles and bounced. It made his vision go dark, except for little star-like bursts of light. Niall lay on the ground and struggled to draw a breath as his eyes refocused. The match was easily Cathal's, but the other man hesitated. He looked down at Niall with an ashen face and haunted eyes. The sword fell from his hand and clattered on the floor at his feet.

"I yield!" Niall managed to gasp, realizing his opponent would not claim the victory.

Hesitant applause came from a few hands, then was joined by others. Kenna rushed to Niall's side and helped him back to his feet. She gently pressed a folded napkin to his nose to stem the blood that continued to flow. Niall caught her hand and held it. Cathal walked past him without a word and returned to the Royal table with slumped shoulders and bowed head. Niall followed his progress before looking at the King. "I believe the Prince has proven himself. May I take my leave to attend my injuries and make ready for the morrow?"

King Dempsey glared down at him. Niall was beginning to worry that he would be forced to remain and continue the ghastly pageant of civility with blood dripping down his face. Then the King inclined his head and gestured graciously toward the doors. "Goodnight, High Lord. Rest, and we will speak again in the morning."

Kenna helped Niall to his feet and ushered him out of the hall. They made it back to their room without any further interference. His mother joined them a short time later. She insisted on tending Niall's wounds, but left after she was satisfied that they were only superficial. Their final evening at the palace was over, and though it had resulted in a small amount of bloodshed, it would soon be a memory. Niall only hoped his family's lands would be far enough away to satisfy Dempsey and his queen.

* * *

Despite a night of tossing and turning, Niall woke with a renewed sense of hope. He shared the morning meal in the comfort of his own apartment with only his wife and mother for company. No one bothered them, and it seemed that life at court was already moving ahead without them. Everything they were taking was packed and loaded onto the carriage by the time they were finished with their breakfast. The day was an absolutely beautiful one. It felt like the heavens themselves were rejoicing at the prospect of the journey.

Niall stood outside the palace with Kenna, waiting for the driver to arrive and the final necessities of travel to be put in place. His mother was a short distance away, bidding farewell to some of her friends. She'd been at court for months and established friendships with many of the people there.

"If it's all right with you, I thought we could take our lunch in the carriage and stop as little as possible. I want to cover as much distance today as we can," Niall commented to Kenna. "Is your stomach feeling any better?"

"It's not too bad now that breakfast has settled," Kenna answered. She was smiling softly to herself. "And I agree entirely. I'm eager to be away from here and to set up our family's new home." Her smile broadened and she laughed a little.

"You're in very good spirits," Niall commented happily. He brought her hand to his lips and kissed the back of her fingers. "Shall we stop in some of the towns to reprise our act?"

Kenna laughed again. "I doubt your mother would enjoy seeing us take aim at each other. But yes, I am in good spirits. There's much to celebrate." She paused, then looked at him with a mischievous sparkle in her eye. "I've a surprise for you once we're well away from this place."

"Oh? What sort of surprise?" Niall asked. He was intrigued, and couldn't help but enjoy the sense of liberation in the air.

"You're going to have to wait and see," Kenna answered playfully and kissed his cheek.

Niall was about to whisper a guess into her ear when one of the King's stewards came hurrying out the doors and down the steps toward them. "High Lord, King Dempsey wishes to speak with you before you depart."

Niall's spirits came crashing back toward the earth like a felled dove. The clear blue sky lost some of its brightness. He wasn't surprised, but he'd hoped to leave without any parting shots being fired. He kissed Kenna's hand again. "I'll be back straight away."

He followed the steward into the palace and past the bustle of courtiers and servants. There was nothing different to the daily business of the place. For all the fuss made over Niall's return, his departure seemed to have little impact. The hallway leading to the King's study was quieter than usual.

Niall was ushered through the doors and then directly into the King's presence. He bowed low, happy to show the man any amount of flattery he had to in order to put the court and everything about Rosehaven behind him. "Your Majesty, I was told you sent for me?"

"Ah, yes," King Dempsey casually looked up from a piece of parchment on his desk. "I trust your wife and mother are prepared for the long trek back to the estate?"

"Yes, everything is ready. We'll leave as soon as you dismiss me." Niall straightened. "Is there anything in particular you required, or is this a farewell?"

"I'm afraid that's why I've called you here," King Dempsey leaned back in his chair and studied Niall. "There's been a change of plans."

Niall could have sworn the floor fell out from beneath him, reality seemed to tilt strangely. His face felt numb, his palms began to sweat. "Your Majesty, my wife is still unwell. I cannot allow her to remain in a place that has such a negative impact on her health."

"Have no fear, Niall. I would not ask you to keep your wife here. In fact, I insist that she retire to your estate and see to her well-being," the King answered quickly, putting his hands up as if trying to reassure Niall of his concern and understanding. "But there is much to be done yet. My advisors believe it would be unwise for you to leave court at this time."

"But... I cannot be parted from—please." Niall choked on his words. He could barely form a coherent thought, much less put a sentence together. He felt like the jaws of a trap were snapping around him. Kenna was being sent away, and he would not be allowed to follow. "You said we could leave. I can't send her away alone."

"Of course not," King Dempsey stood up and walked around the table to wrap an arm around Niall's shoulder. The grip was painfully tight; possessive and unrelenting. "Which is why your mother must go as well. They can see to your affairs back home, and you will be here with me."

Niall drew a shaky breath. He wanted to knock the King's arm off his shoulders but was too shocked to make his body obey. They were so close to being free, and now he knew that freedom would never be granted.

"You should be honored. I recall how diligently you served King Fergal. I must have that level of service myself. Your presence at court is absolutely essential." The King wasn't even bothering to hide his delight at

Niall's distress. "Now, go and see your wife off. Your home is quite a long way from Rosehaven. You don't want to delay them."

"Y—yes, Your Majesty," Niall barely recognized his own voice, it was so quiet and defeated. The thought of delivering this news to Kenna and his mother made him feel physically ill. Yet, somehow, he had to find a way to do it. The King would not hesitate to send a servant to deliver the news for him and Niall would be forced to watch their departure from behind a window. "I'll be back shortly."

"That's a good lad," King Dempsey gave Niall's shoulder a firm pat. He moved back to his desk and began rifling through the papers there but stopped when Niall opened the door. "And Niall, do impart to them my wishes for a safe journey. Tell them to use wisdom in their travels. Foolhardy behavior can cost lives in these troubled times."

Niall stopped and turned to the King. Whether in the palace or not, none of them were safe, and all would suffer for the actions of one. "I will impart your regard, and trust their safety to your good grace."

"I'm glad you understand my concern." King Dempsey's lips curved in a slow predatory sneer. "Off you go then."

Niall stepped outside and closed the door behind him. He barely noticed his passage from the King's study to the palace doors. He walked out into the sunny courtyard and felt nothing of the day's warmth. Kenna was happily chatting with his mother beside the carriage. She looked up at his approach and her smile faded.

Niall pulled her into his arms and clung to her. His tongue felt thick and stiff when he spoke. "The King has changed his mind. He shares my concerns for your health and insists that you and my mother return to the estate, but I am to remain here in his service."

"No, no. You're coming with us," Kenna said. She reached for his hands and tried to pull him toward the carriage. "Just get in the carriage with me, and we'll go."

Niall shook his head, fighting against the urge to defy the King and do as she asked. "I wish that I could."

"Niall, I can't leave you here. I can't."

"You must, my love," Niall whispered. He pulled her close again. "I swear, I will follow as soon as I'm able." They both knew it was unlikely King Dempsey would ever willingly allow him to leave. Niall held his hand out to his mother. "Take Kenna home. Look after each other. Know that you will both be in my thoughts every minute that we're apart."

"I'll speak with the Queen. She's a mother. Some part of her must know this is wrong," Lady Carene responded. She gripped him protectively. "I will not leave my only child here to suffer alone."

"Listen to me, both of you," Niall insisted, pulling back to meet their eyes. "You must get in that carriage, and you must leave. King Dempsey will strike at you both if we resist this. I need to know that you're safe." Then in a quieter voice. "Do not stop at the estate. Go to Kenna's family. You'll be protected there, and in a better position to negotiate for my release."

His mother took his face in her hands and kissed each cheek, then his forehead. "Be careful, Niall. I love you, and I will do everything in my power to see you away from this place."

"Thank you," Niall whispered. He hugged her tightly. "May I have a moment with Kenna?"

She hugged him again and then climbed into the carriage. Niall could hear her sniffling as he took Kenna's hands in his.

"I love you, Kenna. Please, don't put yourself in harm's way to fight this." Niall stroked her cheek with his thumb. He wanted to preserve every detail of her face in his memory. He'd hold to it in the days to come and let it be the image that kept him from giving up entirely. "I wish I could give you the life I promised when I married you. I so wanted to build that home with you."

"This isn't how it was supposed to be," Kenna whispered in a voice broken with tears. "I don't want to leave you behind. I don't know how to go without you."

"I know, but I'm safer with you out of their reach," Niall replied. He tried to smile bravely, but his heart was too heavy to make it convincing. "And now you can set up a home for us in Arthan. Surprise me with all the wonders of a water garden of our own."

Kenna kissed him deeply. She threaded her fingers into his hair and clung to him, lips and tongue conveying her sorrow without words. Niall returned the kiss, desperate, his heart breaking as he held her. When they finally pulled apart, he rested his forehead against hers. "I loved you from the very moment we met, and I will love you until I draw my last breath."

"We will see each other again, Niall. I swear this will not be our last embrace," Kenna vowed before she kissed him again, this one was fleeting and chaste compared to the other. She whimpered a little as she pulled away. "Promise me that you won't lose hope."

"I promise," Niall replied with solemn sincerity. "Now go, before the King summons me back or changes his mind and insists that you stay as well. I'll write to you every single day. We'll get through this."

Niall guided her to the carriage and helped her into her seat. Her eyes remained on his face even as he closed the door behind her. The driver climbed into his seat but before he clucked at the horses to move, Kenna reached out of the window for Niall. He took her hand, their fingers lacing together.

The carriage started to move forward. Niall walked beside the coach and clung to Kenna's hand for as long as he could. Then the animals' pace increased and Kenna's fingers slipped through his. Niall's heart split down the middle, a deep, painful ache radiating through his chest. It took all the resolve he possessed to remain upright as he watched his world drive away. If he only had himself to worry about, he would have collapsed on the cobblestones, but Niall didn't want Kenna's last view to be the moment he broke. He was alone now, and adrift in a sea of enemies.

CHAPTER 19

A New Act

The carriage dragged Kenna away from Niall like a predator with more strength than she could fight. She was still in a state of shock, not quite able to believe they were being torn apart. Her heart was broken, but the breaking was a slow, agonizing process. New cracks appeared and widened with each mile. It wasn't until Lady Carene pulled her close and dabbed a handkerchief at the tears on her cheeks that Kenna even realized she was weeping. The realization turned silent tears into body-wracking sobs.

"They took him from me. He should have fought back. I should have stayed with him," she cried, angry and devastated. She was outraged at the way the King and Queen toyed with them. She was angry at Niall for not ignoring them and coming anyway, and she was livid with herself for letting it happen. She clenched her hands into fists at her side and slammed them against the cushioned seat. Despite her anguish and anger, Kenna knew they couldn't fight the King's order. It wasn't just a matter of her own safety, or Niall's. It would have been so much worse for them all if she'd refused to leave.

"I know, darling, and so does Niall," Lady Carene soothed. She held tightly to Kenna, stroking her hair and weeping along with her. "We will find a way to get him back safely, but that is a discussion best left for later." She jerked her head toward the front of the enclosed carriage, reminding Kenna that they weren't completely alone.

Kenna took a breath and hiccupped as she released it. Falling to pieces wasn't the answer. It wouldn't change their situation; it would only make finding the solution more difficult. Her face crumpled again and a fresh batch of tears flowed down her cheeks. Lady Carene pulled her closer still and held tightly as Kenna poured out her grief and rage in powerless sobs.

It was several minutes before Kenna pulled herself together again. The countryside that passed by the carriage window was lush and green, and it helped her focus past the pain. She wiped her face and smoothed hands over her skirt. The simple actions were mundane, but that was as close as she could come to feeling normal right now. Her sense of composure was tenuous but there.

One thing became certain; King Dempsey never intended to allow Niall out of his sight. Sir Liam's comments at dinner were foolish, even dangerous, but ultimately not the cause of this situation. The King and Queen demonstrated a special skill in knowing exactly how to cause the most harm to those they considered a threat. They were meticulous and ruthless in the application of that talent. That told Kenna their positions were not as secure as they liked.

Niall might have more friends and support in Rosehaven than he thought. That support was both good and dangerous. If King Dempsey and his Queen wished to get rid of Niall, they would have to find a way to do it that would silence his supporters and keep them from mounting an uprising in his name. Whatever action they took it would be exact and merciless.

Kenna crossed her arms, fuming. *They're fools. If they had any sense at all they would have let Niall leave. He's done nothing to demonstrate an interest in the throne. With time and distance things would have settled on their own. Niall would be here with me, and Rosehaven would have forgotten us.*

The view outside came into focus again. A happy life far from court was a pretty dream, and one Kenna wanted to cling to. Her lips trembled and she could feel her composure cracking again. *But the moment King Fergal chose Niall, we lost that chance. It wouldn't matter where we were, his claim would put him at odds with anyone who wanted that kind of power.*

A familiar two-story building appeared through the opening in the curtains. The sight of it shook Kenna from her sorrow. She suddenly sat up straighter. They'd stopped here on the return to Rosehaven. This was where Niall hid the weapon used against Ian. "Stop the carriage! I feel ill. I need to step out." She banged on the far wall until the vehicle heaved to a stop.

"Is it your stomach again?" Lady Carene asked. She was watching Kenna closely.

"It is," Kenna answered with an absent nod. She jumped out of her seat and flung the door wide. "I'll just be a moment."

"Shall I come with you?" Lady Carene asked.

Kenna waved a dismissive hand at her mother-in-law and kept moving, making straight for the chicken coop. There was a clump of bushes a few feet past it, and this was where Kenna stopped. She was only partially obscured by the bushes, but having blamed the stop on illness, she simply doubled over with her back to them and began to dig. Lady Carene would take her for her word, and the shrubbery concealed her work. Kenna was too focused on the task to care beyond those details.

Luck was on her side; there'd been little rain over the past weeks and the signs of Niall's work were still visible beneath the foliage if one knew what to look for. The wretched weapon wasn't buried deeply, Niall hadn't had the time or tools to do a comprehensive job when they were here before. The weapon was still wrapped in the shirt he'd worn the night they left Britwylde. Kenna snatched the thing up and twisted it into the folds of her underskirt. She brushed her hands off as best she could and returned to the carriage.

"You should drink some water, Kenna," Lady Carene said as they climbed back into the coach. "Maybe we should take a break, give you time to rest and recover."

Kenna shook her head. "No, we need to get back on the road if we hope to make it to the next town before dark."

"I really believe it would be better for you if we took a break. Traveling is tiring, and you shouldn't strain yourself." The older woman was studying Kenna carefully.

"I'm well enough to keep going. Please, I'll drink some water, and sleep on the way." Kenna knocked against the side of the carriage to signal to the driver. She fixed a pointed look on her mother-in-law. "It would be best if we were on our way again. There's important work to do and we shouldn't delay any further."

Lady Carene considered Kenna silently, then nodded with understanding. She settled back in her seat, and their journey continued. Kenna pulled the bundled weapon from her skirt and stuffed it into the bag with her night clothes. She didn't tell her companion what it was. There was still a risk of being overheard, and it was the instrument of Ian's death. Something like that was not to be mentioned casually in a place where safety and secrecy were concerns.

They made impressive progress after that, and were far from Rosehaven by the end of the day. It was well past dinner time when they finally pulled off the road and took rooms at an inn on the outskirts of a quiet town. Kenna's body ached from the drive, and her heart ached from Niall's absence. She wanted to curl up and sleep, but there was much that needed to be discussed. Not the least of which was how they would save Niall from King Dempsey and Queen Elanor's brutality.

Claiming fatigue, Kenna excused herself from the dinner table early. It wasn't a lie, and she didn't have to exert herself to convince anyone of her weariness. The only untruth was the implication that Kenna intended to go straight to bed. Sleep had to wait. Lady Carene made her own excuses and followed Kenna up to the room they were sharing for the night.

"Are you going to tell me why we really stopped earlier today?" Lady Carene asked after she finished bolting the door.

Kenna placed the bag with the murder weapon on the bed and turned to look Niall's mother in the eye. She didn't know how Lady Carene would respond, but the news would not be pleasant for her. After a little consideration, Kenna decided that the direct approach was the best one. "That was where Niall hid the weapon used against Ian. I needed to retrieve it."

Lady Carene inhaled sharply and placed a hand over her heart. She didn't weep, nor did she sink into a chair, but met Kenna's statement with courage and responded calmly. "To what end?"

"We both know that Niall is not safe at the palace," Kenna began. She placed her fingertips on the bag and rallied what little energy remained to her. "I believe it's likely King Dempsey will find some crime to charge him with. This weapon proves that Ian's death was no accident. It gives us something to barter for Niall's release."

"Or it could spur King Dempsey to take immediate action," Niall's mother pointed out gently. "We must remember that they have the power to kill Niall without us ever drawing near enough to prevent it. Anything we do must be handled with caution to ensure he won't pay the price of a misstep."

Kenna bit her lower lip to keep it from trembling, and the physical discomfort helped her to hold her tears at bay. She felt helpless and terrified, and that made her angry. But she tried to keep her temper in check, worried that she might lose the tenuous grip on her composure if she let that anger get the better of her. She sank onto the bed, rubbing her temples. "I know whatever we do puts Niall at risk, but doing nothing can't be our only option," she said, staring down at her lap. "I have the weapon and King Fergal's declaration naming Niall. There must be a way to turn that to our advantage."

Lady Carene moved to sit next to Kenna and took her hands. "We should go to your family. We'll be in a better position to take action when we have their backing."

"Getting there takes too long, and we'll be too far from Niall to act quickly when Dempsey does enact whatever sick plans he has in mind," Kenna replied. She rose to pace off the anxious energy. She didn't know how they could save Niall, but everything in her screamed that they shouldn't go too far. "We have to stay close. I can't say with any certainty when the King will act, but I think it's likely he plans to strike once we're too far to intervene. Going much further than this will be giving him exactly what he wants."

"My instincts say the same," Lady Carene agreed. She bit her thumb and frowned. "No doubt our driver's been instructed to notify Dempsey and Elanor if we deviate from our course."

Kenna nodded. "And he will be expected to report back as soon as we've reached Britwylde. If he doesn't, we may as well go knock on the palace doors and announce our defiance."

They fell into silent contemplation. Every option seemed to put Niall in greater danger. Kenna continued to pace, ignoring the way her body screamed for rest. There would be plenty of time for her to indulge her physical condition later. What she needed to do now was find a way out of this mess. "Do you think the driver could be paid off, convinced to say he delivered us to Britwylde?"

"Possibly, but we'd be asking him to lie to the King, an offense that could lead to execution. I doubt it could be done cheaply, and our fortunes are not what they once were," Lady Carene answered thoughtfully.

"We shouldn't dismiss it entirely," Kenna stated. It was a slim hope, but better than nothing. She stopped her restless wandering and stared into the flames. Resolve hardened around her fear and grief; a shell of composure to help her think clearly. One way or another, she would remain close to Rosehaven. "We'll put an offer to him tomorrow once we've stopped for the day. I'm not willing to travel any further than that, but the added distance might make him more receptive to the idea. If he refuses," she paused, her stomach twisting ominously, "we'll do what must be done, and then return to Rosehaven."

Lady Carene's eyes locked with Kenna's. She took a deep breath and squared her shoulders. "Agreed, whatever must be done." She stood up and took hold of Kenna. "But now, you need to rest. You'll feel worse if you over-exert yourself. Niall wouldn't want that, and neither do I."

Kenna didn't argue. She allowed her mother-in-law to help her undress, and tuck her into bed. Tired as she was, her mind raced with worry that made it difficult for her to relax enough for sleep. She wondered if Niall was able to sleep, if he felt as alone and defeated as she did now. Her heart broke at the idea that he was lying there without anyone to hold him and soothe away his fears. Were her own safety all she had to be concerned with, Kenna would have jumped out of bed, stolen a horse from the stable, and ridden all night to get back to him.

* * *

After a restless night, Kenna was even less enthused about another day on the move. Each mile they covered further dampened her spirits. It didn't help matters that the roads were poorly maintained. The constant rocking and jolting of the carriage worked in tandem with her stress to aggravate her digestion. This time when she called for a sudden halt, her illness was not a pretense.

It was late afternoon when they finally approached a drab and cheerless village, though Kenna suspected her impression of it might be the result of her misery and nothing in particular about the town itself. Per Lady Carene's insistence, they pulled to a stop and climbed out of the carriage. She had been watching

Kenna with the focus of a hawk for the past several hours, and would hear no arguments against taking a break.

The driver said little to them; if he was eager to continue, he didn't show it. Kenna herself was grateful for the reprieve. The seats inside the carriage were cushioned, but after so many hours they felt hard and uncomfortable. The chance to stretch her legs and work out the cramping in her lower back was a welcome one.

She stayed by the carriage for a few minutes, watching as the driver filled buckets of water for the horses. He didn't seem to be a cruel man. He wasn't overly friendly or talkative, but he was courteous when they did interact. It wasn't surprising that he maintained his distance. This was not the pleasant and lively treks of the traveling folk, and the division between classes was a harsher reality when one person was in obvious service to the other.

Kenna closed her eyes and thought back on those happy days. She smiled to herself, remembering the playful banter and never-ceasing jingle of bells when the caravan moved down the country roads. The memory of how Niall would often whistle to himself as they trekked along made Kenna's smile broaden. At first, he'd whistled songs from his youth or time at court, but after time, his tunes shifted to the bawdier ballads sung by their companions. Thoughts of those happy times were so vivid and precious. Kenna could hear the music even now. Happy fiddling echoed in her ears, followed by the sound of applause.

Her eyes flew open. It wasn't her imagination at all. The music was real, it had life and the sweet familiarity of home. After months of performing her act with Niall, Kenna knew the melodies in her sleep. It wasn't just any troupe, it was hers.

She hiked up her skirts and took off down the muddy streets, following the tune like a siren's song. The music grew louder and Kenna couldn't help but feel that it was welcoming her home. She turned a corner and was greeted with the joyful vision of red, blue, green, and yellow banners festooning a circle of wagons. A crowd was pressed close to the unfolded stage, clapping and cheering as Daris and Elize performed the final tricks in their act.

Kenna's spirit soared as the show ended in an uproar of cheers and applause. Remmy jumped up to give his usual closing plea for compensation. Baskets and coins filtered through the crowd. Some of the villagers lingered nearby but most tossed a few coins and wandered away to return to the doldrums of their daily lives. It didn't take long for the people to notice Kenna's rich, fine clothing amidst their own simple garb. They did doubletakes, then hurried to lower themselves in bows or curtsies. The presence of a noblewoman was not something they were accustomed to, or expecting.

In minutes, Kenna found herself surrounded by the townsfolk. She stood on tip toe, and scanned the sides of the stage, where she knew the performers waited to receive their share of what was gathered after a performance. The commotion quickly drew the notice of the travelers. Kenna saw heads turning, eyes focusing. and the light of recognition when they saw her face.

An exuberant female voice rang out over the murmurs of the surprised townsfolk. "Kenna!" Elize pushed past the crowd and ran toward Kenna with open arms.

The muscles in Kenna's back and shoulders relaxed, and some of the gloom cleared. Her time among the travelers represented safety and freedom. The friendship that Elize and Daris offered was genuine, and the hug that Elize wrapped Kenna in was proof of that. Kenna clung to the other woman, as though that embrace would keep her afloat in the midst of all the misery that was pulling her under.

"Oh, Kenna! I'm so happy to see you," Elize squeezed tighter, then stepped back and held her at arm's length. "What's happened? You look terrible." She glanced around the immediate area. "Where is Niall?"

There was only one answer Kenna could give. She slumped into her friend's arms and felt the tears tumble from her lashes and down her cheeks. "He wasn't allowed to leave, and I wasn't allowed to stay."

"Kenna, no," Elize guided her away from the crowd to the safety of the other performers. "Tell me everything."

"It was awful." Kenna could barely get the short sentence out between hiccupping breaths. "They were... so... cruel." She breathed in deeply, trying to steady herself, wiping the tears from her eyes. She thought of the courtly games, the fight with Cathal, Dempsey's cold and calculating words. The memories fueled the tears that fell fast and hot down her cheeks. Elize pulled her into a hug, shushing her and whispering that everything would be all right.

Kenna took a shuddering breath and rallied her composure. "There is so much I have to tell you, but I shouldn't speak of it here. I'm sure Niall's mother is wondering where I am."

"We'll take you back to her," Daris spoke up as he joined his wife. He wrapped one of his arms around Kenna protectively. "Whatever it is, you aren't facing it alone. That's why we're here. We were coming to Rosehaven to check on the two of you."

"I doubt you would have been allowed entrance. The King knows we were taken in by a band of travelers. You would have been turned away or cast into the dungeon. Niall was right. The King would have hurt us by hurting you," Kenna explained. She'd longed for their company, but the thought of what Dempsey and Elanor would have done to them was too much to bear.

"It looks like he caused enough pain without our presence," Elize's voice was sharp with anger.

"Well, you're among friends now, Kenna. We'll get things sorted." Daris kept an arm wrapped around her as they started back toward the inn. His grip was warm and strong, shielding Kenna from the eyes of those they passed.

Despite her words, Kenna was torn between wishing her friends had made it before she was forced to leave Niall, and being relieved that they weren't subjected to the pitiless machinations of King Dempsey and Queen Elanor. The dream of a safe escape in the presence of their adopted family was one she wished could have become reality. That path was full of sunshine and warmth, compared to the murky one she now walked.

Kenna felt a surge of guilt when they rounded the corner and she caught sight of Niall's mother. Lady Carene was pacing back and forth at the rear of the vehicle. Even from a distance it was obvious that she was sick with worry. Her face was red, as if she was holding back tears, and her shoulders were rigid. When she looked up and saw Kenna approaching, she let out a small, half-strangled sound and ran to meet them. "Are you well? Where did you go, my dear?" She pulled Kenna from Daris and Elize to examine her with the fretful gaze of a mother.

"I'm sorry. I shouldn't have taken off without letting you know where I was going," Kenna apologized sincerely. She hadn't thought of the toll her absence would take and was immediately ashamed for the lack of consideration she'd shown. "I heard music and went to investigate."

Lady Carene's eyes raked over Elize and Daris, not unkindly, but with a fiercely protective glint. "As long as you're safe, but please let me know where you're going next time. I couldn't bear to lose you too."

"Of course, I promise. There's enough to worry about without my recklessness on top of everything," Kenna looked from Lady Carene to Elize and Daris. "But I think our fortunes may have changed. Lady Carene, let me introduce you to my friends. These are the people Niall and I spoke of, Elize and Daris. Elize, Daris, this is Lady Carene of Britwylde, Niall's mother."

The two travelers lowered themselves into a bow and a curtsy respectfully. Lady Carene released Kenna and held her hands out to the two of them. "No, rise. You of all people owe me no displays of respect. Niall and Kenna told me of all you did for them. You saved my family. It is I who owes you."

Elize and Daris rose slowly. They looked surprised and uncomfortable by the response. Kenna held back a laugh, something that she hadn't done in weeks. Daris and Elize frequently accepted the impersonal adoration of an audience but now balked at the unfeigned gratitude of one woman.

"My Lady, please," Daris managed awkwardly. He offered a hand to Lady Carene as she stood back up. "We did only what we thought was right."

"Niall and Kenna have become dear friends. Their friendship has been enough reward," Elize added.

Kenna smiled at them both until the hollowness of Niall's absence caused her to sober. "He should be here with us now. Niall missed you as much as I did."

"Which brings us to the source of our woes and worries," Lady Carene commented. "The driver went inside to see to our lodgings for the night. I know we hoped to put a little more distance between us and the palace before we made our proposal to Phineas, but I think the extra rest will do you good."

"Extra rest? What's happened?" Elize looked at Kenna in alarm.

"I took ill while we were at court. It was the reason King Dempsey allowed me to leave," Kenna explained. "Niall was to join us," Kenna felt her anger and hurt building again, "but the King decided that he should remain behind."

"Who is Phineas, and what sort of proposal did you plan to put before him?" Daris glanced at the door anxiously. Though he'd never spent a day at court, Kenna could see that the gravity of their predicament was not lost on the traveling performer.

"He's the man the King charged with driving us to our family lands." Lady Carene looked at him frankly. "We intend to ask him to allow us to go our own way, but to make it appear as though he delivered us to Britwylde."

"To deceive the King, until we can secure Niall's freedom," Kenna said, making certain her friends understood the gravity of what they were going to ask of the man.

"And if he refuses?" Elize asked quietly.

Kenna met her eyes and lifted her chin in determination. "For his sake, I hope he does not."

Daris and Elize exchanged quick, but meaningful glances. They settled into stances that Kenna knew well. They were determined to be a part of this, and there was nothing that could be said to dissuade them. It lifted a terrible weight off Kenna's shoulders. She blinked back a fresh batch of tears. "Thank you."

"Of course," Daris replied. He met her eyes and continued in a grave tone. "Come to the caravan tonight. We'll do whatever we must."

Kenna took his meaning with absolute clarity. If things went poorly with the driver, Daris was prepared to be the one to ensure the man's silence. She hated to expose them to such a dark reality, but there was too much on the line for her to refuse help. "I will get my husband back, no matter the cost." Daris nodded and laid out a plan to help them achieve their aims.

Phineas returned a few minutes later, reporting that their rooms were secured and dinner would be brought up at the appropriate hour. He eyed Daris and Elize with curiosity but not hostility. Kenna thanked him and introduced her friends. It wasn't the first time her experience on stage had served her well in the past weeks.

"Which brings me to another matter, good sir," Kenna smiled warmly at him. "Our evening meal is already taken care of. My friends have invited us to their camp for dinner and a private performance. You've shown us such care that we would be honored if you'd join us."

"You want me to join the two of you ladies for dinner?" he looked at her with disbelief.

"Of course we do," Lady Carene spoke up smoothly. She was the model of composure and grace. The woman could have held her own with any of the actors in a skit. "It would hardly be fair to deprive you of the experience. Especially since my daughter-in-law's illness has slowed our progress for the day."

Kenna smiled apologetically at Phineas. "It's the least we can do, and the traveling folk will think nothing of another person to view the show."

"In fact, the more the merrier. We're performers; we love a good audience," Elize added cheerily. "If you agree now, we can make all the preparations well before you arrive."

"But dinner's only a few hours away," Phineas cocked his head in surprise. "Is that all the time you need to prepare?"

"It's what we do." Daris nodded emphatically. "We'll be ready with time to spare."

"Well, I suppose it would be ungallant of me to allow two fine ladies to go into a place like that unescorted." Phineas scratched the whiskers on his chin thoughtfully, then nodded. "All right then, ladies. I'll come along."

Kenna let out a sigh of relief that she hoped would play off as pleasure. "Then we'll just go in and change out of our traveling clothes while Daris and Elize take care of everything else."

Phineas looked singularly pleased now. He bowed to Kenna and Lady Carene before excusing himself to see to the horses, and then clean the dust of travel off his cloak and boots. Daris and Elize waited until he was gone before confirming the time and details with Kenna. Then they made their own farewells and returned to the caravan to inform their fellow performers of the plan.

Lady Carene insisted that Kenna lay down and rest before they departed for the travelers' camp. Kenna's body seemed to be in complete agreement. The minute her head hit the pillow she fell fast asleep. The sleep was a deep and dreamless one, for which Kenna was exceedingly grateful. The strain of everything she faced felt heavier without her partner by her side, and the few hours of rest greatly refreshed her. It gave her the boost she needed to put on a brave face when they walked to the grassy knoll where the caravan was set up for the night.

Elize and Daris had done their job well. The stage was unfolded and dressed as it would be for any of the performances, though it was rarely opened in camp unless repairs were required. The other travelers greeted Kenna with smiles, but said nothing of what was planned. A blanket was laid out in front of the stage, with plates of bread and cheese. Mugs of ale were handed to Kenna, Lady Carene, and Phineas as they settled down for the night's entertainment. Everything was perfect, and Kenna could see that it was having the desired effect on their target audience.

Phineas was smiling from ear to ear as he gulped down his first mug of ale and lifted his cup to be refilled. He laughed at the jokes told by the brothers as they juggled, and cheered boisterously at the fire eaters. He watched in absolute captivation as Daris and Elize rolled out their plethora of flips and catches. The ale continued to flow throughout the hearty meal as salted pork and summer vegetables were added to the bread and cheese. Kenna vowed inwardly to pay whoever had donated such a feast, once they had Niall back and were safely away from the palace.

"Did you enjoy yourself?" Lady Carene leaned over to Phineas and filled his cup again as the show came to a close.

"Oh, aye!" he replied without a trace of formality. "It's been years since I saw a production like that. There was a troupe that used to visit the village I grew up in. They never had anyone eating fire though."

"I'm glad to hear it, Phineas," Kenna turned her mug in her hand, she'd hardly touched her meal. "My husband was fond of the juggling act. He would have liked the show they put on tonight."

Phineas took a deep drink from his cup. "They were good, but I've seen several acts like that. The fire eaters are harder to come by. The acrobats were good as well. That Elize is quite fetching."

"I couldn't agree more. My wife is a stunning and talented woman," Daris said, jumping off the edge of the stage to join them. "It's a pity you're traveling away from Rosehaven. We were hoping to be allowed to put on a special performance to honor the new King and Queen."

"Perhaps we need not return to my family's lands with such haste." Lady Carene spoke conversationally.

"No, no, the King charged me with getting the two of you home safely." Phineas shook his head. "Besides, such groups aren't allowed within the city walls. Even if they were granted permission, I'd not risk the wrath of a King to see it." He gave Daris and Elize a little nod. "Not to imply that your group is lacking in talent, mind you."

"I'm sure we could speak to the King on your behalf." Kenna's stomach was doing uncomfortable flips. "It would be such a pity to deprive the citizens of Rosehaven of such a wonderful show. Perhaps if we were to speak to him in person, we could convince the King to allow it."

Phineas frowned. "No disrespect intended, High Lady, but common folk like myself do what the King commands. There is no persuading me to do otherwise."

"Please, I beg you." Kenna gave up the pretense. She took hold of one of his hands. "My husband is alone there. We are newlyweds, and I miss him so terribly. If you cannot take us back then leave us here, continue on as if we were still in your charge, and we'll find our own method of return."

"My Lady, I have the King's express command to take you and Lady Carene to Britwylde estate." Phineas pulled his hand from Kenna's. "I am to take you there and report back to His Majesty as soon as the deed is done."

"We can pay you for your efforts. Take the money and enjoy yourself somewhere." Lady Carene pulled a pouch of gold from her skirts. "Simply return to court when enough time has passed to convince him that you discharged your duty. With clever wording, it need not be a lie."

"It would be a deception all the same. You ask me to willfully disobey King Dempsey and then deceive him." Phineas put his cup down and crossed his arms. "You might be willing to play such games, but I am not."

Kenna looked at Daris, who gave her a grim nod and moved away. He spoke to Remmy then returned, taking up a position behind Phineas. It was all so subtle, as if what was to come was completely mundane. Kenna's stomach churned angrily.

"If you don't wish to deceive the King, then you could simply take the money and leave," Kenna pleaded, hoping beyond hope that Phineas would accept the offer and let them go. "It would be weeks before anyone suspected things were amiss. You could be far from Venallis before anyone was the wiser."

"I would be the wiser." Phineas glared at her. "And to be honest, I'm beginning to see why they say the King dislikes the High Lord. If this conversation is any indication of your family's loya—"

Daris knelt down in a flash and hooked his right arm around Phineas' neck. He locked his left arm around his right wrist and squeezed, cutting off the man's speech and his airway. Phineas clawed at the iron grip and kicked out. His flailing feet sent the cups and plates on the blanket flying across the grass. Ale splashed Kenna's cheeks.

Lady Carene took hold of Kenna and turned her face away from the grisly scene, but she could still hear the sounds of the man's desperate struggle. Every choked wheeze burrowed into her soul and left a dark, empty spot behind. The scuffling sounds of movement slowed; one of Phineas' feet bumped against Kenna's leg in a weak, listless manner. Then everything went still and quiet.

Kenna pulled herself free of her mother-in-law's grip and turned back to see Daris lowering Phineas' limp and lifeless form to the ground. Daris looked down at the body, blinking and breathing deeply. He was as still as the corpse for a moment, then clapped a hand over his mouth and hurried away. Elize followed after him as Remmy and three of the other men came over to take Phineas' body to buried.

Kenna stumbled to her feet and backed away from the disarray of their deadly picnic. She'd killed in self-defense when Britwylde was attacked, but this was a different situation. Phineas hadn't been trying to hurt her. He was just a simple man who was obeying an order given by his King. He was just doing what he thought was right, and he'd died for it.

"We tried to convince him to let us go," Lady Carene spoke softly at her side. "He didn't deserve to die, but neither does Niall."

Kenna dashed at the tears that were falling down her cheeks. Rationally, she knew Phineas had forced them to take action, but it didn't ease the guilt that twisted through her. "He made his choice. We had to make ours." She said the words out loud, trying to convince herself.

Kenna's limbs felt numb and cold. She walked away from Lady Carene and headed instinctively toward the yellow and blue wagon that had provided shelter for so many months. She couldn't face Niall's mother right now. She couldn't face anyone. *I chose one life over another. There's no going back, and there's no time for regret as long as Niall is in danger. But what sort of person does that make me?*

Her mind replayed the sounds of the life leaving Phineas over and over again. She closed her eyes and focused on the rustling of the wind through the nearby trees, and the gentle calls of the birds. Kenna drew a slow, steadying breath, knowing that when all of this was over with, and Niall was back at her side, she would feel the full impact of this evening's deeds. She suspected it might haunt her for years to come.

It was over an hour before anyone came to check on her. Elize knocked on the wooden side of the wagon as she stepped around the corner. "Everything is finished. They buried him in the woods. One of the men will take his place at the inn and then drive your carriage to Britwylde in case the King has people watching the roads."

"Is Daris all right?" Kenna asked, staring at the ground, still trying to sort through the implications of everything they'd done tonight.

"He's shaken. He's never killed a man. We've fended off hobgoblins, but..." Elize let her words drift off. She took a step closer and reached for Kenna's hand. "He knows it had to be done. Leaving Phineas alive would have risked word reaching the King."

"I'm sorry, Elize." Kenna turned to embrace her friend and clung tightly. From the moment she'd left Arthan, nothing had gone the way it was supposed to. It felt like a different woman had departed the halls of her family home. She wasn't sure who she'd become, or if there was anything left of the person she was. "We never should have involved you in this. If the King learns you played a part in it, he'll show no mercy. He's ruthless, Elize. His wife is even worse than he is."

"Nonsense," Elize replied firmly. "You didn't involve us. We involved ourselves. Daris and I both knew something like this was a possibility when we learned who the two of you are. We knew, and we wanted to go with you anyway."

Kenna shook her head. "It's one thing to know of the danger, it's another to look it in the eye and face the consequences."

"Kenna, the world is full of powerful people who think they can do whatever they want to those beneath them." Elize held Kenna at arm's length so she could look her in the eyes. "What they don't understand is that we are just as strong as they are, and there are so many more of us. Alone, we can be picked off one at a time. Together, we're a force to be reckoned with, and someday they will be made to understand that. We won't let him hurt Niall."

"You sound like you want to start a revolution," Kenna commented.

"Who says I don't?" Elize stared back at her solemnly. "Niall should be King and you should be Queen. You could change things. There is suffering and hardship now, but it would be worth the pain you've faced if the two of you took the throne. You could make the world a better place."

"A rebellion would only hurt the people of this kingdom. I will not be the cause of any more unnecessary suffering," Kenna stated firmly. "We're only going to get Niall back. We'll get him back, and then we'll carry on with our original plan."

Elize looked like she might push the conversation further, but after a second of silence she nodded in agreement.

"We should go check on the others," Kenna said. "I'm sure I've caused worry with my absence."

They walked hand in hand to join the rest of the group. Daris was standing near the stage. His face was still tinged with green, but his expression was resolute. Lady Carene was standing at his side. It seemed that she'd decided Daris and Elize now fell under the canopy of her motherly devotion.

"Elize explained the plan to you?" Remmy asked.

"She did, and thank you all. I know this is far more than any of you ever bargained for when you took us in." Kenna moved past them and took up a position near Daris and her mother-in-law. "We have a little time before King Dempsey and Queen Elanor realize the situation has changed. It's an advantage. A small one, but we can't take anything for granted."

"How do you propose we get back into the city?" Lady Carene asked.

Kenna contemplated that for a moment. The guards at the wall would recognize them in an instant. Even in disguises they would risk detection. If they were discovered, then Phineas would have died for nothing, and Niall's life would be forfeit. She wished her family wasn't so far away. The Rihtall Vashirat was respected. It wouldn't stay Dempsey's hand for long, but diplomacy would demand he tread carefully if he were dealing with a member of Kenna's family.

"Couldn't we just go in under the guise of asking permission to perform?" Daris asked.

Kenna looked up at him and an idea began to take shape. The troupe's arrival at Rosehaven's gates would put Dempsey on high alert, but a single performer, under the right circumstances, could be exactly what they needed to get inside without raising suspicion. "Oh, there'll be a performance, but it won't be one with juggling or acrobatics."

"What do you mean?" Daris asked. He frowned at her, his demeanor tensing. "Kenna, why are you looking at me like that?"

"If I draw up some sketches of Arthan garb, how fast do you think you could make a costume for Daris?" Kenna asked Remmy's wife. The idea was taking solid form now.

"A few days, as long as I can get the correct fabric and the designs aren't too complicated," Dana replied.

Kenna looked back at Daris. "Then we need to start working on your Arthan accent, and I'll have to teach you as much as I can about the customs of my Vashirat."

"What are you suggesting?" Elize asked. She released Kenna's hand and moved to her husband's side.

"I think a diplomatic approach might be exactly what we need, and it's rather fortunate that I have a brother just about the same age as Daris. They wouldn't turn a high-ranking member of the Rihtall Vashirat away," Kenna smiled broadly, eyeing Daris. "Are you ready to perform before a King?"

His jaw dropped. "Have you lost your mind? No one is going to believe I'm Arthan nobility. Besides, don't all you nobles know each other?"

"No, it's actually quite brilliant," Lady Carene piped in. She put a finger to her lips thoughtfully. "The Venallian nobles know one another, but few, if any, are familiar with all of Kenna's siblings. In fact, aside from Kenna herself, I'd say none are known well in the court at Rosehaven. You'd be admitted into the palace, and that gives us a way to contact my son."

"Don't worry, with the right clothes and a little practice you'll blend right in," Kenna assured Daris. "I have one of Niall's cloaks in our trunk back at the inn, and I'm willing to donate my own gowns for fabric."

"But I'm not even Arthan," Daris sputtered. "Don't you think they'll notice that?"

Lady Carene made a noise of disdain. "Please. Most of them are barely able to see past their own noses. They'll see your darker complexion and hair and believe you're whatever you say you are."

Kenna took Daris' hand. "I know you can do this. It's a lot, yes. We are asking you to be the key to Niall's rescue; but I believe in you, and I trust you to do what you can to keep my husband safe."

"And aside from my playing dress-up, how are we going to do that?" Daris asked.

"We'll figure that out on the way back to Rosehaven," Kenna insisted. "Whatever we do, Niall will need to know before we act."

Daris looked at Elize, who watched him with a pained expression. The risk was not just Daris', but also Elize's. She began to speak, but stopped, and the uncertainty she felt flashed across her face. "This has to be your decision, and yours alone, Daris. You are risking your life in doing this. I will support whatever decision you make."

He sighed heavily. "Then I suppose we'd better get to work. It's going to take more than a new outfit and a little acting to pull this off."

CHAPTER 20

Gilded Cage

Hours passed by at a slow and relentless pace. Despite King Dempsey's insistence that he required Niall at court, he was rarely called upon. Niall spent most of his time alone in his rooms. On the rare occasions he did pass the threshold of his chambers, he felt the eyes of guards and servants following him wherever he went. It had been a nearly a week since Kenna left, but it felt more like a year.

The only solace that he took was knowing that Kenna and his mother were getting further and further from the influence of the King and Queen. He tried to avoid contemplating when, or if, he would ever see his wife again. Were it not for the promise he'd made to Kenna, Niall would have given into darkness and despair the moment he lost sight of her. When he lay awake at night, with Kenna's side of the bed so cold and empty, it was difficult to stand against the crushing sense of hopelessness.

On this particular evening Niall was resigned to yet another dinner alone. Earlier in the day, he had made a rare foray out of his room to the library in search of something to help pass the idle hours. After a lengthy search, he came across a volume of legends and myths from Arthan. The book was dusty and looked like it had gone unnoticed for months, if not years. It reminded him of Kenna and that was worth the sneezing fit that resulted from disturbing the book's place among the cobwebs.

After finding his literary companion he made a stop at the kitchen to acquire another bottle of wine. The wine steward lifted a brow, but withheld comment when Niall took the last bottle of one of Dempsey's favorite vintages. Though it was obvious that Niall's rank as High Lord meant little to the King, the servants were still obliged to heed his authority. The pilfering of a bottle of wine was a small victory, but knowing that it would frustrate Dempsey was all the amusement left to Niall.

Armed with entertainment and refreshment, he settled in his room and prepared for dinner to be delivered. The knock at the door came earlier than it typically did, surprising Niall slightly. He closed the book and made for the door, but when he opened it, it was not a servant carrying a tray of food, but a young page.

"Please forgive the disturbance, High Lord, but there is a visitor come to call on you," he delivered his message with a hurried bow. "He awaits you in the great hall."

"A visitor?" Niall frowned. Everyone he knew was already here at court or traveling far from the palace. Were it a messenger with word from Kenna, the missive would simply have been delivered to his room, if the King allowed it to be delivered at all. "Who is it? Do you know their purpose?"

"Begging your pardon, High Lord, but I know only that I was instructed to call you to the great hall," the boy replied.

Niall nodded and dismissed the young man. He took a quick account of his appearance in the looking glass and made for the door. As usual, he detected the presence of the King's spies keeping pace with him, subtle though they tried to be. He exchanged quiet greetings with a few people along the way, but with dinnertime so near, most were already in the dining hall.

As he approached the room, Niall found that each step brought greater apprehension. It was strange that the King would allow anyone to call on him. It was even stranger that Dempsey required him to receive a guest in public. Niall began to wonder what Dempsey thought to gain from such a spectacle. Whatever the case, it was likely to be an unpleasant experience.

The doors swung open and Niall was greeted by the eyes of most of the court. At the end of the room a man faced the King and Queen. His dark, shoulder-length hair was tied in a knot at the nape of his neck. Even with his back turned, there was something about the figure that struck Niall as familiar. He was dressed in traditional Arthan garb, the fabric of which Niall could have sworn he'd seen before, but it was more than that...

"Ah, here is the High Lord now," King Dempsey stated when Niall entered the room. "Lord Niall, come quickly and assure your brother-in-law of your good health. Lord Jaik has been most insistent on seeing you himself."

"My brother-in-law?" Niall's footsteps slowed. He knew Kenna had several siblings, but he'd never laid eyes on any of them. An irrational glimmer of hope sputtered to life. Perhaps Kenna and his mother had made extraordinary time, and already enlisted the help of her family to negotiate his release. But no, it would take magical, and miraculous, intervention for them to have arrived in Arthan so soon. "Lord Jaik, have you word from my wife?"

Lord Jaik flicked his cape imperiously. He lifted his chin and turned slowly to set a rather smug, incredibly pompous grin in Niall's direction. Niall's jaw almost dropped to the floor, but by the grace of the gods he managed to retain his composure. Standing at the end of the hall, in clothes made from what Niall now recognized as fabric from Kenna's own wardrobe, was none other than Daris.

"And there he is! Just as Your Majesty said," Daris proclaimed with a thick, rather ridiculous Arthan accent. He smiled broadly at Niall and opened his arms in a gesture of welcome. "Come, don't look so surprised! We are family now!"

Niall blinked, then bit his lip to keep from bursting into a fit of laughter. "Lord Jaik, your presence at court is something of a shock."

"As is yours, brother. Are you not still within the first year of marriage?" Daris asked. He frowned disapprovingly and tutted at Niall. "In Arthan, it is customary for a man and his wife to remain in the same dwelling during that time." He turned to King Dempsey, waving his hand as he explained his meaning. "It is with a mind toward the production of children. Are not your own people concerned with heirs?"

"We are indeed, sir," King Dempsey said, clearing his throat. To Niall's express delight, it was obvious that the King was taken aback by the bold manner of this newcomer. "But the High Lord has duties to attend here at court."

"Ah, I see! But, begging your pardon, noble Majesty, can he not attend to both you and his familial duties? In Arthan we are able to balance our time between the two," Daris strutted toward Niall with the swagger of a peacock. "Or do you claim some issue with my sister?"

"Of course not, brother," Niall responded quickly. "I had concerns for my lady's health. I assure you, I intend to join her as soon as the King deems the time right." Niall glanced pointedly at the King. "But perhaps such matters would be better addressed in private. I'm sure they are of little interest to anyone but us."

"Why not stay and dine with us, at least?" King Dempsey leaned forward. Niall thought he saw traces of amusement on the older man's face. No doubt, Dempsey saw an opportunity to heap humiliations and torment upon him. "After all, a son of Vashirat Rihtall is a noteworthy guest. Surely, High Lord, you agree that members of your wife's family are deserving of the highest honor?"

If the suggestion made Daris uncomfortable he did nothing to betray it. Niall, on the other hand, felt every muscle in his body tensing. Daris was no fool, but the intrigues of court could be treacherous even to those raised to navigate them. Not only that, Niall was dying to know what Daris was doing there dressed as a member of Kenna's family. "If Your Majesty wills it," he said, shrugging in the hope that he appeared relaxed. The less he seemed to care, the less interest King Dempsey would take in forcing the matter.

"Actually, most gracious and magnificent Majesty," Daris bowed, flipping his cape once again. "I must beg your indulgence. The journey has left me quite weary, and I fear the food in your country does not agree with my digestion. It would be far better if I took my meal in private, with foods prepared by my own servants."

Niall's eyes shifted between Daris and King Dempsey. The King's smile took on a distinctly strained quality, evidently frustrated to have his game thwarted, but compelled to observe diplomatic considerations. He took a deep, slow breath, the smile never leaving his face.

"I could see to Lord Jaik's accommodations myself. That way Your Majesty need not be troubled by such details," Niall offered slowly. "He is, after all, my family."

"A gracious offer." It was Queen Elanor who responded. She placed a hand on her husband's sleeve. "Such simple tasks are well-suited to your abilities, High Lord."

Queen Elanor's talent for finding ways to make an insult appear as a compliment seemed to pull the King from his irritated silence. "Quite right, my darling. By all means, High Lord Niall. You have been rather idle since the High Lady departed. I've tried to be patient, but really, one cannot spend all their time drinking in their rooms."

"As wise as ever, Your Majesty," Niall managed, though the words stuck in his throat. "I'll see to it right away."

"Then get thee to your work," Queen Elanor replied. She waved her hand dismissively in Niall's direction as she turned back to her meal.

Niall bowed and gestured toward the doors at the opposite end of the room. "Lord Jaik, if you'll come with me. You may take your dinner in my chamber whilst accommodations are made ready for you."

"As is right and good, sister's husband." Daris looked to the King and Queen. "I wish both Your

Majesties a most pleasant evening. You are truly... Ah, what is the word I'm looking for? Oh yes! Immense."

"I beg your pardon?" King Dempsey looked at him, brows furrowing. "What exactly are you implying?"

"You know," Daris looked to Niall, as though he sought help with the language. "When someone or something leaves a mark upon your thoughts? Is immense not the correct word?"

"Oh, um, I believe the word you seek is impressive," Niall answered. As amusing as the expression on Dempsey's face was, Daris was tempting the wrath of an ill-tempered lion.

Daris clapped his hands together and his smile brightened. "Ah, yes! Impressive, that is it! For truly, they leave an *impression* on all who perceive them."

"Ha! Yes, languages can be difficult. I see your sister has a far better grasp of ours." Niall clamped a hand down on Daris' shoulder and squeezed hard. He dipped his head toward the monarchs again and then started to pull Daris toward the doors with urgency. "To that end, I think we ought to go get you fed and settled in."

"Fantastic! Farewell, Your Majesties!" Daris gave one final half-bow to the King and Queen, then allowed Niall to usher him out of the room.

Niall practically dragged Daris through the corridors and passages of the castle. Curious gazes followed them. Some offered brief greetings, but most allowed them to pass without a word. Daris continued his flamboyant performance throughout the palace. He strutted down the halls as though he owned everything his eyes fell on.

As usual, a servant waited outside the door to Niall's chamber. Niall was certain the King instructed them to listen to anything that happened inside and report back immediately. He ground his teeth in frustration, he needed to know Daris' true purpose but couldn't risk being overheard. He was wracking his brain for some excuse to send them away when Daris himself provided it.

"You there, serving boy!" Daris snapped his fingers at the young man. "Fetch us wine and goblets. I must have a dry vintage with my meal."

"Good sir, I am ordered to remain near the High Lord, lest he require my aid," the man replied.

"Where I come from, a lowly servant would never dare speak to a man of my stature in this way." Daris' eyes narrowed. He approached the servant with a convincing show of snobbish superiority. "I gave you an order, young man. Fetch me the wine or I shall report to your King that you have been a slothful and disobedient wretch."

The serving boy glanced helplessly from Daris to Niall, who jerked his chin in the direction of the kitchens. The young fellow looked as though he wanted to persist, but a scowl from Daris sent him scurrying down the hallway. The moment he vanished around the corner, Niall opened his door and pulled Daris in after him. He slammed the door shut and turned to his friend.

"It seems we've gained a level of affinity," he remarked with a raised brow. "What exactly has gotten into your head? If the King realizes you aren't who you claim to be, he won't bother to throw you into a dungeon, he'll simply have the guards run you through."

"I'm pleased to see you too," Daris huffed, still using the accent. "Some people have no appreciation for the theatrical arts."

"That is the worst attempt at an Arthan accent I have ever heard," Niall commented. "You're lucky they were all too shocked by that absurd performance to notice."

"I thought it was—" he started with the accent, then winced and dropped the charade. "I thought I was rather convincing, actually."

"What are you doing here, Daris?" Niall ignored his friend's rebuttal and went straight to the point.

"I'm getting you out and back where you belong, at Kenna's side," Daris untied his cloak and tossed it on the bed. "She's waiting with your mother and the rest of the caravan in the forest a few miles outside the city."

"For the love of the gods, Daris! Why isn't she safely away?" Niall hissed, fighting to keep from shouting. He ran his hands through his hair and paced around the room anxiously. "She should be on her way back to Arthan by now. If they learn that Kenna's nearby—that she did not obey the command to return to our home, the King and Queen could level charges against her, and my mother, for that matter."

"The plan is to have you out of here tonight. We'll sneak out and meet the others as soon as the palace is abed." Daris explained as he wandered around the room. He stopped at the table and picked up the bottle of wine Niall had taken from the kitchens earlier. "Were they speaking the truth? Have you been spending all your time in here drinking?"

Niall snatched the bottle from his friend. "Yes and no. I have been spending all of my time in my room, and I've certainly had the occasional drink, but not to the degree they think." He crossed to the wardrobe and flung the doors open wide, revealing several unopened bottles. "I want them to think I've given up. I'm hoping that if I seem to be as much a drunk as Cathal, they'll no longer see me as a threat and let me go."

"Then you should have done a better job of playing the part back there in the dining hall," Daris said. "You can hardly stand there making comment on my performance when you didn't even pretend at being muddled by drink."

"I was too surprised to see you pretending to be my brother-in-law, wearing clothing made from one my wife's cloaks, if I'm not mistaken." Niall was quick to shoot back. Despite the situation, he did smile. At a different time, the whole thing would have been hilarious, and it did feel good to be in the presence of a friend. He only wished this charade weren't for nothing. "But Daris, this plan will never work. You should go before someone finds out who you really are."

"This is hardly a dungeon. It can't be that difficult to get out," replied Daris. "Aren't castles full of secret passages and things like that?"

"I'm watched all the time. That boy you sent after the wine isn't the only person the King has keeping an eye on me. At night there are guards posted by my door. The King claims it's for my protection, but it's to keep me from slipping away." Niall closed the doors to the wardrobe and crossed to the window to stare out at the boring patch of courtyard that served as his only view of the outside world. "I haven't been allowed to set foot out of doors since I said goodbye to Kenna. This may not be a dungeon, but make no mistake, it is a cage. I am not a free man." Niall shook his head and looked back at his friend. "If I give him any cause, Dempsey will throw me in a real dungeon and lose the key forever."

"All the more reason to act quickly," Daris came to stand by his side. "We'll get you out of here, and then continue with the plan we made before you left Brittendell."

"You should go. Take Kenna and my mother to Arthan." Niall sighed. "There is hope that I'll be allowed to join them, but one misstep could cost me my head, and then that hope will be gone forever."

Footsteps outside heralded the return of the servant before Daris could reply to Niall's declaration. The footsteps grew louder—louder and more numerous than those of a solitary servant. They were also not the sound of the softer soled shoes of a palace page. Rather, it was the scattered thuds of several heavily booted feet marching down the hall. Suddenly his statement held an ominous sense of prophecy.

The door swung open without the courtesy of a knock or any sort of warning. Niall didn't jump, nor did he flinch, but he felt the blood drain from his face when he saw the contingent of armed guards standing on the threshold. It seemed the arrival of a potential ally was all the provocation Dempsey needed to take action. "Is there a problem, sirs?"

"High Lord Niall," the captain of the guard strode into the center of the room. "You are hereby placed under arrest by order of their Royal Majesties King Dempsey and Queen Elanor."

"And what is it I am to have done to warrant such action?" Niall crossed his arms and levelled a stern look at them.

"You are charged with the poisoning and murder of King Fergal," the captain answered succinctly.

"What?" Niall could hardly believe what he'd heard. He wasn't surprised that Dempsey had acted so suddenly, but to level an accusation of regicide was more drastic than anything Niall would have guessed at. "I wasn't even here when the King died. I hadn't been for months."

"You are to be taken to the dungeons this night, by force if you do not surrender willingly," he held a pair of irons out toward Niall. "I suggest you come with us quietly."

"What is the meaning of this?!" Daris exploded. To his credit, he'd had enough presence of mind to slip back into the Arthan accent. "I demand to know what evidence there is to support such an outrageous claim!"

The captain looked over at Daris with little concern for the display of indignation. "All evidence will be presented at the trial, scheduled three days from now. King Dempsey has given permission for you to attend, but says he will not speak to you or any other member of the accused's family. He also stated that you should seek accommodation outside the palace in the meantime."

Daris looked as though he might punch the man. He took a step toward the captain, hands balling into fists. Niall knew his friend stood no chance against four armed and trained palace guards. If things escalated, he would be thrown into a cell as well.

"I'll go without complaint," Niall stepped between Daris and the guard. He held his arms out for the shackles. As the iron cuffs were locked around his wrists, Niall turned to Daris. "Please get word to your sister. Tell her to take heart. I am innocent of these charges, and I trust the King's justice will prove that." It was a lie, an obvious one, and everyone in that room knew it. He was stepping into the noose, whether he was guilty or not.

"Brother," Daris reached for Niall's hand. "You will not be abandoned."

Niall smiled sadly. Daris' words offered comfort, even if they could do little to help him out of the predicament. Still, hearing his friend refer to him as a brother, and knowing that it wasn't part of an act, eased some of the turmoil that was forming a whirlpool in Niall's mind. "Go, see to your lodgings. Send word to Kenna."

Daris opened this mouth to argue, but stopped before uttering a single word. His shoulders slumped and he nodded. Then the guards tugged on the chains that bound Niall to his fate. He walked out of his room surrounded by armed men.

Niall was paraded through the palace in full view of the court. King Dempsey had planned his production well. Though Daris' arrival might have spurred the act sooner, it was clear that the King had set this into motion long before the guards arrived to take Niall into custody. Niall didn't make eye contact with anyone. It took all his focus to put one foot in front of the other. The charge of regicide could have but one sentence.

Every step he took now was leading him closer to that end, and he knew it well. He hadn't poisoned King Fergal, but it was easy enough for him to surmise who had. The King and Queen didn't just need him out of the way, they needed someone to take the blame for their crimes. If it wasn't him, another would have sufficed. This was just a convenient way for them to be rid of two problems at once. Niall would be found guilty, and he would be killed.

The entrance to the dungeons was in a far corner of the palace grounds. Niall's feet faltered as the door opened and he was presented with a stairwell that led to a pit of darkness. He could almost imagine he was being shown the maws of death itself, and he couldn't quite summon the courage needed to descend those stairs. It took a powerful push from the captain to get him to move again.

Niall's footsteps echoed off the dank stone walls and mingled with the cries of the other hapless prisoners that dwelled in the shadows. His hands started to shake. The movement was betrayed by the jingling of the chains that held him. He laced his fingers together and pressed his wrists close to his body. If he couldn't stop the trembling, then at least he could hide the evidence of fear from his captors.

They led him through a few passages, lined with iron-barred cells, and dimly illuminated by flickering torches that were spread too far to provide adequate illumination. Now and then, Niall would glance into the dark corners of the cells and find his gaze met by eyes that looked like two glowing pinpricks shining back. A moan or plea occasionally drifted toward him from the prisoners who stared as he passed. This was a place without hope, and what little remained to Niall was fading quickly.

It felt like they walked for miles before the guards stopped in front of an imposing door of wood and iron. The captain pulled keys from his tunic and unlocked the padlock that sealed the barrier. He swung the door open and pushed Niall into a room with a single, isolated cell. Once inside, the shackles were removed, and he was stripped of his fine outer tunic and the ring that bore his family crest. It was the symbol of who he was, of the power and influence his family once held. The captain took it and any other ornament that indicated his nobility. Reduced to a stature no better than any of the other nameless prisoners, Niall was shoved into the cell and left alone in the shadows.

Niall sat in bleak solitude for two days. The only person he saw was the guard who brought food. His meals consisted of bread spotted by mold and a watery, flavorless porridge. The only courtesy his rank seemed to allow was that instead of one meal, he was provided with three. The food was so bad that Niall almost wondered if the act was meant more as torture than mercy.

Midway through the third day of his imprisonment, Niall was taken from his cell and provided a bucket of water to clean his face and hands. The water was cold, but fresh, and it pulled Niall from his miserable stupor. His face was shaved and his tunic returned. It was the most he was given in the way of preparation before the guards led him back through the prison and into the bright light of the afternoon to attend his trial.

Niall was marched through the streets to the imposing stone structure where all such business was carried out: Rosehaven's Hall of Judgement. The public display was meant to add to his disgrace, but the people who gathered to watch his progress did not look at him with contempt. The eyes that Niall dared to meet were filled with pity. Not a single item was thrown at him, and no one jeered. For all Dempsey's attempts, the people were not against him nor convinced of his guilt. It gave Niall heart. If the common folk could see the manipulation, then perhaps the Lords who sat in judgement would see it too. Maybe, by some miracle of justice, they would rule in his favor.

That hope died the instant Niall entered the courtroom. Sitting to the right of the judges was King Dempsey himself. He was dressed in a black velvet greatcoat, trimmed in ermine. Atop his head was the most ornate crown in the Royal treasury. His attire was a subtle reminder that he held power over them all. There could be no other conclusion but that he was here to ensure they gave the verdict he desired. The trial was nothing but a pretense to satisfy the letter of the law.

The guards who escorted Niall through the city pulled him roughly toward the center of the room. Niall held his head high and raked his eyes over the people assembled. Several off his former peers looked away quickly. Some, those counted among Dempsey's friends, returned his gaze with cold hostility. Yet, even with the King looking on, Niall saw sympathy and compassion from others. Even so, he knew there was little hope that anyone would have the courage to stand up to this sham of a trial. There was only one person's presence that truly comforted Niall.

Daris was among the crowd. He still wore his Arthan attire, but he'd removed some pieces, and had managed to make the outfit look like it differed from that which he wore in the palace. He inclined his head toward Niall when their eyes met, but made no other indication of friendship or greeting.

"Noble lords, you are brought here today to sit in judgement on a sad and serious matter," King Dempsey said, opening the proceedings himself. He rose from his elegant seat and stood before the nobles assembled. "Our beloved King Fergal was taken from us by means of treachery and poison. Evidence indicates that this act was carried out by one held most dear in our former King's heart. I admit that even I was shocked and horrified when it was brought to me. My heart is heavy with the burden of it."

Niall glared at the King. *If the man had a heart, it shriveled up and died long ago.*

"I charge you to judge this case with the gravity it deserves." King Dempsey looked at each of the lords who sat in the judgement seats. "Pay no heed to the youth of this man or the familiarity you may feel for him, for even the threat of killing a King is high treason. The act is one of the greatest depravity, and deserves the most serious of punishments." He cast a cold look in Niall's direction and returned to his seat.

"High Lord Niall of Britwylde, you stand accused of high treason and the murder of King Fergal," Lord Bowen, a former comrade of Niall's father, spoke from the first judge's seat. He folded his fingers together and looked down at Niall behind a carefully composed expression of impartial authority. "How do you plead to these charges?"

"Does it truly matter whether I plead innocent or guilty?" Niall countered. He straightened his shoulders and met the eyes of the man who addressed him. "For it seems amazing to me that I should be charged with poisoning a man when I was not even in Rosehaven at the time of his death. Furthermore, I have been told that I was presumed dead myself when King Fergal passed."

Lord Bowen shook his head. "Young man, you will get nowhere by avoiding the questions presented to you. You were asked whether or not you are guilty of the charge laid against you."

"Not guilty," Niall snapped. "I thought my response implied that."

"Very well. Then we shall hear the evidence gathered by the court," Lord Bowen answered. He shifted his attention from Niall to a piece of parchment on the desk before him. "Where is the servant who cleaned the accused's chamber in the castle when he left King Fergal's service to attend his brother's wedding?"

A young woman stepped forward. She was dressed in the uniform of a palace maid and looked utterly terrified. Niall almost pitied her and would have if it weren't for the knowledge that she was only there to condemn him.

"You were the one put to the task of cleaning the rooms occupied by the High Lord when he worked in service to King Fergal?"

"Yes, my Lord," she replied, glancing at Niall. "Though he was not a High Lord at the time."

"That is of little relevance to these proceedings," Lord Bowen waved a hand dismissively. "Is it also true that you found a vial hidden among his belongings?"

She looked at the floor, face turning red. "I did, my Lord."

"And what was in this vial?"

"It looked to be a blue liquid, with a strange sort of shimmer to it," the poor maid answered. She kept her eyes fixed on the floor, only glancing occasionally at the Lord who addressed her. "I did not know what sort of brew it was, but the bottle was pretty and I thought to keep it for myself."

"And how long had I been away from court before my rooms were cleaned?" Niall asked, speaking before Lord Bowen could ask another question.

"That is quite enough from you!" Lord Bowen slammed a gavel down on the table and pointed a finger at Niall. "You will be granted an opportunity to refute these claims when all the evidence has been heard. If you cannot control your tongue in the meantime, you will be gagged."

Niall clenched his jaw and gripped the railing in front of him but offered no further argument or interruption.

"And when did you suspect the vial might contain something of a dangerous nature?" Lord Bowen asked, returning his attention to the maid.

"I forgot about the vial in the months after I took it. Two weeks past I found it when I was cleaning my own rooms. I poured out what was in it, then filled the vial with water and put a rosebud in it. It was just past noon at the time," she replied. Here she did stop and glanced at Niall again. "When I finished with my duties for the day and returned to my room, the bud was dead and blackened."

Niall had to bite his tongue to keep from shouting a rebuttal. He could have made a number of arguments against the notion that this was evidence to prove his involvement in King Fergal's death. There was nothing to prove the bottle had been in his possession prior to leaving for Brittendell. He was being led to the slaughter like a lamb.

"And what did you do when you found the dead flower?"

"I brought it to the head housekeeper, my Lord. I told her where I found the thing. She said we must take it to the Queen at once." The maid was trembling, and the shaking seemed to grow greater with each word. It was increasingly obvious that she was under some kind of coercion, perhaps the threat of death herself.

"That will be all, thank you," Lord Bowen indicated that she could return to her seat.

He then called another witness, and another after that. Niall was forced to stand in silence as one person after the next came forward to offer up flimsy evidence and anecdotes of his time in service to King Fergal. Each fictitious claim painted the portrait of an ambitious and ruthless man. People with whom Niall had rarely interacted came forward to besmirch his character. Casual statements that he'd made in passing were now twisted and turned into proof of his murderous intent. It was a brutal assault, designed to make him a monster in the eyes of the people bearing witness to the proceedings. By the end of it, Niall felt more alone than he thought possible.

"And are there any who might refute these charges, and speak to the honor of High Lord Niall?" Lord Bowen asked after dragging the character assassination out for two agonizing hours.

Niall looked around the room, fully expecting to find himself standing without a friend in the world. He couldn't blame anyone for being cowed into silence. The people who sat in judgement, and many of those who spoke against him, were among the most powerful nobles in Venallis. King Dempsey was watching him with a sickening sparkle of joy in his eyes, though his mouth remained tight and grim.

"I would, Lord Bowen," Sir Liam rose from his seat and came to stand at Niall's side. He gave Niall a sympathetic look.

"Very well, Sir Liam. You may speak," the Lord judge replied. He leaned back in his chair and seemed to turn his attention away from the proceedings.

"I have known this young man since he arrived at court, a lad of no more than fifteen. I say to you all that I do not know the man described by those who have come forth to speak against him." He looked around the room sternly. It was the most fearsome Niall had ever seen the man appear. Sir Liam turned his gaze back on Lord Bowen, unperturbed by the lack of interest shown. "I emphatically deny what is being presented as evidence, and I would also assert that anyone who claims this young man is ruthless or power-hungry has never actually conversed with him, nor spent any meaningful amount of time in his presence."

Niall could have wept at Sir Liam's words. The man was putting himself and his family in danger by standing up in his defense. In all likelihood, he would come to pay a price for his honesty and courage sooner or later.

"Your objections to these proceedings have been noted, Sir Liam. But unless you have some evidence to dispute the charges, I must ask you to return to your seat," Lord Bowen replied, and his tone with Sir Liam was surprisingly kind. Niall suddenly realized that what he'd thought was disinterest was something else entirely. The man looked weary and uncomfortable, even ashamed. He leaned forward again and turned his attention to Niall. "And now, High Lord, you may speak in your defense. Have you any means of proving your innocence or disputing the claims against you?"

"How am I to offer proof against baseless slander, impressions formed from years-old conversations?" Niall asked. He looked around the room, knowing that it didn't matter what he said, he was already judged guilty. "I left the palace four months before King Fergal's death to attend my brother's wedding. In the span of a few hours, residue from assumed poison is said to have killed a flowering bud. Is it to be believed that the same toxin took months to kill King Fergal? Even if it did, why would I poison the King and then leave the instrument of my crime behind for anyone to find? I have been painted as a vicious schemer who has the intelligence and will to commit murder. What could I possibly have hoped to achieve by killing King Fergal?"

Niall paused and shook his head woefully. "I can't claim that I didn't hope to gain advantage or position in my time at King Fergal's side. I doubt any of the nobles here at court can claim that. I was his godson and the second son of a High Lord. The most I ever hoped for was that King Fergal might reward my service with the ability to make a life for myself. All my goals and ambition rested firmly on his generosity and survival."

He looked around the room again, then fixed his eyes on the King. "My entire household was brutally slaughtered. My wife and I barely escaped with our lives. We could have returned to court, but we did not. I would have happily lived out the rest of my days as a poor entertainer. In fact, that was what I'd set my mind to do. I only returned when I learned my mother survived the attack and was here. You would have been rid of me entirely were it not for that."

"And what is that in relation to the matter we discuss today?" Lord Bowen asked.

"King Fergal was like another father to me," Niall returned his attention to the judges. "If I were so hungry for power that I would kill a man I held so dear, why would I choose to live in obscurity? Why would I stay away after the King died if his death benefitted me? What purpose would that serve?"

A murmur went up among those sitting in the stands. It wasn't evidence, but Niall's words seemed to stir some to his cause. He found Daris in the crowd and wished for all the world that they were standing before a different audience. The plays and tricks performed by the traveling folk were honest and brought joy to those who watched. This mockery of justice was nothing more than a pretense to make his death look lawful.

Lord Bowen conferred with his fellow judges. They were losing the room, and the King was glowering at them. The commotion continued until Lord Bowen turned from his fellows and slammed the gavel on the table several times, calling for silence. "We are now ready to pass judgement on the accused."

Niall looked up. He took slow deep breaths to keep his heart from pounding. The room gradually hushed, but the tension was so thick that it made the air feel heavy.

"High Lord Niall, after hearing all the evidence brought before this court, and taking into account those who spoke of your character, as well as your own claims. We, the Lords and masters of this realm find you guilty of the act of high treason, and the murder of King Fergal," Lord Bowen was forced to pause at the uproar of the crowd. He didn't use the gavel this time, but waited for the cries to settle on their own. When the noise finally died down, he continued. "In two days' time you will be taken from your cell, drawn through the streets of Rosehaven to the town square. There your entrails will be removed and burned before you, your head cut from your neck, and your body divided into four pieces to be displayed in the four corners of the kingdom."

The room erupted a third time. People jumped to their feet in surprise, some shouted insults at Niall, others wept. It became a strange, distant buzz in Niall's ears. His whole body went numb, his face tingled, and the floor beneath his feet felt like it was swaying. Each breath became quick and shallow.

Everything that he'd endured over the past six months came crashing down on Niall. He saw Ian's bleeding body, heard his final words. The mangled corpses of their household servants flashed in front of him as vividly as if he'd stepped back through time. He saw Kenna's beautiful face, her dark brown eyes sparkling with love, he heard her voice begging him to get in the carriage and leave with her. Any need to maintain a dignified pretense crumbled in an explosive burst.

"Murderer!" Niall shouted over the din. He glared at Dempsey and took a step forward. "You killed my father, my brother, an entire household!"

"Silence!" Lord Bowen began pounding the table with his gavel.

But Niall would not hold his words back this time. He turned his attention to the judges. "I will not be silent! I have been silent for weeks as I was forced to bow to a King and Queen who orchestrated the destruction of everything I held dear. I will hold my tongue no longer!" Niall was almost blind with rage. "If I am sentenced to die so that a murderer and usurper can sit on the throne, then I will at least speak the truth before I'm added to their list of victims. That crown belongs to me! I was named heir by King Fergal himself, and my family has paid the price for it."

"Shut that traitor up!" King Dempsey roared. He jumped from his seat, face purple, eyes bulging.

Guards started to move toward Niall but he did not stop. "Death to the false King!"

The guards fell upon Niall without mercy. They slammed him to the ground, punching and kicking, but he felt none of it. Niall fought as best he could with his hands bound, wrapping the chains around the ankles of his attackers, and kicking wildly. He didn't care how badly they beat him. He'd tried so hard to play by the rules of the court, to escape with his life and it meant nothing. He continued to scream his rage, spitting insults at Dempsey and the lords who condemned him.

It took a brutal boot to the stomach to silence Niall, and only because it knocked the wind from him, making it impossible to form words. The guards hauled Niall to his feet as he gasped and coughed. He still jerked away from their grip and refused to be subdued. There was nothing left in him but defiance and absolute loathing even if it only sealed his fate.

"Get that man out of here!" King Dempsey demanded. "If he dares speak another word, cut his tongue out."

"Go to the underworld and rot!" Niall managed, having regained himself enough to snap a final curse as he was dragged from the court. He caught one last glimpse of Daris before the doors shut. Niall continued to struggle and fight the entire trek back through the city. He didn't care if it cost him his tongue. He would denounce Dempsey as a murderer and a false King until they took his voice from him.

When they returned to the prison, Niall dug his heels in at the door. The guards had to use such force to move him that they all tumbled halfway down the stairs and landed in a tangled, bruised heap at the bottom. Even after they regained their bearings and Niall was forced to his feet, he continued to resist. He raged at Dempsey with words and fists.

Niall's protests and flailing riled the other prisoners, whose shouts joined his. It earned him several brutal blows to the torso. Still, he fought back. He kicked and swung his bound hands, even throwing his head back into the faces of his captors any time they tried to grab him from behind. Every tear he'd shed for his family turned into combustive fuel to feed the explosive outburst.

By the time they reached his cell again, more than one of the guards were sporting bloody noses, and Niall was bleeding and bruised from head to toe. They threw him into his cage and slammed the door with vicious force. One of them called for a knife and a length of rope to tie Niall down. Broken and bleeding, Niall crawled into the corner and curled his body in a tight ball to await the Dempsey's cruel brand of "justice."

CHAPTER 21

Family's Fate

Kenna stood at the edge of camp, anxiously watching the path that led toward Rosehaven for any sign of Daris. She hadn't slept well since he brought word of Niall's arrest. Most of the lonely nighttime hours were spent in tears or restless pacing.

They were hidden within a forest that grew tall and thick a few miles outside the city walls. Even at the edge of the wood, the tallest towers of the castle appeared grey and hazy in the distance. Kenna spent hours of her time staring through the tree trunks toward Rosehaven and willing Niall to feel her presence. She felt his presence grow stronger every day that passed. No matter what happened now, a part of him would always be with her.

"The trial was scheduled for midday. The ride from Rosehaven takes two hours," Lady Carene stated, gently approaching Kenna from behind. Her tone was that of a parent offering comfort and reassurance, but the lines of concern on her face were stark. She wrapped an arm around Kenna and stroked her hair. "It will be some time before Daris returns. Waiting on the road will not bring him here sooner."

"I know, but it's easier to stand here and look at an empty road than it is to sit in the camp and pretend there is anything that can take my mind from what Niall faces," Kenna admitted. She didn't take her eyes from the leaf-strewn path. It was not yet fall, but already some of the leaves were beginning to shift from green to gold.

"I won't argue with that," Lady Carene answered calmly. The older woman was quiet for a brief time. She seemed to contemplate the rustic road that twisted through the trees. "Things have changed between you and my son, haven't they? You've grown closer through all of this."

Kenna nodded. She'd never been as close to anyone else. Niall was the other half of her. If he perished, she didn't know how she'd move forward. Yet she would have no choice but to plow ahead, broken heart or not.

"One only needs to see the way Niall looks at you to know that he's in love," Lady Carene continued. She gave Kenna a little squeeze. "Both my boys loved you in their own way. No matter what the future brings, I am grateful for the happiness you've brought to them. I hope that you have found love and joy as well."

"I have." Kenna exhaled, tears pricking at the corners of her eyes. Somehow, in all of the fear and suffering that had passed in her time in Venallis, she'd found unimaginable happiness too; happiness with Niall. The prospect of losing him when they'd so recently found one another was overwhelming, unbearable, and all too close to becoming reality. She would have screamed into the trees if she thought it could ease the unyielding emptiness that threatened to break her.

"Are you in love with Niall?" Lady Carene asked quietly.

The question pulled Kenna from the brink of hopelessness and brought her back to the moment. "I am. I love him with all of my heart," Kenna replied with the solemn truth. She laid her head on her mother-in-law's shoulder. "I need him to be safe. I need him to come home."

"I know. So do I." Lady Carene kissed her temple. She was such a soothing presence, so nurturing. Though Kenna loved her own mother, and knew her mother loved her, their relationship had never been as affectionate, nor as effortlessly supportive. Until now, Kenna never realized how much she'd longed for this kind of nurturing.

Lady Carene took a breath and stroked Kenna's back tenderly. The silent pause was not an uncomfortable one. When she did speak, her voice was full of motherly wisdom, understanding, and hope. "Kenna, does Niall know you're carrying his child?"

Kenna broke down, releasing the fear and worry that she'd held in solitude. Her hand drifted to her still small waist. She shook her head, hastening the tears that fell from her lashes. She'd suspected her condition for a few weeks, but hadn't been positive until days before their departure. To have another person know of the tiny life that thrived within her made the reality of its existence feel solid and undeniable. It was a relief and a burden all at once.

"I wasn't certain until shortly before we left Rosehaven. Niall was already under so much strain, I didn't want to add to his concerns until I knew without a doubt," Kenna sniffled. "When we were given leave to return to Britwylde I made up my mind to tell him as soon as we were away from the city. But then—" She melted into tears again. "Oh gods! What if we can't save him? What if he dies never knowing his child, or even that he will have a child to carry on his memory?"

"Kenna, hear me now," Lady Carene's hands moved to Kenna's shoulders and turned her until they were facing one another. "We will find a way to save Niall. This child will know its father."

"How can you be certain?" Kenna asked. She wanted to cling to hope, but was afraid that doing so would make the pain impossible to bear if Niall was lost.

Lady Carene pulled her close again and rocked her back and forth. "Because I know that neither one of you will give up. The past months alone have proven that." She paused for a moment before continuing. "The world has always judged Niall the weaker of my sons, but I knew from the day of his birth that of the two, my youngest was the fighter. He came to us early. I still remember how small he was, how delicate. The midwife was so certain that he would not survive that she cautioned me against naming him. But Niall fought for every tiny breath and clung to life with such fierce determination. I knew he would survive then, and I know he will survive now."

Kenna didn't say anything. She knew Niall was a fighter, but sometimes it didn't matter how hard a person fought, fate would take them from you regardless. She just wanted it to be over. It didn't matter to her where they went or how they made their way in the world. The only thing that was important was that they did it together, as a family. Until Niall was away from Rosehaven, there was no way to be sure they would get that chance.

"Now, come along: my grandchild needs you to take care of yourself. I know it's difficult with so much hanging on uncertainty, but you need to eat something and try to sleep." Lady Carene stood up and offered her hand to Kenna. "Daris will not arrive any sooner if you make yourself ill with worry. Until Niall is here to see that his family is safe, the task falls to me."

"You're not going to take no for an answer, are you?" Kenna asked, with a small, teary smile. Allowing another to take the lead was a relief and made it oddly easier to consider the trivial matters of rest and sustenance.

"I am not, and Niall will not thank either one of us if he returns to find you in worse shape than when you were parted," the Lady replied, with enough resolve to bar any argument.

Kenna took the proffered hand and allowed Lady Carene to lead her back toward the camp. "How are you so calm through all of this? I can't breathe without feeling like the world is crashing down on top of me."

"Looks can be deceiving, my dear. Outwardly, I may appear calm, but that is not a reflection of my feelings," Lady Carene patted Kenna's hand as she spoke. "No matter how old your children get, they are always your babies. You'll experience that yourself soon enough." She cast a sideways glance at Kenna. "And in all honesty, I do not have to contend with the added difficulties of carrying a child. Blessed as your condition may be, it is not a comfortable state of being, even under the best of circumstances."

They came to a stop outside Kenna's wagon. Despite her desire to remain on watch for Daris, she was quite tired, and as a result, her stomach was beginning to rebel once again. "I'm learning that with greater clarity every day. No matter how much I sleep, I never feel that I've rested at all."

"I'm afraid that will not change soon. Babies are even more exhausting after they're born."

"Then it's a good thing that Niall and I will have you here to help us," Kenna responded, trying to smile, but with little success. She grew quiet again. She wished she could be as certain of Niall's safe return as his mother was.

"This will all be over soon, and then you can tell Niall he's to be a father. Try to hold on to those hopes, and to what joys will come when all of this is over." Lady Carene pulled her into a comforting hug. "Go lay down. I'll come for you as soon as Daris has returned."

Kenna released her hold on the other woman and stepped inside. She walked through the familiar space and curled into a ball on the bed. A sense of dread pulled at her heart no matter how much she tried to heed her mother-in-law's advice. She lay her hand across her belly and thought of the child that grew there. Would it look like Niall? If things went badly, would this little person be the only thing she had left of her husband and the all-too-brief time they'd shared together? She closed her eyes and tried to imagine a bright future, but no matter what images she conjured they were tainted and shadowed by doubt.

Even mired by fear and uncertainty, weariness prevailed. It slipped in and dulled the worried aching that permeated everything in Kenna's world. The bed was warm and comfortable, and in its soft embrace, Kenna was able to dream of happier days. It was a short-lived, but precious relief, brought to an end an hour later with the announcement of Daris' return.

Kenna sat up groggily. She took a few minutes to wake up fully and prepare herself for whatever news her friend brought. It was impossible to strike any kind of balance between hope and fear. Hope whispered that Niall would somehow be standing there with Daris. Fear mocked that, and supposed Niall was already past any chance of rescue. Rationally, Kenna knew she should ignore both, but the argument continued as she tried to summon the courage to face either possibility.

With a resolute nod, she climbed from her bed and stepped out the door. She could see a small crowd gathered around Daris, and even from this distance knew he returned alone. A bitter sense of sadness rippled through her, but she continued to take one step after the other. Daris would have word, and from that she could determine her reaction and how to move forward.

Niall's mother was already there. She turned as Kenna approached and held a hand out to her. "Daris was eager to speak, but I told him to wait for you before he shared his news."

"Thank you," Kenna replied. She looked at Daris and her heart clenched. From the expression of tortured despair on his face the news was not good. Elize stood at his side, but she looked torn between comforting her husband and supporting Kenna. Kenna offered her friend a reassuring nod, or at least hoped it was reassuring. In truth, she felt too chilled with fear to suppose the gesture had been convincing. "What happened, Daris? What did the court decide?"

Daris looked more miserable than Kenna had ever seen. He took a shaky breath and his face turned a little red. "Guilty. I'm sorry, Kenna, Lady Carene. The trial was an utter sham. Everyone there knew it. Niall never had a chance."

"And the sentence?" Kenna asked, eyes closing, heartbeat thundering in her ears until it seemed to stop beating entirely. The weighted pause that followed forced her to open her eyes again and look at her friend. "Daris, what was the sentence?"

"Niall is to be drawn and quartered in two days' time." Daris wasn't weeping, but he looked near to it.

"No, no, no, no," Kenna shook her head, unable to form any other response. Her knees wobbled. The world felt like it was spinning out of control. It was too much, too terrible, and Niall was facing it alone, with only his enemies to bear witness. Yet, somehow Kenna remained upright.

"Is there any chance of an appeal? Or that King Dempsey would commute the sentence to a less severe punishment?" Elize asked, glancing at Kenna with a look of sad desperation.

"I don't see how. When they pronounced the sentence, Niall... It was like something inside him snapped. He openly charged the King with the murder of his father and brother." Daris paused, rubbing his temples. "He publicly laid claim to the crown, as the rightful heir of King Fergal."

"My boy, my poor boy!" Lady Carene clapped her hand over her mouth, shaking her head. She knew, as well as Kenna did, that Niall's declaration was enough to seal his fate.

"The guards fell upon him as he denounced the court and the King. Dempsey ordered them to cut out Niall's tongue if he said another word. The threat did nothing to silence him. They dragged him from the building—I followed as far as I could but was not allowed on palace grounds. Niall continued to fight and rail against the King through the streets. Riots broke out after he was taken into the dungeons. I was nearly mobbed on my way to the city gates." Daris shook his head and looked at them apologetically. "I'm so sorry I could not do more for him. The King's order to have Niall's tongue removed has almost certainly been carried out by now."

Kenna's stomach gave a violent heave and she doubled over. The convulsions were so intense that she could barely take a breath before the next came. She wretched until her ribs ached and her limbs were shaking. Lady Carene dropped to her side. She was weeping but tended to Kenna all the same.

When the vomiting finally ceased, Daris picked Kenna up and carried her to some cushions arranged on a blanket near one of the campfires. Elize filled a cup with water, and pushed it into Kenna's hand. Lady Carene was led to a cushion beside her. Dana put a kettle over the fire and brought cups of warm tea to them a few minutes later. The traveling folk stood close by, ready to see to any small comfort that might be required.

Kenna couldn't stop shaking, she felt like all the warmth in her body had been sucked away. She could have sworn her blood turned to ice and was no longer pumping through her veins at all. Eventually, Elize took the cup away again, wrapped her in a blanket, and pressed a wet cloth to Kenna's cheeks and forehead.

Kenna shuddered and forced herself to focus on regaining something akin to composure. *I have to snap out of this. Falling apart will... delay our ability to—to come up with a solution. Niall needs me to be strong now, to form a plan and do whatever it takes to pry him from those monsters. It doesn't matter what they've done to him, he's still the man I love. I'll be his voice if that's what he needs. As long as we're together, we will find a way through it.*

"We have two days to put together a rescue," said Daris, once things had settled a little. "It's not a great deal of time, but I believe it's enough. We can see to whatever injuries Niall's suffered once we have him out of the city."

Kenna nodded mutely. Even with her resolve she was still fighting through an ever-twisting cyclone of thoughts and feelings. She hurt for Niall, she felt outraged, helpless, determined, terrified. The tempest was crushing.

"Sir Liam spoke up in Niall's defense," Daris was still talking, and Kenna realized he had been for some time. "I think he would be willing to help us get Niall out of the dungeons. It was Sir Liam who helped me leave the city. He recognized me from Brittendell, and knows we're nearby."

"But even if we do find a way to free Niall from the dungeons, how are we to get him out of Venallis?" Elize asked. "He's been convicted of high treason, of killing a King. If he slips free of their cage, they'll be watching every border—every port. The roads will be impossible to travel without discovery."

"Kenna is in no condition to live life as a fugitive," Lady Carene declared before Kenna could form words herself.

"What do you mean?" Daris looked up, perplexed.

Kenna found her voice at last, though it was rough and shaky. "I'm with child. Niall and I will be parents when spring comes again."

Daris and Elize exchanged mirrored looks of surprise, and the mood around the fire changed. It devastated Kenna that what should have been a happy announcement was sullied by the knowledge that the child's father faced torment and death.

"Does Niall know?" Daris asked.

Kenna shook her head. "Not yet, and if we don't find a way to prevent his execution, he never will."

"We can't just save him. We have to clear his name," Elize stated firmly. She looked like she was about to march into Rosehaven and charge the dungeon herself. "You have the weapon used against his brother, and the document that proves he's the person King Fergal named. There has to be a way to use those."

"We've no way of proving who used that weapon," Lady Carene replied. "And King Fergal's declaration only adds motivation for Niall to have killed him. Even if we can exonerate him, once the truth comes out, he will be expected to take the throne. Have you considered that he may not be in a state to do that?"

"Then we get him out of there and make a run for the borders," Daris reiterated.

"I don't care if we end up running for the rest our lives or seated on thrones," Kenna interrupted. She pushed Elize's hand away and stood up to look down at them all. "Niall must survive. I'm more worried about his physical condition than my own right now. We need to stop arguing about what to do after we rescue him, and start focusing on actually getting him out of there. I will march into that city alone, if need be, but I swear by the gods, I will not leave Rosehaven again unless my husband is at my side." Kenna didn't wait for anyone's response before walking away. Practical details needed to be decided, and concern over where and how they lived after the rescue were only distracting them from taking action.

She charged to the edge of the camp and took up her position at the road to clear her mind and settle enough to form a plan that provided a reasonable chance of success. The earth-beaten path wound through the trees and stretched out between Niall and herself like an enormous snake. At its head sat a devil, whose wrath urged the beast to strike Niall down. That couldn't happen. Kenna wouldn't let it. Niall was hers, and she was his completely.

As Kenna's eyes focused on the distance, she caught sight of a figure moving along the dusty forest road. In the deepening shadows, it was difficult to make out many details, but from the stature it looked to be a man on horseback. She took a step forward and strained her eyes, willing them to pick out some identifying factors.

Footsteps crunched on the bits of leaves and twigs that littered the ground behind Kenna. "Are you all right?" Elize asked.

Kenna ignored her question. The answer was obvious: She was not. Instead, she pointed toward the approaching rider. "Was there someone else away from camp today?"

"No, Daris was the only one," Elize squinted. She pointed as well. "Whoever it is, they aren't alone. Look! There's another rider coming round the bend."

Sure enough, as Elize spoke, another figure emerged from the trees. The first was close enough now that Kenna could see his cloak was a deep burgundy velvet, trimmed in gold. It was one she'd seen before, but couldn't remember who the wearer was. The second figure was not as tall as the first, and rounder in stature. This one was not dressed as richly, though it was obvious that both were members of the noble class. Kenna took a step back, fearful that Daris had been followed and these men were enemies.

"We should warn the rest of the camp." Kenna whispered to Elize. If they were found out now, it could destroy any chance of a successful rescue.

They hurried back and raised the alarm. Though not fighters, the travelers had a small array of weapons, mostly used for hunting or the occasional encounter with highwaymen. Kenna watched the strangers draw closer. They didn't appear to be armed, but she'd put nothing past King Dempsey and his ruthless wife. These riders could simply be a distraction to lull them into a false sense of safety as a larger ambush was put in place. She pulled her bow from her trunk and nocked an arrow to the string but waited to pull back and take aim.

Daris and the others who had weapons handy moved to block the road where it opened into their camp. The riders pulled their horses to a stop and dismounted slowly. Both men held out their hands to show they were unarmed and came in peace. Then, the second, shorter man lifted one of his hands to pull the hood away from his face.

"Hold your weapons. We mean you no harm," Sir Liam called out. He scanned the faces of those who stood to block his approach, eyes settling on Daris. "Please, call off your men. My companion and I wish to help."

Daris' eyes shifted to the second rider. "And who is your companion?"

"Cathal, son of the usurper, Dempsey," Cathal pushed his own hood back and bowed.

Kenna pulled her bow tight and approached him slowly. The men standing between them parted. "How dare you show your face here!"

"Please, my Lady—my Queen," Cathal dropped to his knees before her. "I have not come to challenge you or your family. I've come to offer my service, and my life, if that is the price for my part in the harms served upon you and the rightful King."

His actions caught Kenna off-guard. She lowered her bow slightly and stared down at the kneeling man. Part of her struggled to believe his words. Yet Sir Liam was with him, and he'd proven to be an ally to Niall.

"You took my son from me! Ian trusted you and you betrayed him." It was Lady Carene who broke the stillness. She pushed past the crowd, hauled Cathal to his feet and struck him across the face with surprising force. She pulled her hand back and slammed it across Cathal's face a second time before Sir Liam stepped in to stop her.

"Peace madam, I beg you!" He held her gently but firmly. "It is Dempsey who orchestrated the entire thing."

"As he orchestrated the cutting out of my husband's tongue?" Kenna asked. She took hold of Sir Liam's arms and pulled them away from her mother-in-law, but Lady Carene didn't raise a hand to Cathal again. "Tell me, where was Cathal when Niall was subjected to that torment? Drinking himself into a stupor in his rooms, perhaps?"

"He has not lost his tongue. I swear to you, Niall is whole, and as yet unharmed," Cathal answered mildly. He kept his eyes cast to the ground and his hands lowered.

"What does he mean?" Kenna looked from Cathal to Sir Liam.

"We intervened before the deed could be carried out," Sir Liam explained. "Cathal's arguments against the mutilation were what spared Niall. The King rescinded the order. I was allowed to see Niall before we left the city."

"You saw him?" Kenna put her bow aside. She was desperate for any details about Niall's state. "How is he holding up against all of this?"

"He was rather battered from fighting the guards, and his spirits are low. But I do not believe he has given up hope entirely," Sir Liam replied. "I've been assured by the King, and the guards, that Niall will come to no further harm until..." He let his words drift off.

Kenna looked toward the heavens and offered small thanks for Niall being spared the torture of losing his tongue. Her heart yearned to go to him straight away and shield him from any further suffering. Since the night his family was attacked, they'd shared every hurt and fear. Each one had been faced together and overcome standing hand in hand. It was what had made the pain and uncertainty bearable for them both.

"Then let's go get him now, before another moment can be wasted," Daris stated firmly. "If you're counting on the word of that liar and murderer who sits on the throne, I doubt we can be certain of Niall's well-being."

"My father stated it publicly," Cathal insisted, though he did not try to defend his father's character. "There's nothing for him to gain by going back on such a statement. It would only make Niall's claims more believable. To his mind, he's won already."

"Your father also claimed to be my husband's friend. He swore loyalty to King Fergal. Both are dead, along with one of my children. Their blood soaks Dempsey's hands," Lady Carene spoke, disdain dripping from her words. "Forgive me if I don't put much stock in what he, or you, have to say."

Cathal flinched as though her words were a physical blow. "I know I can never expect forgiveness for the part I played in those deaths. I do not deserve it and, therefore, will not ask for it. The only thing I can do is tell you that were I offered the chance to change my deeds, I would not carry them out a second time."

"That is of little comfort to my husband and sons," Lady Carene snapped. She turned her back on Cathal and walked away from the group to resume her place by the fire.

Kenna watched Lady Carene as she considered this unexpected turn of events. She looked at Cathal again. *I will never forgive him nor find it in my heart to pity what he's become. I don't want his help, but I can't turn it away either.* She glanced at Sir Liam and the others standing nearby. Though no one said it, she could sense that they were waiting for her to proceed. They were looking to her to lead them.

"There will be time for regret later. When my husband is free, I will leave it to him to judge your crimes," Kenna began, staring at Cathal coolly. "We need a plan to free him from the dungeons. I'd prefer to make the attempt as soon as possible. I share Daris' concerns and Lady Carene's lack of trust."

"We cannot hope to break him free of his prison," Sir Liam was shaking his head. "After the riots, Dempsey doubled the guards at his cell. I was the last person allowed admittance."

"Word of Niall's claim to the throne has spread throughout the city. My father and mother have barred the gates to the palace. Every available soldier is at arms," Cathal explained.

"If there's no hope of rescuing Niall, why have you bothered to come?" Elize crossed her arms and glared at them both.

"We did not say there was no hope of rescuing him," Sir Liam raised a placating palm. "Only that we would not be able to break him free of the dungeons. Cathal and I both believe it will be possible to save him. Not only save him, but see that he ascends to the throne of Venallis as King Fergal wished."

"What do the two of you have in mind?" Kenna asked with a frown. This was turning into more than a rescue, it was a revolution, one that centered on Niall's claim to the crown and their ability to prevent his death. *How can I make this decision without speaking to Niall first?*

"The execution is to be carried out publicly, in the town square. We can hide people within the crowds. The executioner has been in my father's employ for years and would never betray him. But I believe that I can pay off some of the guards who will be present on the scaffold," Cathal explained.

"That's only half a plan. Even if you pay off some of the guards, there are still the loyal ones to contend with," Elize pointed out.

"Yes, but they'll be taken by surprise. The guards we bribe will turn on those loyal to Dempsey and give our people the time needed to free Niall of his bonds," Sir Liam stated. "The people are already restless, and now they doubt the legitimacy of Dempsey's rule. Cathal and I believe that it will take very little to get them to rise up. The current King is not a popular one."

Cathal looked at Kenna. "Have you any proof that Niall was named heir to the throne?"

The question took Kenna aback. King Fergal's choice of heir was the source of all their suffering. Cathal was still an enemy in her mind, and it didn't feel safe to speak openly with him. Yet, the proposed plan required revealing the truth to the entire kingdom. They were past the point of hiding.

"I do," Kenna reached into one of the pockets of her skirt and pulled out the worn square of fabric with its glittering letters. She unfolded it and showed it to Sir Liam and Cathal. "This is the source of all our troubles. Perhaps it can be the end to them as well."

Cathal reached for it, but Kenna snatched her hand away. Regardless of his claim to want to help, she didn't trust him. If this document could save Niall, there was no way she'd allow Cathal to lay a finger on it.

"This only proves Niall's right to the throne," Daris pointed out. "Dempsey could easily claim the only reason he took the crown was because Niall was thought to be dead. Like it or not, the man is the King. Niall's outburst at the trial is still enough to convict him of treason. Dempsey would only have to argue that Niall threatened a ruling monarch."

"This is not the only piece of evidence I hold," Kenna met Cathal's eyes. "We found the weapon you used against Ian."

Cathal's composure shattered, and he sank to his knees. He covered his face with his hands. "I would that it had killed me instead."

"The past cannot be changed," Kenna replied, utterly unmoved by the show of repentance. Her thoughts turned toward the two brothers, connecting oddly between what she faced now and the life that might have been. She felt a strange sort of conflict. *Ian didn't deserve the death he was dealt. I would do anything to spare his family the pain of that loss. But if Ian hadn't died, I never would have married Niall. Our child wouldn't exist now. I liked and admired Ian, but I wouldn't have loved him as deeply as I love Niall.*

"Kenna?" Elize placed a hand on her shoulder. "What do you think we should do?"

"We need to decide who's going and who's staying behind," Kenna replied, firmly. She gripped her bow tightly. "And I will hear no suggestions of my remaining here at camp. Niall is my husband, and the father of my child. I will no longer sit back and wait for others to determine our fate.

CHAPTER 22

Marked For Death

Except for a sickly glow from the tiny, barred window on the door leading to the outer dungeon, it was perpetually dark in the miserable room that contained Niall's cell. After the trial, any semblance of courtesy or respect for his noble birth was gone. The three rancid meals he was given before were reduced to a crust of dry, moldy bread once a day, and a cup of water. Niall carefully rationed out the water, but left the bread for the rats. He had no appetite and only drank the water to ease the discomfort of a parched tongue. Since he'd been spared the torment of having it cut out, it seemed only fitting to seek that simple comfort in the time he had remaining.

Sir Liam was the last person, aside from his jailors, with whom Niall had any contact. The guard who delivered the food and water was sporting a black eye from the rage-fueled fight after the trial. He occasionally spat in Niall's direction, but that was as close to conversation as it ever came. Sometimes Niall would comment on the status of the black eye, noting a reduction in swelling or the change in color as the bruise healed. It was a small and petty jab, but he took whatever minor entertainment or victories he could.

Niall had a multitude of bruises from that day, as well as a nasty gash on his left cheek from the tumble down the stairs. In fact, most of his body hurt in one way or another. His wrists were raw from the metal cuffs that encircled them. The guards hadn't bothered to remove them after the scuffle. Each breath brought pain, likely the result of a cracked rib from the brutal kick that stopped his initial tirade at the trial. There was a general ache from spending long hours on the cold, hard floor, and Niall felt dizzy and sluggish from lack of food. It was of little consequence though. By sundown tomorrow he'd be gone and past such concerns.

More than any physical injury, Niall's heart felt torn and beaten. His own pain would end soon, but Kenna would be left with the burden of his conviction and execution. He would have given anything to see her face one last time, to tell her how much he loved her and that his final thoughts would be of her. Even if she could come to him, he wouldn't want her to see him brought so low. It would only make the days and months after his death more difficult for her to endure. If his loneliness spared Kenna any measure of pain, Niall would gladly carry that burden.

Time had no meaning in such isolation, and knowing he was advancing toward his death was too surreal to wrap his mind around. The idleness was the worst for Niall. Sometimes he caught snippets of conversations between the guards standing outside his door. Most of those discussions were mundane and uninteresting. The day-to-day concerns no longer held meaning either. Those things seemed as unreal as his impending execution

The rats offered brief bouts of entertainment after meal times. There were many rats, and only a small piece of bread each day. The battles fought over those crumbs were intense and devious. Niall even named a few of his cellmates. His favorite rodent warrior was brave enough to take pieces of bread from his fingers. The rat was smaller than the others, and missing half its tail, but was as bold as any of its larger counterparts when it came to the contest for food. Niall referred to the rat as Sir Terrance the Tailless. The friendship was rather lop-sided, but Niall was in no position to be picky. After all, he was a convicted traitor and King-slayer. If Sir Terrance could look past that, Niall was willing to forgive his taciturn nature.

It was in the midst of one of these one-way conversations that the door to the outer dungeon swung open. Niall cast the bread he was holding into the far corner of his cell and pressed himself against the wall. The day's meal had been delivered in the morning and it had to be nearing evening by now. Niall could only guess at the reasons for this visitor's arrival; none of the options were pleasant.

Candlelight flooded the meager space that had become his world, painfully bright after so many hours in near total darkness. Niall had to look away and shield his eyes until they could adjust to this fresh assault. When they finally did, he was shocked to find himself confronted with the cause of his captivity.

Dempsey stood outside the cell with a three-armed candlestick in his hand. He stared down at Niall with a strange expression on his face. It was not the look of contempt or victory that Niall might have expected. The King's countenance was cold and contemplative. His features seemed to twist in the dancing candlelight and the shadows it cast. At times, Dempsey looked softer—the familiar friend known to King Fergal and Niall's father. Then the light twisted and settled on the face of a man whose thirst for power had drowned those friendships in a river of blood.

"What do you want?" Niall hissed. The question was full of loathing and disgust, and he remained as far from the bars as he could. "If you're hoping I'll beg for mercy, you'll be disappointed. I'll accept nothing from a murderer and traitor. Not even mercy."

Dempsey shook his head and set the candlestick on the table that stood in the center of the far wall. A servant entered to place a chair beside the table, then left again. Dempsey watched the process, but didn't say a word until the door was closed and the sound of footsteps growing distant indicated they were alone.

"Still defiant, I see," he commented as he settled into his seat. "You should mind your words. I could still have them remove your tongue if you cannot control it."

Niall scoffed. "You'd all but prove the truth of my statements if you did. Which, I suspect, is why you relented in the first place."

"You always were a proud little shit, weren't you?" Dempsey growled. "I never really understood why. You were such a frail, pathetic thing growing up. Your parents would have been better off if you'd died the day you were born."

"Funny, I was thinking something along the same lines about you," Niall shot back. He resituated to a more comfortable position but remained sitting. "If you'd died in the wars, my family would be alive and well, and yours would never have existed."

Dempsey shook his head. "A petty and weak attempt at an insult, boy."

"You've left me with little else," Niall muttered.

"I was right to prevent you from taking the throne. Venallis requires strength in its ruler. Fergal should have been a strong King, but he allowed heartache and sentiment to cloud his judgement. This kingdom has the potential for greatness. Fergal squandered that. I will not."

"He trusted you, as did my father. They both counted you among their dearest friends. Do you consider deceit and betrayal signs of strength?" Niall asked.

"I am a patriot. I thought they were as well. It took years to bring the provinces of this country together. Countless lives were lost." Dempsey gazed into the flames as he spoke, seeming to view another time and place entirely. "I would have spared them, but I saw how complacent they were becoming. Fergal lost himself when his wife died giving birth to a son that never took a breath. The realm required an heir, but he couldn't see past his own grief to do what had to be done. Your father was content to hide away in the countryside, counting sheep and watching his coffers grow as fat as the cattle that grazed on his lands. All the while *I* looked to the needs of the kingdom. My wife worked tirelessly to pick up the dead Queen's duties so that the kingdom did not fall apart when Fergal refused to wed another. Without us, Venallis would have fallen back to its old divisions and chaos."

"My father and King Fergal were both better men than you could ever hope to be. They understood that their position was not to rule, but to serve," Niall replied. He'd understood that principle logically before, but now he spoke with conviction. "They knew that the people of a realm are the true strength and value. Without the people, the nobles are nothing."

"You're as foolish and naïve as they were," Dempsey said, looking at Niall again. "The people don't know what they need. They're uneducated rubes. I've sacrificed my closest friends to see to the survival of this realm."

"Is that what you tell yourself to sleep at night?" Niall stared at him in disbelief. "You're no patriot. You're only a small man who has to destroy his betters so that he can pretend to be their equal."

"You will remember that you speak to your King," Dempsey growled.

"We both know who should be wearing that crown, and it isn't you." Niall met his eyes steadily. "Besides, what will you do about it? Have me executed?"

"Despite what you may think, it gives me no joy to see how your family has fallen—to know that the last of Edan's line will die a traitor's death."

Niall jumped to his feet and pressed against the bars, ignoring the way the room spun. "I'm no traitor! You may be able to fool or bully the other nobles into conceding that lie, but don't dare pretend you're innocent with me! I'm paying the price for your crimes."

"You're paying the price for your ambition," Dempsey shot back.

"I'm going to be marched out in the streets tomorrow to literally be torn apart," Niall turned away in disgust and paced a few steps. "The least you could offer me is the truth. How is it a threat to you if it dies with me tomorrow?"

Dempsey stared long and hard at him. Then he slowly rose from his seat and approached the cell. "Very well. If you want the truth, I'll give it to you. I willingly stepped aside when the leaders of the clans decided that Fergal was the better candidate for King. I was already married, I came from the greater family, I held more wealth, but Fergal, your father, and the other chieftains decided those things didn't matter. I allowed it. I held my tongue for years as Fergal pined for a dead wife, and refused to remarry and produce an heir that would ensure the continued stability of this kingdom. It was I who held the factions together when Fergal went into his rooms to mourn for half a year. *I* stayed at his side when your father left to tend his lands. Yet he saw none of it, neither of them did. And when the time came, Fergal chose you, a boy, barely in his twenties to follow in his footsteps. Yet again, sentiment was placed before what was best for the kingdom. I could not allow it a second time."

"And somehow your actions are justified because you think they didn't value you, and that I'm not worthy of the throne," Niall shook his head. "You could have simply killed me and been done with it. Why murder my entire family? Why destroy your own son by forcing him to kill Ian?"

For the first time since Niall's return to Rosehaven, Dempsey showed a small sign of remorse. He looked away from the cell, wiping a hand over his face. For a moment, Niall thought he'd get no answer, but then the older man turned back to him.

"It was obvious to me that Fergal intended to name you over my son. Even before your family sought the wealth and power of an Arthan Vashirat. Despite my every effort, Cathal has never applied himself to a task. It wasn't until I revealed Fergal's plans that he showed even the slightest motivation to consider the future of our family." The King wandered through the small space as though the movement helped him to order his own thoughts.

"Your death would have been far too convenient. King Fergal only told your parents and myself that you and Cathal were contending for the succession. Questions would have been asked, and suspicion would have immediately fallen on my family. Cathal's chance at the throne would have dwindled even with you out of the way. So, I sought my own Arthan alliance and did what needed to be done to make my family the stronger option. I had hoped that if your brother were dead and your father left with only one son to follow him, and no alliance with the Rihtall, Fergal would choose Cathal, leaving you to follow in Edan's footsteps. Bedalia could inherit my lands, and her brother could take the throne."

"But I secured the alliance by marrying Kenna, and Fergal didn't change his mind," Niall replied, the pieces falling into place. He turned away from King Dempsey and sank back to the floor slowly. "My father knew Cathal was being considered, and he suspected you would act against us without that alliance."

"I cannot say what your father did or did not suspect of my plans." Dempsey shrugged. "What I can say is that your family would have been spared if you'd only drank the poisoned cup my son offered you on the morning of your wedding."

"What?" Niall frowned. The song of the banshee echoed in the dark. He'd been warned of poison, and those words had spurred his family into taking extra precautions in the days leading to the wedding.

"Oh yes. It would have spoiled your wedding day to be sure, but your household would have remained intact," Dempsey replied conversationally. "When you did not, my Arthan allies were willing to play their part and accept the blame. The rivalry between the Rihtall and the Stratham is a bitter one, it was the perfect cover for my men. They were provided Stratham uniforms and weapons for the attack. My forces were in place by the time you reached your family's lands, ready and waiting near Britwylde for Fergal to make his decision."

"That's why there was no warning, no signs of the Stratham crossing into Venallis." Niall rose again to pace the confines of his cell, processing this information with each step. "You speak of Venallis needing a strong ruler—insist that your family could provide that, but even you admit Cathal's lack of interest in leadership and responsibility. If you think my family was unsuited to the post, surely you see that your son is even less capable of governing the realm."

"Cathal did what had to be done at the time. He is facing a crisis of conscience right now, nothing more," Dempsey answered dismissively. "In time, he will set aside his scruples and see that everything I've arranged was for the greater good."

"And the attack on my home? You say your soldiers wore the colors of the Stratham. Then you and your Queen used those same colors when you welcomed me back to court." Niall returned to the edge of his cell. The thought that her family's enemies were to blame for the attack on Britwylde had plagued Kenna for months. Dempsey had admitted to having allies in Arthan, and hinted at the Stratham, but Niall needed to hear it outright. "You did not simply use the rivalry between Vashirats as cover for your crimes. The Stratham are your Arthan allies, aren't they?"

Dempsey shrugged a second time, the gesture was infuriatingly nonchalant, as if they were discussing something as mundane as the weather. "Your father knew ties to Arthan's power would strengthen your claim; I understood the same. He chose the Rihtall and I, the Stratham. They were willing enough to take the blame for the death of your family in exchange for a union between Cathal and the niece of their leader when my family ascended the throne."

"And you really think the people of Venallis would support allying the country with those who so recently massacred a respected family?" Niall could hardly believe what he was hearing, yet knew Dempsey would have an answer for that problem as well. He'd worked it out so perfectly and convinced himself that his was the path of righteousness.

"As to that, I was going to lay the blame of King Fergal's death on agents of the Rihtall," Dempsey replied. He paused and half-smiled at Niall. "But by surviving that night you've provided a much simpler solution."

"And what solution is that?" Niall asked.

Dempsey leaned forward. "That your family plotted with the Rihtall to kill the King and take power. The Stratham discovered the treachery and took action to try to prevent it. The people will view them as heroes and celebrate the union between the crown Prince and a Stratham lady. My place on the throne will be secure, and the Stratham will have the power and backing of Venallis to rid themselves of the Rihtall. Everyone will be satisfied with the end result, and those who are not—like yourself—will be dead."

Niall's mouth was dry, his knees felt weak. He looked back on all the times their families had interacted. Dempsey and his father had been like brothers. They frequently spent holidays together, Niall and Ian grew up playing with Cathal and Bedalia. None of that mattered to Dempsey. Niall's family was gone. The Stratham would have the power to destroy the Rihtall, and his mother and his wife would be marked as traitors. At best they would be stripped of their lands and cast out, at worst they'd be sent to the scaffold as well.

Silence filled the room, and Dempsey returned to his seat, leaning back to study Niall in the dim candlelight. Apparently, he'd said all he was going to and felt no need to offer Niall anything else.

"Have you no sense of compassion? No concept of right or wrong?" Niall asked finally. "Is nothing but power sacred to you?"

"Venallis is sacred to me. It's a young nation; if it is to grow strong, it must shed its weaknesses. I wish that it were not so—that your family, and Fergal, could have been spared, but they were the sacrifices I had to make," Dempsey answered, clapping his hands together to punctuate the end of his statement. He looked to the outer door and then back at Niall. "You asked for the truth, I have given it to you. And now I shall leave you with another truth."

The King moved to the door and signaled the guards outside. Niall thought the interview was over, but the door swung wide to allow another to enter. The newcomer was a tall, broad-shouldered man, in a heavy jerkin and a cowl. He held a rolled bundle of leather in his arms and moved with brutish purpose. He glanced at Niall, then bowed to the King. "You sent for me, Your Majesty?"

"I did, Conall," Dempsey replied before turning back to Niall. "And here is the final bit of honesty I shall leave you with. One last truth to ensure you understand your fate, and that of your loved ones should you choose to have another outburst tomorrow."

Dempsey stepped aside so that the other man could approach the table. Conall laid his leather parcel on the tabletop and unrolled it with meticulous care, as though it held something precious within its folds. Niall craned his neck to see what lay hidden inside. Candlelight glinted off metal as the leather was laid flat. Niall backed away from the bars, stopping when his back pressed against the cold wall of his prison.

"Conall is my executioner. These are the tools he will use on you tomorrow." Dempsey gestured to the array of instruments glistening in the light of the flames. "Well, some of them. I did not think it necessary for Conall to drag the axe all the way down here." He moved to the door. "Now, I must return to the business of the kingdom. Conall, spare no detail when you explain to the King-killer how you will use each of these tools. Leave them here when you finish, I want the traitor to spend the night in the company of his own destruction."

Conall watched Dempsey leave, then turned his attention to Niall with a cruel sneer. He lifted a knife with a hooked point from the leather case and held it out for Niall to see. "I like to name my tools, gives the experience a more personal touch. I designed this one myself. I call it 'Slisne'. I'll be using it to slice open your gut, the hooked end will help me to take hold of your entrails."

Niall slowly slid down the wall as Conall continued to describe, in devastatingly gruesome detail, all the steps of the death that awaited him. Niall wanted to plug his ears and close his eyes tightly but knew that his reaction would be reported to Dempsey. Any show of fear would be considered a victory. He would not let Dempsey have this one.

So Niall sat in helpless horror and tried to drown out the words by imagining that he was far away with Kenna. They were happy and surrounded by golden, sandy dunes, free of the cold, harsh grip of death. He did his best to cling to that dream, but the grisly details of what awaited him still managed to break through. The blue skies of his fantasy turned grey, and words of love were twisted into a soliloquy of torture.

At last the oration came to a close and Conall left Niall to sit alone in the dark. Niall pushed away from the wall. A strange, tingling sensation skittered across the skin on his lower abdomen, as if his body was already bracing for the assault. Niall slipped his hand through the gaps in the bars and pressed against the cold metal, trying to reach the knives on the table. If he was to die, he would rather do it on his own terms; quickly, with as little pain as possible, and in private. The table was several feet away and his hands were still shackled. Though there was a fair amount of chain between his wrists, the bars of the cell were not widely spaced and even if they had been, the table was too far to be reached.

Broken, terrified, and robbed of even this modest measure of defiance, Niall sank to the floor and began to sob. He was isolated and powerless. Tomorrow he would be forced to stand before the masses and pay the ultimate price for the crimes of another. There was nothing he could do but wait for the end to come.

It was hours before his tears abated and any semblance of self-control returned. Niall stoically lay on the ground staring at the table that held his death. He couldn't form coherent thoughts. There was only darkness, the knives, and the inevitability of his tragic end. Sleep would not come this night.

In the morning a servant was sent to retrieve the executioner's tools, but no final meal was delivered. The hours passed slowly, yet far too quickly. Niall was sitting up in the corner, subdued and resigned to his fate when the door opened again.

"Stand up," the guard barked. He fitted a key to the lock and turned it as several other men shuffled in behind him.

Niall did as he was told. There was no point in fighting them now. That anger was spent, and he couldn't overpower so many when he stood alone and had gone without food or proper rest for days. The shackles were removed long enough for Niall to be stripped of the tunic he wore over his shirt. The brief reprieve from the metal cuffs brought a moment of relief to his raw wrists, one that came to an end seconds later, when his bonds were returned.

The guards pushed him out of the cell and toward the stairs. Niall's life became measured in steps, each one leading him closer to his final breath. He barely marked his passage through the rest of the prison. The space around him was a dreamlike jumble of sights and sounds. To know the hour of one's death, and to understand the manner of that death, put all other things into an odd and unreal perspective.

The sunlight outside was blinding. Its brilliance forced Niall to stop as soon as he stepped out into the open, and it took several seconds for his eyes to stop burning. It wasn't just the light that required adjustment; it was the openness and wind. This was a world of freedom and light, one that Niall no longer felt he belonged to but cherished anyway.

He took note of all the commonplace details taken for granted before. The stone wall that surrounded the castle grounds was made up of countless granite bricks that shimmered slightly in the sunlight. He'd never taken the time to appreciate the beauty. There was a pleasant breeze that drifted down from the mountains near the city. It offered relief from the usual sweltering heat of late summer, and it carried the scent of pine.

Mingled with the aroma of the rose gardens, it created a heady, fresh smell that helped to wash the stink of the dungeon from Niall's nose. *Has the air here always been so sweet, or was I just too preoccupied to notice it before?*

A man dressed in the livery of Dempsey's household waited on a horse a few feet from the prison door. As the guards pushed Niall forward, he noted the rope fixed to the horn of the saddle. That rope was then secured to the chain that ran between the shackles binding Niall's hands. When the guards were certain the knots would hold, they signaled to the horseman. He clicked at his mount and began to ride toward the gates that led to the city proper.

The pace was slow enough for Niall to follow behind at a walk. The streets were lined with people who came to watch the execution of King Fergal's killer. Once, a few years after coming to court, Niall had been present at the execution of a man convicted of treason. The crowds that gathered for that spectacle had been boisterous and angry. Rotten fruits and vegetables were hurled at the condemned man as he made his way to the place of death. In contrast, those who gathered today were solemn and many looked sympathetic. The stony silence continued as Niall was led closer to the town square. There was no spectacle, no displays of support for the day's deed.

As they started down a portion of poorly maintained road the rider suddenly spurred his horse to a greater pace. It was no more than a fast trot, but caught Niall off guard, and he was yanked forward mercilessly. The sudden change caused him to stumble a few steps before falling onto his stomach. He landed in a wet and muddy patch of street where the cobblestones were few and far between.

Niall twisted and slid behind the horse, unable to regain his footing while the animal continued to move. His arms were on fire, the raw skin on his wrists started to bleed, and every joint protested the strain. Each bump in the street jolted through his entire body, adding insult to already existing injuries. If the animal was spurred to a run Niall doubted there'd be enough of him left to carry out the sentence once they reached the scaffold.

Now the people did cry out. They yelled for mercy and when the first tomato was launched into the lane, it was the rider who was spattered with fetid juice.

More spoiled vegetation flew into the streets. Some bounced off the horse and hit Niall, but the target was obviously the oppressor and not the prisoner. The rider finally pulled the horse back to a slower speed, but Niall was too battered to get to his feet, even with the animal's gait reduced.

There was no further concession to the crowd, and the march didn't halt until they reached their destination. Niall lay on the ground panting. His body was wracked with pain from head to toe. The breeze, which had felt so soothing before, was now cold against his soaked and muddy clothing. He couldn't move and didn't feel any motivation to do so.

The people gathered here were not as compassionate as those who lined the route to the square. Niall imagined Dempsey had paid some of them to make a show of scorn. He opened his eyes and looked around at the faces of those nearest, wondering if any of them would be kind. He found nothing but the cold and unfeeling gaze of enemies.

A pair of strong hands clamped down on Niall's shoulders and started to tug him to his feet. The action stirred a glimmer of rebellion in Niall. He jerked away from the touch and planted his hands beneath him. It took reserves of strength he didn't realize he possessed, but Niall managed to push himself back to his feet without assistance. The effort cost him dearly. A wave of dizziness caused him to sway weakly, but he gritted his teeth and forced his body to remain upright to begin the walk to the scaffold under his own power.

Niall's determination faltered when he reached the bottom of the stairs. He looked up at the wooden platform and the long rectangular table that waited for him. The sight stopped him in his tracks. Niall hung his head and his knees started to give way again. Calls from those who saw this farce for what it was drowned out the people who were spewing hatred and vitriol. One of the guards on the scaffold descended and slipped Niall's arm around his shoulder, offering support as he ascended the steps.

"Thank you," Niall whispered hoarsely when they reached the top. It seemed odd to thank a man for helping him to his death, but the guard handled him gently, and it was a moment of humanity amid the nightmare.

Conall stood beside the long rectangular table with sturdy wooden rods attached to each end. He wore a dark mask over his face, but Niall could see the glimmer of anticipation in his eyes. On the opposite end of the scaffold another smaller table held the knives that he'd introduced Niall to the night before. A long, curved axe leaned against the table.

"Make yourself comfortable," Conall mocked, gesturing to the surface in front of him. "We'll begin as soon as King Dempsey arrives."

Niall's entire body began to tremble. He couldn't force his feet to obey. Every instinct screamed for him to run, though he knew there was no hope of escape. He stared wordlessly at the table, trying to keep his breathing steady. The guard who helped him up the stairs took hold of him again. Assisted by another man, they lifted Niall up, one at his shoulders, the other at his feet, and carried him toward the table.

The hopelessness of the situation was overwhelmed by the instinct to resist death. Niall started to fight. He twisted and struggled against the hands that held him. Tired and weak though he was, the guards had trouble keeping their grip. Hampered by his resistance, they clumsily slammed Niall onto the tabletop. Conall stepped in to help when they had to resituate their grips to pull Niall's arms over his head and secure them tightly to the rod nearest his head. The process was repeated with his feet at the other end of the table.

Panting and bound, Niall lay stretched out in front of Conall; a helpless sacrifice to Dempsey's ambition. Fanfare rent the air as if by design. Niall lifted his head to watch King Dempsey take his place on a balcony opposite the scaffold. Queen Elanor was at his side, but there was no sign of Cathal. The King nodded to the guards and a steady, horrible drumroll began.

Conall leaned close to Niall's ear. "Slisne has been looking forward to this."

Niall jumped violently when Conall grabbed the edge of his shirt and pushed it up to expose his torso. He was gasping, each breath heaving in and out. Conall turned to fetch his tools. Niall couldn't catch his breath nor control the way his body shook. All he could do was watch as the executioner picked up his weapon and turned back toward him. Time slowed strangely. The voices of the people assembled faded to a low, monotone buzz. Niall's eyes followed the hooked blade as it moved down through the air toward his exposed skin.

CHAPTER 23

The Still Small Hours

Kenna watched the preparations for Niall's execution, each passing moment unimaginable torture. If this rescue was to succeed, everything had to be perfectly timed—and that meant staying hidden and calm, no matter how loudly the desire to act pulsed through Kenna's soul. It was bad enough to see the axman arrange his tools, but her heart shattered when she saw Niall appear, dragged into the square behind the horse. He looked broken and beaten, even more than he did in the days following the terrible attack on his family. Every move he made betrayed the physical pain he was in, and an aura of hopelessness seemed to surround him. It went against every instinct for Kenna to turn from him and move into position. *I have to be patient, keep my mind focused, and act when the time is right. Looking away now is not turning away from Niall.*

All eyes were fixated on the spectacle unfolding around the scaffold, and no one was paying the slightest attention to the dark-haired girl in peasant's garb as she lifted her skirts and ran toward the building opposite the execution site. Kenna skidded to a stop a few feet away. Cathal walked past her without a glance in her direction. He marched ahead and called out to the guard who stood at the base of the stairs. After a few tense moments, the guard bowed and left his post, unable to disobey an order from the son of the man who wore the crown.

Doubt crept into Kenna's mind for a few seconds as she waited in the shadows for a signal from Cathal. Niall's life depended on the very man who had killed Ian and beckoned the force that destroyed his home. Kenna suddenly feared that she'd been foolish to accept Cathal's change of allegiance. For all she knew, this was just another game orchestrated by his parents, designed to lure her back into their grasp. But just as she was tensing for an attack, Cathal waved for her to move forward.

Kenna steeled her nerves and stepped into the light. Cathal nodded as she passed, but Kenna barely looked at him. She ran up the steps to a railed ledge that surrounded the enclosed Royal balcony, creeping along the walkway that lined the upper story of the building and making her way to an inconspicuous barrel standing near the edge of the wall. Cathal had placed it there during the night, along with her bow and quiver.

She was mere feet from where King Dempsey and Queen Elanor sat, waiting to watch the terrible display of cruelty, hidden from their view by nothing more than a thin barrier of wood and the banners that adorned it. A single creaking floorboard could alert them to her presence. If one of the guards were to look around the corner she'd be spotted in an instant, and all hope would be lost.

The drumroll began. Kenna snatched up her bow and quiver from their hiding place inside the barrel. She counted each heartbeat that thundered in her ears, pulsing in sync with the drums. Focusing past the heads of onlookers, Kenna raised her bow and fit the arrow to the string. The executioner turned and lifted a wicked blade with a curved tip. Time stilled; the voices of the people assembled faded to a low, monotone buzz. Kenna took a slow, deep breath. *Steady, patience; wait for Daris' signal.*

The knife glinted in the sun as the executioner raised it over Niall's exposed torso. Kenna took another breath. She pulled the string back a fraction further. *Come on, Daris.*

Then there was another flash, at the base of the stairs. Kenna's fingers opened. The arrow flew from her bow, whistling over the heads of those who surrounded the scaffold. She watched its course, holding her breath until the arrow struck its target. It landed, perfectly centered, in the executioner's throat. Time returned to normal. The knife fell from the axman's grip and bounced harmlessly on Niall's stomach, accompanied by the spray of its owner's blood.

Chaos erupted in the town square. On the other side of the wall, Kenna could hear Dempsey barking enraged orders that went unheard in the clamor. She didn't try to make sense of the commands—the guards would be charging after her in seconds. Clutching her bow, she turned, flung the quiver over her shoulder, and ran down the stairs as fast as she was able.

Kenna jumped the last few steps and threw herself into the throng of people. Most were still too confused and surprised by what happened to pay any attention to her. She kept her eyes fixed on the scaffold where her husband remained bound and helpless. Daris was racing up the scaffold steps; the hood that had concealed his face had fallen down. He dodged a guard, grabbed the rails and somersaulted to land firmly at the top. A second later he was at Niall's side, untying him, and pulling him away from the table. The guards Cathal bribed were fighting off the men loyal to King Dempsey, and shielding Niall and Daris from attack.

"Niall!" Kenna shrieked over the madness that was filling the streets. She needed her husband to know she was here, that she'd come for him.

Niall was no longer visible, but Kenna reassured herself that Daris was with him and would not leave his side. She surged past the final groups of onlookers and pushed toward the guards who fought on their side. They were bracing themselves for the inevitable rush of men loyal to Dempsey, but stepped aside when she approached. Kenna took those final steps two at a time and practically fell forward in her rush to get to Niall.

Daris was crouched beside him near the back railing of the scaffold. He moved out of the way as soon as he saw Kenna coming. She closed the final feet between them and threw her arms around Niall. He looked terrible: weak, tired, and covered in bruises.

Even in such a sad state, new life seemed to pump back through his body at their embrace. He clung to Kenna, fingers digging into the fabric of her bodice. "Kenna! Oh, Kenna!" He kissed her, despite the madness playing out in the square. Kenna returned the embrace tenderly.

She broke the kiss a second later, and cupped his cheeks in her hands. Even battered and filthy as he looked right now, Niall's face was the most beautiful thing she'd ever laid eyes on. She stroked the matted and muddy hair from his forehead and hugged him again and again. "I'm here, love. I'm here."

"I thought I'd never see you again," Niall admitted. He studied her face when she pulled back, and she could see hope and fear warring in his cerulean eyes. After everything he'd been through, his confusion wasn't surprising. "I didn't dare to hold out hope of a rescue."

"It's all right now, Niall. I swear to you, I'm never letting you out of my sight again," Kenna kissed him again, then moved to help him back to his feet. She looked at Daris. "Sir Liam and Cathal should have Dempsey under control."

"What?" Niall froze. "Cathal can't be trusted. He'll turn on us. We have to escape Rosehaven."

"I don't like it either, but he helped us get into the city, and it was his money that supplied the guards who stand in our defense now," Kenna explained. Just admitting that Cathal provided aid made her feel sick.

Niall didn't argue; instead, he gripped Daris' arms and moved to stand. The strain of his ordeal was evident in the way his body shook at the effort. Kenna slipped his arm around her shoulders and lent her strength to his. She seethed inwardly at the suffering her husband had endured, but held her temper in check. Niall needed her support, not her anger. She was about to offer him words of encouragement when another voice rang out over the din. Kenna froze; she knew what was coming and hadn't had the chance to prepare Niall for it.

"People of Rosehaven, hear me!" Sir Liam shouted. He was standing on the balcony with Dempsey, Elanor, and Cathal. An assortment of people stood with them. They were an armed mixture of the traveling folk and Sir Liam's own guards. The King and Queen, along with their bodyguards, were subdued, with blades pointed at them.

Sir Liam lifted his arms high and continued to call for calm. It took a few minutes but the crowd settled and trained their focus on him. "We have gathered in this place to see justice served. But the death of High Lord Niall will bring no justice for the murders and misdeeds that have been done. Indeed, we do stand in the presence of King Fergal's killer, but it is not the man who was led to the scaffold. I speak of the former High Lord Dempsey, and of his wife the High Lady Elanor. They are the murderers, and they sought to claim yet another victim—another King, this day."

Niall almost fell back to the floor of the wooden platform. Daris wrapped an arm around his waist, and Kenna's grip tightened. Niall looked at one, then the other. "What is he doing?"

"Following King Fergal's command," Kenna replied in a quiet, steely voice. She would have spared her husband this, but it was the only way they could live without being hunted—the only way their child would be safe. Niall's expression grew panicked. He started shaking his head, as if the action would silence Sir Liam.

"Our beloved King Fergal chose his heir wisely, but it was not the man upon whose head the crown sits now. Behold your true monarchs!" Sir Liam pointed down to the scaffold. "King Niall and Queen Kenna!"

There was a stunned silence, and all eyes turned to settle on Kenna and Niall. The weight of it hit Kenna like a cart full of bricks. There was no going back now. Niall had laid claim at his trial, and Sir Liam now named them before the people. Kenna's arm tightened around her husband. No matter the outcome, they were together and would be to the end.

"Lies!" Dempsey shrieked. He shook off the man who held him and rushed to the railing to stand at Sir Liam's side. "You claim this traitor is the King, yet you provide nothing to back up your assertions. *I* was crowned. *I* am the King of Venallis. You are a traitor and will suffer the same fate as this so-called King of yours."

"Father, stop!" Cathal stepped forward. "There has been enough bloodshed—it's over. You cannot live forever, and I will not take a crown that is gilded in blood. You ask for proof; you shall have it." Sir Liam reached into a pouch at his waist and lifted two objects. He held them high over the railing of the Royal box, visible for all gathered.

Niall squinted, but Kenna didn't need to look to know what Sir Liam brought forth. In one hand he held the cloth with King Fergal's command for the succession, and in the other was the weapon used against Ian.

Cathal pointed at King Fergal's decree, training his eyes on his father. "This is the evidence of your crimes—of *our* crimes, and I am the witness. I confess my part in the plot to destroy High Lord Edan's family. On your orders, I killed his eldest son with that weapon. I unlatched the gates that allowed our soldiers and the Stratham to massacre Britwylde. I may not have poisoned King Fergal myself, but I knew that the toxin came from my mother's stores, and I did nothing to stop it." A collective gasp rose up from the people gathered in the square. Dempsey gaped at his son. His mouth opened and shut several times.

"Murderer!" a voice rang out from someone standing near the scaffold.

"Usurper!" another followed.

Dempsey backed away from the railing, looking out at the people with growing panic on his face. There was a moment of stillness on the balcony, and then a flurry of activity. Dempsey's personal guards reacted to the shift of attention. They fought back against the men that held them. Weapons changed hands and the disgraced King's men started to gain control of the small space.

Dempsey ripped the sharpened antler from his son and charged toward Sir Liam. "I will kill you for this, and your head will sit on a pike next to Niall's!"

Cathal jumped forward, pushing Sir Liam out of the way. The movement caught his father by surprise, and the momentum of his attack carried through, the blade of bone driving deep into Cathal's torso. The young man's mouth dropped open, and his hand lifted to the hilt of the weapon. He began to slump forward, his lips were moving, but the balcony was too far for Kenna to make out what he was saying.

Dempsey caught his son and eased him to the ground. Elanor screamed and threw herself at her husband. She pushed him away from their child and clutched Cathal to her chest. Sir Liam staggered back in shock. The guards who had been fighting for Dempsey stopped and stared in horror.

Dempsey stumbled to his feet. He gazed down at his wife and son for a moment; then, before anyone could react, he turned and bolted through the doorway at the back of the balcony.

Remmy regained his composure before the others. He stepped away from Sir Liam and disarmed the leader of Dempsey's bodyguards. Sir Liam's men followed the traveling leader's example and quickly returned order to the balcony. Sir Liam shouted for two of his men to go after the disgraced King. The last of Dempsey's loyal followers surrendered as Cathal drew his final breath.

Stunned silence filled the square. Not even the birds seemed willing to shatter the stillness. People turned from the balcony one by one to stare up at Niall and Kenna. Then, almost in unison, the crowd began to kneel before them. A single voice rang out, echoing off the cobblestones: "Long live King Niall! Long live Queen Kenna!"

More people took up the call; the few who had remained upright sank to their knees as well. Kenna turned to her husband. "This was the only way for us to be safe." She nodded toward the people. "It's time to address your subjects."

Niall stopped leaning on Kenna and took her hand in his. He stepped away from Daris and slowly moved toward the edge of the scaffold. He raised his hands and the shouts of support dwindled until it was quiet once again. Tears brimmed in Kenna's eyes. She wished they could simply disappear into the crowd and leave the crowns behind. Yet, she felt a sense of immeasurable pride as she watched Niall step into the role he was meant to play.

"I did not seek this out," Niall began. He looked commanding, despite the mud that stained his clothing. "But I swear that I will do everything in my power to be worthy of the position and trust you place upon me. I will strive to honor the faith King Fergal has shown in naming me, and I will do all in my power to respect and cherish the memories of the lives lost to put me on the throne."

"We will start by seeking justice for the wrongs committed by King Dempsey and Queen Elanor," Kenna stated firmly, assuming her place at his side, and the responsibilities that came with it. She squeezed Niall's hand and looked out at the upturned faces of the people. "I am a stranger in your land, but I've walked among you. I've shared in your laughter and in your tears. I love this kingdom as I love the land of my birth, and I would see the wrongs made right and the people cared for."

Cheers and applause erupted for the new King and Queen. Niall wobbled, his legs buckling a bit. Kenna gently wrapped her arm around his waist to subtly support him. Daris stepped forward and looped an arm around Niall as well. King or not, he'd reached the limits of his strength. Together they led him back down the steps and turned toward the palace.

Sir Liam ordered the arrest of the former Queen and had Cathal's body removed from the square. After checking on Niall and swearing his loyalty to the new King, he ordered his men to protect Niall and Kenna, then took a contingent of guards and hurried ahead to alert those within the palace of the change in leadership. Kenna and Daris helped Niall into the saddle of the very horse that had dragged him through the streets. When he was seated securely, Kenna climbed up and settled behind him, taking the reins to steer the animal. Daris followed along, joined by Elize, who emerged from the throng of people with a dagger in her hand.

It was hardly a kingly procession, but appearances were the least of Kenna's concerns. Niall's breathing was growing labored, and he was shaking from head to toe. By the time they made it through the gates to the castle courtyard he was beginning to lean to the side. It took much of Kenna's concentration to guide the horse and keep her husband in the saddle at the same time; when Daris saw her struggling, he took hold of the reins and led the horse through the gate to the palace, leaving Kenna with only Niall to worry about.

Once they were within the royal courtyard, Daris helped Niall off the horse and up the steps leading to the palace. Kenna dismounted and ran to help Niall. The second the palace doors closed behind them, Niall's legs gave out completely. Daris managed to catch him as he lost consciousness, while Kenna sank to Niall's side and cradled his head on her lap as Elize hurried further into the castle, calling for help.

Away from the eyes of the public and the horrors of the scaffold, Kenna examined her husband. Under the filth, Niall's sleeves were stained red from wrist to elbow. His breathing was shallow, and his left cheek bore a deep gash that ran almost to his temple. Kenna stroked the matted hair from his forehead and clung to him protectively. Even under the grime she could see the disturbing lack of color in his cheeks.

It seemed like it took hours for Elize to return with help, but Kenna knew it was only impatience and concern for her beloved that made the seconds creep by. Soon enough, Niall was being gently lifted off the ground and carried to the residential wing. Kenna followed behind, never taking her eyes from her husband. The treatment they'd received in their time here, and the strain of the past week, was still too fresh in her mind to trust him to the care of the court.

They carried Niall through the corridors and to the royal apartments. Warm water was brought up and a fresh set of clothes placed in the room while Kenna herself saw to cleaning Niall's battered body. She did the work meticulously, revealing a myriad of cuts and bruises as she wiped away the blood and dirt. Each injury was a fresh barb to her heart. The wounds bore silent testimony of his ordeal. Niall didn't stir once, not even when she eased his head over a basin and poured water through his sullied golden curls.

By the time the Soulbound healer arrived, Niall was clean, his clothes were changed, and he was comfortably arranged in the enormous bed. Were it not for the gash on his cheek and the angry bruises spattered across his skin, he would have looked like he was peacefully napping.

"My name is Aliace. I was told the King was in poor condition." Aliace spoke softly and curtseyed before Kenna. She was of middling years, with pale brown hair that showed several streaks of white. "With your permission, my Soulmate and I will see to his wounds."

Kenna nodded and shifted to make room for the healer, but she remained close to the bed. She clung to Niall's hand as the Soulbound moved closer and placed her hands on Niall's chest. Without another word, she closed her eyes, and Kenna saw a soft silvery-blue light flicker beneath her palms. Niall took a deeper breath, then sighed.

The bruises began to fade before Kenna's eyes. The skin on Niall's cheek knit back together until there was nothing but a pale pink mark left behind. Niall's pallor improved, though the circles under his eyes remained dark and sunken. It was like watching the natural healing process take place in seconds, rather than the days and weeks it would have required without magical intervention.

After several minutes Aliace opened her eyes and looked up, pulling her hands away from Niall's chest. She turned to Kenna reassuringly. "The King will recover. I've healed his injuries, but he will need food and a few days of rest before he should return to normal activities, Your Majesty."

"Thank you," Kenna replied, blushing slightly. Here in the quiet and peace of the bedroom it felt strange to be addressed so formally, and she wasn't entirely sure how to handle it. She shifted the attention back to Niall. "Were his injuries severe?"

"He had a broken rib, and the cut on his cheek was deep. His face will bear a scar for the remainder of his life, but most of the wounds were superficial," she looked at Kenna kindly, but seriously. "Your husband has been through much, but he will recover physically.

Unfortunately, I can do nothing for the harm that such an ordeal leaves on the spirit."

"I understand. Thank you, Lady Aliace," Kenna offered her a tired but grateful smile. The other woman curtsied and turned to leave, but Kenna called out, halting her progress. "Please inform Lady Carene of her son's condition, and tell her I will call her in momentarily. I just need a minute with him. I'm certain she will be waiting right outside."

"Of course, Your Majesty. Is there anything else I can do for you?" Aliace asked.

Kenna shook her head and turned her attention back to her husband. "No, that's all I require. Thank you again."

She knew Lady Carene would be eager to see her son, and wouldn't keep her waiting long, but so much had happened in so short a time. Now that Niall's injuries were tended to, Kenna needed a few quiet moments alone with him. Though the official details had yet to be addressed, they were the King and Queen now; it was not a reality Kenna relished. She wished there had been a way to save him without laying that burden on his shoulders. If it were only Niall and herself to be considered, she would have run as far and as fast from Rosehaven as his condition allowed. Accepting the thrones of Venallis wasn't freedom, but it was safer than the alternatives. Still, their lives would never be their own now, and the child she carried now had its destiny determined, well before it took its first breath.

After a few minutes, Kenna released Niall's hand and smoothed her skirts, trying to gather herself. Lady Carene should not be kept waiting any longer. Niall was her only living child, and she'd nearly lost him. As predicted, his mother was waiting just outside. She heaved a sigh of relief when Kenna opened the door, then hurried to son.

Kenna resumed her place at Niall's bedside, taking his hand once again. Lady Carene settled on the other side of the bed and lovingly stroked back Niall's hair. She tucked the blankets more tightly around him as she hummed softly. Kenna was awestruck by the quiet tenderness of Lady Carene's caregiving. It didn't matter that he was a grown man, or a King; Niall was her child and right now, her baby. After an hour, Lady Carene kissed the scar on his cheek and went to her chambers to rest, leaving instructions that Kenna send for her when he woke.

Hours passed and Niall slumbered on. Kenna stayed at his side and never released his hand. It was well past dinner—the evening sun all but set—before Niall stirred. He made a slight sound and his fingers tightened around Kenna's. His eyes fluttered open, clouding with confusion as he scanned the room until his gaze settled on Kenna. A small, weary smile spread across his face. "It was real... you're here."

"I am, my love, and you're safe now," Kenna replied gently. She reached out to caress the side of his face.

"I thought I might have dreamed it," he whispered, closing his eyes again.

"No, it wasn't a dream. We're truly together again," Kenna said, as much to reassure herself as him. "How are you feeling?"

Niall sighed and opened his eyes again before he moved to push himself up cautiously. "Better; there's less pain, though I feel a bit stiff. How long was I asleep?"

"Nearly eight hours," Kenna lifted his fingers to her lips and kissed them. "I considered waking you for dinner, but the Soulbound who attended your injuries said you needed sleep. She also said you should take rest for a few days to fully recover."

"How am I to rest? I was made King..." Niall replied contemplatively. He frowned and stared down at the blankets for a brief time. "Our lives will belong to the people... we're no longer free to decide our course."

"Are you angry?" Kenna asked.

"No, I—I don't really know how I feel about it," Niall admitted. "I thought I'd be dead by now. Yet, I'm here with you, and I'm King of Venallis... and you're the Queen of Venallis. It isn't real enough to feel anything more than shock."

Kenna chuckled a little. "I may not have been facing execution, but I find my new station equally surreal." She paused and shook her head, thinking over all the changes they were facing. "Among other things."

"Other things? Is it not enough to become the rulers of an entire nation?" Niall asked. He ran a hand through his hair and looked around the room again.

Kenna took a breath, unsure how this next piece of news would be received, or if it was even the right time for it. Niall had already been through so much today. She didn't know if the added pressure of impending parenthood would be too much in his exhausted state. He'd know soon enough; her condition was not one that could be hidden for long. Eventually he'd notice her growing belly and realize a child was on the way. She already thought it was less flat than it had been a few weeks ago, though that was likely her own imagining.

"Kenna? What's the matter?" He was eyeing her with open concern. "Has something happened to my mother?"

"No!" Kenna answered quickly. "No, it's nothing like that. Everyone is fine... our family is well," she took his hand placing it over her abdomen. "It's well—and it's growing."

"Growing?" Niall frowned for a moment, then his eyes grew wide and locked on the place where their hands rested. "Kenna, are you saying what I think you're saying?"

"I am," Kenna nodded. "I wanted to tell you once we were away from Rosehaven, but those plans went a bit awry." She blinked back tears of joy. "I am carrying our child, Niall."

He was very still for several long seconds and Kenna started to worry that the news was too much for him. Then an enormous smile spread slowly across his face. He let out a laugh that was punctuated with a sniffle. Niall pulled Kenna into his arms and clung to her. "I thought I'd lost everything, and in one moment you've given me the entire world."

"You're really happy? We've been through so much these past months—this isn't too much for you?" Kenna asked. It was a silly question, since the baby would come whether he was ready for it or not.

"Of course I am," Niall lifted her chin and kissed her with such sweetness that it stole Kenna's breath. He released her slowly, and huffed out a breathy laugh. "To think that while all of these terrible things were taking place, this small wonder was happening—it *is* happening! We're having a baby—a little prince or princess to follow in our steps."

Kenna smiled through tears of joy, feeling a bit foolish for being so worried. Finally sharing this with him made the world feel right and whole once more. Niall was safe, Dempsey and Elanor could no longer harm them, and in a matter of months they would welcome their child into a world of safety and love. She realized that it didn't matter where they were, or what titles they held, the path ahead was one they would forge together.

"Are you alright? Do you need to rest or eat something?" Niall asked, still grinning like a fool. "I could call for a tray to be sent up." He pushed the blankets and started to move to get out of bed.

"You just spent a week in a dungeon and narrowly escaped execution, and you're worried about my well-being?" Kenna shook her head.

"Well, yes—you're with child. I want you to have everything you need." Niall cast the blankets aside and started to get out of bed.

"What do you think you're doing?" Kenna asked. She gently pushed him back onto the pillows and resituated the blankets across his lap. "You are supposed to rest. I will send for a tray of food and you will eat it—all of it. You're the one who needs looking after just now."

"Yes, Your Majesty," Niall answered playfully. "Have you any other commands for me, my Queen?"

Kenna leaned back down to kiss Niall's forehead. "Yes, I—we nearly lost you. Never scare me like that again."

"I'll do my best, love," Niall replied. He leaned back and relaxed with a yawn, despite having just arisen from several hours of sleep. Kenna stroked his cheek, indulging her need to touch him and reassure herself that all was well, then left to call for the servants.

Lady Carene returned before the food arrived. She doted over her son, and Niall seemed willing enough to let her. When the food was brought in, he ate it without a word of complaint about the way they watched over him. He tired quickly after that, leaning back on his pillows with a yawn. Lady Carene tucked him in again and bid them both a goodnight.

Kenna made for the door, but Niall called her back. She argued that he needed a restful night, but he insisted she sleep at his side. Kenna hesitated, but climbed into bed with only a perfunctory protest for his comfort. She snuggled next to her husband, and within minutes they were both fast asleep.

Niall slept for most of the next day as well. When he woke, he told her of the trial and imprisonment. Dempsey had spared no effort in tormenting him. Niall sometimes fell silent and his expression grew haunted; when Kenna asked him what he was thinking, he would merely shake his head and tell her not to worry, he was only remembering a nightmare. She didn't push him for more, trusting that he would share his thoughts when he was ready, but she worried the scars of what he'd endured ran deeper than the mark he bore on his cheek.

Kenna was confronted with the responsibilities of her new position before the day was through. As Queen, she was equal in power and command to Niall. With the King still abed, she found herself at the center of a kingdom that was in a state of flux. Though her own upbringing included an education in leadership, Venallis was not the land of her birth, and some of their rules and customs were still unfamiliar. Lady Carene and Sir Liam did what they could to help her navigate the currents of power, but the decisions ultimately rested on her.

By midday, Kenna was more than a little frazzled and absolutely relieved when she was finally able to slip away to the quiet of the royal chambers for lunch. It was strange to find these rooms a sanctuary after everything Dempsey and Elanor did. Removing the usurper's personal belongings did much to remove the memories that lingered, but having their friends nearby did even more.

Daris and Elize kept a close watch on them both. Daris stood with the guards outside the room most of the time, and Elize was at Kenna's side nearly day and night. They rarely left the palace, and joined Kenna for most meals.

"How is Niall doing?" Elize asked as the servants cleared away lunch. "I've wanted to pay him a visit, but Lady Carene said he was still quite worn out from his ordeal. You wouldn't believe the rumors flying around the court."

"After everything that's happened, I don't think any rumor could shock me," Kenna replied. She poured herself a cup of water, pushing her wine away, the smell of it made her stomach churn uncomfortably.

"There are varying accounts of how far things were taken when he was imprisoned," Elize said.

Daris pinched one last grape from the tray before it was taken away. "According to some, the new King is unable to speak, having suffered the loss of his tongue at the hands of Dempsey's torturers."

"He spoke to the people before we came to the palace." Kenna gaped, aghast by the nonsense. "How do things get twisted into such ridiculous nonsense?"

Elize shrugged. "I think it's just a way for those who were not involved to feel like they had a stake in things." She reached for Kenna's hand. "As you say, it's nonsense—It doesn't change Niall's condition for the worse. Don't let it trouble you; there's enough for you to deal with as it is."

"The rumors will persist only as long as the King is in bed and away from the public eye," Daris assured her.

"Then perhaps it's time I was out of bed and seeing to the business of the kingdom," Niall's voice rang out. He was fully dressed and leaning casually against the door frame.

Kenna jumped out of her chair and hurried to his side. "What are you doing up? Lady Aliace sad you needed to rest for a few days. It's only been a day and a half since you were healed."

"Kenna, I'm fine, my injuries weren't severe; exhaustion was her concern. While I may not feel quite myself yet, I am well enough to get out of bed," he responded, taking her hand and tucking it into the crook of his arm. He led her back to her seat and settled in one of the empty chairs. "Besides, I spent the better part of a week alone and confined to a single room against my will. I find that the luxury of roaming is one I can no longer resist."

"You certainly look better than the last time I saw you," Daris observed. He filled a goblet with wine and passed it to Niall. "I've been enjoying the King's bounty. I figure I earned it after practically carrying you up the palace steps."

Niall accepted the cup and took a deep drink before responding. "Indeed, you clearly had the worst of it that day. Next time I'm to be torn apart, I'll be sure to check that it won't inconvenience you."

"I doubt I'll be available for something like that again. I suggest you avoid it altogether," Daris replied, lifting his glass and taking a drink as well.

Kenna took Niall's hand. "I insist you avoid it. Seeing my husband dragged through the streets once was one time too many. I don't even want to think of it happening again."

"Niall is King now, he can abolish the practice completely if he chooses to," Elize pointed out.

"Which reminds me," Daris said. He put his goblet on the table and stood up to offer Niall an incredibly deep, and obviously practiced bow. "How may I serve you, Your Majesty?"

Niall got back to his feet and pulled Daris up. "By never doing that again. Never ever—I mean it. You saved my life, not once, but twice. I never want to see you take a knee before me—you or Elize, I don't give a fig what the protocol is."

"I'm inclined to agree with my husband. We would not be here if it weren't for the friendship the two of you have offered," Kenna smiled at them both. "I hope that you'll consider staying with us, though we'd both understand if you'd rather not. The court is hardly a place of adventure and excitement."

"I don't know about that; it seems to me that seeing the beginning of a new dynasty could be quite exciting. Besides, the two of you wander into trouble anytime we let you out of our sight," Daris answered. He looked at Elize and grinned. "And you owe me a new jug of whiskey. I imagine the King and Queen of Venallis could get their hands on some of the finest ever made."

"Then you'll stay?" Kenna asked, hopefully. Daris and Elize were family now, whether they shared blood or not.

"We were going to ask to stay, even if you hadn't said anything," Elize replied, and glanced at Daris. "In fact, we've been talking, and we think it might be time to consider starting a family of our own. If we stay here, we won't have to be concerned with our performances. Your little one will need a playmate after all."

"Who knows, perhaps they'll become more than friends," Kenna pointed out. "Though, I suppose it's a bit early to discuss such things—you aren't even with child yet." Kenna looked at her for a moment. "Are you?" Elize started to laugh.

Daris half-laughed before furrowing his brow in concern. "You aren't, are you?"

Still laughing, Elize shook her head. "No, of course not. We only just talked about it this morning, Daris."

"True," Daris agreed. The relief on his face was enough to make Kenna chuckle as well. He settled back in his seat and downed the last of his wine in one long gulp. "I mean, we did agree. I'm just not ready for it to happen today."

Kenna exchanged an amused glance with Niall who leaned forward in his chair. "Try becoming a King on the same day you learn you're to be a father. It was a good thing I was already laying down when Kenna told me, or I would have fallen on my backside."

"In fairness, you brought those things on yourself. I was there when you publicly announced your claim to the throne," Daris pointed out. "And the entire caravan was aware of your efforts in the production of an heir." Kenna and Niall exchanged glances and turned similar shades of red.

It was Elize who came to their rescue. "You should mind what you say, husband. They are the King and Queen now. You could find yourself ordered to clean the chamber pots for the entire palace."

"We could, you know," Kenna teased him, keeping her expression absolutely serious. "We could heap all manner of responsibility on you."

"Quite right, my love," Niall joined in.

Daris looked at all three of them in turn before shaking his head and refilling his cup. "You are all the worst people—you know that, right?"

"You adore us," Elize said with a twinkle in her eye. "Don't even bother pretending otherwise."

"I adore you," Daris agreed. He cast a quick look at Kenna and Niall. "I'm feeling a bit conflicted about those two."

This response was met with good nature, and for a little while they were able to forget the pressure of court. They spoke for another hour, laughing and teasing one another as they had when they were traveling through Venallis and putting on shows. It was the first time Kenna felt that she could let her guard down within the palace walls.

When the time for leisure came to an end, Niall joined Kenna as she returned to the business of the kingdom. It was a relief to have him by her side this time, but it brought a deeper sense of reality to their new positions. Once again, she was stepping out of the comfortable and familiar to embrace something new.

With Niall back on his feet, Kenna was able to relax some of her duties and see to her own body's needs. At first it was difficult to view the palace as home, so little of her experience had been pleasant. Aside from Niall and Lady Carene, and those she'd formed bonds with before being named Queen, Kenna wasn't certain of any members of the court. There were too many who were quick to offer friendship when someone was in power, and even faster to snatch it away when the winds changed direction. The courtiers to the former Queen was a perfect example of this: those who once flocked to Elanor's side and took part in her cruel games were now simpering at Kenna's door.

Kenna was cautious in who she allowed into her inner circle. Lady Carene, Elize, and Lisbeth were the ones she truly trusted. She was polite, and observed the ranks and status of the other noblewomen, allowing them to attend her, but it took time for Kenna to feel comfortable with most of them.

Niall was equally selective, though he had a slightly larger group of people to choose from, due to his time spent in the service of King Fergal. Still, the trusted circles were smaller than some thought fitting for a King and Queen, and many resented the inclusion of Elize and Daris, neither of whom carried noble blood or titles.

It was for that reason that Kenna found herself strolling through the gardens with Niall, Elize, and Daris on a sunny afternoon two weeks past the rescue. After a lengthy discussion, Niall and Kenna had come to the conclusion that for the great loyalty shown—and for their safety—Daris and Elize should be granted titles and patents of nobility.

Kenna walked at Niall's side, her arm hooked through his, with Daris and Elize keeping pace. A small contingent of guards walked several feet behind them, keeping watch at a respectful distance. Summer was ending and turning to the deep russets and bright golds of autumn. The roses were going dormant and the chrysanthemums flaunted their vibrant blossoms.

"Kenna and I have been giving the arrangement of our court a great deal of thought," Niall said once they were well away from the palace walls and deep within the tall, leafy hedges of the gardens.

"And we want the two of you to hold places of honor in that court," Kenna added. "We trust you with our lives and the life of our child."

"You've said as much before," Elize replied. "Why take such a formal tone now?"

"Of all the people here, we're the last to expect the two of you to stand on etiquette," Daris plucked a bloom from one of the nearby plants and handed it to his wife. There was nothing formal in the exchange, just a small token of affection given freely. Kenna smiled at the little interaction. It was a reminder of simpler days. She hoped that time at court would never coat their genuine natures in the polished veneer of wealth and responsibility.

"I know that, Daris, and it's something that Kenna and I appreciate about you both." Niall answered. "It's why we've asked to speak to the two of you. We need people with whom we can be our true selves."

"We want to show our gratitude, and wish for you to feel that you have as much right to be here as anyone else," Kenna added to Niall's statement. They turned a corner and found themselves in a quiet alcove, with a majestic weeping willow, and an elegant stone bench nestled under its vine-like boughs.

"Now you're scaring me," Daris looked at them with a raised brow. "Elize and I haven't felt unwelcome. We're the best friends of the King and Queen of Venallis. Who could be more welcome?"

"A High Lord and High Lady," Niall replied as he ushered Kenna to the bench. "Which is what the two of you will be, if you're willing to accept the positions."

Daris and Elize both stopped and stared at Niall and Kenna as if they'd started speaking a foreign language. Elize lowered herself onto the bench beside Kenna. "But we're not nobility. We're just a pair of acrobats from a traveling troupe, who happened to save you from a band of hobgoblins. Surely, those of noble birth would object."

"The ranks and titles of Rosehaven's court are not simply a matter of blood. They can, and often are, given when one has offered service to the kingdom. Half the court attained titles this way. My own father was not noble-born—King Fergal issued patents of nobility for him, as I wish to do for the two of you," Niall explained.

"Niall and I would have died at the hands of hobgoblins, or starved to death long ago if it weren't for the kindness you've shown," Kenna stated, wrapping a friendly arm around the other woman. "It is within our rights to grant this."

"Niall, Kenna... I—I don't know what to say," Daris stammered. "You're not just offering us titles. This would place us above everyone at court but the two of you. Surely there are those better qualified for such honors."

"Technically that is true, and there will be those who take issue with it, but there are none we trust more. I will smooth any ruffled feathers that happen as a result of this decision," Niall assured them. "Will you accept?"

Daris and Elize exchanged wide-eyed looks, visibly overwhelmed by the conversation. Kenna could tell they were at a loss for words. Having just become a Queen herself, she could relate to their shock. "You don't have to answer right away. I can assure you that Niall and I both understand how—"

There was a commotion from the bushes to their right, within a shaded corridor of greenery that obscured the details of the movement. Kenna felt Elize's arms wrap around her and pull her to the side. She saw Daris yank Niall toward the bench. A figure emerged from the shadows, a man in tattered velvet robes, his beard unkempt, hair wild—but Kenna knew his face and caught the glimmer of gold atop his head. Dempsey still wore the crown, though he'd been stripped of the title of King.

"Watch out, Your Majesty!" Daris yelled, pivoting to place himself between Niall and Dempsey as a knife flashed in the air. The deadly blade arched toward Niall's chest. Daris caught Dempsey's arm at the wrist. He pushed the older man back as Niall shouted for the guards.

"Common filth! How dare you try to stop the hand of a true king!" Dempsey growled like a mad dog. He reached into his tunic with the lightning speed of a man who'd seen more than one battle. Daris didn't have time to react before a second blade drove deep into his side, burying to the hilt between his ribs.

The sound Daris made tore at Kenna's heart. It was a sickening gasp that gurgled off into something like a tearless sob. He stumbled back, releasing Dempsey's hand as he looked down at the weapon that protruded from his body.

"No!" Elize screamed. She flung herself forward and sank to the ground with her husband. "Daris, no, love... It's all right, you're all right. Hold on, please hold on."

Dempsey snarled and charged toward Niall a second time. Niall reacted quickly, having recovered from the suddenness of the initial attack. He jumped on the former King and pinned him to the ground. The two of them struggled over the first dagger, still in Dempsey's hand.

"You'll never be King! I won't allow it!" Dempsey screamed. "I will die to protect this country from another weak man!"

Niall slammed his hand against the paving stones, over and over until Dempsey's fingers loosened their grip on the hilt. Kenna dove for the blade and snatched it up before their attacker could make a bid to regain control. She pressed it to his neck as the guards flooded into the area and brought their weapons to bear on their former master.

Though he was disarmed, Dempsey continued to struggle and curse. Two guards pinned him to the ground, another wrapped his arms around Niall's waist and pulled him away from the scuffle and back to his feet. Outnumbered, held down, and staring at the points of several swords, Dempsey finally stopped fighting, and was hauled to his feet none too gently.

"Take him to the dungeons!" Niall commanded. "Lock him in the cell he put me in."

"Call for the Soulbound, quickly!" Kenna shouted as she fell to Elize's side and held her while she wept over Daris. Niall joined them as soon as Dempsey was away.

"The healer will be here soon," Elize said, crying and stroking the side of her husband's face. "Just... just... you'll be better in no time."

"I don't think... I don't think I can," Daris coughed. Blood was starting to seep from the corner of his mouth.

"No, it's not that bad," Niall reassured him, looking at the wound for a moment. Kenna could see from the expression on his face that the words were a lie. "You'll be fine. I'm the King now. I'll make it an order if I have to."

"I never was good at following orders," Daris mumbled. His skin was taking on a sickly grey color. His eyes were growing distant. "Elize, I'm sorry. I couldn't let—I wanted to give you everything."

"You will, love," Elize wept. "Please, don't give up." She clung to his hand desperately. "Don't leave me, Daris. I need you."

He started to shake, and each breath was accompanied by a terrible gurgle and wheeze. "Be strong. Promise... you'll be..." He gasped again. "Elize..."

"I'm here," she whispered, but even as she did the light was fading from Daris' eyes. He took one final shallow breath before his hand slipped from Elize's. She took hold of his shoulders and tried to pull him into her lap, clinging to him frantically. "Daris! Daris! No, you cannot go. You cannot leave me!"

Tears streamed down Kenna's face and words were choked off by grief. She wrapped her arms around Elize and tried to comfort her, but the other woman shook her off. "Elize, he's resting with the gods now."

"No!" Elize replied. She laid her head down on his chest and began keening. "Come back. Please come back."

None of them moved from Daris' side until Lady Aliace and several other members of court arrived. Niall's mother knelt beside Elize and Kenna, but Elize would not be consoled or pulled from Daris. Aliace placed her hands over the wound but moved them away a second later, confirming what Kenna already knew: Daris was gone, beyond even the magical intervention of the Soulbound.

Elize refused to release him. She continued to call to Daris and shake him, as though doing so could summon him back. After several minutes, Aliace touched Elize's brow and used magic to calm her enough for Kenna and Lady Carene to pull her away. Niall, Sir Liam, Remmy, and other members of the traveling band who had come with their leader, lifted Daris from the ground and carried him back to the palace. Walking behind with Elize, Kenna could see Niall's shoulders shaking and knew he was weeping.

That night Kenna clung to Niall and sobbed against his chest. She couldn't stop the tears once they started. The pain of Elize's cries echoed in her ears, it ripped through her heart and added to the loss of a dear friend. It was worse still, knowing how close she'd come to losing Niall again—and that had he been the one to die, Daris would still be here now.

Niall wept with her. He stroked her back and held on tightly. Were it not for his grip, Kenna feared she'd be swept away by the tidal wave of her emotions. Just like Mairi, Daris and Elize were paying the ultimate price for their loyalty.

* * *

In the sad days that followed, all honors were shown to Daris. Niall bestowed the title of High Lord posthumously, even though he'd never actually accepted it. They held two funerals for him. The first was a formal event, one befitting his rank. When the final words of farewell were spoken, Niall stood before the nobles assembled and announced that the rank of

High Lord would forever be retired; Daris would be the last to hold that title. If anyone objected, they didn't have the nerve to say so.

That same evening another smaller, intimate ceremony was held among the travelers. It was far more genuine, and suited the man they honored. According to their customs, music was played and his costume was retired. When his body was laid to rest, drinks were poured, with the final glass filled and left on his grave. Kenna tried to speak to Elize, but her friend simply stared into the distance. Her eyes remained always fixed on something just outside the activity around her. She lingered at Daris' gravesite long after the rest of the travelers went back to their tents and wagons.

Kenna and Niall stayed close by, despite the protests of their guards, who had been on high alert in the two days since the attack. Kenna finally put her foot down and stated that she would not leave Elize outside the palace alone; Niall would not leave either of them behind. The captain agreed to keep a distant watch, but would not be convinced of their safety outside the security of the castle.

It wasn't until the sun sank below the horizon and the stars came out that Elize could be led away. She walked at Kenna's side without saying a word to her. They made their way through the halls of the palace and back to Elize's apartment in utter silence. Kenna bit her lower lip and looked at her friend with concern before turning to Niall. "Go on to our rooms; I'll meet you there when Elize is settled and ready for bed."

"As you wish," Niall replied. He tried to bid Elize a good night, but she only blinked at him in response.

Once he was away, Kenna ushered Elize into the room, poured a glass of wine and led her to a chair by the fire. Kenna silently unpinned Elize's hair, combed the long, dark tresses, and then plaited them into a single braid for the night. All the while, Elize sat and stared into the flames without uttering a word. She held the cup in her hands but never once lifted it to her lips.

"Shall I help you into your nightdress?" Kenna asked anxiously. Elize shook her head, it was as much of a response as Kenna had received since Daris' death. "I can stay and sit with you for a while, if you like," Kenna offered. She put the brush down and settled into a seat near Elize. "Daris wouldn't want you to shut yourself off like this. He wouldn't want you to be alone right now."

"But I'm not alone," Elize said, looking into the shadowy corner of the room. "He's here still, I see him... I hear his voice."

"I know you want him to be here." Kenna put a hand on the other woman's knee. "I can't imagine what you're going through."

"No, you can't," Elize answered coldly. She finally looked at Kenna. "Daris died so that you don't have to go through this."

Kenna pulled her hand away slowly. The look on Elize's face sent chills down her spine. There was no warmth, no hope, nothing of the woman she'd shared so many hours with over the past months.

"We spent our whole lives together. We were paired for the stage almost from the time we could walk." Elize turned back to the flames as she spoke. "I cannot remember a time when he was not a part of my existence. I don't even know who I am without him."

"You're you," Kenna answered quietly. "I know it doesn't feel like it now, but you're strong. I know you'll find a way forward."

"I don't want to," Elize replied. She got up and moved through the room aimlessly, arms wrapped around herself. "I'm leaving Rosehaven soon."

Kenna blinked back tears, though this announcement wasn't a surprise. She'd hoped Elize would stay, but didn't want to ask her to remain in a place that held so much pain. "I'll miss you terribly, but I do understand why you need to go."

"Do you?" Elize turned to her. "Do you understand what it is like to have your heart ripped out and shredded before your eyes?"

"I wish I could do something to make this easier." Kenna rose and took a few steps toward Elize but stopped short. "Please, Elize, don't push me away. I care about you—Niall and I both care about you. We want to help."

"I know you do," Elize answered. Her shoulders relaxed slightly. She took a breath and shook her head. "But you can't." She started walking away. "Aliace says that Daris and I are bound. I have to go to the City of the Blessed to train as one of the Soulbound, or I will lose what little sanity is left to me."

"Then Daris really is still here?" Kenna replied, not entirely surprised to know that the bond between Elize and Daris ran deeply enough to form that magical connection. "But... that's good, isn't it?"

Elize turned back to her. "I am left with nothing of the life I hoped to live. I can choose a half-life with the man I love, away from everything I held dear, or I can have this bond severed and give him up forever."

"I'm so sorry," Kenna whispered. She looked down at her hands helplessly. "I would do almost anything to spare you this."

"I know you would, but there's nothing you can do." Elize looked away from her. "And I can't look at you without knowing that Daris died to save Niall.

Everything you have now was taken from me. I know it's unfair, but I wish we'd never met."

A fresh batch of tears welled up in Kenna's eyes, but she held them back, though Elize's words hurt more than any physical blow would have. "I don't know what to say to that. I wish I could make this right somehow."

"Just go." Elize bowed her head and started to cry. Kenna stood rooted to the floor. Her heart screamed to go to her friend and hold her, but her instincts warned that the action would not be well-received. Elize dashed at the tears and turned her head slightly. "Please, Kenna, leave me to find what little peace this life has to offer now."

Kenna nodded and walked to the door with heavy feet and a heavier heart. She managed to hold the pain at bay until she made it to the room she shared with her husband. Niall looked up when she stepped inside, the moment he saw her face he opened his arms. Kenna ran to him and buried her face in his tunic.

CHAPTER 24

A New Day

Justice was a difficult thing for Niall to wrap his head around in the days that followed Daris' funeral. So many had lost their lives as a result of King Fergal's choice; so many were still suffering the consequences of King Dempsey and Queen Elanor's ambition. He would have been willing to leave Dempsey and Elanor's fates up to the courts, but the magnitude and number of their crimes dictated that Niall and Kenna were the only ones deemed high enough in rank to decide their sentences. After lengthy consideration, Niall volunteered to spare Kenna the strain and deal with the matter himself.

There was nothing he could do that would bring back those who were gone now. Ian, his father, Fergal, the men and women who'd served Britwylde so loyally for so many years, and Daris. Their sacrifices were beyond any idea of justice Niall could mete out. It was those who were left behind that preoccupied his mind.

How could he bring any kind of satisfaction to the people who were experiencing such devastating loss? His mother and Elize were both facing lives they'd never asked for. His mother was moving forward by focusing on the legacy of their line, but Elize was utterly lost. She had left for the City of the Blessed a few days after her husband's funeral, without a word of farewell to Kenna or himself.

"Is there something wrong with your food?" Kenna asked. She was starting in on her second serving. The queasiness seemed to be easing now, and her appetite was returning with a vengeance.

Niall sat across the table from Kenna in their private dining room. Though the food was skillfully prepared, he had little appetite for it. "No, I'm just preoccupied."

"You should have a care for your health. It was not so long ago that you were in need of healing," Kenna fretted. "I don't wish to see you take to your bed again."

"I'm recovered, Kenna. At least, in body. My spirits will take more time, and those are what trouble me now," he reassured, but tucked into the meal of cheeses, fruits, and meats to ease her mind.

Kenna watched with approval. When he'd eaten most of what was on his plate she spoke again. "What troubles you?"

"The council reviewed Elanor's crimes today. She made no attempt to excuse herself for taking part in forming the plots against my family," Niall admitted, pushing the remainder of his meal away. "The council pushed for me to pass down the sentence of drawing and quartering."

Kenna reached for her cup and took a long drink before responding. "How do you feel about that?"

"To be honest, the whole thing makes me ill," Niall replied with a sigh. He wiped his hands on a napkin and signaled for the servants to take his plate away. "She took part in high treason. Her hands are as stained with blood as her husband's—but I know what it is to face that death. I would not wish it on anyone, not even her."

"We can see that her execution is less... barbaric," Kenna reminded him. She placed a hand on her abdomen. "The woman is terrible, but she's lost her son. I find myself more inclined to mercy now that we have our own child on the way. I'm determined to build a better world for him or her to live in."

"I know, and I'm in complete agreement. I share your conviction to create a brighter world." Niall nodded and grasped her hand to kiss it. He took a deep breath and released her. "But there is still the matter of Dempsey's punishment."

Kenna reached for the wine and refilled Niall's goblet herself. He watched her, noting the way the muscles in her jaw tightened. They'd been married long enough for Niall to know that she was trying to form a measured response. The battle between her personal feelings and her duty to be fair-minded played out on her face as boldly as if she'd spoken.

"As King I am expected to dole out fair and unbiased judgement," Niall continued, feeling anger bubbling to the surface. "But I despise that man. I cannot look at him without wishing him dead, and yet death is too merciful an end for him."

Kenna was slow to respond. When she did, her eyes did not meet Niall's. "Are you considering the death he planned for you?"

"To be honest, I have, but I won't spare Elanor that only to order it carried out on Dempsey... I think it's what he expects." Niall shook his head. "I wish I could say it is a sense of mercy or honor that stills my hand, but it is not. He would see it as confirmation that his own actions were justified self-preservation. I don't want to give him even that level of satisfaction. I want him to feel what he's inflicted on so many others."

"Then make your decision based upon the suffering of others and not the pain you've endured at his hands," Kenna responded gently. "He'll get no pity from me, and I doubt there are many who will speak out on his behalf."

Niall considered her words carefully. It was one thing to harbor anger against someone. It was another thing entirely to act on that rage. As the new King and Queen, they had the power to do as they willed, but if they used their power to enact vengeance, were they any better than Dempsey and Elanor? He didn't want to be that kind of ruler. Such action held a heavy cost, and would leave a stain on the souls of those who chose to take it.

"I can't forgive what he's done," Niall stated quietly. "I don't want to. I simply want to move forward and put all of it behind us."

"Then do what you must to bring that about and never let him trouble you again, my love," Kenna replied. "You have my support, no matter how you choose to proceed against him."

Niall nodded contemplatively; Kenna's words brought a strange sense of clarity to his thoughts. Perhaps all he really needed was the knowledge that she would not judge him if he chose to deal with Dempsey harshly. Or maybe it was just a need to mull the matter over with another voice, to filter his emotions out of the decision.

Even so, it was two days before Niall felt mentally prepared to face Dempsey. Once he was outside the dungeons, it took several minutes of pacing for him to summon the courage to take the first step back into that world of darkness and despair. Niall hadn't returned to this place since the day he was led out to face death; there was but one purpose for his return now, and when that was resolved he had no intentions of ever setting foot here again. Niall steeled his nerves and pushed the heavy oak door open.

The smells and sounds brought every second of his imprisonment back. It was surreal to move through the dimly-lit space and receive bows from the same men who a few weeks earlier were responsible for overseeing his captivity. The guards looked at him now with apprehension, and were overly eager to win his favor. Niall found that he didn't harbor any ill will toward them. They were under the orders of a King and had no choice but to carry out their duties. But that understanding didn't motivate him to offer them any reassurances, either.

The door to the lowest level of the dungeon appeared in the gloom. Niall felt a twinge of panic as he approached it. There was an irrational fear that if he stepped back inside that room, he would find himself helpless and caged again, and the life he lived now would be nothing more than a dream. The sound of the lock clicking shook Niall from his nightmarish flight of fancy. He remained outside the threshold as the warden entered to light the candles inside. The pause gave Niall a few minutes to gain control of his fear before he came face-to-face with the former King.

Still shaken, but determined to see this through, Niall stepped inside and looked around the room with revulsion. He hated every crack in the wall, every shadow cast by the candlelight, and each bar that formed the cell in which Dempsey now resided. The acrid scent of damp stone and rodent droppings that permeated the air made him want to vomit. He knew that smell all too well and hoped never to encounter it again after this day.

"So, the high and mighty King Niall has finally deigned to look upon his predecessor," Dempsey sneered from his cell. "How does it feel to see me brought so low? Do you enjoy it as much as I did when our places were reversed?"

Niall stared at him in disgust. "I take no pleasure in this meeting. I hoped never to return to this pit again. I certainly do not relish being in your presence, regardless of the circumstances."

"Then why come at all?" Dempsey asked, approaching the bars. "I assume you're here to tell me what my punishment is. You could have saved yourself that trouble and simply had one of the courtiers deliver my sentence."

"Your fate was my responsibility. I won't ask another to deliver my decision to you," Niall answered calmly. "Nor will I hide behind the throne to justify my actions."

"Don't fool yourself into pretending that you're here out of a sense of honor." Dempsey pressed his face against the bars. "You're here because you want to see me suffer as I made you suffer."

Niall grabbed the man's shirt front and held him in place. "Yes, I do. Is that what you want to hear? I want to subject you to every hurt and humiliation you inflicted on me."

"Huh; perhaps I was wrong about you," Dempsey replied with infuriating superiority. "It seems you're not as spineless as you appear."

"You're pathetic," Niall said with a snarl before he released the man. He turned away from the cell and paced the room until his temper was under control again. "Your family has been destroyed by your ambition and you still think you were right."

"I assume I'm to be executed then?"

"No, I'm not going to kill you," Niall replied. He turned slowly and looked at the older man. "I'm going to forget you."

Dempsey let loose a derisive snort. "As weak and foolish as I thought. You will be the end of this kingdom. I suppose you think showing mercy will endear you and your wife to the people."

"Oh, I don't intend to show you an ounce of mercy. No, I'm not going to kill you because I want you to understand the pain you put so many other people through," Niall said. He approached the cell slowly, eyes locked with Dempsey's. "Your wife was executed today. Did you know that? She climbed the stairs of the very scaffold you intended for me and laid her head on the block. Do you know what her final words were?"

Dempsey remained silent, but Niall could see the impact of his statement. A part of him considered stopping, but the broken, jagged edges left in the wake of so many deaths urged him on. "She disavowed herself from you. She confessed her guilt and died with your son's name on her lips."

"Cathal died because he was weak and a fool," Dempsey answered abruptly. Despite his words, his eyes glistened with tears that were barely visible in the dim light. "I will not spend my days allowing his actions to make me question my choices."

Niall thought of his own child. The baby hadn't even arrived yet, and already he would lay down his life to protect it. That Dempsey could stand before him now, after killing his own son, and so callously deny the tragedy was beyond comprehension. Any faint glimmer of compassion Niall might have harbored for Dempsey sputtered out of existence.

"That is exactly what you will do. I will leave you with nothing but time to consider the price of your actions," Niall hissed. He paused and stared hard at the man before him, loathing the fact that he had ever been considered a friend. "My decision concerning your fate is this: you will spend the rest of your days in this room with no one but the ghosts of your dead family to keep you company."

"You know that if I ever escape, I will come after you," Dempsey shot back.

"I do, which is why I'm going to have the door bricked over as soon as I leave here," Niall replied coolly. He watched as his words made their full impact. "No doubt you've noticed the chute they put into your cell. It's big enough for food and water to pass through, but not for a grown man."

"You haven't the stomach for it, boy." Dempsey's words may have doubted Niall's intent, but his voice shook enough to betray his fear.

"I promise you, I do," Niall replied without remorse. He stepped right up to the bars and met Dempsey's eyes. "When I leave here, I will return to the rooms that were once yours. I will go to my wife, who is already carrying an heir to the throne, and I'll enjoy all the power and luxuries you sacrificed your honor for. It will be my line that leads Venallis into a new age, and you will never be anything more than footnote in the history of this kingdom. A pathetic man who failed as King."

"What of my daughter?" he asked, for the first time displaying something other than feigned bravado. "Bedalia knew nothing of my deeds—she played no part in any of this."

"I'm not like you. I don't punish the innocent for things beyond their control." Niall turned away and reached for a candlestick. He could have told Dempsey that he'd already made arrangements for Bedalia to be taken into one of the noble households far from court, but he wanted the man to feel as hopeless and lost as he had when they last spoke. "I cannot forgive what you've done, but I swear I will forget you when I leave here and never think of you again." He took a step toward the door.

"Wait! Don't leave me here alone," Dempsey called out, true terror in his voice. "I beg you—kill me!"

Niall stopped on the threshold. He glanced over his shoulder but didn't face Dempsey. "You're not alone. You'll have the rats and the memory of your deeds to keep you company."

"Mercy!" Dempsey cried out. "For pity's sake, mercy!"

Niall faced forward and started walking. As he stepped into the outer chamber, he gave the order for the stonemason to begin work. The man nodded and closed the door. The sound of Dempsey's pleas turned to screams that bounced helplessly off the walls. The echoes followed Niall all through the dungeons, only fading once he stepped into the sunlit courtyard. Niall took a deep breath, wiped Dempsey from his mind, and went to find Kenna.

The next task that faced Niall was bittersweet. He wanted to honor Daris' memory in a way more tangible than a symbolic title. Elize was now a member of the Soulbound and there was little he could offer her; and even if he could think of something suitable, he doubted she would accept it.

There was one other person Daris held dear, and Niall focused his efforts there. Word of Daris' death was sent to Brittendell, with a request that Brenin and his wife come to Rosehaven as soon as it was possible for them to travel. To make the journey easier, Niall sent one of the finest carriages at his disposal to transport them.

Nearly three weeks passed before the carriage returned with Brenin and his family. They stepped out into the courtyard with wide-eyed and curious stares. Protocol and business kept Niall from meeting them at the doors, but the first chance he was able to steal a moment away, he sent a message asking Brenin to join him in the royal stables.

During his time in King Fergal's service Niall had escaped to the quiet solitude of the stables on the rare occasions he found himself free of work. The shuffling of the horses in their stalls and the scent of hay reminded him of Britwylde. It still did, though the reminder was tinged with a deep sense of loss now. Even if he weren't bound by the throne, there was nothing left of that life. He hoped that time would allow those memories to bring happiness instead of regret.

Niall pulled off his tunic and hung it on a hook that was already burdened with ropes and halters. He ordered his personal guards to take up posts outside the door, and allow Brenin entrance when he arrived. With brush in hand, Niall opened the door to his newest horse's stall and began stroking the beast's silky, copper flank. It felt good to slip off the formality and responsibility of ruling for a few precious minutes.

The stable doors opened a short time later and the sound of slow, uncertain footsteps shuffled through the straw. Niall put his task aside and popped his head outside the stall. Brenin was wandering down the aisle between the stalls with an expression of wonder. Niall chuckled softly. The younger man looked like a child in a room full of delicious sweets.

"Over here," Niall called, stepping out to greet him. "Thank you for coming. I know it's a long journey, especially with a little one."

"Well, one can hardly ignore the summons of a King," Brenin replied. He took off his cap and bowed before Niall.

Niall blushed and gestured for Brenin to rise. "Please don't. I told your brother he need never lower himself to me, and that extends to you and your family as well."

Brenin's eyes and nose went red. He rose, swallowed, and looked away. The deep impact of losing a brother was something Niall understood all too well.

"Daris was one of bravest and best people I ever met. I would gladly sacrifice the crown, and the trappings that come with it, to have him back with us." Niall said. He had to blink away tears of his own before continuing. "But he died protecting his King, and I will spend my entire reign trying to be worthy of that. Which is why I've asked you to come here."

"I heard that you bestowed the rank of High Lord on my brother. I'm certain he would have been delighted—complained about the duties, but would have served them with honor," Brenin began slowly. "Rowan and I prefer a simpler life. We've worked hard for what we have in Brittendell, and we have no wish to give that up."

"And I'd never dream of asking you to leave it behind. On the contrary, I asked you here so that I could make a contribution to that life," Niall replied. He'd considered offering Brenin a title but had predicted that the man would refuse it. "You mentioned that you were hoping to meet with High Lord Edan to ask for his help in acquiring horses for breeding."

"We've both had to move forward, despite the losses of those we held dear," said Brenin. "Your father was a good man. I'm certain he would have helped, but it wasn't to be."

"He took the needs of his tenants seriously, which is what I wish to discuss. When my father died, I became the High Lord. I may be the King now, but the welfare of those tenants is still important to me," Niall began. A grin spread across his face and he gestured to the animals that surrounded them. "All of the horses here belong to the crown, to me. I offer you the choice of any three mares and three stallions. Will six horses be enough for you to start your farm?"

Brenin dropped his cap and gaped at Niall in shock. He turned a slow circle, looking at each of the splendid beasts in turn. He came back around, still speechless.

Niall muffled a slight laugh before he continued. "Are they not satisfactory? I could ask for horses to be sent from Arthan as well."

"No—I mean, yes... are you serious?" Brenin ducked to pick up his hat. When he stood upright again, he was slightly more composed. "Thank you, Your Majesty. Six is more than enough, but these are the finest horses in Venallis; they're far too magnificent for a humble place like mine. Animals less grand than these would still be better than anything offered at the markets near Brittendell."

"Nonsense, there are more here than I could ever need, and I want to do this. I know it won't bring Daris back or ease the pain of that loss, but he was proud of the life you were building there. Please, accept this gift. For Daris, if not for yourself," Niall pleaded. The fact that he was a King speaking to someone of common birth was irrelevant.

Brenin looked at the horses again. He moved closer to one of the stalls and reached inside to pet the muzzle of a sweet-natured, grey mare. "How am I to choose? They're all beautiful."

"Take your time," said Niall, giving Brenin a pat on the shoulder. "I've told my stablemaster to give you any information you ask for. You, Rowan, and the baby are welcome to stay at the palace as long as you like."

"We will, thank you," Brenin repeated. But his tone was distant now, his concentration focused on the horses. Niall would have liked to stay and help Brenin make his selections, but there was a pile of work waiting to be attended. He bid Brenin farewell, adding an invitation for a private lunch the next day. It was enough to stir the younger man from his thoughts momentarily, but before Niall had reached the door, he had the mare out of her stall, and was running his hands down her legs.

* * *

The autumn months that followed were temperate and warm. The trees lost their leaves, but a sense of peace and rebirth seemed to hang in the air. Kenna and Niall were at the center of a court bustling with anticipation for the coronation of a new King and Queen. With Dempsey and Elanor gone, the atmosphere at the palace became one of hope. The people seemed eager to embrace their young leaders, and as the weeks passed and the promise of a little prince or princess started to become visible, it only added to the optimistic mood.

The official coronation was to take place in a few weeks and the castle was an absolute frenzy of preparations. Were it not for the tireless efforts and attention to detail by Lady Carene, Niall and Kenna would have been happy to avoid the pomp and pageantry entirely. But Niall's mother would hear nothing of it; she insisted that as the first of a new dynasty, the coronation had to be grand enough to be engraved in the minds of the people for generations to come.

The pressures of their new positions were relentless, especially with the added apprehension of parenthood looming on the horizon. Niall fretted over Kenna constantly, jumping to his feet to run to her side at the slightest indication of discomfort. She took it in good stride and repeatedly assured him that all was well. Niall would simply kiss her forehead, ask if there was anything he could do for her, and continue to dote whenever their duties didn't keep them apart.

One responsibility they were both looking forward to was greeting Kenna's family upon their arrival at the palace. Two days before the coronation, a messenger rode through the gates at dawn. She delivered the happy news that the party from Arthan was nearby and would be arriving before dinner. By late afternoon a sentry announced their approach. Niall put aside the documents he was reading and went in search of his wife, who met him in the hallway, practically bouncing with excitement.

They took their place at the top of the palace steps as the carriages carrying Kenna's parents and siblings drove through the gates. Under normal circumstances, visitors were brought into the throne room to be presented to the King and Queen, but Kenna hadn't seen her parents since they left Britwylde, and her siblings since she departed their estate in Arthan. She was too eager for the reunion to delay it to satisfy ceremony, and Niall suspected her family was just as impatient for the reunion. They'd mourned her death for months before learning of the escape, and according to their letters, the revelation of her survival was like having her miraculously returned from the dead.

Niall smiled at his wife as the transports pulled to a stop. Her unbridled joy and enthusiasm were infectious. For his own part, Niall was a little nervous about the meeting. Up to this point he'd only been introduced to Kenna's parents, and in the time since their departure, he'd hardly been able to provide the safe life that was expected when they left her in his care.

Bugles blared and grooms in the royal livery stepped forward to open the carriage doors. Lady Isla stepped out of the first carriage, followed by her husband. Kenna let out a little squeal of delight and would have run down the stairs if Niall had not been clutching her hand. He began to move forward with urgency, mostly keeping pace, but still half-dragged.

"Kenna!" Lady Isla exclaimed. The dignified and stoic veneer that Niall saw from her at Britwylde was dropped entirely. She was a mother, desperate to see the child thought lost.

"Mother!" Kenna called back. She broke away from Niall when they were down the stairs and ran into her mother's outstretched arms. Lady Isla clung tightly to her daughter, eyes closed, whispering soundless prayers of thanks. Her father encircled them both in his arms. They held on to one another for several minutes, crying tears of joy.

"I have dreamed of holding you like this, but went so long without hope that I would ever have the chance to do so again." Kenna's mother pulled back and looked her daughter over. Her eyes stopped on the small curve that was just visible under the layers of Kenna's gown. "You're with child!"

"I wanted to tell you in person." Kenna nodded. "I'm at the beginning of my fifth month."

Lady Isla kissed Kenna's cheeks, and the tears already coating her face were joined by a fresh batch. "To see you happy and safe, with a little one on the way... Kenna, there are no words to describe the elation that I feel. I almost fear to close my eyes and find it's nothing but a sweet dream."

Niall approached then and found himself yanked into the matriarch's embrace. It was as tight as the one his own mother gave him when they were reunited. Lady Isla kissed his cheeks as well, and then pulled both of them close again as the rest of the family filed out of their carriages. There were several small children among them, giggling with excitement, and restless after the long ride. Kenna's siblings greeted her and Niall in turn, with no less enthusiasm than their parents. The sheer volume of the reunion was enough to make the servants working nearby stop their tasks and turn to gaze in curiosity.

"Niall, this is my eldest sister, Iyari, her husband, Harrus, and daughter Lali," Kenna introduced the first of her siblings to approach. "Iyari, this is my Niall."

"It's an honor to meet all of you. Kenna speaks of you often," Niall replied with genuine delight. "I almost feel as though we've already met—I'm pleased to make that a reality now."

Iyari offered him a warm, dimpled grin. She bore a strong resemblance to Lady Isla, but her eyes held a spark of mischief that was absent in the matriarch's. "See if you continue to feel that way after our family has been in residence for a few days."

"I'm sure I'll be even more delighted then," Niall replied. He tilted his head to look at the little girl clinging to Iyari's skirts. "Hello Lali, Kenna tells me that you were very fond of my brother Ian." Lali looked up at him with wide eyes and inched a little further behind her mother's legs.

Niall crouched, lowering himself to her level and held out a hand to her. "I was hoping that we could be good friends as well. After all, I am your uncle now, and I was quite fond of Ian too."

"He took me horseback riding and let me have sweets when no one was looking," Lali answered shyly. She was still holding Iyari's dress, but stepped closer to Niall. "Do you like sweets?"

"As a matter of fact, I do," Niall replied with a smile. "One of the very best things about being a King is that I can have all the sweets that I want, and I can share them with whomever I choose, whenever I choose. I don't even have to sneak them."

Now she did release her mother's skirts and took a step toward Niall. "Truly? Any kind you want?"

"Indeed, any kind you can imagine," said Niall, as though swearing a solemn oath. "And the cooks are preparing a mountain of treats for the coronation."

Lali looked up at her mother, then back at Niall; but instead of addressing him she wandered over to Kenna and hugged her legs. "You were right. He is very nice. I like my new uncle."

"I like him too." Kenna laughed, bending down to cuddle the little girl.

The family shifted, and Kenna introduced her siblings one after another. She had an elder brother named Pharid, a younger brother, Andren, who was more interested in the soldiers practicing nearby, and her littlest sister, Veda. She was only four and still rubbing sleep from her eyes, having napped for the last hour of the journey.

Niall took a moment to speak to each of them as they stepped forward. Kenna had spent hours talking about her siblings in the days leading to their arrival. Niall made a point of noting any shared interests and tried to make each meeting personal. Kenna's family was close-knit and it was important to him that they feel comfortable and welcomed.

Only two of Kenna's siblings remained to be introduced. Her sister Stazia stepped forward, head bowed, cheeks and nose a vivid shade of red. Niall frowned and looked at Kenna in confusion. This was not the outspoken woman that had been described to him.

"Stazi, what's the matter?" Kenna asked. She reached out and took her sister's hands.

Stazia shook her head and Niall realized she was weeping. It took several seconds for her to gain enough composure to speak. "I thought you dead, and I was so wretched to you the day you left. I was jealous and mean-spirited. Oh, Kenna, I was so afraid you died thinking I didn't..."

"I know you didn't mean any of it," Kenna responded gently. She put a hand on Stazia's arm. "I left our home knowing that you loved me, and with love in my heart for you."

"I do love you, Kenna," Stazia said, finally looking at her sister. She pulled Kenna close and sobbed on her shoulder. "I'll never take that bond for granted again. Please forgive me for letting my petty jealousy get the better of me."

Kenna held her close, stroking her back. "You had my forgiveness long ago. We're sisters, even when we don't behave as kindly as we should."

They stayed locked in one another's arms for some time before Kenna finally pulled away and introduced Niall. Stazia granted him an equally tight hug and gave him strict instructions to guard her little sister and future niece or nephew with his life. Niall assured his sister-in-law that he had every intention of spending his days doing exactly that.

A male voice called out from behind the rest of Kenna's siblings. "I suppose you think I'll let you win at all the games now that you're a Queen."

Kenna looked away from the rest of her family and a wide smile spread across her lips. "Jaik!"

"I kept your secret, Kenna. Have you any notion how difficult it is to keep something like a grandchild hidden from our mother?" Jaik said as he moved closer. He gave her a look of playful displeasure before giving up on the pretense and grinning from ear to ear.

The two of them bore a striking similarity to one another; both had the same wide, rich brown eyes and high cheek bones, and their smiles were matched in brightness and warmth. He lifted Kenna up gently and hugged her close. When he put her back on the ground, he turned an assessing look on Niall.

"And you must be my sister's new husband," Jaik remarked. "After so many letters filled with the details of your many charms and virtues, I did not expect to meet a mere mortal. Perhaps my twin has been a bit biased in her descriptions."

"My charms and virtues?" Niall asked with a glance in Kenna's direction. "I'm not sure what those might be, but I will defer to your sister's judgement on the matter. I've come to trust her opinions, but I think she may see more in me than is actually there. She's told me a great deal about you as well."

Jaik clapped Niall on the back in a comfortable and companionable manner. "All true, I assure you—except for anything that might paint me in a less-than-favorable light. Then I'm certain you were told the most astonishing lies."

"I'm sure," Niall laughed, but there was a twinge of pain beneath it. He couldn't help but think of Daris, and how he'd once claimed to be the man now standing in front of Niall. In less than a year he'd lost his brother, and a friend who'd become as close as a brother. Jaik's playful demeanor was refreshing, but it made him yearn for that brotherly connection. "I look forward to getting to know you better, Jaik."

"As long as he behaves himself," Kenna said with a raised brow and a half-smile. "The last thing I need is to have you picking up some of my brother's bad habits before the baby comes."

Jaik put a hand over his heart as if mortally wounded. "I would never do such a thing... but I will be sure to tell the King of all our lovely adventures as children. He must know of his Queen's boldness."

"Oh, you really are the worst," Kenna grumbled, but her eyes were twinkling with affection all the same. She shook her head and turned back to the rest of her family, gesturing toward the palace. "Shall we go inside and get you all settled? I've had the kitchen working on all of your favorite dishes for dinner tonight." She hooked her arm through Stazia's. "And I promise, everything has been properly seasoned." Niall frowned at that last remark and made a mental note to ask why she felt the need to offer such an odd reassurance.

The arrival of the Queen's family caused quite a commotion. Kenna's younger brothers and sisters were sources of endless energy. They skipped through the austere halls and chambers of the palace with unabashed exuberance. Compared to the usual atmosphere of reserved dignity it was a breath of fresh air. Niall found the noise and enthusiasm delightful. It reminded him of their time with the caravan and helped to ease the tension of the impending coronation ceremony.

The next days passed in a blur. Kenna spent much of her time with her family, and Niall was happy to take the burden of extra work in exchange for the delight that their presence brought her. Though there was much to be done, Niall still made a point to spend time with his in-laws. It was in the hours with family that he could set aside the larger concerns of the kingdom and be himself. He hoped that with Kenna as Queen, the court would abandon some of their rigid habits and embrace a warmer, more open, and more joyful atmosphere; some, like Lisbeth, already had.

There was an enormous banquet on the evening prior to the coronation. Representatives from Wiettan were in attendance, as well as some members of the smaller Vashirats of Arthan. The night was filled with long-winded speeches, toasts to the health and long life of Niall and Kenna, well-wishes for a healthy heir, gifts, and endless meetings with the nobles and dignitaries in attendance. By the time the festivities came to a close, Niall thought his hand would be chapped from all the people who kissed it.

The quiet that settled over the castle was charged with a sense of anticipation. Despite the weariness that Niall felt, sleep was elusive. He lay in bed beside Kenna, listening to the steady rhythm of her breath as she slumbered peacefully. He wished his own rest would come as easily, but didn't begrudge her the respite. She tired more and more easily as her pregnancy progressed and the activity of this week had taken its toll. Tomorrow would be the busiest of all.

Niall let out a quiet, exasperated groan. He knew he needed to sleep to make it through all of the ceremonies and celebrations ahead of him. It was ridiculous that he couldn't drift off after such a long evening, and yet an endless barrage of thoughts kept him from his dreams. He climbed out of bed in frustration and crossed to the window to stare out at the night sky. The stars were the same whether he was the second son of a High Lord, a knife thrower in a band of traveling entertainers, or a King on the eve of his coronation.

Now that he was nearing what some might consider the end of his adventures, Niall found that he fervently wished he could go back to relive them. He sighed heavily and reached for the shirt and pair of trousers draped over the back of a nearby chair. *If I stay here, I'll wake Kenna with my restlessness. A brief walk might bring some peace or at least wear me out enough to sleep.* With that thought, he left the bedroom and slipped out of their chambers.

The corridors were empty and the castle quiet. The guests and members of court were all slumbering in their beds, wholly oblivious to anyone who passed by their doors. Niall wandered without purpose or aim until he came to the audience chamber. The thrones stood tall and silent at the end of the room. At the side of each was a six-foot candlestand, holding a single, thick candle that provided the only light in the room. A pillow sat upon each seat, cradling the crowns that would be placed upon Niall and Kenna's heads at the ceremony.

Niall approached the golden circlets in silence. The way the light played across the metal and jeweled bands almost made it look like tiny flames flickered within the gems themselves; it was beautiful and ominous. Once upon a time, Niall might have met this honor with more enthusiasm, but now he understood the price of rising so high. He stopped just before the steps that led to the thrones, and sat down on the cold marble tiles to stare up at the symbols of the office he held.

He remained there for several minutes before the sound of soft, unshod footsteps padded through the room. Niall didn't need to turn to know who approached. He took a deep breath and turned to offer Kenna an apologetic smile as she stopped at his side.

"I was worried when I woke to find the bed empty," she said, smoothing a hand over the curve of her belly. "How long have you been awake?"

"I'm sorry, I didn't mean to disturb you. In fact, I was trying to avoid that," Niall admitted. He looked back up at the crowns. "I've not been able to sleep yet."

Kenna lowered herself to the floor beside him. "Niall, you should have sent for something to aid your sleep. Tomorrow will be a difficult enough day without being exhausted."

"I know. I just couldn't stop thinking about everything that brought us to this point."

"It's a lot to take in," Kenna laced her fingers through his. "We've been the King and Queen for over a month now; tomorrow is only a formality."

"But one that makes it real, and official. I know that it's ridiculous, but it feels like I've only been pretending at being King," Niall replied. "Once we put those crowns on—once the blessings for our reign are spoken—there won't be any going back." He looked down at her hand in his. "And I desperately wish that we could."

"So do I," Kenna answered quietly. "I miss having the freedom of simply being Niall and Kenna, and Spending quiet evenings by a campfire. I miss..."

Niall wrapped an arm around her and pulled her closer. Kenna didn't need to mention their friends by name for him to know where her thoughts rested. "I miss them too." He looked back at the thrones. "When I think of all the people who died so that we could come to this point, it makes me hate the very idea of putting those crowns on. I would give all of it up in a heartbeat if it would bring any of them back."

"But that's exactly why we must accept this burden, Niall." Kenna rested her head on his shoulder. "We cannot let the deaths of so many be in vain. As the King and Queen, we can take measures to prevent others from suffering such cruel fates."

"Which is why I haven't run screaming from the palace yet," Niall replied. He kissed Kenna's hair. "Though, we still have a little time; say the word and we can bolt. I'm sure Remmy would allow us to take up our old act."

Kenna laughed a little. "Yes, but I'm less willing to have knives thrown at me with our little one in residence."

"That's all it would have taken to convince you not to do that act in first place? I wish you'd told me that sooner. I could have been spared endless hours of fretting," Niall teased. He stood up and offered her his hand. "Come, the little one needs rest too, and if you aren't willing to go back to hurling weapons at one another I suppose we'll have to settle for the monarchy."

"Well, life is full of compromise," Kenna replied playfully as she accepted the hand he offered and allowed him to pull her to her feet.

When they returned to their room and bed. Niall wrapped his arms around his wife and closed his eyes. He set aside the thoughts of crowns and nobles and imagined they were back in their little wagon. The mattress had been filled with straw instead of feathers, and the wool blankets were not as fine as the ones that dressed their bed now, but it was there that they'd fallen in love, and it was where a part of their hearts would always dwell.

It rained during the night, but when the morning dawned it was as beautiful a day as anyone could have asked for. Niall and Kenna were excused from all of the usual business of their day to prepare for the coronation. They were each drawn warm baths of rose-scented water and attended by their most trusted family and friends. Every moment and detail of preparation was perfectly organized and executed, thanks to the efforts of Niall's mother. The day was one of special significance, and the entire city of Rosehaven seemed to be waiting with bated breath for the hour of the coronation to arrive.

Niall felt the same nervous panic that he'd experienced on the morning of his wedding. In many ways he was a groom again, but this time he was being wed to the whole of Venallis. It was the bond he shared with Kenna that would get him through it. Knowing she would be at his side, an equal partner in the tremendous task that lay ahead, was the one thing that made the pressure bearable. From this day forward, their lives would belong to the people of Venallis, and it would be their sacred duty to serve the needs of the realm.

Niall felt like a boy in his tunic of purple and gold brocade. It was the finest garment he'd ever worn, and it bore the weight of the world in its seams. His mother straightened the bejeweled chain draped across his shoulders and chest, and then reached up to fuss over his unruly curls.

"Your father and brother would have been so proud," she whispered, fixing a teary smile on him. "They both knew you'd go far."

Niall reached for her hand. "I only hope that I'm up to this task. I feel so small and insignificant in the face of it."

"As anyone would if they had any sense," she replied.

The doors opened and Niall's breath caught in his throat. Kenna stood on the threshold in a gown of golden silk and plum velvet. It was trimmed with an intricate, deep purple lace, that shimmered with shining strands of thread that reflected in the light like mother of pearl. Diamonds and amethyst lined the neckline. The waist was high, almost hiding the little bulge of their growing child.

"Your Majesty," Niall bowed before her, taking her hand to kiss it reverently. "I fear the gods themselves cannot compare with you today."

Kenna blushed. "It's all flash and dazzle. I feel I might suffocate in all these yards of finery."

"I assure you, the gown pales in comparison to the one who wears it," Niall replied. He was utterly besotted and didn't care who knew it. "The people won't even notice me at your side."

"You don't do yourself justice," Kenna answered. She took Niall's hand and allowed him to lead her out of the room. "There will be many an eye on the King of Venallis."

"Not at all, for he is standing next to the sun herself," he returned solemnly. The doors to their outer chamber opened and they stepped into the hallway. Niall kissed Kenna's hand again before they turned to leave the residential wing. They made their way through the castle and out into the courtyard, where they were led to a gilded carriage, pulled by a pair of white stallions with shining harnesses, and flowers woven through their manes and tails.

The carriage processed through the streets of Rosehaven at the head of a marvelous parade. The people cheered with open and genuine adoration as they passed. Hats were tossed in the air and petals were cast onto the street before the carriage. It was a strange and stark contrast to the last time Niall was led through the city. He'd been the definition of defeat that day. Now he was the epitome of triumph.

Thunderous applause erupted when their coach arrived at the city square. Lady Carene had managed to wipe all evidence of the previous events from existence; not a single nail was left from the scaffold. Banners hung from every rooftop, garlands of flowers and ribbons ran from one building to the next. Faeries flitted around the square, sprinkling the area with their glittering dust, but the most brilliant touch of all was the presence of the traveling troupe of entertainers. For the first time ever, they were performing within the walls of Rosehaven. The fanfare provided was not that of the royal orchestra, but rather the musicians of the troupe with their drums, flutes, and fiddles.

Niall and Kenna exchanged delighted smiles and waved to their friends and adopted family, heedless of the demands of propriety. It was the perfect touch to help them relax, and a beautiful acknowledgement of a treasured time in their lives. Niall looked to his mother and mouthed words of thanks before they climbed the steps of the dais to be officially proclaimed the King and Queen of Venallis.

Niall barely registered the words of the Head Wizard as he pronounced a magical blessing over the proceedings. They swore their pledges of service with solemn, measured voices that only shook a little. Niall could feel the world shifting around him, and he sensed every pair of eyes resting on them. It was a moment that he would never forget.

The Head Wizard lifted the crowns high for all to see. Then he turned and lowered them toward Niall and Kenna. Niall reached for Kenna's hand and found it waiting for his. Their fingers wove together as the crowns settled atop their heads. No matter how heavy the burden might become, they would carry it together.

EPILOGUE

The sound of water splashing down on granite was punctuated by elated squeals and childish giggles. Kenna leaned against a pillar and watched her sons splash and frolic in the spray of one of the fountains of her family's water garden. Their raven ringlets were dripping, and their clothes were equally soaked.

It was past time for lunch, but the boys were playing so pleasantly with one another that she hated to disturb them, and the picnic would hold until they were ready to come sit down. They loved the water gardens of Arthan as much as Kenna had when she was a little girl. It filled her with delight to see them enjoying such simple pleasures, and they were so rarely able to find the time to leave Rosehaven and visit her childhood home.

This reprieve from the palace was greatly needed by the entire family. Though Venallis was prospering under their rule, there was always something to intrude upon their peace. In recent weeks they'd received disturbing news from the City of the Blessed. After five years, Elize was still struggling in her life there, and her choices since joining the Soulbound were causing problems for the sisterhood. There was nothing Kenna could do to help her, and even if she could, Elize continued to refuse their help or friendship. To be back in Arthan for an occasion as happy as Jaik and Lisbeth's wedding provided distance and a sense of peace that the court at Rosehaven lacked.

Unfortunately, the peace was short-lived. A well-aimed splash from her eldest son turned laughter into tears. Kenna sighed and moved to intervene when she heard Niall's voice from the picnic blanket behind her.

"Ian! Be nice to your little brother; Daris looks up to you." His tone was stern but patient. He held their daughter in his arms as she slept. The baby had had a full belly, and was completely unperturbed by her older brothers' rambunctious play. In fact, she usually slept better amid chaos.

"He splashed me first and I didn't cry like a baby!" Ian argued. He was five and full of opinions.

Niall sighed and shook his head in exasperation. "Did he do it on purpose?"

Ian bit his lower lip and fixed a set of large, bright blue eyes on his father. "No, Papa, he was just playing." For all his energy and strong will, he was an honest child.

"So you threw water in his face to retaliate? That's not how we handle accidents, Ian," Niall replied, shifting to put Aillee in her bassinet. "You both need to apologize, and then it's time to come eat your lunch."

In the meantime, Daris was approaching Kenna with his arms outstretched. His mouth was open wide in a wail that was disproportionate to the amount of water that had been splashed. Tears were running down his round cheeks, side by side with the droplets from the assault. He was not as bold as his namesake and was past due for a nap. Kenna stooped to lift the crying three-year old, soaking her own clothes in the process.

"I'm not hungry," Ian replied. He went further into the frothing spray. "And I'm not sorry, either."

"Well, at least he admits it," Kenna remarked to her husband. She wrapped a blanket around Daris' shoulders and sat him down with a plate of dried fruits and cheese. "I'll go get him. I'm already soaked. No need for you to get drenched chasing him down."

"An admission of guilt is not going to get him out of an apology, or a nap if his attitude doesn't improve," Niall replied. Despite the frustration in his voice, he offered Kenna a playful salute. "But I commend your courage in facing our angry little water sprite."

"You can commend my courage by being the one to wrestle him into bed tonight," Kenna shot over her shoulder as she struck out to collect her eldest son.

By the time Kenna caught up with him, Ian had wandered further into the garden and was seated at the edge of one of the pools. He was dangling his feet in the water but had his hands over his face. Kenna approached him gently. She could see that his little shoulders were shaking and could hear his muffled crying. The journey from Rosehaven to Arthan was a long and arduous one, and all the children were still fighting fatigue as a result.

"I'm sorry, Mama," Ian looked up at her with heartbreaking earnestness. "Daris is just little."

"Yes, he is 'just little', and he's still learning how to be careful when he plays," Kenna sat down next to Ian. She wiped the sodden hair from his forehead. Aside from his curls and blue eyes, Ian resembled her more than Niall. "I know you love your little brother and sister, which is why you have to be an example to them. How will Daris know how to treat Aillee if you don't show him how to be a good big brother?"

"I'll try, I promise," Ian answered quietly. He looked out over the pool to the glittering phoenix of water that stood in the middle. "Mama?"

"Yes, Ian?" she asked.

"Why did you leave this place? It's better than Rosehaven. Home is boring."

Kenna laughed a little; having grown up here, she'd often thought Arthan boring compared to other places. "So that I could marry your father and be your mother," she replied simply. Ian was still too young to hear all the details of how their marriage came to pass. It was a sad beginning to a life that had brought her more joy than she'd ever imagined.

"And to be the Queen?"

"Yes, but I didn't know I would be a Queen when I met your Papa." Kenna explained.

Ian seemed to consider this for a little while. He looked up at her thoughtfully. "And someday I'll be the King?"

"You will, and then your son or daughter will follow you, and their child, and theirs after that," Kenna answered. She smiled and tapped his nose. "But that will be a long, long time from now. Today, you need to go tell your brother you're sorry, and then eat your lunch."

Ian let loose with a greatly put-upon sigh but didn't argue. Kenna took his hand and led him back to the rest of the family. He dutifully apologized to Daris, hugging him afterward, and the soggy offenses were laid to rest. Peace was once again restored within their little kingdom. Kenna nestled next to Niall when Ian was settled with his lunch. It was one of those rare occasions when she felt like they were simply Niall and Kenna, instead of the King and Queen.

"You know, I think things turned out quite well for us," she said, kissing her husband's cheek.

He smiled down at her warmly. "I couldn't agree more."

ABOUT THE AUTHOR

Christen is an avid reader who enjoys going on adventures whenever she can. Her love of fantasy started at an early age with fairytales and The Hobbit. She lives in Kansas in the home she shared with her late husband. She first discovered a love of storytelling on the stage. In her late teens she began writing, a hobby that helped her through her husband's death. Christen enjoys spending days in her gardens and having adventures with her friends and family.